KINDRED

A Jefferson Tayte Genealogical Mystery

Other books in this series:

KINDRED

A Jefferson Tayte Genealogical Mystery

by

STEVE ROBINSON

THOMAS & MERCER

Published by Thomas & Mercer, Seattle
www.apub.com

Amazon, the Amazon logo, and Thomas & Mercer are trademarks of Amazon.com, Inc., or its affiliates.

ISBN-13: 9781503954694
ISBN-10: 1503954692

Cover design by Lisa Horton

Printed in the United States of America

For my wife Karen

Prologue

Karwendel Mountains. Bavaria, Germany. November 1973.

He wished now that he had taken the road. The road would have led him down to a town or village where he could have sought help. But he knew that if he had tried to escape by the road, he would already be dead. The mountains, on the other hand, gave him places to hide, but beneath an overcast sky, amidst frozen rocks that were already partly settled with snow, he felt so cold. He pulled his jumper up over his mouth and tried to calm himself. His breath, swirling up into the chill morning air, could certainly give him away. Despite trying to warm his hands in his pockets and in the folds of his jumper, his pale, blueing fingertips were already losing sensation and he had only stopped to rest for a few minutes.

He had to keep moving.

These mountains were no strangers to him. He had spent much of his youth among them, a rope and harness and all manner of equipment to aid his ascent and descent. But he had none of that equipment with him now. He looked up to his right and saw an uninviting snow-capped peak he knew he was ill-prepared for. Yet for now it was the only direction open to him. To his left was a sheer drop of thirty metres or more, and before him in the direction he was heading, away from his pursuers, was a high overhanging rock face, impassable to all but the very best mountaineers. Going up and around it was his only option.

He peered out from his cover, out over the sprawling green valley below him. Looking back he could see no movement among the rocks, and for a moment he wondered whether the people hunting him had given up. It was mere wishful thinking; he knew they would not. There was too much at stake. He blew warm air into his hands in an ineffective attempt to breathe life back into them. He reached beneath his jumper and pulled out the hem of his shirt, which he ripped against the edge of a jagged rock. Then he tore off enough material to wrap around his hands before he began to climb.

The first few metres were relatively easy, barely more than a scramble. After that he had to rely on cracks in the rock to gain any kind of purchase. His progress became slow, and he felt certain he was losing the early advantage he had made over his adversaries. As the angle of ascent became more shallow again he caught movement out of the corner of his eye and he froze, his heart suddenly thumping. A second later he heard a familiar sound and he breathed again. It was a goat, perched at a seemingly impossible angle on the mountain face to his right. He smiled to himself, and then another sound almost caused him to lose his footing. It was a gunshot, loud enough in the quiet still of the mountains to cause an avalanche in more favourable conditions.

He didn't dare look back. The fact that he had heard the shot at all meant the bullet had missed him, but it also meant that the hunters had spotted their quarry. He made haste, tempering speed with safety. He would not give whoever had fired the rifle a second shot at a stationary target. He scrambled again, moving higher. He was almost there. Another shot was fired, and this time he saw the bullet ricochet off the rocks above him.

He kept going, knowing that all the while he was out in the open, life or death would be determined only by chance, and the skill of the rifleman below him. A third shot caught his boot. His ankle spun around and he slipped momentarily, but he felt no pain. Looking down, he saw that the bullet must have glanced off his heel. There was a tear in the leather, but nothing more.

Hand over hand he continued to climb the remaining distance, aware now that several of his fingers were cut and bleeding. But before another shot was fired he managed to slip over the high point he had been heading for, dropping from view on the other side, where he lay panting for several seconds. Assessing his new surroundings, he saw the ever-present mountain peaks on his right, and there was now a shallow slope ahead of him, which led his eye to a trail of smoke. It was further down, perhaps half a kilometre away beneath the ledge he had been traversing. He was unable to determine its source, but he thought that where there was smoke there was a strong probability of finding other people— perhaps someone who could help him. His hopes lifted as he began to descend the slope, but then he heard a sound that instantly rekindled his despair. Dogs, at least two of them, were suddenly baying for his blood.

He imagined his pursuers had brought the dogs out from the secluded mountain retreat he had escaped from, further back towards the road. He supposed the beasts were well-suited to the mountains, and he knew it would not take them long to find him. The only question in his mind now was whether he could make it to the source of the smoke before they reached him. He began to run. The loose ground beneath his boots made for treacherous footing and he was soon out of control, barely managing to stay on his feet as his momentum grew. As the slope levelled out and his pace slowed, he ventured closer to the ledge and peered down into the valley, his eyes trained on the smoke trail. He could see a chimney now. It had to be a climbers' hut and there was clearly someone there. But how to reach it?

The dogs kept howling. They sounded closer and their vicious din spurred him on. He tracked the ledge, looking for a way down. The hut was in full view now, less than a few hundred metres away. On level ground, he knew he could have sprinted to it in no time, but this was not level ground. Far from it. Taking the direct route he saw that there were two steep descents between him and the hut. He saw a wide ledge, perhaps ten metres below him, where the mountain levelled off, then he had to hope there was a way down from there. He lowered himself and began to climb.

The dogs now sounded terrifyingly close—so close that he paused to look back at the slope he had just run down. Then he saw the first of them. He realised they must have found another route, a longer but flatter way around perhaps, but with speed on their side they had quickly made up lost ground. The hound paused momentarily, and as if it had just seen him, it began to bound down the slope after him as the second dog came into view.

He wasted no time. As he descended lower and lower, he thought the angle of his descent would surely slow the dogs down. They would have to find another way again, but he knew it would not stop them. They were so fast that it was only a matter of seconds before they were above him, snapping and growling, their teeth bared, their jowls drooling. At first he thought they would try to follow after him, such was their hunger, but as he sank lower, further distancing himself from them, they hesitated. A moment later they were gone.

The rest of the descent to the ledge below came and went in a blur. He reached it and ran to the next ledge. The hut was so close now that he could smell the wood-smoke coming from the chimney, but it was still tantalisingly out of reach. The way down from here appeared even steeper and he doubted his skills. His hands were shredded, the shirt rags he had wrapped them with now red through with his blood.

He ran along the ledge, looking for a better way down. There was another slope. It was covered with scree from the cliff face. He ran towards it, but as he came closer, he heard the dogs again. They were ahead of him now, picking their way down through the rocks, between him and the slope he was heading for. His first thought was to turn and run back the other way, but he already knew there was no way down for him in that direction, and he supposed that if he tried to climb again, the men driving the dogs would be there waiting for him. So he ran faster, hoping to reach the scree first.

But he did not.

He stopped just a few strides away as the first of the dogs came at him, all snarling teeth and muscle. It pounced and he fell. He tried to hold the beast by the neck, but it was too strong. A moment later he felt its teeth bite into his arm. Then with the other he reached out and found a rock, which he drove hard into the animal's skull. It whimpered and fell back. He had no time to consider his injured arm. He was on his feet again at once, but now the second dog was bounding and howling towards him. There was only one option open to him and he took it. As the dog arrived, he ran to the scree slope and leapt for his life, hurling himself down onto his stomach. Beneath him the loose stone began to slip and slide, until they were moving together, like water along a fast flowing stream that built and built as he descended further. Both dogs continued after him. He saw one and then the other, sliding with him, but they were no longer in control of their destiny any more than he was.

They slid like this for several fast seconds, rolling in a chaotic tangle of limbs and gnashing teeth, until ahead of him he glimpsed an edge where the scree slope seemed to end abruptly, either to a further slope or perhaps a precipice. Fearing the latter, he began to grapple for purchase, trying to slow himself down. He rolled again and tried to dig the toes of his boots into the stones. He pushed himself up to further arrest his slide. It was working. One of the dogs passed him as he slowed, but he did not appear to be slowing fast enough. The edge was close, and now he could hear the scree cascading like a waterfall, crashing onto the rocks below.

He looked around, certain that he would not be able to stop himself in time. A large rock sat close to the edge, and knowing it was his only hope, he began to roll towards it, sliding fast again as he picked up speed. As he crashed into it, the pain in his chest was intense. He thought he must have broken several ribs. He cried out as he clung to the rock, watching as the dogs continued to slide towards the precipice, howling and gnashing. They whimpered as first one, and then the other slid over the edge, and moments later the dull thuds of their bodies signalled their end.

He could hardly breathe. He supposed one of his broken ribs must have punctured a lung. Slowly, he stood up, clutching his chest. The pain made him dizzy, but he knew he had to keep going. The dogs' handlers would not be far behind. The hut was close now, the way down to it, easier—perhaps no more than a steep walk if he traversed it in stages. It would take a little longer, but with his injuries he felt it was all he could manage. If his pursuers caught up with him he knew he could no longer outrun or outclimb them.

He chose his path carefully and was soon there. Beside the hut was a narrow, rocky track where he saw an all-terrain vehicle, and with it his salvation. He practically collapsed at the hut's door. It opened freely. On his hands and knees he looked up to see a man adding another log to the fire.

'*Bitte helfen Sie mir!*' he called, pleading for the man's help.

As the man turned around to face him, a wry smile creasing his lips, he saw that it was the very man he had been running from. Despair sapped the last of his strength and he crashed to the floor, knowing all was lost.

Chapter One

Present day.

Pacing along a highly polished corridor at the German Heart Centre in Munich, his tan suit still creased from the flight, Jefferson Tayte glanced apprehensively at Jean, and for the umpteenth time he hoped they weren't too late.

They had flown in from Heathrow Airport that afternoon for an appointment with a ninety-seven-year-old man called Johann Langner, and it had come as a shock to hear that he had suffered a heart attack the day before, not least because Tayte was pinning so much hope on what he believed Langner might be able to tell him.

His excitement over the meeting, and Jean Summer's hand as she sat beside him in the window seat, had pulled Tayte through the relatively short flight, helping to overcome his fear of flying. Now his stomach was in knots for entirely different reasons.

'And you're sure Mr Langner still wants to see us?' Tayte said to the grey-suited man they were following.

Tayte didn't know his name, only that he appeared to be a chauffeur of sorts. He was tall like Tayte, but slim like Jean. He'd met them off the plane and taken their bags to the Mercedes that had been waiting for them outside the arrivals terminal, but instead of conveying them to their hotel as Tayte had expected, he'd brought them straight to the hospital. He had Tayte's suit carrier over one arm and Jean's backpack was slung across his shoulder.

'Herr Langner's instructions were quite explicit,' the man said, with only the slightest trace of a German accent. 'He's sufficiently recovered and wants to see you as soon as possible.' He slowed down as he turned to face Tayte and added, 'While he still can.'

Tayte nodded back. He understood that at Johann Langner's age, and in his present state of ill health, tomorrow might not be an option.

Jean almost had to jog to keep up with Tayte's long strides. So much so that the tablet PC she'd recently bought nearly fell out of the denim jacket she was wearing over her yellow summer dress. Being a professor of history, she was no stranger to research, and since meeting up with Tayte again in London after his previous assignment, she'd spent the two weeks that followed surfing the Internet at every opportunity, having taken it upon herself to learn all she could about the man Tayte was pinning so much hope on.

'I read in *Der Spiegel*,' she said to the man they were following, 'that a painting by Matisse has just been sold through Mr Langner's gallery for a record sum.'

'Yes, that's correct,' the man said. 'And it was no small achievement on Herr Langner's part. He started out with next to nothing, and it took several years to make what you would consider to be a proper living, but then both his business and his reputation began to grow. He even managed to reunite a few of the paintings that passed through his hands with their rightful owners after they had been stolen during the war.'

'What keeps him going?' Tayte asked. 'And can I get some?'

The man gave a small laugh. 'His son, Rudolf, has managed the business for some years now, but on this occasion Herr Langner handled the sale personally.'

'Maybe the excitement proved too much for him.'

'That's quite possible. It was a lot of money.'

They stopped walking beside a door to their right. The man knocked once, opened it, and set their bags down. Inside, the room was bright, predominantly white, with splashes of pale blue on the few items of furniture and on the blinds at the window, which looked out over a communal recreational garden in full summer bloom.

The bespectacled Johann Langner was sitting up in bed, wired to the electrocardiograph machine beside him, staring at his guests through the right-hand side of his glasses; the left lens was blacked out. He raised a wavering hand, crooked with arthritis, and brushed his wispy white hair back off his brow as Tayte and Jean approached. The man they had been following made the introductions.

'Herr Langner, this is Mr Tayte, the American genealogist, and his associate, Professor Summer.'

Langner smiled, exaggerating the facial disfigurement around his cheekbones and jawline, revealing crooked teeth that were stained brown from old age and tobacco. 'I lost it during the war,' Langner said, clearly noticing that Tayte was staring at the blacked-out lens. In contrast to the man who had just shown them in, his German accent was decidedly pronounced.

Tayte returned Langner's smile. 'I'm sorry,' he said. 'I didn't mean to stare.'

'That's quite all right,' Langner said. 'Most people do the first time, and believe me, you'd stare harder if I took my glasses off.'

The notion seemed to amuse Langner. He chuckled quietly to himself, then turned to the man by the door and said, 'You can leave us now, Christoph.'

Christoph frowned. 'Where's Ingrid? Perhaps I should wait with you until she returns.'

'Ingrid is my personal nurse,' Langner said to Tayte and Jean. 'This is my third heart attack and Ingrid has literally saved my life every time. She should return shortly.' Langner reached for something beside the bed. He fumbled for a moment, and then he brought a cabled switch into view. 'I'm not so old and weak that I'm incapable of pressing this button if I need help,' he said to Christoph. 'Besides, I'm sure I'm in good hands.' He smiled at his guests again.

'Very well,' Christoph said, 'but I must insist on waiting outside.'

'Yes, yes. If you must,' Langner said. Once Christoph was out of earshot, he added, 'He means well, but he treats me like a child.'

Tayte just smiled, and realising that he was still holding his briefcase, he put it down by the side of the bed and pulled two chairs closer so that he and Jean could sit down. As he did so, he wondered why such chair manufacturers didn't make them wider. Maybe then he wouldn't have to push the arms down so hard just to get up again.

'Now, Mr Tayte,' Langner said once they had settled, 'I feel I must apologise to you for not being able to see you sooner.'

'That's perfectly understandable,' Tayte said. 'I'm just glad to have the opportunity now.'

Tayte had first tried to meet with Johann Langner the year before, soon after he returned home to Washington, DC from a visit to London, but every time he'd tried to contact Langner he'd been informed that his health was in too poor a state for him to see anyone. That is, until recently.

'Very well,' Langner said. 'Now you mentioned in your letter that you believe I can help you to find your birth parents.'

Tayte drew a deep breath and held on to it as he thought through the implications of that simple statement. For now at least, he felt that all the failed research he had conducted into his own family history over the years really came down to this man and what he may or may not be able to tell him. When the call he'd been waiting on throughout his previous assignment had at last come in, confirming that Langner was able to see him, he'd been all the more anxious to meet the man. He reached inside his jacket and pulled out the photograph his mother had left for him when she'd abandoned him in Mexico forty years ago, when he was just a few months old.

'As I'm sure you know,' Tayte said, 'I trace people's family history for a living. I've been trying to trace my own, so far without success, ever since I found out I was adopted.'

'Really?' Langner said. 'A genealogist who knows nothing of his own family history. How painfully ironic that must be for you.'

'You can say that again,' Tayte said. 'But it keeps me going. In a way I feel it drives me to be better at what I do, in the hope that I'll someday be good enough to find the answers I'm looking for. I was told I'd been adopted soon after my adoptive parents died in a plane crash, when I was in my teens. They left me this.' Tayte handed the photograph to Langner. 'I believe the woman in the picture is my birth mother. I'm trying to find her, or at least find out who she is. The photo was taken in 1963.'

Langner studied the image. 'You seem very sure of the year. How can you be so certain?'

'I'll come to that in a minute, if you don't mind,' Tayte said. 'Do you recognise her?'

Langner seemed to give it some thought. He took his time before answering. Then he began to shake his head. 'No, I'm sorry.'

Tayte had been prepared for that. He didn't expect it to be so simple. 'But you do recognise the building she's standing in front of.' It wasn't a question.

Langner brought the photograph closer to his good eye and scrutinised it.

Jean joined the conversation. 'You bought the building from the government in 1958 after it was earmarked for demolition as part of an area regeneration project.'

Langner began to nod his head as he set the photograph down onto the bed. 'Yes, this is one of my buildings. It's on the outskirts of the city, not far from here. The stone lions were originally placed there as representations of strength and courage. They're quite unmistakable.' He smiled at Jean. 'You've certainly done your research. I can see that you already know a good deal more about me than I know about you.'

The remark caused Jean to fidget in her seat. She pushed her shoulder-length brown hair back over one ear and returned an awkward smile. 'It's made a welcome change to the historical figures I usually find myself researching.'

Langner laughed. 'The living over the dead, eh? It will not be long now before I am one of your historical figures myself.' He turned to Tayte. 'So your mother was outside one of my buildings when this picture was taken, and you've come all this way in the hope that I can help you to identify her?'

'Perhaps not directly,' Tayte said.

The months of research that had begun when he'd opened the safety deposit box his late friend and mentor, Marcus Brown, had bequeathed to him had led him here, and now he only hoped his hunch was right—he was desperate for it to be right. He reached into his briefcase and pulled out a folder, which he placed on his knees. Opening it, he withdrew a photocopy of a newspaper cutting Marcus had left for him, along with a brief letter explaining that he hadn't told him about it before because he didn't want Tayte to get his hopes up until he had more to go on. That's all there was, and Tayte supposed Marcus must have made the discovery close to his death or there would have been more. However little, Tayte believed it was enough.

'I'm sure you remember the day this picture was taken for the local newspaper, the *Abendzeitung*,' he said, handing it to Langner.

Langner took the photocopy. It showed two images of the same neo-classical building. One was clearly more recent than the other and had been taken when the newspaper article was printed in 1963. The other was from an unforgettable time in world history. Both images showed a wide three-storey building, with what Tayte considered to be an oppressive central portico, whose towering concrete pillars reached almost to the full height of the structure. In the centre were the two stone lions, exactly as they appeared in the photograph Tayte had of his mother.

The letters above the main doorway were obscured in the photograph, showing only part of the words spelled out above it: 'nd E'. With only the limited elements of the photograph to go on, Tayte had come to think of the building as a hotel somewhere, and he'd spent many hours trying to work out possible names for it—the Grand Excelsior perhaps. He'd spent a great many more hours researching those hotels whose names fitted, but he'd found nothing that matched. And it was no wonder, because he now knew he'd been looking in the wrong places. The words above the main entrance weren't even English, they were German: '*Blut und Ehre*'— 'Blood and Honour'.

Tayte heard Langner say something then, but it was spoken too softly to make out. 'I'm sorry, what was that?'

'*Hitlerjugend*,' Langner repeated, gazing now at the newspaper copy as though the older image, with its tall Nazi Party flags adorning the pillars, had stirred old memories within him. '*Blut und Ehre* was the motto of the Hitler Youth. The building was established for promising young boys from all over Germany.' He shook his head. 'I wanted to do something good with that place, although many of Munich's people at the time would sooner have seen it destroyed. I believed it was important to preserve it.'

He paused. 'What's that British phrase I'm looking for? Ah, yes . . . Lest we forget.'

'So you turned it into a museum?' Jean said.

'I suppose you could call it that. Although, I prefer to think of it as an education centre. It's been overshadowed now of course by the *NS-Dokumentationszentrum*, the Munich Documentation Centre for the History of National Socialism, which was built on the site of what used to be the headquarters of the former NSDAP—the National Socialist German Workers' Party, which you will no doubt better know as the Nazi Party.'

Langner looked down at the photocopy of the newspaper cutting again. '1963,' he said, smiling to himself. 'I remember the mayor of Munich cutting the ribbons as though it were yesterday.' He looked up at Tayte. 'How can a former Hitler Youth training academy possibly help you in your search to find your mother?'

It was a good question, and one which Tayte had already asked himself many times since he'd embarked on this most personal of assignments. When it came to his own family history, Tayte knew he'd been clutching at straws his whole life, and he had to admit to himself that this time was no great exception, but this time he knew for a fact that this former Hitler Youth building was somewhere his mother had once been. He had never found such a concrete connection to his family before, and Marcus had clearly thought it important, which had helped to spur Tayte on. All he figured he had to do now was to find out why his mother had gone there, and then follow the clues. He reached a hand towards Langner and pointed to another image on the newspaper copy. It showed a crowd and several protest placards. He singled someone out.

'Going back to your earlier question, I know the photo I have of my mother was taken in 1963 because she was there the day your education centre was officially opened. She was at the ceremony.'

Tayte paused as he wondered again whether his father had perhaps taken the photograph. 'See the dogtooth 1960s baker-boy hat this woman's wearing?'

Langner looked more closely and nodded. Tayte drew his attention back to the photograph of his mother.

'Her face is a little obscured in the newspaper image, but that's very clearly the same hat my mother's holding in the photo she left me. The style and pattern are identical.'

'So your mother was a *Demonstrant*? She was protesting against my having saved this former Hitler Youth building from demolition?'

'Maybe,' Tayte said. 'Or maybe she was there for some other reason and just got caught up in the crowd. It's the reason she was there at all that interests me—whether it was because of the building or perhaps someone connected with it.'

'Which is what brought you to me,' Langner said.

Tayte nodded. 'I figure if I can find out what or who my mother was interested in, and why, it could lead me to someone who can identify her.'

'But I've already told you I don't know the woman in this picture. I can't see how I can be of any further help to you.'

'Volker Strobel,' Jean said, sitting forward as her eyes locked on Langner.

Langner's eyebrows twitched at hearing the name and he smiled. 'Ah,' he said. 'Now I begin to see where this is going.'

Tayte elaborated. 'According to the article in this newspaper, Volker Strobel was the main reason for the protests at your opening ceremony that day—the day my mother was there. As I'm sure you can imagine, when I set out to identify why she was there, Strobel went straight to the top of my list.'

Jean leaned in and picked up the newspaper copy. 'This article shows that the protestors were strongly against preserving the institution that had, and I quote, "spawned such evil as Volker Strobel, the Demon of Dachau".'

Langner's features had taken on a solemn appearance. He slowly nodded his head in recognition of the facts being presented to him as Tayte continued.

'I spent a considerable amount of time trying to find out about Strobel—trying to understand why my mother might have been interested in him. I soon learned that researching a most-wanted war criminal, whom no one's been able to find since the war ended, is no walk in the park. Coupled with the seemingly impossible task of trying to connect this man with a mother I know nothing about made the job of finding my family seem as impossible as ever.'

'But something has given you hope?' Langner said.

'Possibly, which of course is why we're here. I managed to identify a few people in Strobel's family line, but no one wanted to talk to me about him. They all gave me the same answer—the answer I'm sure they've given to many Nazi hunters over the years. They said they knew nothing about him. They were ashamed of him and wanted to be left alone, and for the past to be left where they felt it belonged. So, after that avenue was closed to me, I returned to the archives and kept digging in the hope that I might turn something up. Then I found a reference to Volker Strobel that made it all the more imperative that I see you.'

'Do you remember the magazines of the Hitler Youth?' Jean asked. 'One was called *Will and Power*. Issued bi-monthly.'

'Yes, of course, the *Wille und Macht*,' Langner said. 'It was familiar to most members of the *Hitlerjugend*. There may be many things wrong with me, my dear, but there's nothing whatsoever wrong with my memory.'

Tayte reached into his folder again and slid out another of the records he'd collected. 'During my research I came across a digital copy of the magazine on the San Francisco based Internet Archive.

It was filed under Baldur von Schirach, the magazine's editor at the time. I had a translated copy made and this is a printout of the page that caught my attention as it appeared in *Will and Power* magazine in May 1937.'

Langner took the copy and studied the page for several seconds before a gentle smile creased his lips. 'So young,' he said, his tone distant and melancholic. His smile dropped. 'We had become perfect little soldiers—we sons of the *Führer*. I was nineteen years old when this picture was taken—a young man swept along by a wave so strong no one could have stopped it, let alone imagine the devastation it would ultimately cause.'

Langner turned the copy of the magazine page around to face Tayte and Jean. Amidst the text, which was written in the Fraktur blackletter typeface so synonymous with Nazi Germany, were the portraits of two Hitler Youth members. The image was in black and white, but having seen so many photographs of similar Hitler Youth members during his research, it was not difficult for Tayte to imagine their blonde hair and blue eyes, their black trousers and brown shirts, with black ties and cross straps over their chests. With their strong jawlines and proud, authoritative stances, they looked the epitome of Nazi Germany's perfect Aryan race.

'We had grown out of our shorts by the time this picture was taken,' Langner said. 'We were being honoured for our conduct in the *Hitlerjugend,* and for becoming two of the youngest members to make the rank of *Bannführer* at the time, although when the war began and the majority of adult leaders were conscripted into the *Wehrmacht* and the *Waffen-SS,* the minimum age was reduced to as young as sixteen to make up for the sudden deficit in leadership.'

'The article tells of your friendship with Strobel,' Tayte said.

'Yes, and of course the HJ, as we commonly referred to it, encouraged such comradeship.' He gazed down at the image again. 'Look at us,' he added, offering the image closer to Jean. 'We were the very best of friends when this picture was taken. But how quickly the war, among other things, changed all that.'

'You fell out?' Tayte asked.

'What about?' Jean added. 'If that's not too personal a question.'

'No, it's quite all right. It was a long time ago. I had once thought that nothing could come between us, but I was clearly very naive. In simple terms I suppose we fell out over a girl, and because the war brought out the very worst in Volker Strobel. I came to hate and despise the man I had once considered my friend.'

'Could you tell us about him?' Tayte asked.

'To a point, yes, I could.'

'And will you?' Jean said.

Langner turned to Tayte and regarded him seriously. 'If your mother was interested in a man such as Volker Strobel, are you completely sure you want to find out why?'

Tayte gave a single, determined nod.

'Wherever it may lead? Whatever the repercussions?'

When it came to understanding his own ancestry, Tayte had always felt a degree of apprehension about what he might someday find. Nevertheless, he had to know where this new lead would take him. He looked at Jean and then back at Langner. 'Yes, I'm absolutely sure,' he said. 'If there's something about Volker Strobel that could help point me in the right direction, I'd be glad to know it, wherever it might lead.'

Langner sat up and took a sip of water from the glass beside his bed. 'Very well,' he said, adjusting his posture. 'Let me tell you about the man who was once my closest friend. As it remains unclear about what you hope to find, I suppose I should commence the story of my acquaintance with Herr Strobel, *Der Dämon von Dachau*, from the day I first met him. It was in 1933 and I had just turned fifteen. It wasn't mandatory to join the *Hitlerjugend* until 1936, but I come from a long line of military forefathers, and so

I had been a member of the *Deutsches Jungvolk*—the junior branch of the *Hitlerjugend*—from the age of ten. I can still remember the very first time I saw Volker. Out of nowhere he came striding confidently towards me. His hair as bright as fire and his blue eyes so piercing it was impossible to look away, despite the somewhat difficult circumstances I had found myself in.' Langner paused, as though momentarily lost to his memories. 'Yes, I remember Volker Strobel very well,' he added. 'But then, it was a very memorable introduction.'

Chapter Two

Munich. 1933.

'Kick him again, Erich! Never let your opponent gain the upper hand.'

The boy's lip was already swollen and bleeding profusely from the blow that had knocked him to the ground. It was three against one and he knew this was a fight he could not win.

'Like this, Günther?' Erich kicked the boy again, and this time it felt as if the blow had cracked a rib.

'That's it,' Günther said with obvious satisfaction. 'The strong dominate the weak. Remember that.' He was suddenly towering over the defenceless boy. 'What's your name?'

The boy spat blood at him. A moment later he felt a tug at the neck of his shirt as his head and shoulders were pulled up, only to be smashed back down again by Günther's fist. Laughter rang in the boy's ears. Another blow sent his head crashing into the parquet floor that lined the corridor he had previously been running along on his way to class. He wanted to cry, but he didn't. Had his father been there, he knew he would have beaten him all the harder if he had. Instead, he rolled onto his side and curled his knees up to his chest in supplication.

Then, through the blood in his eyes, he saw a pair of knee-length white socks striding towards him, and a pair of black shorts and a brown shirt like his own. It was another boy of about his age approaching along the otherwise empty corridor. Their eyes met, and even while he was being kicked repeatedly in the back, by all three of the older boys for all he knew, the boy couldn't take his eyes off the newcomer.

The approaching boy called out. 'Hey, *Blödmann!*'

The kicking stopped and somehow the pain in the boy's back and ribs seemed to intensify.

'Who's this, then?' Günther said. 'Has your little brother come to help you?' He laughed. 'We'll soon see who the stupid one is. It's still three against two, and we're older and stronger.'

The size and strength of the opposition seemed to make no difference to the newcomer, who was suddenly in their midst, standing with his hands on his hips in a defiant, mocking posture.

'And what are you going to do, little man?' Günther continued. 'Do you want some of the same med—'

Günther wasn't allowed to finish his sentence. The newcomer cracked his fist into Günther's nose with such speed and determination, it would have been impossible to see it coming. The other two boys backed away, as though suddenly less sure of themselves.

Günther quickly recovered. He wiped the blood from his nose and studied it momentarily before looking up again. 'You're going to pay for that!' He lunged at the newcomer and landed a glancing blow to his chin, jolting his head sideways. Then Günther leapt at him and pulled him to the ground. 'Can you wrestle, little man?'

The newcomer lashed out again, but this time his punch was easily blocked.

'I'm a very good wrestler,' Günther said as he twisted his legs around the other boy and rolled him over, pinning him onto his back.

The newcomer jabbed again, and now he cut his opponent's lip. He threw another punch, but any advantage he might have had was fleeting.

Günther blocked him again and he knelt on his upper arms, immobilising them. 'See how you like this,' he said, and then he began to rain blow after blow into the newcomer's face, like a blacksmith hammering steel, until his knuckles were wet with blood.

Beside them, the boy stirred. He sat up and the pain in his ribs caused him to wince and clutch his side. He saw Günther's friends move closer and he knew he would not be allowed to help this bright-haired boy who had come to his aid. He could do no more than watch and hope that the bully would soon let up. Blow after blow continued to fall until the boy saw the fight go from the newcomer. He had stopped bucking and twisting, and his head seemed limp now as it rocked from side to side as Günther kept hitting him. The boy thought Günther would never let up. He thought he was going to kill the newcomer if he didn't do something. He was about to, for what good he thought it would do, but the beating suddenly stopped. Günther seemed to freeze mid-blow.

He groaned. 'Oh, *Scheisse!*'

Very slowly Günther began to fall sideways towards the boy. He landed heavily just a few feet from him, and it was then that the boy saw the reason he had stopped the beating. Protruding from his side was the unmistakable black and polished nickel plate handle of the newcomer's Hitler Youth dagger.

The newcomer began to move again. He slowly sat up, blood in his teeth and all over his face from the beating he'd just taken. He kicked Günther's legs away from him and the other two boys who had been with him turned and ran for the doors at the end of the corridor.

The newcomer got to his feet. 'You must learn to stand up for yourself—show your enemies you're not scared. I'll teach you.' He straightened his shirt and tie. 'Well, are you just going to sit there all day?' He extended his arm to help the boy up. 'I'm Volker. Volker Strobel.'

'Johann Langner,' the boy said. 'Is he dead?'

Volker kicked Günther and he groaned again. 'He'll live. He's probably just in shock, that's all.'

Günther stirred and tried to remove the dagger from his side.

'You should leave that,' Volker said. 'If you take it out, you'll bleed to death.' To Johann, he added, 'It's true. I've seen it happen.'

Johann scrunched his brow. 'You have?'

Volker nodded. 'It was a pig, but what's the difference?' He turned back to Günther. 'Lie still, *Schweinchen,* or you'll make things worse.'

Volker took Johann's arm. 'Come on. We should leave.'

Johann resisted. 'He could still die.'

'He'll be fine.'

'Why did you stab him?'

'I had to do something. He was going to kill me, I swear it. Now let's go. His friends saw what happened. They'll soon come back with help, and then I'll be in trouble.'

'No,' Johann said. 'We can't leave him.'

Volker sighed. He seemed to think about it. 'All right then, as we're going to be friends I'll stay and take my punishment. But only for you. Only because you want me to. How's that for friendship?'

Johann didn't know how to respond, so he gave no reply. In truth, he thought Volker Strobel an odd boy, but he didn't dare tell him so.

'My family are from Austria, but my parents live in Munich now,' Volker said. 'Do your parents live in Munich?'

'No, Dresden.' Johann scrunched his brow. 'Why do you want to be friends?'

'Perhaps it's because you remind me of myself.'

'How?'

Volker smiled. 'We both have fair hair and blue eyes, don't we?'

Johann laughed. It made his lip hurt. 'So does half the academy.'

'That's true, but I just took a beating for you, didn't I? That makes us friends.'

'Does it?'

Volker nodded with enthusiasm. 'Of course it does, *Blödmann*. And besides, you owe me now. We'll have to remain friends at least until you can pay me back.'

The door at the end of the corridor slammed open then and Günther's friends returned. Pacing ahead of them was *Scharführer* Henkel, one of the squad leaders.

'Don't worry. I'll tell them you came to my rescue,' Johann said. 'I'll tell them how brave you were.'

'I'm not worried. If I am in trouble, my father will sort it out.'

'How will he do that?'

'He's an important man in the party. He knows people—important people. He can pull strings.'

'Let's hope he doesn't have to,' Johann said, and as the *Scharführer* arrived, he thought again how odd Volker Strobel was, and how interesting he supposed their friendship was going to be.

Chapter Three

Present day.

A knock at the door to Johann Langner's private room at the German Heart Centre interrupted the nonagenarian's recollections of Volker Strobel. A moment later the door opened and a woman Tayte put in her mid-fifties entered. She was wearing white trousers and a light-green nurse's tunic, and Langner's face lit up at the sight of her.

'Ingrid! You have returned to me at last. I was about to send Christoph to look for you.'

'*Es ist Zeit für Ihre Pillen,*' she said, her lips barely moving as she spoke.

'In English, if you please, Ingrid,' Langner said. 'We have company. This is Herr Tayte and Professor Summer. They have come to examine the skeletons in my closet.' He laughed as he turned to Tayte and Jean and winked at them. At least, Tayte thought it was a wink. It was difficult to tell on account of Langner only having one eye. 'Herr Tayte . . . Professor Summer . . . this is *meine Lebensretterin*, my life-saver, Ingrid Keller. In case you're not so familiar with the German language, she's telling me that it's time for my pills.'

Keller did not respond to Langner's witticism. She simply tutted and poured him a glass of water. 'Here.' She offered a fistful of tablets to Langner and waited as he put half of them into his mouth at once. She passed him the water. 'Swallow.'

She was very direct, Tayte thought, and thus far a woman of few words. Her features were decidedly masculine. She was stockily built with thick forearms and a square jawline that framed an unadorned, no nonsense face. Even her black hair was styled like a man's, so short it was almost a buzz-cut. Tayte figured it was at least a hygienic hairstyle for a nurse to have. He watched Langner swallow the last of his pills, and then he looked on in fascination as Keller began to massage his throat.

'Did the boy die?' Tayte asked as soon as the massaging stopped. 'The boy Strobel stabbed?'

'No,' Langner said. 'That is to say, he did not die then.' He paused as Keller moved away and sat in front of the ECG monitor, where she began checking what appeared to be the recent activity logs. 'Volker had inflicted no more than a flesh wound to the older boy's side,' Langner continued. 'But instead of being punished for it, he was rewarded for bravery, would you believe? Against the odds, he had come gallantly to the aid of a fallen *Kamerad* and single-handedly defeated the bullies. No, it was the older boys who were punished. Fighting was tolerated, even encouraged, but these boys had shown themselves to be cowards, and that most certainly was not tolerated. The boy Volker stabbed, however, did not forget the incident. It set up a bitter rivalry that would see him dead within a year.'

'Strobel killed him?' Jean asked.

'The report showed Günther's death to be an accident. He was apparently running with his dagger drawn—every boy in the *Hitlerjugend* carried one on his hip. He tripped and fell and the knife pierced his heart, killing him instantly. At least, that is how it appeared, but I know better. I had no part in it, but Volker used to talk about how he was going to sort him out.

Afterwards, he made no secret of what he'd done, and of course, his reputation grew.'

'If you don't mind me saying so,' Tayte said, 'Volker Strobel seems an odd choice of friend. And a best friend at that.'

'Odd, yes, he was certainly that, but we soon settled down to our education and training—our continued indoctrination in national socialist ideology—and in those early days I looked up to Volker. He had saved me from a terrible beating on my first day at the *Hitlerjugend-Akademie,* and he was so very charismatic that it was difficult not to be swept along with him. Besides, he had chosen me as his friend, and believe me, I would not have wished to be his enemy. That came much later.'

'Yes, you said you fell out,' Tayte said. 'You mentioned a girl.'

Langner sighed and sank his head back onto his pillow. 'Ah, there is always a girl, isn't there?'

Tayte glanced at Jean and she returned a coy smile. A year ago, he would have given a very different answer, but now he simply nodded in agreement and said, 'What was her name?'

'Her name was Ava Bauer,' Langner said. 'She had the softest dark blonde hair and a smile that made me want to know everything about her. She was a little older than Volker and me, but our education had matured us beyond our years by the time I met her.' He paused thoughtfully. 'That was in November 1938. I was twenty and she had just turned twenty-one. She lived in Munich on a quiet little street in the southwest district of Sendling.'

'Were you still in the Hitler Youth?' Jean asked.

'Yes, it was all either of us knew. Many boys joined the ranks of the SS or SA when they turned eighteen, but because the *Hitlerjugend* needed leadership, some of us were encouraged to stay on. We had both progressed along the chain of command by the time we met Ava. We were each responsible for thousands of boys, and I know the power had intoxicated Volker. By the time the war broke out a year later, the ranks of the *Hitlerjugend* had swollen to over eight million. If we had not remained, I'm sure I would never have met Ava, and seeing her for the first time remains one of the highlights of my life. In more ways than one it was another unforgettable encounter. You see, we met on *Kristallnacht*.'

Chapter Four

Munich. 9 November 1938. *Kristallnacht.*

The chill November air caused a shiver to run through Johann Langner, despite the sight of the flames that were licking out from the synagogue windows in the near distance on Herzog-Max-Strasse, which appeared intensely bright against the fading afternoon sky. He stamped his feet and blew warm air into his hands as he continued to survey the scene: the smashed doors and broken windows, the stormtroopers and older members of the Hitler Youth, such as himself, running here and there in their brown shirts, carrying knives and broom handles. Some also had axes to smash down any door whose Jewish owner refused to open it.

'This is wrong, Volker.'

'They are Jews,' Volker said with disdain. *'Untermenschen*! Subhumans who will destroy our entire way of life if we let them.'

Johann shook his head. 'They are citizens of Germany, Volker. It's the Bolsheviks who threaten our way of life, not the Jews.'

Following the recent assassination of a senior diplomat at the German Embassy in Paris, Ernst vom Rath, by a Polish Jew called Herschel Grynszpan, notice had been given for a nationwide riot in retaliation—a pogrom against Jews all over Germany and its annexed territories. Alongside the SA or *Sturmabteilung*—the assault division known as 'stormtroopers'—the Hitler Youth were to join in, and since Johann and Volker were now adult leaders within the organisation it was their duty to take part. At least, that was how Volker saw it.

'You have to do something now you're here,' Volker said. 'The other leaders will talk. They'll say you like the Jews.'

'I don't care. This is going too far. I'll have no part in it.'

'Here, take this.' Volker handed Johann an empty bottle. 'Throw it at that shop window. Surely that won't affect your conscience too much. See, the glass is already broken.'

Johann took the bottle. He gazed at it thoughtfully for a moment, and then he dropped it. 'I won't do it.'

'Hey, Strobel! Langner!'

The two friends turned to see a young man they had known well while earning their achievement badges as they moved up through the ranks of the Hitler Youth. They had not seen him since he turned eighteen and became an SA stormtrooper. He was with several other men, all of whom were armed with a weapon or blunt instrument of some kind. They were not all dressed in the brown shirts of the SA. Some had been instructed to wear casual clothing to make it look as though the German people had risen up in anger against the Jews for the assassination earlier that month, rather than a coordinated effort by the Nazi regime to help deal with *die Judenfrage*—the Jewish Question.

'Heinrich!' Volker called back, smiling. 'What a night this is going to be, eh? I hear the Gestapo have already made a great many arrests.'

Heinrich came over. 'Yes, it will be a night to remember so that we can tell our grandchildren about it when we're all grey-haired and toothless! How is it you're not with your units?'

Volker laughed. He put a hand on Johann's shoulder. 'It seems my friend's lunch has disagreed with him. He's feeling sick.'

At hearing that, the angular features of Heinrich's face creased in disbelief. 'You're queasy, Johann? A strong fighter like you?' He slapped Johann's back. 'I won't believe it.'

Johann offered him only a weak smile in return, as if to corroborate the lie.

'Look, now it's me who's falling behind,' Heinrich said. 'I'll see you.'

'Wait,' Volker said. 'We'll come with you. We were about to rejoin the party anyway.' He threw Johann a serious stare. 'Weren't we, my friend?'

Johann raised his eyebrows apologetically. 'I'll be along shortly. Perhaps a few more minutes.'

Heinrich laughed again. 'You must have it very bad. It's a pity. You're missing all the fun.'

Johann watched them leave, thinking it no pity at all. Whatever the consequences, he would sooner stay where he was, in a street where it appeared no more damage could be done. Somewhere in the near distance the shouting suddenly grew louder and he covered his ears. It made little difference. Another window shattered, and above it all came the high-pitched wailing of women and children as another Jewish home or business was raided. It reaffirmed Johann's resolve to have no part in it. He began walking back along the street, away from the flaming synagogue that was now all but indistinguishable amidst the consuming flames and the onset of night. He was leaving, and to hell with it.

But fate, it seemed, had other plans for him.

A scream so close that it startled him rang shrill in his ears and he turned back. His eyes quickly scanned the buildings, some now with lights at their windows, others in darkness. Where had the sound come from? It was a woman's cry, of that he was certain, or perhaps it was a child. His strides grew longer until he was almost at a sprint, wondering why, on this of all nights, he should care. And yet, he could not help himself.

Another sound drew his attention. He heard raised voices to his left, and then an upstairs light above a watchmaker's shop caught his eye as someone moved in front of it, momentarily blocking the window. The business clearly belonged to a Jewish family. The walkway outside was littered with broken glass and other items that had been destroyed and hurled out. The scream came again and Johann ran in through what remained of the smashed-in entrance door. The voices became louder and he fought his way across the debris towards the lighted stairway he could see at the back of the shop. He began to climb the stairs and was met by two Hitler Youth boys who were hurrying down. He thought them no more than fifteen years old, and they were each carrying an assortment of household items that clearly did not belong to them. They must have recognised the HJ-*Bannführer* insignia on Johann's shirt, because they both froze at seeing him.

'What have you got there?' Johann asked, his tone sharp.

'Just some pans for my mother,' one of the boys said.

'Everyone's taking things,' the other boy said. He handed Johann a watch. 'Go on, have it. I'll find another one.'

The voices coming from the apartment above drew Johann's attention again and he moved past the boys, dismissing them. 'Go home, both of you. And no more looting, you understand?'

The boys nodded and went on their way as Johann continued to climb the stairs. At the top he heard a woman whimpering, and then came one of the voices he'd heard before. It was a man's voice.

'Tell me the combination or I'll beat your daughter this time.'

The whimpering woman was crying. 'Please, no! I told you, my husband is the only one who knows it and the Gestapo have taken him.'

There was another woman in the room. 'Leave her alone,' she said. She sounded younger, but it was difficult to be sure. 'It's clear she doesn't know the combination to the safe. Can't you see she's been through enough today?'

Johann heard the man's voice again. 'You know, there's only one thing worse than a Jew,' he said. 'And that's anyone else who looks out for them. Is that what you are? A Jew lover?'

At that moment Johann burst into the room. It was a sitting room, although it was now barely recognisable as such. Every painting and every item of soft furniture had been slashed. All the other furniture lay broken on the floor, which was covered with fragments of china and glass. In the middle of the room stood two non-uniformed men, each holding a crowbar. The taller of the two—a wiry man with a pronounced nose—was waving his crowbar at a young blonde woman, whom Johann took to be the person who had spoken out in defence of the woman these men were threatening. She had a young girl of about four years old clutched to her side. The older woman, whom Johann presumed was the child's mother, was standing beside the safe these men were interested in. Her dark hair was knotted and unkempt. Her face was bloody and her clothes were torn to such an extent that she had to hold the top half of her dress up to maintain what little dignity she had been spared.

'Did you do this?' Johann said to the men, indicating the older woman, drawing attention to her beaten and dishevelled state. 'Did you rape her?'

The wiry man shook his head. He gave a derisive laugh. 'I wouldn't touch a filthy Jew.'

The other man stepped closer to Johann. He was much heavier set than the other, with a bald head, and eyes that were dark and deeply set. He spoke with obvious offence at Johann's intrusion.

'That safe is ours. Now go away, little soldier boy, and find somewhere else to loot, while you still can.'

The man stabbed his crowbar at Johann as he spoke, making it clear that he intended to beat him with it if he didn't leave. Johann looked at the older woman again and saw the terror in her eyes. He looked over at the younger woman and wondered what she was doing there. Clearly she wasn't a Jew; her long grey coat bore the emblem of the *Bund Deutscher Mädel–Werk Glaube und Schönheit*— the League of German Girls' Faith and Beauty Society—which was a section of the BDM for young women too old for the BDM and too young for the NSFrauenschaft. She wore a green, narrow brimmed felt hat, which suggested to Johann that she might also have come in from the street on hearing the older woman's cries. He looked down at the child then. He wondered what terror she had been forced to witness and rage engulfed him. He could not let this continue.

The bald man's crowbar was still outstretched towards Johann. With great speed and determination, he grabbed the man's wrist and twisted his arm around, pulling him down. Then he hit him hard in the face and he fell instantly. The wiry man took a swing at Johann. His crowbar caught the side of Johann's back, and he turned and locked his arm around the other's, holding him in place as he slammed the base of his palm into that prominent nose of his. The man screamed in pain, and Johann continued to hold him so he could hit him again for good measure. When he let go, the man ran bleeding from the room, leaving his bald friend to fight for himself.

But he did not.

It was clear to Johann that there had never been any real fight in either of them when it came down to it. It was one thing to hit a woman or a child—a despicable and cowardly thing to his mind— but it was another matter entirely to go hand-to-hand with some-one who had known fighting all his life. Johann had seen the traits many times before. Over the years he had become adept at reading the signs, and he had read this situation well. The bald man could not leave the room fast enough. He was running even before he had fully stood up, and like his wiry friend before him, he made a clatter on the stairs as he bowled down them.

Johann went to the older woman. If he'd had a coat, he would have put it around her, as much to ward off the coming night's chill as to help restore her dignity. As he did not have a coat, he turned to the window, thinking that the material from the curtains would suffice, but as he did so, the younger woman held her own coat out for him to take.

'Thank you,' Johann said as he took it.

He looked at her properly then for the first time, and he thought her smile as kindly as her gesture. She was slim, medium height, and she had a small, button nose that made her blue-grey eyes appear all the bigger as he held them in his for a moment and smiled back at her.

'Her need is greater,' the woman said.

'Yes,' Johann agreed. He looked down at the little girl standing beside them. She was still clinging to the young woman as though afraid to let go. 'And who might you be?' Johann asked.

The girl did not answer. She just stared up at Johann, her cheeks glistening with tears.

'Is this your mother?' Johann asked her, pointing to the older woman.

The girl nodded. She let go of the younger woman then and ran to her mother. Johann followed her and put the coat over the woman's shoulders. She was bent over with her face in her hands, quietly sobbing.

'Is there somewhere you can go?' Johann asked her. 'Somewhere safe. I've no idea how long this will last.'

The woman looked up. She shook her head.

'Then you should hide somewhere. The attic perhaps?'

The woman nodded.

'Good. Take your daughter. I'll find food and water and bring it to you.'

The woman stood up. 'Where have they taken my husband?'

Johann paused before answering. 'I don't know. Perhaps you should ask at the police station when all this is over.'

'What will they do to him?'

Johann gave no reply. Instead, he looked pensively at the younger woman, whose blank expression offered no more answers than he had himself.

———⌣———

Outside the watchmaker's shop, having found provisions and warm clothing for the watchmaker's wife and daughter, Johann continued to look upon the woman he had just met as she buttoned up her coat, and not for the first time that day he silently wished he had brought his own. The onset of night had chilled the air further, and he imagined the woman was glad to have it back again. Without such comforts, the cold forced Johann to cross his arms around his chest as they made their way through the forever altered streets of Munich in search of more hospitable surroundings.

'What were you doing in there?' Johann asked. 'They are Jews. Why were you trying to help them?'

'I was on my way home from a BDM meeting. We were told what was going to happen to the Jews and I just wanted to get home safely, but as I approached the watchmaker's shop I heard a child crying. Then I saw the broken glass where the shop windows had been smashed, so I went inside. I know I shouldn't have, but a crying child is hard to ignore, Jew or otherwise. Those two men you hit must have been close behind me.'

They stopped walking and the woman offered out her hand. 'I'm Ava, by the way. Ava Bauer.'

Johann took her hand. It felt clammy, despite the cold. 'Johann Langner,' he said. 'I'm pleased to meet you. I only wish it could have been under better circumstances.'

'Yes,' Ava agreed.

A moment later, Johann asked, 'Do you live far from here?'

'Forty minutes on foot. I usually ride my bicycle, but it has a flat tyre. I don't mind. I like walking.'

'So do I. I'll see you safely home.'

'But you're already cold.'

'I don't care. I could do with the fresh air tonight.'

They continued walking by the pale light of the streetlamps, still heading away from the burning synagogue. The red, white and black flags and banners of the Nazi Party adorned almost every building they passed, reminding Johann of the political and military machine that was behind everything he had just witnessed, which he knew was just one of many such acts of violence and destruction currently taking place in every town and city across Germany.

'Why did *you* go in there?' Ava asked. 'I took you for another looter when I first saw you.'

'For similar reasons. I heard screaming. I suppose that was the child's mother?'

'Yes, the men started hitting her. I expect my turn would have come soon enough.'

Johann shook his head. 'I really don't have the stomach for what's going on here. Give me a fair fight for something I believe in and you'll find no man more dedicated to his duty. But this . . .' He waved a hand back in the direction they had come from. 'It's certainly not my idea of soldiering.'

'How old are you, Johann?'

'Twenty.'

'Why didn't you join the *Wehrmacht* as soon as you had the chance? How come you stayed on in the HJ?'

'In a word, Volker.'

'A friend?'

Johann nodded. 'He enjoyed the leadership and the power, I suppose. We've known each other since joining the HJ academy here in Munich, and we'd made it a competition between us to see who could earn his achievement badges first, and who could move up the ranks before the other. It was always a close race, and one we carried on into adult leadership, even to this day. I was enjoying myself enough to let him talk me into staying on when we were invited to do so, and as Volker always says, it will put us in good stead when it's time to become real soldiers. I suppose we're more like brothers.'

'Do you have any real brothers?'

Johann gazed up into the sky. It now appeared dark against the city rooftops, which were awash with moonlight. 'No,' he said, then feeling the need to correct himself he added, 'that is, I had a brother, but he died before I was born. My mother told me he contracted a lung infection when he was a year old.'

'I'm sorry,' Ava said. 'What was his name?'

'He was also called Johann. The name belonged to my grandfather—a common man who rose to become quite a celebrated war hero of his time. I suppose my parents were set on honouring his name.'

'It's a good name,' Ava said.

Johann smiled. 'As good as any, I suppose. You know, I often wonder what my brother would look like if he were still alive, and whether we would be friends, as it is with Volker and me.' He laughed to himself. 'It's silly, I know, but I feel that since I've been given his name, I must live up to my father's expectations of what my brother's life might have been, as well as my own.'

'That must be quite a burden for you.'

'I don't mind. When I need to push myself to be better than I am, I think of my brother and he spurs me on. In my mind he's a great hero, like my grandfather. But because he's dead I can never best him, however hard I try.' He paused, thinking about his father and recalling how he'd often scolded him for his mistakes, letting him know that he doubted his brother would have made them were he alive.

'But what about you?' Johann added, preferring to talk about Ava instead. 'Do you have any brothers or sisters?'

'No. When I was a little girl my mother told me that as soon as I was born she knew one child was enough.' She laughed to herself. 'I've never quite known what she meant by that.'

Johann thought it was because her mother knew she had created perfection, but he didn't dare say it. 'I see that you volunteered to stay on in the BDM.'

'Yes, for my music, mostly.'

'What do you play?'

'Piano. My father's a teacher. Now I've started teaching some of the other girls.'

'I should very much like to hear you play sometime.'

'Yes, perhaps. Sometime.'

They continued walking at an amble. Johann had become so wrapped up in Ava that he no longer felt the cold. 'As you're in the BDM,' he said, 'you must be over eighteen.'

'I'm twenty-one.'

'Really? You look younger.'

Ava gave him a playful smile. 'I bet you've used that line on girls before.'

'N-no,' Johann stammered. 'I meant it. I wasn't even trying to—' He paused as he noticed Ava's smile begin to drop. 'That is, you look very nice and I *would* try to, but I'm sure I could come up with something better to say if that was my intention.'

'And what would you say?'

Johann felt his cheeks flush, and he thought Ava must have noticed the sudden burst of colour in them. He stuttered and stammered again briefly as he tried to find an answer that wouldn't embarrass him further. Then Ava began to laugh.

'It's okay,' she said. 'I'm just teasing you.'

Johann laughed with her, glad to make light of his embarrassment. He was about to speak again when the low rasp of a car horn sounded close behind them. They turned to see who it was.

'It's my papa,' Ava said.

The car pulled up ahead of them and a smartly dressed man in his mid-forties got out. He stood by the open door with his elbow on the roof. 'Ava! Thank goodness! With everything that's going on tonight, I was worried about you.'

Ava looked into Johann's eyes. 'I have to go,' she said. 'Can we take you somewhere?'

'No, that's okay. I really should find my friend.'

'Well, stay out of trouble.' Ava made for the car, and as she reached it she turned back with a smile and said, 'Thank you for rescuing me.'

'It was my pleasure.'

Johann watched her open the passenger door and slip delicately into the car. It began to pull away and he wished then that he'd asked to see her again. However was he going to find her in such a big city?

He called out. 'I'm glad your bicycle has a flat tyre!'

Ava leaned out of the car window. She was still smiling, yet at the same time she looked confused. 'Why?'

Johann returned her smile. He could feel his face beaming as he said, 'Because if you had taken your bicycle today I might never have met you!' He waved as the car sped off, and knowing that she was now too distant to hear him, he added, 'And I'm very glad I did.'

Chapter Five

Present day.

All at once, Johann Langner's voice broke off and the ECG monitor he was wired to went into a state of alarm. It began to beep and flash, and Langner began to convulse as if he were having a seizure. Ingrid Keller was on her feet in an instant.

'Out! Now!'

However caught up in Langner's reminiscences Tayte and Jean were, they both did as they were told. They jumped to their feet and Tayte grabbed his briefcase while Jean gathered from the bed the documents they had previously shown to Langner. They were at the door, and Tayte was about to open it when Langner's voice stopped them.

First he coughed, and then in a hoarse whisper he said, 'Where are you going? I haven't finished my story.'

Keller gave a loud sigh. 'If you don't rest, your story will finish you!'

Tayte didn't know what to do. 'Maybe we can come back later, when you've had some sleep and are feeling better.'

'And what if I don't wake up?'

Tayte glanced at Jean and she gave him a look that said it was his call. 'Are you sure you're up to it?' he asked, concern in his voice.

Keller answered. 'No, he's not up to it.' She pressed a few buttons on the ECG machine and the beeping stopped. 'You should leave.'

'I won't hear of it,' Langner said. 'These little episodes come and go. Sit down again, please.'

Tayte and Jean went back to their seats and Keller shook her head at them. She made Tayte feel uncomfortable, and she was arguably right to want them to leave, but he wanted to hear what Langner had to say, and Langner, it seemed, was keen to tell them.

'Take your time,' Jean said. 'We're in no hurry.'

Langner smiled weakly. 'You're very sweet, my dear.'

Keller helped him to sit up again, and she made him drink some more water before he was allowed to continue.

'Just weeks before the terrible events that came to be known as *Kristallnacht*, Volker and I were invited to attend the *Reichsparteitag Grossdeutschland*—the Rally of Greater Germany, which was the last Nuremberg rally to be held in peacetime. We were having fun, like two of your boy scouts, with little notion of what was ultimately to come. It was held in September, and we'd been given the honour of marching into the city stadium as an eighty thousand strong army of *Hitlerjugend* members to spell out Hitler's name.'

Langner was smiling at the memory by the time he'd finished speaking. Then his expression soured. 'Ah, but those days before the war soon faded. Before long I would be fighting alongside many of those same boys, who were to become my *Kameraden* in the *Waffen-SS*.'

Jean tapped at her tablet PC, calling up some of her prior research. 'It was because of your association with the SS that you faced trial for war crimes after the war ended.'

'Yes. The entire *Schutzstaffel* was declared a criminal organisation, including the combat units of the *Waffen-SS*. Every German soldier who wore the *Sieg* runes of the SS on their tunic was subject to trial at Nuremberg for crimes against humanity—and we were all considered guilty unless proved innocent.'

'I read about your trial,' Jean said. 'You were charged with inciting your troops to give no quarter to surrendering soldiers, and the deaths of seventeen prisoners.'

'Those were the charges, yes, to which I pleaded not guilty. But while I was acquitted of directly ordering the deaths of those soldiers, I was found guilty of allowing their murders. In truth—and at my age I have nothing to gain from lies—I had not known about the murders until it was too late to prevent them.' Langner paused to sip some more water. 'The death sentence was passed and I accepted my fate. It was as I waited to die that I was encouraged to appeal, and then after a good deal of discussion by the prosecuting committee, the sentence was commuted to life imprisonment, of which, as I'm sure you are aware, I served ten years. I later learned that a key consideration for this clemency was due to one of the officers for the prosecution stating that there wasn't a commander on the Allied side, that he knew of, who had not told his troops that this time they did not want to take any prisoners.'

'So you had no involvement with the rounding up or extermination of Jews?' Tayte asked.

Langner gave an emphatic shake of his head. 'I did not, and I would not,' he said, his voice wavering with emotion. 'I was a soldier of the *Leibstandarte*, committed along with the entire youth of Germany to fight what we had been indoctrinated to believe was our common enemy—Bolshevism. I did not hate the Jews.'

'I see,' Tayte said. He saw a tear fall onto Langner's cheek then, and he decided it was best to steer the subject back to kinder memories. 'I guess you bumped into Ava Bauer again. How did that come about?'

Langner wiped his cheek with the back of his hand. He smiled awkwardly, as though still racked by his thoughts, yet keen to change the subject, as Tayte had supposed.

'Bump into her?' Langner began to laugh at the idea until he set himself coughing again. 'Mr Tayte, I didn't just bump into her. I couldn't leave such a thing to chance. I had to find her, and it wasn't as difficult as I'd at first imagined.' His smile dropped again. 'Although I should have gone to find Ava by myself that night. Not that I could have kept her a secret from Volker for long. But I regret with all my heart the day Volker Strobel ever met Ava Bauer.'

Chapter Six

Munich. 23 November 1938.

Beneath a hissing gas lamp, leaning against the stone archway that led into the meeting place of Munich's League of German Girls Faith and Beauty Society, Volker Strobel lit a cigarette and offered the packet to Johann.

Johann shook his head. 'Not just now.'

'Really? It's not like you to turn down a cigarette. Especially on a cold evening like this.'

'I don't feel like one.'

Volker laughed to himself. 'It must be because of the girl, eh? You want to keep your breath fresh, is that it? Have you kissed her yet?'

'How could I have? I've only seen her once, and that was only briefly.'

'Yes, of course. So maybe she'll show up tonight, eh?'

'I hope so.'

After meeting Ava two weeks before, having learned that she was a member of the society tasked with raising girls as torch bearers of the national-socialist world, Johann had made it his mission to find out where the society met every week. He had tried in vain to see Ava on the Wednesday after he'd met her. Now he was trying again in the hope that she had gone to the meeting this week. He had his black winter coat with him tonight, but having stood outside the building with Volker for close to an hour already, the cold was beginning to bite regardless. He crossed his arms and stamped his feet as he took in the busy street before him. He watched a crowded tram go by, and he cast his eyes further along the street and up at the tall buildings whose Nazi Party flags were all flapping in the chill breeze. He rubbed his hands together to warm them, and under his breath he wished that Ava would come out soon.

Volker crossed the steps that divided the archway and stood close beside him. 'You know, you worry me, Johann. I find the circumstances of how you met this girl very disturbing. If you were not my closest friend I would be obliged to report you both. Have you told anyone else?'

'No. Only you.'

'Good. I suggest you keep it that way. It could otherwise be very dangerous for you.' He paused, as if considering the consequences. 'Perhaps it would be for the best if this Ava girl failed to show again tonight. You really shouldn't have anything more to do with her. Let's go and get a drink, eh? What do you say?'

Johann smiled at his friend. He turned and held him by the shoulders forcing their eyes to meet. 'I have to see her again, Volker. Just wait until you meet her. Then you'll understand.'

Volker shook his head. 'I'm sure you must see a great deal in her, but it's freezing out here and I could use a drink to warm me up. Besides, there are hundreds of girls in Munich. Why must it be this one?'

'They're not like Ava. She's special. You'll see.'

The sound of the main doors opening drew Johann's attention then and he turned towards them as light spilled out onto the steps.

'Look, they're coming out now,' Johann said.

He pulled Volker aside, his eyes still on the doors as the first two girls came out. He smiled at them as they passed, and then he quickly turned back to the doorway as several more young women left the building.

'Do you know Ava Bauer?' he asked one of the girls at random. 'Was she at the meeting tonight?'

The girl shook her head and carried on talking to her friend.

Volker blew smoke across Johann's face. 'It's a lost cause, I tell you. Her father's most likely forbidden her to come to these meetings again after all the trouble on the streets the last time she attended. You said her father came to find her because she was late home.'

'Yes, because her bicycle had a flat tyre.'

Johann was paying more attention to the girls now pouring out of the building than he was to his friend. The throng had forced the two of them down onto the pavement and he'd lost track of who he'd looked at and who he'd missed as the seemingly endless parade of girls parted to his left and right. It seemed hopeless. He was about to start calling Ava's name, but at that moment his conversation with Volker caught up with him. His eyes widened.

'Her bicycle! Of course.'

Johann grabbed Volker's arm and pulled him along the street, turning the corner to the bicycle racks he'd seen on their way there. He saw a few girls getting onto their bicycles, and a few others were already cycling away. He ran ahead to see them better, but he didn't recognise Ava among them. There were still dozens of bicycles waiting to be claimed.

He turned back to Volker. 'Her bicycle will have been fixed up by now,' he said. 'She'll be easier to spot if we wait here.'

Volker checked the time on his wristwatch. 'I'll stay another ten minutes, then I'm going for that drink, which you're paying for, by the way. You owe me that much. I've been very patient.'

'Yes, you have. Another ten minutes then.'

During that time, Volker smoked three more cigarettes and Johann watched the bicycle racks gradually deplete. As before, there was no sign of Ava Bauer. Although when he had asked one girl whether she knew Ava, and whether she had seen her at the meeting, she had told him she thought she had. It renewed his hope.

But where was she?

'Time's up, my friend,' Volker said.

Johann felt Volker's hand on his shoulder and he knew it was indeed time to go. There were only a few bicycles left now, and he had to concede that the odds of one of them belonging to Ava were small. He had missed her again.

'Come on, I'm frozen to my bones,' Volker said.

Dejection must have been written all over Johann's face as he turned to his friend because Volker returned a sympathetic smile.

'It's not so bad, Johann. We'll give it one more try next week, eh?'

Johann gave a slow nod. 'You're a good friend, Volker. But I really don't mind coming by myself.'

They set off at an amble, back along the pavement.

'Nonsense, I won't hear of it,' Volker said. 'Besides, you've built her up so much now that I want to see this Ava Bauer almost as much as you do.'

They were laughing together as they turned the corner and crossed the street beneath the pale glow of the lamplight. Then a familiar voice stopped Johann in his tracks.

'Johann?'

He turned back, and at once he caught his breath. It was Ava Bauer.

'Ava!' Johann's face was beaming. 'I thought I'd missed you.'

She was just how he remembered her. She wore the same long grey coat, and her dark blonde hair was rolled up beneath the same felt hat she had been wearing when he first met her. She was standing beside the kerb with her bicycle, and Johann was at a loss to understand how she could have retrieved it without him having seen her sooner.

Ava continued to smile at him, but with a degree of bemusement as she asked, 'Whatever are you doing here?'

Not waiting for an introduction, Volker stepped forward. 'He came to find you. He's besotted with you, aren't you, Johann?' He thumped Johann playfully on the shoulder. 'And now I can see why.'

Johann laughed to hide his embarrassment. 'This is my friend, Volker Strobel. You remember I told you about him?' He turned to Volker. 'Volker,' he said, beaming. 'This is Ava Bauer.'

Ava offered her hand and Volker took it in his. With his eyes fixed on her, he spoke to Johann first. 'You told me how you met Ava, Johann, but you did not tell me how pretty she was.' His eyes seemed to devour her as he leaned in and kissed her hand. '*Fräulein* Bauer.' He clicked his heels. 'It is a pleasure indeed to finally meet you.'

Johann thought Ava was about to start giggling at Volker's flirtatious introduction, but by the time he had lifted his head again, Ava's face was composed, with just the hint of a smile at the corners of her mouth.

'I know the name Strobel,' Ava said. 'Are you related to senior Reich Minister Joseph Strobel?'

Volker raised his chin proudly. 'Baron Joseph von Strobel is my father—although since the German nobility is no longer recognised, my family has stopped using the title.'

'Volker's a very well-connected man,' Johann said.

'Yes, perhaps,' Volker said. 'My father is a great politician, just like our *Führer*. That's where the real power is.' He paused. 'But enough of all that.' He moved closer to Ava and placed his arm loosely around her so that his hand was resting on her bicycle saddle. 'Do you know that Johann here hasn't stopped talking about you since the riots?'

Ava looked as though she wanted to giggle again, and from the mischief written all over Volker's face, it was clear to Johann that his friend was out to embarrass him.

'I wanted to see you again, Ava,' Johann said. His stutter returned. 'I-I hope you don't mind my having found you again like this.'

'No, not at all. I'm quite flattered.'

Johann could feel another blush rising, so he changed the subject. 'I see that you've had your puncture repaired.' He pointed down at the front tyre of Ava's bicycle, having no idea whether it was the right one. 'We were waiting for you by the bicycle racks. I don't know how we missed you.'

'I don't leave my bicycle there any more. The racks get too full. A few of us leave them across the street.'

She gestured behind her, but Johann couldn't take his eyes off her long enough to see where she meant.

'Well, that explains it,' Volker said. 'We were just going for a drink. You'll join us, of course.'

'Well, I—'

'But you must,' Volker insisted. 'We've waited over an hour in the cold for you, haven't we, Johann?'

Johann nodded and gave Ava a sheepish smile. Now that he had found her again, the last thing he wanted was for her to be put off by Volker's overly direct manner.

'It's true that I've been waiting at length in the hope of seeing you again, and that Volker here, like the good friend he is, has been standing in the cold with me. If you do have the time to join us for a drink, I should like it very much.'

'I'd like it, too, but I'll be late home and Papa will worry.'

Volker cut in again. 'What if I told you I know how you can have a drink with us and still be home at your usual time?'

'How?' Ava asked.

Volker lifted her bicycle up onto the pavement. 'Walk with us and I'll explain along the way. We're wasting time here, and you were going in this direction anyway.'

They started walking, Ava pushing her bicycle with Johann to her left and Volker to her right.

'I know a nice place just around the corner,' Volker continued. 'The proprietor has been a friend of my family's for a very long time. He'll serve us the finest brandy to warm us up, and when we've finished, I'll borrow his van and Johann and I will take you and your bicycle home to your papa, who will be none the wiser. Now what do you say to that?'

Ava turned to Johann, and he could see that she was still unsure. He could also see that Volker had changed his opinion of Ava quite considerably now that he had met her. This was a far cry from wanting him to have nothing more to do with her.

'It would just be for one drink,' Johann said. 'And I should very much like the opportunity to continue the conversation we began two weeks ago.'

Ava smiled. 'I don't see why not. As long as I'm not late home.'

'Good!' Volker said. He laughed then as he grabbed Ava's bicycle and began to run with it. 'Come on! If we hurry, we might have time for two drinks.'

Chapter Seven

Present day.

Outside the German Heart Centre on Lazarettstrasse, Tayte and Jean followed their bags into the back of a cream-coloured Mercedes taxi. Although they hadn't had to wait long, Tayte was glad of the cool air-conditioning, which was a welcome respite from the hot afternoon sun. Tayte liked taxis. They took the stress out of driving on unfamiliar streets, and you didn't have to know your way around. He thought back to the last time he'd worked with Jean, in London the previous year, and was glad he didn't have to travel around on the back of her motorcycle again this time.

'Maxburgstrasse,' he said to the driver, and they were on their way, heading towards the city centre.

When the ECG machine Johann Langner was attached to lit up with alarms for the second time during their visit, Ingrid Keller had once again ordered them to leave, and this time Langner had not recovered sufficiently to insist they stay to hear the remainder of his story about his friendship with Volker Strobel and the girl, Ava Bauer, who had come into their lives not long before the war began.

Tayte turned to Jean. 'I hope the old man's okay. Maybe we should have left sooner.'

'I was thinking the same thing,' Jean said. 'But he wanted to talk, didn't he?'

'I know, but I can't help feeling a little responsible. His nurse was right—he needed rest.'

'I think what really set him off that last time was talking about Volker Strobel. Whatever did the man do?'

'A terrible thing,' Tayte said, thoughtfully, repeating Langner's last words to them, knowing that he wasn't referring to the terrible things Strobel had done to earn him the moniker 'Demon of Dachau', but something else. 'I'd love to know what he was referring to, and I'd have really liked to hear what else he had to say.'

Jean agreed. 'Maybe we'll get another chance to talk to him.'

'Yeah, maybe,' Tayte said, but recalling how ashen and drawn Langner had looked as they left his hospital room, he somehow doubted it.

As they continued their taxi ride through the busy streets of Munich, Tayte turned his thoughts to their destination: the registered offices of *Die Freunde der Waffen-SS Kriegsveteranen— The Friends of the Waffen-SS War Veterans*—or the FWK as the organisation was commonly known. It was close by and their bags were light and few. Now that he was in Munich, rather than going to their hotel to check in, Tayte was all the more keen to push on and piece his own family history puzzle together.

'Hopefully we can fill in the rest of Langner's story some other way,' Tayte said. 'The FWK might be able to tell us a thing or two.'

'That's if they'll talk to us.'

'True, but we've nothing else planned until tomorrow. It's worth a shot.'

Jean pulled out her tablet PC. 'I made some more notes about them. While you were staring at the back of the seat in front of you on the plane this morning, I found a newspaper article from the *Guardian* a few years ago.'

Tayte caught Jean's wink as she teased him about the flight and he threw her a playfully sarcastic smile. 'So what have you got, hotshot?'

'Well, it seems that the German government has had a close eye on the FWK for some time. They were established as a non-profit and thus charitable organisation in 1945, but the Federal Finance Court denied them their non-profit status in the early 1990s, when it was discovered that they were not only raising funds to help *Waffen*-SS war veterans and their families, but that they were also assisting families of convicted war criminals. The report goes on to allege that the FWK are even supporting wanted war criminals who are still at large today.'

Tayte scoffed. 'If that's true then I'm not surprised they lost their charitable status. I wonder if they've been helping Volker Strobel. Maybe they know where he is.'

'I'm sure you're not the first person to wonder that.'

'No,' Tayte said, thinking ahead to tomorrow's meeting with Munich's foremost specialist on the Demon of Dachau—an eminent Nazi hunter called Tobias Kaufmann.

The taxi turned off the main road into a narrow street, and out of the window Tayte saw that they had arrived in Maxburgstrasse. He gave the driver the number of the building, thankful that the driver spoke English, as did many of the people he had so far encountered in Munich. As the car crawled along between continuous lines of parked cars, Tayte saw that the area was a hotchpotch of buildings old and new with a few shops here and there, and because the street was narrow, the tall buildings that lined the pavement threw everything into shade. The taxi pulled up in front of a featureless grey wall of offices, whose many dark windows dominated the façade.

Tayte paid the driver and refused the change. '*Danke*,' he said as he and Jean got out, determined as he was to try a few of the more common phrases he'd learned from the app Jean had downloaded to her computer for the trip.

As the taxi pulled away, Tayte wished he'd thought to ask the driver to wait. The dark windows he and Jean were now looking up at made the place look ominously vacant. Jean slung her backpack over her shoulder and Tayte picked up his suit carrier and briefcase. He'd given up offering to carry Jean's bag for her, however much he wanted to. They went closer, taking the few steps that ran up to the aluminium framed double doors. They were closed, and through the glass there was no light to be seen beyond.

Tayte sighed. 'This doesn't look good.'

He tried the door, and as expected, it was locked. There was a letterbox and a doorbell to his right. He pressed the button and heard a buzzer sound somewhere inside, thinking that during office hours it would have brought a security guard to the door.

'At least it's a nice afternoon,' Jean offered. 'I'd like to see the city centre as we're so close. Do you want to get something to eat?'

Tayte had been trying to ignore the groans his stomach was making for the last couple of hours. A kind of brunch had been served on the plane, but however much he liked his food, he was always so tense during a flight that he could never face the in-flight meals. Something to eat sounded good, but a part of him just wanted to check in at the hotel and get on with his research. Several strands of interest had come out of their conversation with Johann Langner that he wanted to explore, but that part of him was the old part—the loner who rarely had anyone with him that he wanted to sit down and share a meal with.

He turned away from the building and gave Jean a smile. 'That sounds great,' he said, thinking it was what couples did on city breaks, but more importantly because he knew it was what Jean wanted to do. He caught a voice in his head then, telling him that the research could wait a few hours, and he almost laughed to himself. Before he'd met Jean such a thought would never have crossed his mind.

'What is it?' Jean asked, clearly noticing his smirk.

'It's nothing.' Tayte grabbed Jean's hand and led her back to the pavement, heading the same way the taxi had gone. 'Let's get another cab and ask the driver to take us to the finest restaurant in Munich.'

Jean laughed. 'Are you paying?'

'Sure, but in that case maybe I'll ask for the second or third finest.'

They were laughing as Tayte turned back to see if there was a taxi coming, although he thought they would have to keep walking until they hit a more touristy part of the city. As he looked over his shoulder his smile turned to excitement when he saw two people, a man and a woman, at the glass doors they had just left. He drew Jean's attention to them.

'Look, someone's going inside.'

He let go of Jean's hand and almost jogged back up the steps to the door. He reached it just as it was closing.

'Excuse me,' he said. He was too excited to recall how to say it in German.

The door opened again and Tayte saw a tall, slim woman in a navy trouser suit, whom he thought was about Jean's age, in her late thirties. The man Tayte had seen with her was standing in the shadows further back. The woman smiled expectantly, as though waiting for Tayte to say what he wanted.

'Do you speak English?' he asked.

'Of course,' the woman said, a little indignantly, Tayte thought, as if he should have known that every German in a business suit spoke English.

Tayte paused to give himself time to get the pronunciation right for his next line. 'Great,' he said. 'I'm looking for *Die Freunde der Waffen-SS Kriegsveteranen*. Is this the right place?'

The woman's formerly pleasant expression changed to a frown. 'We don't have visitors.'

'Well, can I make an appointment?'

'No, I'm sorry. No visitors.'

She began to close the door, but Tayte quickly pulled out the photograph he had of his mother and thrust it across the threshold. He didn't expect anything to come of it, but he didn't think it was a good idea to be so direct as to ask if they were helping Volker Strobel evade the authorities.

'I'm looking for this woman, or trying to find someone who can tell me her name. Can you at least tell me if you recognise her?'

The woman glanced at the photograph. 'No, I'm sorry,' she repeated. She began to close the door again. 'Now if you'll—'

Jean stepped beside Tayte then and cut in. 'Can we talk to you about Volker Strobel?'

The direct approach it is, then, Tayte thought. 'Look, we're not out to expose Strobel,' he said. 'We just want to talk to anyone who knows anything about him in the hope that it might help identify the woman we're trying to find.'

The man came out from the shadows then. He appeared on the other side of the glass briefly before he slammed the door in Tayte's face, rattling the frame. Tayte watched both figures silently recede into the darkness.

'Well, that was a lot of good,' Tayte said as he shoved one of his business cards through the letterbox, more out of habit than the belief that these people might change their minds about talking to him.

'Don't be too disappointed, JT. It went exactly as we expected it would.'

'It did?'

Jean nodded. 'Although, I'd say from the reaction we just got that it's pretty clear the FWK know more than a thing or two about Volker Strobel.'

The taxi Tayte hailed soon after leaving Maxburgstrasse took them further into the centre of Munich, but instead of going straight to a restaurant as Tayte had hoped they would, the driver took them to the edge of the old town because Jean wanted to see the Munich Residence—a former royal palace of the monarchs of Bavaria. Jean had previously described the palace to Tayte, and he couldn't imagine any royal historian wanting to miss the opportunity to see it, but he hadn't let the taxi driver go without first getting a recommendation for a nearby restaurant that served traditional Bavarian cuisine. They spent an hour at the palace, which both Tayte and Jean agreed wasn't nearly long enough to take everything in: the museums, the treasury and the historical gardens, not to mention all the artwork and the tapestries that were spread throughout numerous courts.

It was just after five o'clock when they left, and by now both Tayte and Jean were famished, so they set off south through the bustling streets of the old town, towards the heart of the city, in search of the restaurant the taxi driver had recommended—the *Spatenhaus an der Oper*, which he'd said was on Residenzstrasse opposite Max-Joseph-Platz.

'We'll have to come back before we return to London,' Jean said as they strolled hand in hand across Odeonsplatz in the warm late-afternoon sunshine.

'That's a promise,' Tayte said, looking around for street signs. 'I hope we're heading the right way.'

They kept walking, leaving the plaza and entering into shade along a narrow street that was lined with Baroque architecture. A moment later Jean pointed across the street to a side junction. 'Look. There's a street sign—Viscardigasse. *Gasse* means alley if I'm not mistaken. Residenzstrasse is straight ahead. I think we must be on it now.'

'Great,' Tayte said. 'The restaurant shouldn't be far.'

There were shops to their right, set back beneath the buildings, creating a covered walkway off the street. They crossed and strolled beside them, Jean window browsing while Tayte kept looking for the plaza the taxi driver had said the restaurant was opposite. He noticed the sunlight was splashing onto the front of the buildings a hundred metres or so ahead of them, and he thought that must be where Max-Joseph-Platz was. His stomach groaned when they passed a café and a wonderful scent of coffee and pastries hit him. He was about to increase the pace when Jean suddenly stopped. When he turned around to see why, she wouldn't let him.

'Don't look,' she said, reaching up and covering his eyes. 'I've seen something I want to get for you.'

She pushed Tayte's head away and he thought he heard her giggle. He wondered what she could possibly have seen.

'Go and wait in the sun,' she said, giving Tayte a gentle shove. 'And no peeking.'

Tayte rather liked the cool shade, but he did as he was told and within a minute he was standing at the corner of Max-Joseph-Platz, looking across the sunlit plaza towards an impressive neo-classical portico that led into a building whose purpose he was unable to determine from so far back. He strolled towards it, pausing partway, where he leaned against a circular railing that had numerous bicycles chained to it. He put his bags down, and as he looked back he spotted the restaurant they were heading for and hoped Jean wouldn't be too long. He checked his watch—the same old-fashioned digital throwback from the 1980s with the red LED digits that had served him so faithfully all these years. It told him it was 17.14.

Tayte waited a few minutes, and then he ambled closer to the Corinthian-columned portico that dominated the square, curious to see what the building was used for. As he drew closer to the steps that ran up to the main entrance, he saw that it was the Max-Joseph-Platz National Theatre, and having satisfied his curiosity, he turned away again and slowly headed back, thinking that Jean should be entering the plaza at any minute. He arrived back at the railings and checked his watch again. It was 17.22 and there was still no sign of her.

Maybe there was a line at the checkout, he thought. He closed his eyes and began to think about the research he wanted to do after they checked in at the hotel. *Two friends, whose friendship was torn apart by a girl—Ava Bauer . . .* That was the story Johann Langner was telling them about. *Was it significant?* Tayte didn't know at this point. All he did know was that his mother had seemingly been interested in Volker Strobel or perhaps Johann Langner, or maybe even the building she'd been photographed outside. He made a mental note to visit Langner's former Hitler Youth building, now a museum and education centre, while they were in Munich. Perhaps it held some further clue as to what had drawn his mother there.

Tayte opened his eyes and scanned for Jean again. Nothing. He checked his watch and realised he'd been daydreaming for several minutes because it was now 17.30, which he thought was too long. He strode back to the edge of the plaza onto Residenzstrasse and looked back along the shady street. There were plenty of people about, but he couldn't see Jean among them. He walked over to the shops and began to stroll beside them, conscious of upsetting Jean's surprise, but twenty minutes had passed since he'd left her and he was beginning to worry.

He drew closer to the shops he'd been outside when they stopped. He recognised the jeweller's he'd passed as he set off for the plaza. Ahead was the café, and he thought he had to be close to the shop Jean had been interested in. He kept going and came to a women's fashion boutique, and then a shoe shop. Was that it? Did Jean want to buy him a new pair of shoes? He hoped she wasn't about to start changing his wardrobe for him, because he didn't think he could handle too many changes at once. He liked his wardrobe just the way it was: tan suit, white shirt and loafers. There was no need to complicate his life with anything else. He peered in through the shop window. There was a man and a woman browsing together, and there was someone else paying for something. It wasn't Jean.

Tayte turned away again, but before he could take another step, he saw her. She was further back along the street by the junction they had passed. He began to smile, wondering why she had gone back that way, and what had kept her so long, but when she started to run towards him, his smile changed to a concerned frown. Her hair looked wild and her eyes were glistening with tears.

'Jean!' Tayte ran to meet her. 'What's happened? Are you okay?' Tayte held her shoulders and began to rub them. 'You're shaking.'

She put her arms around him and began to sob into his chest. 'I've been threatened.'

'What? Who by?'

Jean choked back her tears and wiped her cheeks. 'As I left the shop I'd gone into, three men grabbed me. One of them held his hand over my mouth so I couldn't call out. Before I knew it they'd dragged me into a passageway. They pinned me against the wall and one of them pressed a knife against my cheek. He said he'd cut me if I screamed.'

Tayte's blood was already boiling. He could see the impression the knife had left, still fresh on Jean's cheek. He looked around, as though he might still be able to see who had done this, but all he saw were the curious faces of passers-by, looking back at him as if wondering what the upset was about.

'They told me to go home, and to take you with me. They said if we didn't they'd find me again.' Jean paused, still shaking from the shock. 'They said if we didn't they were going to rape me. One of them started to pull my dress up, and then he laughed and they went.'

Tayte shook his head. 'Someone must have followed us after we left those offices earlier,' he said, thinking that whoever it was, they hadn't wasted any time in trying to warn him and Jean off asking questions about Volker Strobel. *So much for leaving my business card,* he thought.

'Two of them had shaved heads,' Jean said. 'I saw a few tattoos. The one with the knife who did all the talking had dark hair, and he had a black skull tattooed on one side of his neck with Nazi SS *Sieg* runes tattooed low on the other.'

'He clearly wasn't worried about you being able to identify him.'

'No, and that's what's so frightening about it. They didn't seem to give a damn.'

'Neo-Nazis?'

'I would imagine so.'

'They're cowards, whoever they were. Singling you out like that.'

Jean reached into her jacket and pulled out a red-and-white-striped paper bag. 'I bought you this,' she said, handing it to him.

Tayte removed the contents and it practically fell apart in his hands. It was a giant Hershey's Mr Goodbar.

Jean tried to laugh at it. 'I know it's your favourite,' she said. 'I couldn't believe it when we passed the shop and you hadn't noticed.' Jean pointed to a small shop front behind them with the words *Welt der Schokolade*—world of chocolate—above the window. 'They sell chocolate from all over the world. I'm sorry it's broken. It must have happened when they shoved me against the wall.'

A part of Tayte wished the people who had done this to Jean were there now, but the sensible part of him hoped they never came within a hundred feet of Jean again.

'Come on,' he said. 'We passed a taxi rank soon after we left the palace. We'll go to the police and report what's happened, and then we'll go and check in at the hotel. We've got some serious decisions to make.'

Chapter Eight

Tayte and Jean were staying at the Hilton Munich City hotel, which was located close to the city centre to the southeast. Tayte preferred the anonymity of larger establishments, where you didn't have to share a table at breakfast with anyone, or get into small talk over dinner with the other guests. It was a failing of his, he knew that, but it was how he liked it and Jean didn't seem to mind.

Their visit to the local police station had been perfunctory at best, but they had reported the incident and Jean had described her attackers to them. There was little the police said they could do, and they seemed to take a less serious view of the incident when they knew Jean had not been physically harmed in any way. They ate as soon as they had checked into the hotel and had dropped their bags off in their room, although Jean had had little appetite. She'd given most of her meal to Tayte, and she'd spent the remainder of their short time in the hotel restaurant pushing the rest of her food around her plate, clearly deep in thought. Tayte had supposed she was going over what had happened, trying to decide whether she wanted to go on or go home.

They found a table in the hotel's Metropolis cocktail bar and lounge and sat down with two large glasses of Jack Daniel's on ice.

'Cheers,' Tayte said, and they both took a big sip. 'Welcome to Munich,' he added with more than a hint of sarcasm.

Jean settled back in her seat. 'At least we learned something after we left Johann Langner at the hospital.'

'We did?'

Jean nodded. 'His old wartime friend, Volker Strobel, must still be alive. Why else would *Die Freunde der Waffen-SS Kriegsveteranen* send a gang of neo-Nazi thugs to warn us off?'

'Hey, that's not a bad accent you've picked up there. Spoken like a true local.'

Jean laughed into her drink. 'How would you know? You've hardly looked at my "Teach Yourself German" app.'

'*Ja, das ist* true,' Tayte said with a grin. He heaved a sigh. 'So what are we going to do?'

'What do you usually do? This isn't the first time someone's tried to warn you off an assignment.'

'That's also true, but I'm a stubborn fool and things are a little different now.'

Jean sat up. 'I knew you'd say that.'

'What?'

'That because I'm here, working on your assignment with you, things are different—that you have me to look out for now, as well as yourself, and you're not comfortable with that.'

'Well, up until now, I've never had anyone else to look out for,' Tayte countered. 'I don't want anything bad to happen to you, that's all.'

Jean sighed, as if she understood where he was coming from, and was even a little touched by it, but Tayte could see she was frustrated.

'I signed up for this, didn't I?' Jean said. 'I told you it had to be all or nothing if we're going to make a go of things together, and you've told me several times that your mother said she gave you up for your own protection. I knew it could be dangerous. And besides, you're not about to pack up and go home, are you?'

'I can't.'

'Exactly, and I wouldn't ask you to.'

'We're on to something here,' Tayte said. 'I know we are. Maybe for the first time in my life I have the chance to find out who I am.'

'I know how much this means to you, JT, but I can't just go home and leave you to it.' She reached across the table and squeezed Tayte's hand. 'I don't want to, and I don't want anything bad to happen to you, either.'

Tayte swallowed the ice cube he'd been sucking. 'Okay,' he said. 'We'll go on together, but we both need to be extra careful. These people aren't playing games.'

Jean nodded. 'So what's our next line of research?'

'Don't you want to get an early night?' Tayte blushed. There was no way he could have said that without it sounding suggestive.

Jean smirked at him, but she quickly got all serious again. 'It isn't even dark outside. Where's your laptop?'

'Right here in my briefcase.'

'Of course it is. So let's get another drink and go over what we've learned so far.'

She laughed as Tayte pulled his briefcase up onto his lap. 'Will you be bringing your "special friend" to dinner with you every night?'

Tayte's travel-worn briefcase went everywhere with him. They had shared many adventures and discoveries on one assignment and another, and he was having a hard time leaving it out of their relationship.

'It saved me a trip to the room, didn't it?'

Jean shook her head. 'You really are incorrigible. So where should we start?'

'Well, that's the thing,' Tayte said as he opened his laptop. 'While I've traced the roots of many of my American clients to Germany, their immigrant ancestors have usually been as far back as I was required to go, and for those assignments where I've been asked to look further back, the records I've needed to see have typically been prior to the time when German civil registration began. Records were held in church archives prior to that, and because the records are so old, no time-based restrictions are imposed. Germany's civil registration records, on the other hand, aren't all that easy to get at. In fact, if you're not a direct family member, or if sufficient time hasn't passed since the event you're looking for, you're flat out of luck. Germany's privacy laws around civil registration records were relaxed a little towards the end of the last decade, but for non-direct family members to access these records, 110 years have to have passed for births, eighty years for marriages and thirty years for deaths, which would be okay for the period we're interested in if you didn't first have to show that the person you're interested in was deceased.'

'I see,' Jean said. 'So what can we do?'

'I think most of the information we can hope to gather will come from talking to people who knew Strobel and Langner, or those people who already have an interest in them, such as the man we're going to see in the morning, Tobias Kaufmann. I'm hoping he'll be able to tell us a thing or two. All we really have for now is what we've already heard from Johann Langner, and that only took us as far as 1938.'

'We know they fell out over a girl called Ava Bauer,' Jean said. 'Can we find out more about her?'

'We could try some general searches, but I don't know that it would be worthwhile at this stage. I prefer to know what I'm looking for and why.'

'We also know that Ava somehow came between Langner and Strobel, and that Langner regretted the day he introduced his friend to her.'

'Jealousy?' Tayte offered. 'Fighting over the girl?'

'That's the impression I got from Langner earlier, although he didn't directly say it.'

Tayte closed his laptop again. 'Jealousy seems most likely,' he said. 'Although we know from the research we conducted into Strobel prior to coming to Germany that he didn't get the girl— not Ava anyway. According to Wikipedia Strobel married someone called Trudi Scheffler.'

'That doesn't mean he didn't want Ava.'

'No, it doesn't. And if that's the case, what terrible thing did Strobel do in connection with it? Langner was very clear that Strobel had done something.'

'Jealousy can certainly bring out the worst in people,' Jean said. 'And by all accounts, Strobel was already on his way to becoming the very worst kind of person by the time the war broke out. When I found out that my ex-husband was cheating on me, I was jealous of the other woman for a very long time. What did she have to offer that I didn't? It can eat away at you unless you get a hold of it. I wanted to do some terrible things to her, I can tell you. Sometimes I scared myself.'

'But you didn't, did you?'

'No, of course not, but I thought about it.'

'Thinking and doing are two very different beasts,' Tayte said.

'Yes, and Volker Strobel was clearly something else entirely. Who knows what a man like that was capable of.'

Tayte agreed. He took a slow and thoughtful sip of his drink, considering that whatever had happened back then, the two friends and the girl, Ava, were clearly on some kind of collision course by the time the war began.

Chapter Nine

Munich. April 1940.

More than a year had passed since Johann Langner first met Ava Bauer, and the thought of seeing her again that evening made for a restless journey as the train he'd been travelling on for close to an hour carried him north to Munich. During that time they had seen one another far less frequently than Johann would have liked, not least because 1939 saw a new chapter in his life.

At the beginning of that year, he and his friend, Volker Strobel, had left the Hitler Youth to join the enlisted ranks of the *Waffen-SS*, where they spent six months prior to their enrolment in the SS officers' training school in the Bavarian town of Bad Tölz, which was thirty miles south of Munich. It was a paramilitary career path they had both been cultivated for over the years because of their exemplary service and leadership potential in the Hitler Youth, but the relocation had made any kind of contact with Ava very difficult.

She had agreed to write to both Johann and Volker, all having become good friends during their brief time together, but so far, Ava had committed herself to neither man. Because of this, Johann and Volker often found themselves vying for her attention whenever the opportunity arose, and they would often compare the number of letters each had received from Ava, as though it were a benchmark for Ava's affection. To date, Johann was ahead by five letters, which he took to be a good sign.

SS-*Junkerschule* Bad Tölz was Germany's equivalent of Britain's Sandhurst Royal Military Academy and the United States Military Academy at West Point, and it had impressed Johann from the moment he had entered the complex between the two conical towers that framed its arched main gate. It was there that they had quickly refined their leadership skills, but with the advent of war that September, their time at the training school lasted only seven months.

Johann stopped trying to read his newspaper and neatly folded it and placed it beside his peaked cap on the empty seat beside him. He had thought it might help to distract him during the journey, but every time he picked it up he found himself unable to concentrate. He gazed out of the carriage window instead and noticed that dusk had begun its inevitable descent, obscuring the buildings on the outskirts of Munich into featureless shapes, darkening the glass to a pale mirror in which he saw the reflection of a young man who seemed to have grown up so fast in recent years that he barely recognised himself. Perhaps it was his officer's uniform, or the responsibility that came with it.

Soon to join the ranks of the elite *Leibstandarte SS Adolf Hitler*, which was originally established as Hitler's personal bodyguard, he wore the field-grey duty uniform of an SS-*Untersturmführer*, having welcomed the honour of serving with the regiment as a Junior Storm Leader attached to the Reconnaissance Battalion— not least because he knew there were appointments for SS officers that he had no taste for, such as within the ranks of the Security Police—the *Sicherheitsdienst*, commonly referred to as the SD.

He considered that the only thing about him that remained unchanged was the hairstyle he had first been introduced to in the *Hitlerjugend*. His hair was just as blonde now as then, and it was tapered down to the skin an inch above his ears and neckline, while the longer crown was slicked back with a pomade hair dressing and combed with a high side parting. He smoothed it back with the palm of his hand and looked down at his newspaper again, catching the headline that informed of Adolf Hitler's meeting with Benito Mussolini at the Brenner Pass, high in the Alps, where they had talked of an alliance between their nations against Britain and France. He wondered what his father would make of this war, and how different it might be from the last, in which his father had fought. As hard to please as Johann's father was, it was Johann's wish to make him proud.

He felt his upper body roll forward as the train slowed down. He checked his watch and noted that it was almost seven thirty. Not long to go now. He had a few days to himself before he had to join his unit and he hoped to spend as much of that time as possible with Ava. They had arranged to meet at eight thirty at the Osteria Bavaria on the corner of Schellingstrasse—a restaurant that Volker, in his usual bullish manner, had insisted they dine at because it was reportedly frequented by Adolf Hitler. In Volker's last letter to Johann, he had informed him that his young cousin, Trudi Scheffler, was visiting Munich with her aunt that weekend, and so he had invited her along to make up a fourth for dinner.

Johann had seen through his friend's plan immediately. It was common knowledge to him that Volker's cousin would marry him if he would have her, but since Volker had made it clear to Johann that he intended to make a play for Ava, Johann could think of no reason why his friend would invite the reputedly beautiful *Fräulein* Scheffler along other than to distract Johann's attention from the girl whose affections they were both vying for. As the train followed a bend in the railway track, Johann glimpsed the covered train terminal ahead. When the train pulled alongside the concourse, he neatly set his cap into place and considered that it didn't matter to him how beautiful Volker's cousin was. To Johann, no woman could outshine Ava Bauer.

———

The Osteria Bavaria was a small, family-run restaurant on Schellingstrasse, close to the centre of Munich to the north. Johann had arrived in good time, and had decided to take a moment to collect his thoughts before going in. He stood at the cross-junction where the main road intersects Schraudolphstrasse and took in the restaurant sign above the arched doorway that told him he was in the right place. He wondered why he had never been to the Osteria before. Volker clearly thought it somewhere special, no doubt because of its connection with the *Führer*, and yet Volker had only ever taken him to fancy establishments before now. If he had been showing off his family wealth, then it appeared particularly odd to Johann that Volker would choose to dine at the Osteria when Ava, whom he surely wished to impress, would be there. Unless Volker had tuned in to Ava's sensibilities enough to know that such lavishness did not impress her.

Unable to keep himself from seeing Ava a moment longer, Johann crossed the street, stepping over the glowing white lines that had been painted alongside the kerb soon after the war began, in an attempt to make the city streets safer in the absence of street lighting. He wondered whether she had arrived yet. Perhaps he was the first. He entered the restaurant and was at once greeted by the smell of wholesome, home-cooked food, which caused his empty stomach to groan.

It was a warm and dimly lit restaurant, already bustling and loud with conversation, the air hazy with cigarette smoke. The general décor appeared to Johann as the epitome of Bavarian charm, with its wood-panelled walls painted with classical scenes, and tightly packed, thin-legged tables adorned with white lace tablecloths. He removed his cap and placed it beneath his arm as he moved further in, trying to catch the attention of the head waiter, but it was Volker's attention he caught first.

'Johann!'

His friend was on his feet, a thin cigarette glowing in his hand as he waved him to their table, which was already set with wine.

Johann couldn't help but smile at the sight of his friend. They greeted one another with a strong embrace and a firm slap on each other's back.

'Volker! It's so good to see you again.'

Over Volker's shoulder, Johann saw that Ava, too, had already arrived, and there was another young woman, a brunette, whom he supposed was Volker's cousin, Trudi.

'Look at you in that uniform,' Volker said as he led Johann to their table. He still had his arm tightly around Johann's shoulders.

'I could say the same thing about you,' Johann said. 'I hardly recognised you.'

Volker laughed. 'So we're grown men at last, and it's no longer make-believe. We're not toy soldiers any more, Johann.'

'No indeed,' Johann said, with a degree of sobriety that clearly surprised his friend.

'Then why the long face? This is what we've been training for, Johann. Surely you must embrace the chance to fight for the Fatherland—for our *Führer*.'

'Yes, of course,' Johann said. He noticed the rank insignia on Volker's tunic then, and he turned the conversation back to it. 'But what's this? You're a captain?'

'I told you my father could pull strings,' Volker said. 'He had me promoted to *Hauptsturmführer*, which means, my good friend, that for the first time since we met, I have advanced ahead of you— and by two ranks!' He laughed at the notion. 'I'm sure you will have the opportunity to climb as high as *Brigadeführer* by the time the war is over.'

As they arrived at the table, Volker finally let go of Johann. Both men were still smiling, only now Johann was smiling at Ava.

'Good evening,' he said, with a slight bow of his head.

'Hello, Johann,' Ava said. 'You look well.'

Before Johann could continue the conversation, Volker interrupted, and it seemed that he couldn't get his cigarette out of his mouth quick enough to do so.

'Johann, this is the cousin I've been telling you so much about. Trudi, this is my best friend, Johann Langner.' Volker slapped Johann's back again. 'And I've told Trudi all about you, too,' he added with another laugh.

Johann smiled and bowed his head again.

'Well?' Volker added, 'Isn't Trudi the beauty I said she was?'

'Yes, of course,' Johann said, not wishing to offend.

Trudi offered him the back of her hand and Johann bent low and kissed it. As he rose again, he smiled more fully. 'Now that I've met you, I see that your cousin's description does you no justice.'

Such flattery might have embarrassed any young woman, but his words merely caused Trudi's smile to flourish further.

'Well, sit down, sit down,' Volker said, taking the seat next to Ava, placing Johann beside Trudi, opposite Ava, which Johann didn't mind at all. It was not, after all, a very large table, and it meant he could look at Ava as much as he liked without making it obvious.

'I hope you don't mind my choice of restaurant,' Volker said. 'It's a little artists' restaurant my father introduced me to. Do you know that he has sat at this very table with Adolf Hitler himself? Our *Führer* is also a keen artist. Perhaps that's why he likes the place so much.'

Johann was only half listening. His eyes were on Ava, taking her in. He liked what she had done with her hair. He was sure he'd only ever seen her wearing it up before. Now it fell to her shoulders, with a clip or pin of some kind holding it off her face to one side. For a moment he was able to block all else out, to the extent that he felt as though they were the only two people there.

'It's very good to see you again, Ava,' he said, quickly adding, 'I've missed Munich,' when what he really wanted to say was that he had missed her.

Ava's lips parted to answer, but it was Volker who spoke again, shattering Johann's illusion.

'You won't find the city much changed from the last time you were here, my friend. Although I'm pleased to see there are now fewer Jews.' He took up his wine glass and laughed. 'And the air is fresher for it, I can tell you.'

Volker had left the officer training school in Bad Tölz a full month ahead of Johann, and he had so far told Johann nothing of his posting.

'You have a position in Munich?' Johann asked, feeling a wave of jealousy wash over him at the idea that his friend should be stationed so close to Ava, while he was off fighting, heaven knows where.

'I wanted to surprise you,' Volker said. 'I'm to help manage the concentration camp at Dachau as *Schutzhaftlagerführer* under the camp commandant, *Sturmbannführer* Alexander Piorkowski.' He laughed to himself. 'And I'm glad to see that our labour camps are being used for the good of the *Reich*. I'll be overseeing the workers who are not only increasing our munitions, but also making our uniforms!'

Johann knew enough about his friend's new role to understand that to be *Schutzhaftlagerführer* was to be part of the SS-*Totenkopfverbände*—the Death's Head Units who took their orders direct from Berlin.

He did not envy his friend the position, so far from the fight. It was certainly no duty for a soldier to his mind. He wanted to change the subject, or risk spoiling the evening before it had begun.

'I see you've had your hair cut very short, Volker,' he said, for want of something better to say.

Volker began to smile. 'After all these years, I thought a fresh look was in order.' Unexpectedly, he reached across to Johann and ruffled his hair. He laughed. 'And I decided it was time I had a different haircut to you, *Blödmann*!' He reached for the wine bottle and emptied it into Johann's glass. 'Drink with me, Johann! Who knows when the chance will come again?'

Everyone raised their glasses and drank, and Johann watched Volker drain his wine. It was becoming clear to him that his friend had already consumed most of the bottle, but it seemed he had not yet had enough. With his arm outstretched, Volker lowered his glass to the table and set it down with a thump. He picked up the empty bottle and spun around on his chair.

'Herr Deutelmoser! More wine, if you please!' To the gathering, he added, 'We might as well have a few drinks before dinner. I'm sure we all have much to catch up on.'

A moment later another bottle of wine was brought to the table by a man in shirt sleeves and a black waistcoat, who looked to be in his late forties.

'And how is your father, Herr Strobel?' the man said as he proceeded to uncork the wine. 'I trust he is well?'

'I expect he is tired, Joseph. He was a busy man before the war began. Now he is a very busy man.'

Deutelmoser poured the wine, and with a bow he left them to it.

'Herr Deutelmoser is the proprietor,' Volker said. 'I insisted he serve us tonight, just as he always serves Herr Hitler whenever he and his entourage visit.' In a lower voice, he added, 'Although I should think he would at least wear a jacket when he serves our *Führer*.'

'It's very warm in here,' Ava said. 'I'm glad I chose to wear one of my summer dresses tonight.'

'You look very pretty in it,' Johann said.

'Yes, the pattern suits you,' added Volker. 'It's a little plain, but I like the flowers.'

Johann doubted that his friend ever spared a thought for such things.

'Do you like *my* dress, Volker?' Trudi asked.

Volker just smiled at her, a little dismissively, Johann thought. He turned to her. 'Your dress is also very pretty,' he said with a warmer smile. 'It puts me in mind of the ocean.'

Trudi giggled and sat forward on her chair. 'It's pure silk,' she said, turning her shoulders from side to side to show it off better.

Volker topped up Ava's wine glass, even though it was still quite full. 'Do you own a silk dress?' he asked her.

'No, I—'

'Then you must allow me to buy you one,' Volker interrupted. 'Cotton is all very well in a place like this, but—'

'You're very kind, Volker, but I couldn't, really.'

'Why ever not? It's just a dress.'

Johann knew the gesture meant more to Volker than that, and he thought Ava knew it, too. He saw that his friend's brow had set into an unpleasant furrow at the thought of Ava refusing him, and not for the first time that evening he thought that his friend was not his usual self. He had seen this expression on Volker's face many times before, and nothing good had ever followed. Now it was Johann who topped up Volker's glass, which was already in need of it.

'Tell me, Ava,' he said, determined to change the subject. 'How are your parents?'

Volker sat back, and Johann saw that he was staring at him with that same furrowed expression, making it clear to Johann that his interruption had annoyed his friend.

Johann thought he heard Ava sigh, perhaps out of relief, as she turned to him. The smile had returned to her lips.

'They're both well,' she said. 'Although business is not as good as it used to be. You remember I said my papa was a music teacher?'

'Yes, of course.'

'Well, perhaps there's little call for learning music when there's a war on, although the business has been in decline for some years now.'

Volker scoffed, puffing cigarette smoke across the table. 'If your papa was in the habit of teaching music to Jews, as I've heard, then it's no wonder.' He stubbed out his cigarette and turned into the restaurant again, as if looking for the attention of Herr Deutelmoser. 'Shall we eat? I'm getting hungry.'

Menus were brought and meals were ordered, and by the time the entrées were served, Johann was glad to see that Volker had settled down to his usual, convivial self again. A pleasant evening ensued, although Johann soon confirmed his earlier thoughts concerning the real reason Volker had invited his cousin to dine with them. He also picked up on a peculiar dynamic that seemed to exist between Volker and his cousin. At every opportunity, Volker would encourage Johann and Trudi into conversation together, confirming to Johann that Trudi was there purely to distract Johann so that Volker could have Ava to himself.

Trudi, on the other hand, seemed oblivious to Volker's machinations. To the contrary, she had barely stopped looking at Volker all evening, just as Johann had not stopped looking at Ava—and he had several times caught her looking back. Trudi's affection for Volker seemed utterly transparent, and Johann was glad to see it, not least because, while Johann found Trudi as easy to talk to as she was on the eye, he thought her very immature, which made perfect sense to him when he discovered during the course of the evening that she had only recently turned seventeen.

At just after eleven, they left the Osteria Bavaria in high spirits, Volker having been the centre of attention throughout the meal—not that Johann minded. He had a few days in Munich before he had to join his unit, and he planned to make them count where Ava Bauer was concerned. She had already agreed to meet him at the Park Café on Sophienstrasse the following afternoon, and as they all made their way along Schellingstrasse in the cool night air, heading for a bar Volker had suggested they visit for a nightcap, Johann was already looking forward to it.

He watched Ava walking ahead of him beneath the lamplight, and for a moment he imagined how good it would feel to hold her soft hand in his. As it was, it was Volker who walked beside her, while he walked with Trudi, which again was all to Volker's plan as far as Johann was concerned. Every now and then Ava would turn back to Johann with a smile that was as much to say that she would rather be beside him. At least, that's what Johann chose to believe she was thinking.

'You like your cousin, don't you, Trudi?' Johann asked her, speaking quietly so that Volker couldn't hear him.

'Is it that obvious?'

Johann smiled and gave a small, almost sympathetic laugh. 'I'm afraid it is.'

Trudi sighed. 'Oh, dear. He must think me very foolish. He's usually very affectionate towards me, but it seems his heart is now set on someone else.'

Johann knew it to be true, but he would not hurt Trudi's feelings any further by telling her as much. He cast his attention ahead and saw that Volker was almost laughing as he spoke to Ava about something he hadn't been able to hear. Ava seemed to be enjoying his company, but there was that look over her shoulder again, and he fancied the smile on her lips was for him. A moment later, Ava glanced back again, and it seemed to interrupt whatever it was that

Volker was saying because he suddenly stopped talking. His face soured as it had in the restaurant earlier.

'Here, Johann,' he said. 'Why don't you walk with Ava. I can see you would both prefer it.'

'Volker,' Ava began, as if to apologise, but Volker cut her short.

'No, no. I must insist.'

As Johann and Trudi caught up to them, Volker grabbed Johann's arm and pulled him closer. Johann couldn't help but see the funny side of the matter. Here was Volker having invited his beautiful cousin along in the hope of beguiling Johann away from Ava, and yet Trudi was so smitten with him that she'd had eyes for no one else all evening. His friend's plan had well and truly backfired. The irony of the situation made Johann laugh.

'What is it?' Volker asked. 'What's so funny, eh?'

'It's nothing,' Johann said, trying not to smile now that he could see how serious his friend had suddenly become. 'Let's go and get that nightcap.'

'No, really. I should like to know what it is about me you find so amusing.'

'It's not you, Volker. Look, forget about it. I'm sorry I laughed. I didn't mean anything.'

Johann put a hand on Volker's shoulder to appease him, but Volker knocked it sharply away again.

'I won't be laughed at,' Volker said. His hand wandered to the dagger on his belt. 'If you were not my closest friend, I—'

'What?' Johann said. 'What would you do? Would you pull out your dagger and stab me in the heart with it? You know you can't beat me in a straight fight any more—dagger or otherwise. You would do better to try and shoot me. And over what?'

Ava came between them. 'Stop it, the pair of you! You've had too much to drink and now you're squabbling like children.' She moved towards Trudi and linked arms with her. 'I'm walking the rest of the way with Trudi, and if you've not settled your differences by the time we reach the bar, I'm going straight home.'

'I'm sorry,' Johann said. He turned to Volker. 'Let's forget about it. What do you say? Blame it on the wine.'

Volker scoffed. 'It's forgotten,' he said, but as they set off again, Johann doubted it was. All the way to the bar, Volker didn't say another word, and although Johann did well to hide it, his friend had unnerved him. While he'd witnessed Volker's temper many times, and seen the often bloody results that followed, he'd never been on the receiving end of it before.

The bar Volker had in mind for a nightcap was no more than a ten minute walk from the restaurant on Ludwigstrasse, one of Munich's four royal avenues, having been named in honour of King Ludwig I of Bavaria. It was more in keeping with the usual type of establishment Volker chose to frequent. It was opulent, with gilt carvings on the ceiling and walls and on the many framed mirrors, whose glass reflected the soft glow of candlelight, lending to the golden aura that greeted the party as they entered.

It soon became apparent that Volker was on good terms with the proprietor here, too, because within a few minutes they were set up with a bottle of *Marillenschnaps* from Austria, at a table in the centre of the room, where everyone had a view of the tables around them, most of which were occupied. The ease with which they had been seated suggested to Johann that his friend had planned for them to go there all along, having reserved what he must have considered to be the best table in the house.

They were all set for a cordial end to what had on the whole been a pleasant evening, despite Volker's unusual temperament, but it seemed that his sour mood continued to stalk him, rendering him silent to the point of brooding as he downed his first glass.

'It's a good bottle, Volker,' Johann said, trying to encourage him into conversation.

Ava joined in. 'Apricot *Schnaps* is my favourite,' she said. 'How did you know?'

'I didn't,' Volker said, and then he picked up the bottle, avoiding eye contact with anyone, and poured himself another glass.

'I like *Himbeergeist* best,' Trudi said with a giggle. 'I love raspberries.'

'What about you, Johann?' Ava asked. 'What's your favourite?'

Johann laughed. 'In truth, I prefer to drink beer.'

Volker scoffed under his breath. 'That's because you have no breeding.'

Not wishing to ruin the evening further, Johann chose to ignore the remark, although he could have thumped Volker there and then for saying it. He watched him down another shot of *Schnaps* and reach for the bottle again.

'Steady there, Volker. You've already had most of the wine this evening.' He smiled to make light of it. 'I don't want to have to carry you home.'

Volker's hand froze on the bottle. He turned to Johann and stared at him. 'Now you think I can't take my drink, is that it?'

Before Johann could answer, Ava stood up. She was frowning. 'I can't stand any more of this,' she said. 'Come on, Trudi. I think we'd better leave this pair to resolve their differences without us. I'll see you back to your accommodation.'

Johann got to his feet. 'Ava, I—'

'I told you what would happen, Johann. Now it's too late.'

'At least let me escort you?'

'We'll be fine by ourselves. It's not far.' Ava signalled for their coats.

'Well, can I still see you tomorrow?' Johann asked, a hint of desperation in his voice.

Ava didn't answer straight away. She made Johann wait as she and Trudi were helped into their coats. They began to leave, and when they were almost at the door, Ava turned back.

'Of course,' she said. 'I'll see you tomorrow.'

'Good night, Volker,' Trudi said, her doe eyes trying to find his.

Volker gave no reply. He didn't even look up from the table as Johann went to the door and watched the girls leave.

Returning to Volker, Johann sat heavily in the chair opposite him and slapped the table, stirring his friend from the funk he had clearly descended into.

'Well, thank you, Volker,' he said with no pretence at hiding the sarcasm in his tone. 'The evening was a total disaster. You know, I'm beginning to think that our eagerness to win Ava's affection could well turn her off both of us altogether.'

Volker stopped turning his empty glass and looked up at last. 'Not you, Johann. I can see now that it's you she wants. I'm sorry.'

'It's a bit late for that, don't you think? It should be Ava and Trudi you're apologising to.'

'And I will. I have to return to my duties at Dachau in the morning, but I'll call on her soon.'

'So, I won't see you again before I join my unit?'

'No.'

'Then this is our farewell drink.' Johann filled both of their glasses and they clinked them together.

'Stay safe, Johann,' Volker said. 'It's a great honour for you to be serving with the *Leibstandarte*. I only wish I were joining the fight with you. Perhaps I will before the end, but my father—'

'I know. Your father has given you camp duties because he wants to protect you.'

Volker nodded. He still appeared somewhat sombre, but Johann was pleased to see his old friend sitting opposite him again, and in part he felt sorry for him. He thought they would have made a formidable pair on the battlefield.

'I'll pass on your apology when I see Ava tomorrow,' he said. 'Perhaps it will help smooth things over before you go to see her.'

Volker smiled. 'You see. You already have another date lined up. Ava has already chosen you, but you're too much of a *Blödmann* to do anything about it.' He laughed and it was refreshing to see. 'You might as well ask her to marry you and be done with it.'

Johann laughed with him. 'And you think she would say yes?'

Volker looked suddenly incredulous. 'Are you blind, Johann? Isn't it obvious? Why do you think I've been so moody since the restaurant?'

'I've been wondering what's come over you.'

'It's because I've lost, Johann, and I don't like it when things don't go my way—you know that. But if you don't do something about it soon, I shall call on Ava every chance I get. It won't be so easy for you to see her. While you're off fighting, I'll woo her into submission.'

Johann laughed again and they both downed their drinks. 'One more *Schnaps* for my courage then,' he said, refilling their glasses.

'And one for friendship. I'll miss you, Johann.'

Volker sat up and reached a hand into his pocket. When he brought it out again he was holding a small, blue velvet box. He slid it across the table.

'I want you to have this. For Ava.'

Johann picked up the box and opened it. A sapphire and diamond ring began to sparkle in the candlelight, like sunlight over a shimmering sea.

'It's beautiful,' Johann said as he took in the imposing central stone and the numerous diamonds that were clustered around it.

'It belonged to my grandmother. I was going to give it to Ava this evening, if I thought she would accept it.'

The revelation surprised Johann. 'You weren't wasting any time, were you?'

'I wanted to beat you to it, but it's you she wants. I'm over her.'

'Just like that?'

'It doesn't happen often, Johann, but I know when I'm beaten.'

Johann shook his head. 'Must everything be a contest between us?' He slid the ring back to Volker. 'I can't accept it. If not to Ava, you should give it to someone else when the time comes.'

'Please take it, Johann. I want Ava to have it. I'm sure she'll accept it from you. Consider it my parting gift.'

Johann didn't know what to say. He could plainly see how much the gesture meant to Volker, and he didn't want to offend him. He supposed it would make Volker happy to know it would still be his ring on Ava's finger, even if he did not have Ava's hand—a consolation prize perhaps, but it had belonged to his grandmother, or so he had said. It seemed odd to Johann that his friend would give something so precious away so easily. But then Volker Strobel had always been an odd boy, and it seemed that manhood had done little to change that.

'Thank you,' Johann said, drawing the ring back across the table. He took another look at it before he closed the box with a snap and slid it into his pocket, considering that a ring was just what he needed if he was going to propose to Ava at the Park Café the following afternoon.

Chapter Ten

Present day.

Although Tayte liked getting around by taxi, for convenience, and to help keep the expenses down, he'd hired a car for the week. It was a small black BMW, which he and Jean collected from the rental company early on the morning of their second day in Munich. Tayte had contacted the German Heart Centre before they set out, to enquire how Johann Langner was and whether he was able to receive visitors again. He had been given little information, other than that a visit was not possible at this time, so instead, he thought to contact Langner's son. He'd arranged to meet him at the Langner art gallery and auction house that afternoon.

Right now, though, they had another appointment to get to, and while the car's navigation system told Tayte that they were close to their destination in the city's northern borough of Schwabing, Munich's former Bohemian quarter, he was cursing himself for not anticipating just how congested Munich's streets were likely to be. They were already running ten minutes late for their meeting with Tobias Kaufmann, a man who had dedicated his life to bringing the Demon of Dachau to justice.

The address Tayte had been given when he'd made the appointment to see Kaufmann was on a tree-lined avenue just wide enough for two cars to pass one another, with parallel parking along both sides of the road for the people working in the various offices located there. When the voice on the sat-nav told Tayte he had reached his destination, he saw the words *Kaufmann und Kaufmann* on the building beside him, and as he pulled into a vacant parking space he realised that the Nazi hunter's day job was as a lawyer, presumably having gone into business with his son or his father.

Briefcase in hand, Tayte pressed the buzzer on the intercom at the entrance. He announced himself, adding, 'I'm sorry we're a little late.'

A moment later the door buzzed. Tayte pushed it open and followed Jean into a stairwell where he read a sign that told him *Kaufmann und Kaufmann* were on the first floor. They went up, and at another door they were greeted by a short, bearded man who looked to be in his mid-fifties. He wore a charcoal-coloured suit and a black skullcap—a kippah or yarmulke depending on whether the wearer spoke Hebrew or Yiddish. Tayte shot a hand out and gave the man a wide smile.

'I'm Jefferson Tayte,' he said. 'This is my friend, Jean Summer.'

'Tobias Kaufmann,' the man replied in accented English. 'Please, come in.'

They followed Kaufmann along a tight walkway between a few desks that were loaded with paperwork and the usual office electronica. At the end of the walkway they entered into a smaller office that was no less drowning beneath stacks of loose paper and lever-arch files. There was another man in dark apparel sitting in a corner of the room. He was a much older man with a long beard that was almost white. He, too, wore a skullcap and he had a walking cane between his legs, upon which his hands were resting.

'This is Herr Kaufmann senior,' Tobias said. 'My father. He still insists on attending meetings whenever the topic is Volker Strobel. My father was ten years old when he and the rest of my family were arrested by the Gestapo. As far as my bloodline is concerned, he is the sole survivor of the holocaust. My family were murdered at Auschwitz and Treblinka, but Elijah, perhaps because he was young and strong, was sent to the work camp at Dachau. That's how he came to live in Munich after the war.'

'I'm pleased to meet you, Herr Kaufmann,' Tayte said to the older man, and Jean smiled at him and nodded.

Elijah Kaufmann just nodded back, saying nothing.

'Don't mind him,' Tobias said. 'He's a quiet man. Did you know that before the Nazis came to power in Germany there were around ten thousand Jews living in Munich? By the end of the war there were fewer than ten. Even now, with the general population of the city having roughly doubled since then, the number has only recently reached pre-war levels.'

'I didn't know that,' Tayte said. 'But given the circumstances, I'm not surprised.'

'No, it's not surprising at all,' Tobias said. 'Please take a seat.'

Tayte had to move some papers off the chair closest to him before he could sit down. He put them on the floor beside his briefcase and they sat around a small pedestal desk as their host began to clear some space for them.

'We call this the Strobel room,' he said. 'It isn't usually in such a mess, but I've been going through some old files and haven't got around to putting them all away again.'

'Don't worry about it,' Tayte said. 'It's knowing where everything is that's important.'

'Very true, Mr Tayte. Very true. Now, you're both interested in Volker Strobel, and that makes me very interested in you. What specifically has brought you here?'

Tayte showed Tobias the photograph of his mother standing outside Johann Langner's building and proceeded to tell him what he'd told Langner the previous day, bringing him up to date with the reason he and Jean were in Munich.

'If my mother was interested in Volker Strobel,' he added, 'it stands to reason that she would know about your efforts to bring him to justice. I believe she must have come to see you about him at some point. Perhaps while she was in Munich in 1963, when she had her picture taken.'

'If your mother did come to see us,' Tobias said, 'her visit will be on file. Where Volker Strobel is concerned, we've always been meticulous about recording the particulars of everyone who visits us, although looking around you, that might seem unlikely.'

The idea of there being a file on his mother right there in that room excited Tayte. He glanced around again and thought that if there was such a file it could take a while to find it. He brought Kaufmann's attention back to the photograph of his mother and asked the question he aimed to ask everyone he showed it to.

'Do you recognise my mother?'

Tobias shook his head. 'I'm fifty-six years old, Mr Tayte. In 1963 I was only a small boy.' He stood up and took Tayte's photograph to show his father. 'Papa, do you recognise this woman?'

Elijah Kaufmann adjusted his glasses and leaned closer.

'It was a long time ago,' Tobias added. 'She might have come to see you in the 1960s.'

The old man shook his head and sat back again.

'I'm sorry,' Tobias said as he returned to the desk and sat down. He handed Tayte's photograph back to him.

'That's okay. As you said, it was a long time ago, and I'm sure your father has seen plenty of people since then.'

'You're welcome to check our files,' Tobias said. 'It might take a while, but we've been in the habit of photographing our visitors since around 1950, when Papa acquired our first Park instamatic camera.' He paused and reached into the desk drawer. 'It's all digital now, of course,' he continued as he withdrew a small digital camera. 'Many of the older pictures have faded beyond recognition, but it could help to locate the file you're looking for if we have one.'

'It's worth a try,' Jean said.

'Where do we start?' Tayte added.

Tobias Kaufmann held up the camera. 'We start with me taking a picture of you for my files before I forget. Now, if you could move closer together so I can get you both in. That's it.' He clicked the shutter and checked the image. Next he had Tayte fill in a form, giving his and Jean's names and the address where they were staying. Tobias began to pull at his beard as he gazed up at the wall of lever-arch files behind Tayte and Jean, as though considering which files to start with. He stood up and went to them, and then he turned back and pointed at Tayte's chair. 'Do you mind?'

Tayte stood up and Tobias pulled the chair closer to the files. He stood on it and slid a couple of boxes out and handed them to Tayte, who was tall enough to reach them without the chair. 'Here, let me help,' he said, and Tobias pointed at a few others to try, which Tayte lifted down.

'There might be something in these,' he said. 'If not, we can try a few more.'

Tayte set the photograph of his mother down onto the desk and they each took a box to go through. The photographs inside were mostly faded, as Tobias had suggested. Some files were no more than a single page, with little information on it. Others contained several pages, but offered no connection for Tayte. The majority were from survivors of the holocaust, in particular the survivors of Dachau, whose accounts of their incarceration at the concentration camp were perhaps of the greatest value to *Kaufmann und Kaufmann*.

An hour passed in relative silence, with only the sound of rustling papers to be heard. Then Jean sat up with a short gasp, drawing Tayte's attention. She was scrutinising one of the photographs, as though she'd seen a possible match. She handed the image to Tayte. It showed a man and a woman standing side by side in that same room, but with a less full wall of files in the background. It was washed out completely in places, and Tayte was glad he'd had a copy made of his mother's photograph before it began to go the same way. He recognised what he could see of the woman's face immediately—he'd stared at his own photograph of his mother long enough to know it was her. He turned back to Jean, whose eyes were wide with interest as she read through the file.

'You're not going to believe this,' she said.

'Here, let me see.'

Jean handed the file to Tayte. 'I don't think you're going to like it, either.'

With a sense of foreboding Tayte took the file and glanced over it. There were two pages, and on the first page his eyes were drawn to the two names that appeared at the top: Sarah and Karl. Status: married. There was no surname.

'So my mother's name is Sarah,' Tayte said under his breath.

His eyes were then drawn to the reason for Sarah's and Karl's interest in Volker Strobel, and as soon as he read it, he knew Jean was right—he couldn't believe it. He didn't want to believe it.

He screwed his face up. 'My mother came here with her husband, Karl, trying to identify Karl's father.'

The spelling of Karl's name hadn't slipped Tayte's attention. It had German or Scandinavian origins, but under the circumstances, Tayte felt it was almost certainly a German given name. The implications of what he'd read left him numb. He looked at the faded instamatic photograph of the couple again, and he studied the pale image of the man standing beside his mother.

'Is this my father?'

Just because Karl was married to his mother, Tayte understood that it didn't necessarily follow that Karl was his father, although there was a strong possibility that he was. He checked the date at the top of the file. It was dated September 1973, which was ten years after the date on the newspaper cutting Marcus Brown had left him, suggesting to Tayte that the trail had gone cold for his mother and Karl after their visit to the former Hitler Youth building. He thought then that it most likely was Karl who had taken the photograph his mother had left for him when she abandoned him. They must have picked up the trail again at some point and it had brought them here. Something else that stood out about the date on the file was that 1973 was close to the year Tayte was born.

Tayte's mind began to wander as he tried to imagine what was going on with his mother and Karl back then, but he was distracted by the facts in front of him. The file stated that Sarah and Karl were trying to identify Karl's father, and they had visited Elijah Kaufmann because they were interested in Volker Strobel. Tayte didn't want to say what he was thinking, but he couldn't deny the possibility.

The file was shaking in his hands as he said, 'Is the Demon of Dachau my paternal grandfather?'

He hoped it wasn't true, yet at the same time he'd never felt closer to the answers he'd been searching for since he'd found out he'd been adopted.

Tobias Kaufmann leaned in across the desk and interrupted Tayte's thoughts. 'It's a curious situation, don't you think?'

'What's that?'

'Well, that if Karl here is your father, then, like yourself, he didn't know who his father was either.'

Tayte nodded. 'Yes, I suppose it is.'

'I expect the circumstances are different, though,' Jean offered.

'Different,' Tayte said, 'but perhaps connected. If Strobel is Karl's father, and my grandfather, maybe my parents came close to proving it. Maybe they found something out about Strobel that he didn't want anyone to know about—Strobel being a man who, for obvious reasons, doesn't want to be found. Maybe they got too close for comfort and that's why I was abandoned—for my own protection.' Tayte turned to Kaufmann and explained. 'I later found out that's what my mother told the sister at the Catholic mission in San Rafael, Mexico, when she handed me over.'

'I think there are a lot of possibilities here, JT,' Jean said. 'You know you're only speculating. It doesn't mean anything without proof to back it up. Aren't you always saying that? All we know for sure is that your mother came here in 1973 with a husband called Karl, looking for a connection to his father. Everything else is guess-work for now.'

'You're right,' Tayte said, thinking that maybe he was allowing his emotions to guide him a little too easily towards what only appeared to be the obvious answers. He didn't even know for sure whether Karl was his father yet, let alone that Volker Strobel was his grandfather. 'So we need to keep digging,' he added. 'I see there's an address in the file here. It's in Munich.'

At that point, Elijah Kaufmann, who so far had been sitting so still and quiet in the corner of the room that Tayte had all but forgotten he was there, said with a heavy Jewish-German accent, 'That was only a temporary address.'

All eyes turned to Elijah. Tayte supposed something about the conversation must have jogged his memory, which meant he had all Tayte's attention.

'Your mother is English,' Elijah said. 'That's right, isn't it?'

'She had an English accent,' Tayte said. 'That's all I know.'

The old man nodded. 'She was an Englishwoman,' he stated. 'I may not recall her face, but I remember her and her husband quite well. It's not every day we get visitors looking for family connections to the Demon of Dachau.' He almost laughed at the idea. 'And you were right.'

'I was? What about?'

'About Sarah and Karl being close to something. When they left here I remember feeling that some vital piece of information had just slipped through my fingers. They were nervous about something. They didn't want to give me their names at first, or have their picture taken. They left a contact address here in Munich in case I had any information for them on Strobel's whereabouts, which of course I didn't, although that might soon be about to change.'

'Papa!' Tobias Kaufmann said, as if his father had said something he shouldn't have.

'It's all right, Tobias. These good people are not our enemy, and the time to catch the Demon of Dachau is running out. Perhaps they were sent to us for a reason. Maybe they can help.' To Tayte and Jean Elijah added, 'I'm sorry, but we have to be careful. You understand?'

'Of course,' Tayte said.

'We understand only too well,' Jean added. 'We were sent a very clear warning not to ask questions about Volker Strobel after we visited *The Friends of the Waffen-SS War Veterans* yesterday.'

'Ah,' Tobias said. 'The FWK. We know all about them.'

'I was threatened,' Jean said.

'By a gang of neo-Nazis,' Tayte added. 'At least we think so.'

'Their leader had tattoos on his neck—a skull on one side and the SS *Sieg* runes on the other.'

'That would probably be Max Fleischer,' Tobias said. 'He's a nasty piece of work. The symbols represent the military insignia of the *SS-Totenkopfverbände*—the SS Death's Head Units. It's illegal in Germany to display these symbols publicly, so the fact that he's been so blatant about it suggests he thought it would add to the intimidation.'

'To let us know who we're up against?' Tayte said.

'Precisely. I expect he keeps his tattoos hidden beneath a shirt collar at other times. I should take his threat most seriously if I were you.'

'We aim to,' Tayte said. 'Although we're not going home just yet.' He brought the conversation back to something Elijah had just said. 'What's about to change?'

Tobias looked uncomfortable for a moment. Then he glanced over at his father.

'Tell them,' Elijah said, his tone impatient.

Tobias sighed. 'We have an insider at the FWK. He's been working under deep cover for three years now. He's heard that Volker Strobel is coming to Munich. Soon. We were beginning to think we were chasing a ghost, but this confirms Strobel is still alive, although as my father just pointed out, the time to bring him to justice is running out. It's for that reason we're working more closely than ever now with the Simon Wiesenthal Centre and the German government.'

'And how can *we* help?' Tayte asked. 'It sounds like you already have all the help you need, and if Strobel's coming to Munich, surely your nets are already closing around him.'

'Volker Strobel has managed to evade capture for seventy years,' Elijah said. 'Let's just say that we don't like to put all of our eggs in the same basket. This lead we have may come to nothing, as it has many times before. But now you two are in Munich asking questions about Strobel, and with a possible family connection that quite frankly I find irresistible. Your skills in genealogy offer us a new angle. You can perhaps ask questions of people who will not talk to us.'

'I see,' Tayte said. 'So, you'd just like us to share our findings with you? Let you know if we hear anything of interest about Strobel?'

'Precisely. Nothing more dangerous than that, although you clearly already have need to exercise caution.'

'I've been having trouble getting access to the records I'd like to see,' Tayte said. 'Primarily for Strobel and Langner, and the people associated with them. Can you help us with that?'

'We can see what we can do,' Tobias said. 'With the German government on board, I don't see why not.'

It was an interesting proposition, and Tayte couldn't see how it put them in any more danger than they were already in, given that he and Jean had already decided to carry on. Access to records which would otherwise be denied him was also a great incentive.

Tobias Kaufmann's next line sealed the deal as far as Tayte was concerned. 'If Volker Strobel does meet with the FWK here in Munich, he'll be arrested, and it's highly unlikely that you'll ever get to speak to him. In return for any information you can give us, we'll make sure you can, before it becomes too late. Maybe then you can confirm whether or not he's your grandfather.'

Tayte was all for it, but he wanted to make sure Jean was, too. 'How about it?'

'I don't see what we've got to lose.'

Tayte reached across the desk and shook Tobias's hand. 'It's a deal.' He handed Tobias a business card. 'My cell number's there, or you can reach us at the address I wrote in the file.'

'Thank you,' Tobias said as he took the card. 'We'll be in touch.'

Chapter Eleven

Following their visit with Tobias and Elijah Kaufmann, Tayte had entered another address into the hire car's sat-nav system, and he and Jean were now heading east to the apartment that his mother, and possibly his father, had given as their temporary address to the Kaufmanns when they visited them in 1973. According to Tobias Kaufmann the apartment was near a man-made waterway called the Eisbach, a tributary of the river Isar that had become popular among surfers because of its shallow, yet fast flowing currents. It took less than twenty minutes to get there, and while Tayte thought it would be great to find the same person still living there from 1973, he somehow doubted it. It was an apartment after all. People moved on and people died. He knew the odds were slim, but it wasn't something he could dismiss without being sure.

Tayte turned the car into the street they had been directed to and drove a short distance to the end of what was no more than a tight lane. There were trees to one side, buildings to the other. He supposed one of the buildings had to be the apartments they were looking for. The street had no through road, but instead ran out to a walkway that, according to the sign he could see, led through a dense cover of foliage to the Eisbach.

He and Jean got out of the car and began to look around for the address. The signs weren't clear, but the building nearest to them gave every indication of being an apartment block, so they went closer. It was a small unit, painted red with a number of shuttered windows on three floors. There was only one entrance as far as Tayte could see. He paused in front of it to check the number for the address he'd written down, and he must have looked as if he needed help because someone called out to him.

'*Kann ich Ihnen helfen?*'

Tayte wheeled around to see an elderly woman in a large straw sun hat, bent double in the small garden to the side of the building. She straightened up with considerable effort and dropped her secateurs into the front pocket of her apron.

Tayte didn't know what she'd just said, and he wasn't sure what to say in reply. He was about to ask whether she spoke English, which was one of the few phrases he had learned, but Jean answered for him.

'*Ich spreche kein Deutsch,*' she said, slowly as though she had to think about it. All the same, Tayte was impressed.

'*Engländer?*' the woman asked.

Tayte recognised that word. '*Ja,*' he said, not wanting to confuse matters by telling her he was American. He threw Jean a smile, in response to which she just rolled her eyes at him.

'You are looking for someone?' the woman said.

'Yes. Someone who lived in apartment twelve in 1973. Possibly someone called Karl, and his wife, Sarah.'

The woman shook her head. 'No, no,' she said. 'In 1973, Geoffrey Johnston lived at number 12. He was English, also. I should know, we shared the same floor.'

'I see,' Tayte said. His hopes were up. If the woman standing in front of him had lived there in 1973 there was every chance this Geoffrey Johnston could still be there, too. 'Does Herr Johnston still live here?'

The woman shook her head. 'He died around forty years ago.'

'I see,' Tayte said again. 'Forty years?' He glanced at Jean and she raised an eyebrow, letting him know that she was thinking the same thing he was—that Johnston had died close to the time his mother and Karl had visited Elijah Kaufmann.

'Do you know how he died?' Jean asked.

'Drowned,' the woman said. She pointed towards the trees and the pathway that led to the nearby Eisbach. 'They found his body caught up by the bridge.'

Tayte looked at Jean again, suspicion of foul play now written all over his face. He made a mental note to look into the particulars of Johnston's death online, sure that the death would have been reported in the newspapers.

Tayte gave the woman a smile. 'Well, thanks for your time.' He was about to head back to the car when he paused and took out the photograph of his mother. 'Before we go, do you recognise this woman?'

The old lady scrunched her face up as she scrutinised the image. She seemed unsure. 'Perhaps.'

'Perhaps?'

'I can't say. She's familiar, yes, but don't ask me why.'

It didn't matter. Tayte already knew that his mother had been staying at this address in 1973, or at least that she and Karl knew Geoffrey Johnston well enough to have given his address to Elijah Kaufmann as a point of contact.

'*Danke*,' Tayte said with a bow.

When he and Jean were halfway back to the car, he said, 'That doesn't sound good.'

'No. Although the timing of Johnston's death could be a coincidence.'

'Yes, it could,' Tayte agreed, but he didn't like it one bit. 'I want to look into Johnston some more when we get back to the hotel.'

They reached the car and Tayte took his notebook out from his jacket pocket. He wrote Johnston's name down, along with 'Eisbach' and 'Bridge' and 'Drowned early to mid-1970s', wondering whether Johnston had in fact been murdered. As they got into the car he couldn't stop himself from thinking that if that were true then perhaps his mother and Karl had shared a similar fate. In which case, he and Jean were clearly dealing with the kind of people who were prepared to kill to keep their secrets.

Chapter Twelve

Following lunch, Tayte and Jean arrived at Johann Langner's art gallery and auction house in plenty of time for their two thirty appointment with Langner's son, Rudolph, who was busy with a client when they first arrived at the modern two-storey building in the Kunstareal—the art district in Munich's city centre. They were waiting on the gallery floor beneath the main auction house, where interested bidders could view the artwork prior to sale. The most expensive pieces were viewable by appointment only in a room off the main gallery, which was where they had been told Rudolph Langner was.

'Fancy taking one home?' Tayte joked as they waited by a painting he didn't really understand. It was little more than a large off-white canvas with a line across the centre in burnt orange. 'What do you suppose this is meant to represent?'

Jean studied it, tilting her head this way and that. She shook her head. 'A sunset of some sort?'

Tayte had never heard of the artist, but judging from the price guide he could see there was clearly a market for his work. He looked around at all the paintings on display. There must have been close to a hundred pieces and it was plain to see that they represented a fortune in commission for the Langner gallery. As his eyes strayed towards the back of the room, he saw a tall, athletic-looking man in a black polo shirt and a tailored silver-grey suit striding purposefully towards them. As the man drew closer he began to smile, and Tayte realised this was who he and Jean had come to see. Tayte thought he was around forty years old. He had coiffed blonde hair and a narrow strip of beard running down the centre of his chin, which Tayte thought was akin to some artistic expression of his own.

The man extended his hand towards Tayte as he arrived. 'Mr Tayte,' he said, with an accent that was more British public school than German. Tayte noticed how piercing his eyes were. They were unnaturally blue, as though he were wearing coloured contact lenses to enhance them. He kissed Jean's hand. 'And you must be Professor Summer.'

'I'm pleased to meet you, Mr Langner,' Jean said.

'Please, call me Rudi.' He turned to Tayte. 'I'm afraid I can't give you long. I've another client to see in just under an hour. Now, you said on the telephone this morning that you'd been talking with my father at the Heart Centre.'

'That's right,' Tayte said. 'Only we had to leave somewhat prematurely.'

'Yes, I heard my father had another turn.'

'Have you seen him since then?' Jean asked. 'Is he okay?'

'I've not seen him, no,' Rudi said. 'His nurse keeps me updated, though. Her latest text message told me he was over the worst. But he needs rest.'

'We met his nurse yesterday,' Tayte said. 'Your father appears to be in good hands. She seems very efficient.'

Rudi gave a small laugh. 'Ingrid Keller might be efficient, but she's the most unpleasant person I know. She's always around him, telling me when I can and can't see him. He seems to like having her around, though, so I let them get on with it.'

Tayte passed Rudi one of his business cards. 'We're keen to see your father again whenever he's up to it. Perhaps you could let either him or his nurse know. I'd appreciate a call if something can be set up.'

'Of course. I'll see what I can do. But you must understand that he's very unwell.'

'I know,' Tayte said. 'Just on the off-chance.'

Rudi smiled and nodded as he slipped the card into his pocket.

As they ambled further into the gallery, Tayte showed Rudi the photograph of his mother. 'You wouldn't have been born when this picture of my mother was taken,' he said, 'so I won't ask you if you recognise her. I was abandoned as a child, eventually adopted, and I've been trying to identify my biological parents ever since.'

'Adopted, eh?' Rudi smiled warmly at Tayte. 'We have something in common then.'

'You were adopted, too?'

'Yes. My father has always been open about it, so I've known from an early age. He had no other children and he wanted an heir to his fortunes, I suppose. Someone to leave everything to when he's gone. He took my unfortunate situation and turned it into something wonderful. He's loved me as well as any child could hope to be loved, and I hope I've loved him as well as any son could. I certainly admire him for all he's done.'

'Do you ever wonder about your real parents?'

'Why should I? My mother didn't want me. Why should I want her?'

Rudi's words sounded cold to Tayte. It was a stark contrast to how he felt about his own mother, but then he'd always believed that his mother had given him up because she'd felt she had no choice. Rudi, on the other hand, seemed entirely comfortable with the situation, so Tayte didn't dwell on it.

'We're trying to find out why my mother visited one of your father's buildings in the 1960s,' he said, moving on.

'And we're hoping the answer lies somewhere in your father's past,' Jean added. 'Maybe in connection with a wanted war criminal called Volker Strobel.'

'Ah, *Der Dämon von Dachau*,' Rudi said with a flash of his eyebrows.

Tayte imagined Rudi's father would have told him about his wartime friend, although he thought it likely that most people living in Munich had at least heard of Volker Strobel.

'Your father was telling us about himself and his friendship with Strobel before the war,' Tayte said. 'I was hoping you could tell us a little more about that time. Has your father spoken to you much about the war years?'

'Very little,' Rudi said. 'And not lately. I think you'll find that most veterans of the Second World War don't really like to talk about it.'

'Your father seemed quite keen,' Jean said.

'Well, that's something new. Perhaps it's because he believes he's not long for this world.'

'We'd appreciate anything you can tell us,' Tayte said.

Rudi stopped walking beside a gilt-framed landscape painting of a rolling cornfield with a distant windmill by a stream. He gazed at it as though trying to recall some of the things his father had told him about the war years. A moment later, he said, 'I know my father was wounded quite badly. That was in 1941, I think he said. On the Eastern Front.' He smiled to himself. 'But they say every dark cloud has a silver lining, and I remember him telling me that something very good came out of it.'

Chapter Thirteen

North of Romanovka, Ukraine. The Eastern Front. July 1941.

The hail of bullets from machine-gun fire arrived without warning, splintering tree and bone without prejudice or distinction.

'Medic! Medic!'

Johann's cries went unanswered in the chaos that quickly erupted around him. To his right, his sergeant, a young *Unterscharführer* who had only recently been assigned to him, fell to his knees as blood began to spread across the shoulder of his camouflage smock. A moment later, another bullet caught the side of his head and spun him around to face Johann, the wide-eyed look of anguish and terror frozen on his face as he went down. Johann dived for the cover of a fallen tree, knowing no medic could save the man now.

A cry went up. 'Ivans! Right flank!'

'Fire at will!' Johann called.

Shots were quickly returned, and the *brr-brr* of the machine gun that had taken the young *Unterscharführer* sounded again, sending splinters of wood showering over his head.

'*Scheisse!*' Johann knew he had to find better cover, and soon.

Having survived multiple engagements on the Western Front since he'd been sent into action in May the previous year, Johann had come to be regarded as an 'old hare' by his *Kameraden*—even though he was barely twenty-three years old. Now the *Leibstandarte* had been called upon to assist with Operation Barbarossa in the east—the *Ostfront*, and Johann had welcomed the opportunity to play his part in defeating communism.

The *Leibstandarte*, as part of Army Group South under *Feldmarschall* Gerd von Rundstedt, had smashed through the Stalin Line at Mirupol, heading towards Zhitomir amidst growing Soviet Army resistance and torrential rain that had rendered the roads so boggy they quickly became unusable. Forced to head across country, the Reconnaissance Battalion had spearheaded the advance, but Johann and his small company had pushed so fast and so deep into enemy territory that they were soon detached from their main division, which, because of the weather and the terrain, had been unable to keep up.

'*Obersturmführer!*'

Johann was still getting used to his recent promotion to First Lieutenant. He rolled onto his side and then crawled on his elbows through the wet woodland ferns towards the rifleman who had called to him as bullets fizzed through the canopy above him. He recognised the rifleman's voice. It was *Schütze* Hartmann—a green recruit, fresh from the *Hitlerjugend*. Johann had thought the experience would be good for him, but he had not anticipated encountering such a fierce Soviet counter-attack so soon.

'Hartmann, how many are with you?'

'None, *Obersturmführer*. What should I do?'

Gunfire was being exchanged to his right and further ahead in the direction his unit had been travelling. He chanced a look above the ferns and saw *Sturmmann* Sachs with two more *Schützen* beside him: a machine-gun crew who were making ready their MG34. That was good, Johann thought, but he needed to draw the enemy's fire, if only to buy them a few more seconds.

'Hartmann, hold your position,' Johann called. 'Return fire!'

He stood up, aimed and fired his MP40 machine pistol at the first thing that moved among the trees ahead, and then he ran through the glistening ferns towards *Schütze* Hartmann. Behind him the buzz of the MG34 began to decimate the woodland at a rate of over 800 rounds per minute.

Two dead *Kameraden* greeted Johann's eyes as he stepped out from the ferns. One was the medic he had called for when the shooting began. Across the clearing where these men had fallen, he could see the young *Schütze*. He was crouching behind a broad tree trunk that had been splintered time and again by enemy fire. Hartmann, armed with a *Gewehr* 98 bolt-action rifle, stopped shooting and turned to Johann with cold fear in his eyes. At that same instant a heavy-set enemy soldier came screaming from the trees to Johann's left with his bayonet fixed. He had flanked Hartmann's position and was now charging straight at him.

The *Gewehr* 98 was a long rifle with a five-round clip. It was well suited to the typically taller men of the *Leibstandarte*, and it was undeniably a useful weapon in the hands of a marksman, but it was less effective in close-range combat, especially as *Schütze* Hartmann had not thought to fix his bayonet. Fortunately, Johann's MP40 was very effective at such close-quarter fighting. By the time the charging 'Ivan' saw him, it was too late. Johann had unleashed a hail of bullets into the man's chest, and he fell just a few feet in front of Hartmann.

'Fall back!' Johann ordered. '*Schnell!*'

It was plain to see that they were heavily outnumbered. They had perhaps encountered a small reconnaissance unit much like their own, but being more used to the conditions, he doubted that their main division was far behind. He knew their position would soon be overrun.

Hartmann arrived beside Johann, bent double to keep low. 'The rest of the unit are pinned down.'

'Where?'

Hartmann pointed off into the tangle of branches and the dripping, rain-soaked leaves. Johann grabbed him by his webbing and pulled him back through the ferns to the machine gun crew and the MG34 that had now fallen silent in the absence of any soldiers left in the immediate area to shoot. He took the MG34 from the hands of the *Schütze* whose white-knuckled fingers were still clenched tightly around the handle.

'*Sturmmann* Sachs, follow me. The rest of you fall back to the farmhouse we passed before we reached the wood.'

Hartmann nodded. '*Jawohl, Obersturmführer.*'

'If we don't make it back,' Johann said, 'try to hold out there until support arrives. It will give you cover and provide good visibility of the surrounding countryside.'

Johann and the *Sturmmann*, another old hare like himself, who had been with Johann since Operation Barbarossa began, headed off with the MG34 to the sound of the gunfire that was now constant. When they drew close enough to see what remained of his unit, and the whites of the enemy's eyes, he dropped behind a tree stump and sat with the MG34 resting between his legs on its bipod. Sachs readied the ammunition, connecting another belt of bullets for sustained firing, and Johann pulled back the bolt, ready to fire. A Soviet bullet disturbed the woodland debris beside him, spitting up twigs. He opened fire and the man fell, but he was soon replaced by another until it seemed that every tree in the woodland had an enemy soldier hiding behind it.

'Fall back!' Johann called to his *Kameraden*. 'Stay low.'

Beside him, *Sturmmann* Sachs opened fire with his P08, the pistol issued to the soldiers of the *Leibstandarte* known as the Luger. An 'Ivan' had tried to charge their position from the cover of the trees, but he had fallen before he reached half way.

Johann's assessment of the situation was dire. He had counted two more of his *Kameraden,* lying lifeless on the woodland's wet undergrowth. Only three now held the position they had been forced to defend when the encounter with the Soviets began, and the enemy, with their increasing numbers, now appeared to be growing more confident. Johann unleashed another burst of bullets as the first of his men crawled towards him. The second man followed soon after, and the third, clearly in a hurry now to join his *Kameraden,* panicked and ran.

It was to his end.

The *Schütze's* agonising scream drew Johann's attention in time to see the blood spatter from the exit wound in the man's chest just before he fell. Without a moment's pause, Johann led the men out of the death trap they had unwittingly stumbled into, retreating fast towards the ferns, pursued all the way by a hail of bullets. Random shots were returned, but Johann and what was left of his small reconnaissance troop were firing blind. There was no time to take proper aim. Just before they reached the cover of the ferns, Johann felt a tug at his right thigh and he knew he'd been hit. He gritted his teeth as the pain hit him, and he was forced to remind himself of the maxim that had been drummed into him during his time at the training school at Bad Tölz.

'Pain is in the brain,' he uttered to himself, biting hard as he threw the heavy MG34 ahead of him and dove into the ferns after it. He didn't know if he was going to make it out of that woodland alive, but he did know that if he were to stand any chance he had to stop his leg from bleeding. When he reached the fallen tree he had first taken cover behind, he stopped and quickly removed his belt.

'Keep going!' he told his *Kameraden,* waving them on. '*Sturmmann,* join up with the rest of the unit at the farmhouse.'

'We won't leave you, *Obersturmführer*. You know what those Ivans will do to you if they capture you.'

Johann knew only too well. He had heard the stories and had seen the evidence first hand. Captured *Waffen-SS* soldiers were often tortured and mutilated before they were allowed to die at the hands of the Soviet Army, who had not signed the Geneva Convention. In some cases, as he had seen for himself, prisoners were subjected to the *Handschuhe* torture, whereby their hands were placed in boiling water until they turned white, and then the skin would be cut around their wrists before being pulled from their flesh. Only then, and if he were lucky, would the soldier be shot in the head to end his suffering.

Johann looked up at the faces of the men before him and knew it would serve no purpose to order them to leave him. It made him hurry all the more. He looped his belt around his thigh as shots were exchanged. As he suspected, the enemy was not holding back. He pulled his belt as tight as he could bear it and tried to stand, hoping that the bullet had passed clean through his leg and not hit the bone. It would have shattered it if it had, making it all but impossible to put any weight on it. *Sturmmann* Sachs helped Johann to his feet as their few *Kameraden* continued to fend off the enemy.

'I can make it,' Johann said.

Sachs, a big man even among a division of *Leibstandarte* soldiers, who were typically chosen for their size and strength, picked up the MG34. As the unit continued its retreat, he sprayed what bullets remained on the ammunition belt into the trees, sweeping left to right to keep the enemy down, hoping to buy them enough distance to make it out of there. But the Soviet bullets kept coming, even if for now the soldiers firing them did not.

The air was alive with the fizzing sound of hot lead and splintering wood. When the MG34's bolt clicked back and stayed back, indicating that the ammunition belt was spent, Sachs dropped the weapon from hands that now seemed too weak to hold it. He wheeled around, and Johann saw that the torso of his camouflage smock was glistening with blood. He appeared to have been shot several times, but had somehow managed to remain standing and firing until his ammunition ran out. A moment later Sachs closed his eyes and slumped to his knees before falling flat onto his face. Dead.

Johann fired several shots in anger before he turned away from the fallen *Sturmmann*. It was easy to blame himself for his death, and he did so without question. Sachs was another *Kamerad* to add to every other who had died under his command.

'*Gehorsam bis in den Tod*,' he told himself. It was the oath they had all sworn to stand by: obedience unto death.

Shortly after Sachs fell, the shooting stopped. His heroic act of bravery had bought Johann and his few remaining men the distance they needed in order to lose themselves from the enemy's sight. Now it became a matter of remaining unseen. They trod carefully through the trees, minding every twig and fallen branch so as to make as little sound as possible, while maintaining as much haste as they could manage. Johann doubted the Soviets would give up the chase so soon, but he was to be proved wrong. At least, the attack soon took on a different form.

'Take cover!'

Johann heard the mortar shell screaming like a banshee over the woodland canopy. It landed ahead with a thump that was followed by exploding steel. Trees began to creak and fall, crushing everything in their path, adding to the danger.

'They're finding their range!' Johann called. His eyes darted here and there, looking for shelter, but there were no trenches here—no foxholes to scurry into. Johann knew they had to clear the trees, and quickly. The next shell would fall shorter. It would not take the Soviets long to find their target.

Another shell went over, this one to the right. Then another landed to their left. To escape the trees Johann realised they would have to pass through this killing zone, and yet to remain where they were, as the enemy advanced on their position, offered no better odds. Around him, Johann's unit had frozen to the spot, unsure what to do next, looking to him for guidance—for leadership. All Johann could think to do was to wait for the next shell to fall ahead of them, and then run after it, hoping the enemy would not fire so soon at the same spot. It was a gamble, but the time to make a decision was fast running out.

'When I run, follow after me,' he told his men.

Another shell erupted, and it was so close that the sound rang in Johann's ears. It was to his right. He waited. Then another shell screamed overhead.

'Ready!'

It thumped down and exploded barely more than fifty metres ahead. Johann ran towards it, limping most of the way. He was quickly overtaken by his *Kameraden*.

'Keep going!' he called. 'Don't stop until you're clear of the trees.'

He reached the site of the last shell and was slowed further by sharp and ragged splinters of wood where several trees had fallen over themselves. The pain in his leg was agonising, but he tried to shut it out. *Pain is in the brain . . . Pain is in the brain . . .*

The last sound he wanted to hear at that moment reached his ears then and he glanced up just as the whistling stopped. He knew that was bad. A second later the shell burst ahead of him and he felt something thump into his chest with such force that it spun him round, stopping him in his tracks. He felt suddenly dizzy. He sat down on the trunk of a fallen tree and tried to make out the scene before him, but his vision was blurred. For a moment he had no idea where he was. Then his arms were raised and two of his

Kameraden were beside him, propping him up onto his feet, which they began to drag through the debris.

'It's *Schütze* Hartmann, *Obersturmführer*. Can you hear me?'

The voice sounded distant and eerily hollow. 'Hartmann?'

Johann recalled that he had ordered the young *Schütze* and the rest of his unit to retreat to the cover of the farmhouse they had passed. He imagined that he had chosen to remain at the edge of the woodland to provide cover for their return. He had disobeyed an order, but Johann was glad. He had to admire the young *Schütze's* initiative and bravery.

'We've seen the main division, *Obersturmführer*. They're close.'

As his men continued to drag him along, Johann felt so light-headed that it was as if he were being borne on wings that would carry him home. No, not home. To Ava. He felt himself trying to smile as he saw her face—her blonde hair pinned up as it had been when he first saw her, her pale complexion and her button nose, and the warmth in her blue-grey eyes that he hoped he would someday see again.

He began to drift, seeing only shadows around him, and the soft green light of the woodland canopy, which every so often seemed to pass over his eyes and close them. He had been such a fool about Ava. He knew that now. The last time he had seen her—when he had met her at the Park Café in Munich over a year ago now—he had intended to ask her to marry him. But his courage, which had since been proven time and time again on the battle-field, had abandoned him that day. They had talked, and they had even held hands once or twice, but the ring his friend had given him—the ring he had so many times imagined slipping onto Ava's finger—had remained in his pocket all the while they were together, and it was still there now.

Johann thought about the ring again—Volker's ring—and was suddenly overcome with worry. In her letters, Ava had told Johann that Volker had been visiting her, not just that once to apologise for his behaviour the evening they had dined at the Osteria Bavaria, but several times since. Had Volker taken his failure to act as a sign that he no longer desired to marry Ava?

Johann feared he had, but it was a matter he was unable to dwell on. The shadows around him suddenly grew darker until all thought and sensation left him, and he was aware of nothing more.

Chapter Fourteen

Vienna, Austria. September 1941.

Johann Langner awoke to the familiar sights and smells of the hospital ward that, as for several of his *Waffen-SS Kameraden,* had been his home for the past few weeks. His bed, the most comfortable he had known in many months, was in a corner of the ward beside a sunlit window that looked down over a busy street and out across the city rooftops towards the Danube. In the bed next to his was a *Scharführer* from *SS-Wiking* Division called Ernst Köhler. The Sergeant Major was an older man, close to thirty, and he had become Johann's jovial companion since he'd been brought in—jovial, despite losing both of his legs during a Soviet mortar bombardment near the Ukrainian city of Tarnopol in one of his Division's early engagements on the *Ostfront.*

'A *Waffen-SS* officer leads from the front, eh, Johann?' he had said when first describing how he received his injuries, which Johann understood to be a dig at the officers of the *Wehrmacht*—the regular army—who on the whole seemed more inclined to lead from a safer distance.

Köhler was already sitting up as Johann stirred, and Johann noticed that he was gazing along the line of beds to his right, towards the entrance. Looking around, Johann saw that he was the last on the ward to wake, and that several of the men were also looking towards the entrance. Johann sat up to get a better look, and the sharp pain in his chest caused him to wince, reminding him that he was not long out of surgery. His movement drew Köhler's attention.

'Looks like an inspection,' Köhler said.

'At this time of the morning? We're in hospital for pity's sake.'

'Well, that's what it looks like from here. Why else would we get a visit so early in the day from such a high-ranking officer?'

Johann tried to glimpse the detail on the officer's uniform to better gauge his rank. He was certainly highly decorated, and Johann noticed that his collar tabs bore silver oak leaves, meaning that he had command of a regiment-sized unit at least. His adjutant was beside him, holding what Johann thought must be the senior officer's briefcase.

'He's working his way along the beds,' Köhler said. He laughed to himself. 'Do you think I should tell him one of my jokes?'

'No, Ernst. I don't.'

'Not even the one about Hitler and the French prostitute?'

'Definitely not that one. Not unless you want to be shot. And keep your voice down. He might hear you and have us both shot.'

When the senior officer arrived beside Ernst Köhler's bed, Köhler sat to attention. He raised his right arm in salute, all trace of mirth gone. Now that Johann could see the officer more clearly, he saw that his collar tabs bore two silver oak leaves, signifying that his rank was that of SS-*Oberführer*—a senior leader of the *Waffen-SS*. He was a slim-figured, softly spoken man who looked to be in his late thirties. As he addressed Köhler, Köhler began to tell him how he came to be at the hospital, and Johann got to hear how *Scharführer* Köhler received his injuries all over again. They spoke for a few minutes, and then the *Oberführer* and his adjutant came to Johann's bedside.

The *Oberführer* studied Johann's chart at the foot of his bed briefly before greeting him with a sympathetic smile. 'And how are you doing today?'

Lying in a bed next to that of a double amputee, Johann felt he had no cause or right to complain. At least his limbs were intact, which meant there was a good chance he would soon be able to rejoin his Division. 'I'm looking forward to seeing my release papers, *Herr Oberführer*.'

'That's the spirit. Your country is most proud of you. How were you wounded?'

Johann recalled his encounter with the Soviet Army in the woods north of Romanovka the previous month—how he and his small Reconnaissance Company had found themselves cut off and heavily outnumbered by the enemy. His account of the events was not of bravery or courage, but of the mistake he felt he had made in his eagerness to push forward, which to his mind had cost the lives of several *Kameraden* under his command. It was a mistake that now haunted his dreams.

'You are too hard on yourself,' the *Oberführer* said. 'And while it does you credit, it does little to serve our cause. It is, after all, a Reconnaissance Company's duty to venture into harm's way. You are often at the very tip of the spearhead of your division. I might add that such fighting spirit that drove you forward in the first place is the very thing that makes the *Leibstandarte* the elite Division it is.'

Johann knew the *Oberführer's* comments were well meant, and he could not deny that they had put him a little more at ease over what had happened, but it was perhaps too soon for Johann to accept that he was without blame for the deaths of his men. He nodded sharply to the *Oberführer*, and had he been standing he would have clicked his heels.

'And what of your wounds?' the *Oberführer* continued. 'I saw on your chart that you received more than one.'

'They tell me I'm lucky to be alive,' Johann said. 'I was shot in the leg, but that was no more than a flesh wound. After that we became caught in mortar fire and a piece of shrapnel struck my chest. From the clearing station I was initially sent to a temporary hospital in Western Ukraine, but the shrapnel was very close to my heart and they didn't have the facilities to remove it without running a high risk of killing me.'

'So they sent you here. I've heard the facilities in Vienna are first class.'

'Yes, *Herr Oberführer*. I'm sure they are.'

'And how is your family bearing up under the strains of war?'

'So far as I know they're managing quite well. I was able to write a few letters before I arrived here, but I suppose the mail service is having a difficult time keeping up with my whereabouts.'

The *Oberführer* nodded. 'Well, good luck,' he said, and with that he moved on to the next bed, across the ward from Johann, to continue what was evidently a morale boosting visit.

'No medals for us yet then,' Köhler said, his shoulders slumping. 'For a moment I thought the *Oberführer* might have had them in that briefcase of his.'

Johann turned to Köhler and smiled. 'I wondered the same thing.'

Just about everyone on the ward had been told they were to receive awards of one kind or another. For Johann, the Wound Badge Third Class in black, and the Iron Cross Second Class for his bravery in combat. He was glad to know that *Sturmmann* Sachs, who had gone with him to rescue their *Kameraden* in the woods near Romanovka, had also been awarded the Iron Cross, albeit posthumously. Ernst Köhler was to be awarded the Wound Badge Second Class in silver for the loss of his limbs, which, following a decree from Adolf Hitler the previous year, meant that he was also automatically awarded the Iron Cross Second Class. Johann thought Köhler deserved it far more than he did.

Later that morning, after they had eaten their breakfast and the nurses had been in to wash those who could not wash themselves, Johann was told that he had a visitor. The news came as something of a surprise to him because he didn't think anyone who knew him enough to want to visit him could possibly know where he was. He had supposed then that it must be another high-ranking *Waffen-SS* officer, come to hand out the medals, but Ernst Köhler had received no such news.

'Then who is it?' Johann asked the nurse who had come to see him. 'What does he want?'

'It's not a man, it's a young woman,' the nurse said. 'And she didn't say why she was here, other than to see you. She told me her name was *Fräulein* Bauer.'

———

Johann couldn't believe it. At first he thought Ernst Köhler was playing another trick on him. Johann had talked about Ava Bauer often enough for the mischievous *Scharführer* to have come up with some self-amusing jape at his expense, but as Köhler was giving nothing away, Johann knew there was only one way to find out.

'Could you please bring my uniform?' Johann asked the nurse. 'I don't want to see her in bed like this. Where is she?'

'She's waiting in a room along the corridor just outside the ward.'

'When you fetch my uniform, would you please tell her that I'll be out to see her shortly. And please don't let her leave,' he added, rushing the words out.

'I'm sure she's not going anywhere until she's seen you. She was very insistent.'

Johann couldn't help but smile to himself as the nurse retreated towards the doors at the far end of the ward. He glanced over at Köhler, who was reading a newspaper, and thought that if he was playing a joke on him, he was being very nonchalant about it.

Within fifteen minutes, Johann was dressed and on his feet, with a crutch beneath his right arm to help take the weight off his leg, which was still painful to walk on unaided. His chest hurt every time he moved, but he was prepared to endure it for Ava, and he'd been told that now he was over the worst, regular exercise would lead to a speedier recovery. As he adjusted to the pain and the awkwardness of movement he felt with every step, it took him a few more minutes to follow the nurse to the room where she'd said his visitor was waiting. When she opened the door for him and he entered, Johann held his breath and continued to hold it as Ava stood up. He began to smile and shake his head at the same time, as though a part of him still needed to be convinced that she was really there.

'Ava!' he said at last. She was wearing a dark green, belted peplum suit, and she had a matching felt hat in her hands. 'But how did you know where to find me? How are you? Oh, it's so good to see you. It's been far too long. However did you get here?'

Ava laughed. 'Slow down, Johann, you're garbling like an excitable child.'

'Looking at you makes me feel like a child again, Ava.'

He let go of his crutch and rushed towards her, throwing his arms around her. He kissed both of her cheeks without waiting for an invitation.

'Shall we get out of this place?' he said. 'Heaven knows, I've had enough of hospitals by now.'

'Are you allowed to leave?'

'I don't know, and I don't care. It looks like a beautiful day outside, and I'm sure the fresh air would be good for my lungs.' He took Ava's hand and stooped to pick up his crutch again. 'Come on. If we don't look suspicious I'm sure no one will question us. There's so much I want to tell you, and I can't wait to hear your news.'

They left the hospital without issue, and the bright, mid-morning sunshine caused Johann's cheeks to flush further. Ava was on his arm to help support him as they made their way towards the nearby Prater—a large area of public parkland where Johann thought they could walk and sit and talk until he felt his presence at the hospital might be missed, which he didn't think would be until at least lunchtime.

'So, first tell me how you knew where I was,' Johann said. 'I couldn't have mentioned it in my letter because at the time I had no idea I was coming here myself.'

'It wasn't so difficult,' Ava said. 'When I received your letter I was very worried about you. I knew I had to come and see you if I could, so I asked Volker to find you for me.' She smiled to herself. 'He's been very helpful to me and my family lately. He sends his wishes and told me not to worry about you because you're a survivor. He said it would take more than a Russian shell to stop you.'

'Someone was certainly looking out for me that day, I'm sure of it.'

'Were you very badly wounded? You didn't say much about it in your letter.'

'It was nothing, really,' Johann said, not wishing to worry Ava with the details. He had survived the ordeal, and he saw no purpose in telling her how lucky he was to be standing there beside her. 'I'm sure everyone has made more fuss over me than was necessary. They tell me that with a little rest I should make a full recovery in a month or so.'

'It must have been terrible for you,' Ava said, gazing into the sky as though trying to imagine the horrors of war.

Johann began to recall some of those horrors, and he began to see the faces of his fallen *Kameraden* again, many of whom had also become good friends.

'Let's talk about you, can we? How have you been? Are your parents well?'

'Well enough, considering. Papa had to stop teaching his music because no one comes to him any more. He's looking for work. Mama and I took laundry jobs, but the pay is very low.'

'I'm sorry to hear that.'

'Mind you,' Ava continued, 'it's not easy to spend what little we do earn. There doesn't seem to be enough food to go around, even for those who can afford it. People are beginning to wonder whether this war was such a good idea.'

'Shh, Ava. Don't let anyone hear you talking like that. It will be different when the war is won.'

They reached the Prater and followed a path beside a lake, heading towards the *Wiener Riesenrad*—a giant Ferris wheel with thirty gondolas that seemed to dominate the skyline. Johann pointed to it.

'I should like to ride the wheel with you before you return to Munich, but perhaps not today. Were you planning to stay in Vienna long?'

'I hadn't really made any plans other than to see you. Now that I have, I'd like to visit you again tomorrow, if that's okay. I'm sure I can find lodgings somewhere close by.'

'I'd see you every day if I could, Ava,' Johann said, turning to her. Their eyes met and neither seemed in any hurry to look away again. 'We'll just go and look at the wheel today then, but tomorrow we'll go for a ride. How about that?'

'Can you make it that far today? Are you sure you wouldn't rather turn back?'

'I can manage,' Johann said, forcing a smile. He supposed his morning medication was wearing off, because in truth every step now seemed to hurt more than the last.

As they followed the course of the pathway through the lush green parkland, neither spoke of the war again, perhaps just to help take their minds off it for a short time as they took in the beauty around them. When they arrived at the *Wiener Riesenrad*, they stopped outside the cinema that was adjacent to it, where the word '*KINO*' was raised high above the building as though competing with the giant wheel for the passing tourists' attention.

'It's quite magnificent,' Johann said as they gazed up at the wheel and the wide gondolas that were slowly turning over the city.

His eyes fell to meet Ava's again. His near fatal wounds had made him all too aware that his life could be over in an instant, and what then was it all for? He reached into his pocket and felt the ring box he'd kept beneath his hospital bed pillow whenever he was out of his uniform. He had come to feel that it somehow kept Ava close to him. At least, it carried the hope of being with her again.

And now he was.

He toyed with the box for several seconds, wondering if he asked her to marry him there and then what her answer would be. Would he spoil the perfect day if he offered it to her? Or would it lead to many more perfect days just like this? There was only one way Johann could know, and his courage did not fail him this time. He let his crutch fall aside as he dropped to one knee, fighting the pain in his leg as he bent it, and in his chest, which was throbbing with nervous joy. At first, Ava looked alarmed, as though she thought Johann had overdone things and had fallen down with fatigue, but then Johann reached towards her and took her hand in his, reassuring her.

He looked up into her eyes as the wheel turned behind him. He was oblivious to the attention he was getting from the passers-by, and he ignored his pain as he pulled out the ring box and opened it with one hand, all the while holding Ava with the other. Then he held the ring up for her to see, and the stones sparkled in the sunlight and reflected in her eyes as she gazed upon them.

'Ava . . .' He paused to suppress a cough, his nerves having parched his throat. 'Ava, would you do me the great honour of being my wife?'

Chapter Fifteen

Present day.

At Langner's art gallery and auction house, Tayte and Jean had moved to the back of the gallery with Rudi Langner, and were now in a room full of Old Masters. Having just been told that Johann had proposed to Ava Bauer in 1941, Tayte was keen to know whether she had accepted.

'So Johann got the girl?'

'Yes, they married the same year,' Rudi said. 'As I mentioned earlier, it was quite a silver lining after my father was wounded. He could have been killed, of course, but had he not been evacuated from the Eastern Front, who knows whether he would have had the chance to propose?'

'That's very interesting,' Tayte said. 'Your father led us to believe that he and Volker fell out over Ava Bauer. Yet we now know that any contest between them over the girl had been won by the end of 1941, and in your father's favour.'

'There has to be more to it,' Jean offered.

'I suspect there is,' Tayte said, thoughtfully, wondering whether Strobel had been able to let the matter go once Ava had married his best friend. He also began to wonder whether a child might have come from Johann's and Ava's marriage, but without access to the vital records he needed to see, he didn't yet know how he was going to find that out. He hoped the Kaufmanns would soon be able to help out there. 'Do you know what became of Ava?' he asked Rudi. 'You must have been curious when you found out about her.'

'I was very curious,' Rudi said. 'But my father would never tell me how or why they separated, or whether she had died during the war or lived on. You'd have to ask him about that yourselves, I'm afraid.'

'I hope we get the opportunity.'

'Yes, so do I,' Rudi said with a slight smile to hide the emotion that had crept into his voice at the idea that his father was unlikely to live much longer.

'You're very close to your father, aren't you?' Jean said.

'Yes, very much so. He's a selfless, hard-working man, and please don't suppose that his wealth is driven by vanity or greed. He donates a great deal to many charities, especially those connected with the holocaust. He's always been someone to look up to. I'm very proud of him.'

Jean offered Rudi a kindly smile. 'And I'm sure he's very proud of you, too.'

'Did your father marry again after the war?' Tayte asked. He'd been wondering why Johann Langner had chosen to adopt rather than father a child of his own.

'No,' Rudi said. 'Perhaps once was enough for him. Or maybe he never got over Ava Bauer. But as I said, he didn't like to talk about it and I didn't like to push him. I could see how upset it made him.'

Tayte wondered then whether the reason Johann Langner didn't like to talk about Ava was related to the terrible thing he'd said Strobel had done. 'Did your father ever talk about Volker Strobel?'

'He mentioned him a few times, mostly from the years when they were growing up as friends before the war. He has many stories to tell about his time in the Hitler Youth, but not so many from the years during the war—at least, not many that he's told me. While we were talking about Ava and how he came to ask her to marry him, he did tell me that Volker Strobel invited him to the concentration camp at Dachau soon after the wedding. Apparently, he had a special wedding gift for my father. When I heard what it was, I was as shocked as my father, I can tell you.'

Chapter Sixteen

Dachau, Germany. December 1941.

Johann Langner and Ava Bauer were married on a bright and cold Saturday morning, just as soon as Johann's recovery was deemed complete and he had been given his release papers. The wedding had been a quiet and somewhat hurried affair because Johann had been allowed no more than three weeks' leave to see his family before he had to return to the *Ostfront*, and because both Ava and Johann had agreed that they didn't want their families and friends to go to any fuss over them when times were so difficult.

Neither had minded in the least, and they cared little for the manner of the proceedings. They simply wanted to be husband and wife, so that it could be recorded for all time that they had once loved each other, and although neither of them had openly said it, Johann knew that to wait any longer was sheer folly in light of the mortal dangers he would again soon find himself in. He was to leave for the *Ostfront* in two days, and the prospect of facing the Russian winter, having heard that temperatures at the Moscow Front had fallen to as low as minus thirty-seven degrees centigrade, made the thought of leaving his new bride so soon after their wedding all the more unbearable.

It was a cold afternoon towards the middle of the month, and for what seemed like the first time since their wedding, Johann had left Ava at her parents' home where he'd been staying while he was in Munich. He hadn't seen anything of Volker during his leave, and while it pained him to be parted from Ava, he had contacted Volker to arrange to see him before returning to his unit. Volker had not been able to escape his responsibilities at the concentration camp, so his friend had suggested Johann visit him there, adding that he had a surprise for him.

Johann had borrowed Herr Bauer's motorcar for the short journey northwest of Munich to the medieval town of Dachau. He drove up to the concentration camp's main entrance gates and took in the thick stonework that surrounded them, and it was impossible for his eyes not to be drawn to the black eagle that sat above them, as tall as a man with its wings spread to either side. He showed his papers to the sentry guard who made a telephone call, and a moment later Johann was admitted through on foot and escorted to the *Kommandantur*—the camp headquarters—where he found Volker Strobel waiting for him, standing in his greatcoat with his hands on his hips at the corner of the building. There were two SS guards with him.

'Johann! It's always so good to see you, my friend.'

They saluted one another and Volker offered out a black-gloved hand. Johann shook it. There was no informal hug or even a slap on the back this time, which Johann understood was because his friend was on duty and that he had his authority to uphold.

'It's good to see you, too, Volker. I missed you at the wedding of course. I was hoping you would be my best man.'

'It would have been my honour, Johann, but duty first, eh? I trust you received the food and champagne I sent.'

'We did. Thank you. It went down very well.'

'I'm sure it did,' Volker said, almost laughing. 'It was very fine champagne.' He pulled his gloves on more firmly and turned away from the building. 'I'm glad you're wearing your coat. I'd like to show you the prisoner camp while you're here, and as I said during our brief telephone conversation yesterday, I've arranged a little something for you. Call it a personal wedding present, if you like, just for you.'

'I'm intrigued,' Johann said as they moved off, the two guards following close behind them.

As they walked, Volker pointed out various parts of the camp, including the SS troop barracks, the administration buildings, the bakery, and the residential officers' housing, making a point of highlighting his own accommodation. He asked Johann about the action he'd seen and of the wounds he'd received at the *Ostfront*, and Johann gave him a potted summary of his life on the front line.

An hour passed as in the blink of an eye, so deep were they in conversation, but it was interrupted when they came to a building with a deep inset arch that led to a single iron gate. It had the words '*Arbeit Macht Frei*' written in iron lettering above it, promising those who were imprisoned in the compound beyond that their work would make them free. They passed through the gate, collecting two more guards for their entourage.

'Being the first camp of its kind,' Volker said, 'Dachau has become the model for all others. We now also have SS doctors at the camp hospital, whose duty it is to regularly determine those who are unfit for work.'

'What happens to them?' Johann asked.

'Special Treatment 14f13,' Volker replied. 'They are no longer of any use to us here, so they are transferred to Hartheim in Austria. This is the prisoner roll-call area. Those buildings beyond are the prisoner barracks.'

They had arrived in a large open space, where Johann saw many rows of single-storey buildings reaching away for as far as he could see. There were prisoners here and there in their striped uniforms, going about their work, and Johann noticed that they wore armbands of different colours. He asked Volker what they signified.

'They represent the authority that sent them here,' Volker said. 'If the Gestapo send us a political prisoner, he wears a red armband. Anyone convicted by the criminal courts wears green. Those sent by the welfare authorities wear black. Jews yellow. Jehovah's Witnesses purple, and so on. It helps us to keep track of everyone.'

'I imagine the security for so many prisoners must be very strong?'

'Indeed. The camp enclosure is heavily guarded. We have seven guard towers and wire fences that are two deep, creating a ten-foot-wide space between them. The guards have orders to shoot anyone found in this forbidden area, and yet even while the prisoners know this, some still enter. The entire compound is surrounded by a combination of electrified, barbed-wire fencing and brick walls. It's impossible to escape, so I can only believe they enter the area with the desire to end their own lives. I really can't understand why.'

As they walked alongside the prisoner barracks and Johann came closer to some of the prisoners, he thought he understood very well. Many were obviously malnourished, and he could only imagine the long work regime they had to endure day in and day out with little or no respite or sustenance. They came to a halt beside a small parade of prisoners who had been lined up three men deep by eight men wide at the end of one of the huts. There were guards to either side of them, clenching their weapons as if threatening to use them at the slightest provocation.

Every prisoner, some wearing thin hats of the same striped material, others with their shaved heads exposed, was visibly shivering in the cold December air. Their otherwise pale skin was tinged with shades of purple at the extremities. It suggested to Johann that they had been standing in the cold for a long time, waiting for Volker to appear. They were all standing to attention, as though they were a fighting unit at an inspection parade, and it was easy for Johann to identify those prisoners who had been at the camp the longest by their drawn faces and hollow-set eyes, and by the way their striped uniforms seemed to hang without substance on their near skeletal frames. As Volker looked upon them, each man seemed to stand more stiffly to attention, forcing his chest out as best he could in an attempt to please their *Lagerführer*. It was clear to Johann from every man's expression that they did so, not out of pride or honour, but out of fear.

Volker turned to Johann and simply smiled at him, saying nothing, as though he was too proud for words at his efforts to instil such discipline at Dachau. A moment later, he turned abruptly on his heel and continued the tour. Johann was glad to move on.

'You know,' Volker said, 'I've a mind to take a bride of my own.'

Johann couldn't imagine what had prompted Volker to think about marriage after what he'd just seen. 'Aren't you going to dismiss those prisoners?' he asked. Looking back, he could see that they were still standing to attention.

Volker waved his hand, as if flicking at a fly that was irritating him. 'They will remain there until we leave the enclosure. Do not feel sorry for them, Johann. Those workers were selected because they are in need of discipline. Now where was I? Ah, yes, you remember Trudi, don't you? The beautiful Trudi Scheffler?'

'Yes, of course.'

'Well, I think I'll marry her after all. I'm sure she'd like that. Then you and I will both be married. And someday, when this war is won, our children, and perhaps even our grandchildren, will be the best of friends, just like us. Wouldn't that be something?'

Johann just nodded and feigned a weak smile, distracted by everything around him. He considered himself fortunate that he was not in Volker's shoes. The perils awaiting him on the *Ostfront* were a far greater enticement to a fighting soldier of the *Waffen-SS* than to be assigned duties at a work camp such as this, where discipline was seemingly demanded through cruelty over a sense of honour.

'You're a very lucky man,' Volker continued.

'How so?'

'For marrying Ava, of course. For winning the girl.'

Johann had wanted to believe that Volker was over Ava Bauer, as he had told him that night in the bar after they dined at the Osteria Bavaria. He wondered then whether his friend was only interested in marrying Trudi because he himself was now married. It was a childish thought, but if there was any truth to it then Johann could see that his friend clearly was not over losing Ava Bauer to him at all. He said no more about it as they continued to pace alongside the prisoner barracks, but it concerned him just the same. When they came to the last of the barracks, Volker led them around it.

'We're being sent many Russian prisoners by the *Wehrmacht*,' Volker said. 'I hate those Bolshevik bastards all the more for what they did to you, Johann. The SS Inspectorate of Concentration Camps has recently postponed the execution of prisoners of war who are able to work, but a few more won't be missed. I said I'd arranged something special for you.'

They arrived at the *Desinfektionsgebäude*—the disinfection building at the far corner of the compound where Johann saw a single line of five prisoners, again with guards to either side of them. These men were not standing to attention, but were facing the wall of the building with their shoulders slumped and their heads slightly bowed, as though resigned to their fate.

'Here are your Bolsheviks, Johann. Here are the butchers who defile our women and mutilate our men. They represent those who killed your *Kameraden*—those who tried to kill you.' Volker unholstered his Luger and offered it to Johann. 'Here. They are my gift to you.'

There was no doubt as to what Volker had in mind, but Johann would not do it. 'Your gift to me?' he said, incredulous. 'You want me to shoot these men simply because they're Russians?'

Volker extended the pistol towards Johann again. 'These inmates have been identified as troublemakers. So go ahead, have your revenge. It will do you good, believe me. I shot several of them myself when Ava told me what the Russians had done to you, and I slept better for it, I can tell you. They're usually shot at the SS shooting range at Hebertshausen, but as that's almost two miles away, I had them brought here, just for you.'

Johann began to shake his head. He stepped back. 'I will not shoot them, Volker. It's against the Geneva Convention and you know it. Even if the Russians didn't sign, Germany did. What you're proposing here is not only wrong, it's both immoral and illegal.' Johann shook his head again in disbelief. 'And you call it a gift? You cannot summarily execute prisoners of war like this.'

Volker gave Johann a thin smile that was clearly not well meant. He withdrew his pistol and raised it to the head of the prisoner closest to him, and then he pulled the trigger. The gun's report cracked out and the air around it filled with the familiar reek of cordite. The prisoner Volker had shot had crumpled to the ground before the sound of the shot that killed him had faded.

'As you can see, Johann, at Dachau I can do whatever I wish. I do not take my orders from Geneva.'

He raised his pistol again and shot the next prisoner in the same manner: a single bullet to the back of his head.

'Stop this!' Johann said. It was clear to him now that Volker appeared to take his orders from no one. He had become a law unto himself. 'I've seen enough of your work camp. I'm leaving.' Johann turned to go, but he had only taken three strides before he felt Volker's hand on his arm.

'Wait, Johann! I thought this was what you wanted.'

Johann turned to Volker with an expression of loathing. His eyes narrowed. 'Well, I don't. When I kill Russians, it's because they're trying to kill me!' He shook his arm free. 'I can see myself back to the main gate,' he added, and then he set off at a march, unable to endure Volker's company a moment longer.

Chapter Seventeen

Present day.

Following what had proved to be a very informative visit with Rudi Langner, it was just after three thirty in the afternoon when Tayte and Jean climbed back into their hire car. With no other appointments in their schedule, Tayte thought now would be a good time to pay a visit to the building in his mother's photograph: the former Hitler Youth training academy, which Johann Langner had turned into an education centre. They drove northwest in the ever-present traffic, talking over what Rudi had just told them about Volker Strobel.

'I sincerely hope Strobel isn't my grandfather,' Tayte said, reflecting on how anyone could think that giving their friend a free hand to execute people was a great idea for a wedding present. 'But I guess you never really know where you come from until you look,' he continued, thinking that he was always finding surprises in other people's family trees and now the surprise was potentially on him. 'I mean, what if the Strobel gene is kicking around inside me? Am I capable of such things?'

'I think you'd probably know about it by now,' Jean said. 'And we can't choose our ancestors. You of all people know that.'

'You sound just like Marcus Brown.'

'Well, I did have the privilege of knowing him for quite a few years, and I'm sure he would have told you the same thing. We're not accountable for the things our ancestors may or may not have done. It's what we do during our own lives that counts.'

Tayte laughed to himself. 'Marcus would definitely have said that.'

'That's because he was a very wise man.'

Tayte nodded, and slowly his smile faded. He'd first met Jean on a visit to London to see Marcus, unaware that his friend had set them both up on a blind date. He recalled the day with startling clarity—the day Marcus was murdered.

'I still miss him.'

'Of course you do. So do I. I can picture him smiling down at us, feeling very pleased with the way things are going between us. And he'd be over the moon to know that his research has brought you closer to finding your family.'

'I owe him so much,' Tayte said. 'Did you know he used to teach family history back home in DC? This is going way back. It's how we met.'

'Yes, he mentioned it when he first told me about you.'

'Of course he did.' Tayte thought back to those times and smiled to himself. 'I'm sure he was just as keen to find my family as I was. It hurts to know I can never repay him.'

'Find your family,' Jean said. 'For yourself and for Marcus. That's how you can repay him. I can't imagine anything would have made him happier.'

Tayte reached over and put his hand on the back of Jean's. He'd never been one to show his emotions too readily, and he was finding it hard to tell Jean exactly how he felt about her now. But he sensed Jean understood that about him. They exchanged smiles, and in that moment he knew his message had been received and understood. Then the voice on the sat-nav interrupted the moment to let them know that they had arrived at their destination.

'There it is,' Tayte said, gazing through the windscreen at the wide, neo-classical structure with its high, pillared portico.

Apart from the grand entrance, it was little more than a dressed-up blot of concrete and windows—a lot of windows. Tayte thought the building looked even more oppressive in reality than it did in the newspaper clipping Marcus had left him, despite the obvious effort to enhance the surrounding space with trees and shrubs, and what appeared to be a picnic area with wooden bench tables. The building's façade was in shade, which didn't help. Tayte drove into the car park at the front of the building, which he supposed was once a Hitler Youth parade ground, and found a space with ease.

'It's not very busy,' Jean said, reading his thoughts. 'I suppose it gets busier at weekends.'

They got out of the car and strode up to the entrance. Tayte's eyes immediately fixed on the two stone lions at the top of the steps to either side of the main doors. He pictured his mother standing between them a little over fifty years ago and his eyes wandered up to the restored words above the entrance: 'Blut und Ehre'. Tayte climbed the steps and put his hands on one of the lions, feeling the cool stone against his palms. He wondered whether his mother had perhaps touched that very spot, and for a moment he felt so close to her that a shiver ran through him.

As he followed Jean into the building, he felt as if he had just stepped back in time to the 1930s. He heard faint but rousing classical music that crackled as though being played through an old gramophone or Bakelite radio set. It was disconcerting at first to see Nazi Party flags being displayed so flagrantly in the hall they had just entered, but he supposed it was all part of the experience, and he had to admit that it was working. He thought it was going a bit too far, though, when he saw the young attendant waiting to sell them their tickets. He was kitted out in a Hitler Youth costume, replete with achievement badges, and he even wore a short blonde wig to complete the stereotypical Aryan look, although it was poorly fitted and curled at the edges.

'*Zwei, bitte,*' Jean said, while Tayte was still staring at the young man in disbelief.

They followed the guide book they had been given to their left, into a room full of cabinets displaying items from the period. One wall showed a line of boy-sized mannequins dressed in the various iterations of the Hitler Youth uniform through the years.

'I don't know about you,' Tayte said once he thought the attendant was out of earshot, 'but I found that more than a little unsettling.'

'I know what you mean,' Jean said. 'You can't knock the place for authenticity, though, can you?'

They came to a display of Hitler Youth daggers and Tayte wondered why none of these boys' parents thought it just plain wrong to have their thirteen-year-old child running around with such a weapon attached to his belt. He imagined some mothers must have, but were perhaps too afraid to voice their concerns. On their way around the education centre they saw several other visitors and a few more members of staff in their Hitler Youth costumes, although if this was a typical day's business, Tayte thought Johann Langner must be running the place at a loss in order to keep the past in people's minds. They saw numerous display cabinets as they wandered through lecture rooms, classrooms and a large sports hall, which were all connected through a matrix of corridors whose parquet floors, as with everything else, had been painstakingly restored to their original form.

Over an hour had passed by the time they had gone full circuit, and when they arrived back at the entrance hall Tayte thought it was good to have visited the place, even if he had to concede that it had done nothing to further their understanding of why his mother had gone there.

'I think I'd like to go someplace and get my laptop out,' Tayte said. 'Do some digging around online.'

'Do you want to get a coffee?'

Tayte had seen a sign for the on-site coffee shop. 'You mean, here?'

Jean frowned. 'No, definitely not here. We can't be too far from a decent café, though. Maybe we could stop off somewhere on the way back to the hotel.'

'Sure,' Tayte said. 'That sounds great.'

As they made their way back to the car, Tayte said, 'Would you like to go out for dinner tonight? We can get a coffee first, have a stroll through the city, and find somewhere fancy to eat.'

'I'd love to, but I'd like to get out of this day dress first.'

'You look great,' Tayte said with a grin. 'Sometimes it's nice just to go with the flow and see where it takes you. Don't you think?'

Jean laughed at him. 'And there I was thinking you were a routine kind of guy.'

'Hey, I'm working on it, aren't I?'

'Yes, you are,' Jean said, laughing again. She reached up and gave him a kiss. 'Thank you.'

As they got back into the car, Tayte smiled to himself and thought he would have to work on it more often.

Chapter Eighteen

They found an independent café in a sunny spot set back from the main road just outside Munich's city centre, where it was also easier to find a parking space. Jean ordered a single pastry between them to go with their coffee.

'We should share one,' she said. 'We don't want to ruin our appetites for that fancy dinner you mentioned.'

Tayte had to smile. They were still getting to know one another, and he thought that Jean clearly didn't know him all that well yet, or she would have known he could have eaten her half of the pastry and another two besides without putting so much as a dent in his appetite.

They set up at a table in the window, looking out at the tables and chairs in the forecourt, rather than sitting out in the early evening sunshine, because Tayte's laptop screen didn't handle bright light very well. He got his notebook out and flicked through the pages to find the information he'd written down when they left the elderly lady at the apartments by the waterway earlier. As he opened his laptop, he was glad to see the place offered free Wi-Fi.

'I've been wanting to explore the drowning of Geoffrey Johnston,' he said, 'so why don't we start there. Maybe his death was an accident, but I'd like to satisfy my curiosity.'

'I'll see what I can find on my tablet,' Jean said.

Using Google's translation services to better understand his findings, Tayte started with the German national broadsheet newspaper, *Die Zeit*, which he'd used a few times whilst looking into Volker Strobel before he and Jean left England. It was the country's most widely read weekly newspaper, and it had a good digitised archive available online that dated back to the newspaper's creation in 1946. Tayte started with the year he was most interested in—1973, the year his mother and Karl had gone to see Elijah Kaufmann. He figured Geoffrey Johnston, whoever he was, was likely to still be alive at that point. Tayte entered Geoffrey Johnston's name into the search field. No results were found, so he tried 1974 and was presented with a single result from January that year.

At that moment, Jean looked up from her tablet PC and said, 'You're kidding me.'

'What?' Tayte said. 'What is it?'

Jean put her tablet PC on the table and spun it around for Tayte to see. 'Geoffrey Johnston has his own Wikipedia page. He was a British diplomat with the Foreign Office. His last role was Consul-General, Munich.'

'Are you sure that's the same Geoffrey Johnston?' Tayte asked, scrolling through the information Jean had found.

'It says he drowned in Munich in January 1974.'

'So it does,' Tayte said as his eyes found the details. 'I guess that's why his death made the German national newspapers.' He turned his laptop around so they could both see the screen. 'There's some more information here about the drowning,' he added as he read on, quickly confirming that the drowned man was indeed a British Consul-General, working at the British Consulate in Munich at the time of his death.

'Bloated body found in Eisbach,' Jean read aloud. 'There doesn't seem to be any suspicion of foul play, though.'

'No,' Tayte said, 'although seeing just how close Johnston's death was to my mother's and Karl's visit with Elijah Kaufmann, it still strikes me as highly suspicious. He drowned four months later.'

'I'm sure Elijah Kaufmann didn't have anything to do with it,' Jean said.

'As am I, but perhaps someone could have gained access to Kauffman's files—maybe someone else who worked for him.'

'Or perhaps someone knew your mother and Karl were looking for Strobel and followed them to Johnston's apartment. Just like they followed us after we left the offices of the FWK yesterday. They must also have visited other people during the time before Johnston's death. Maybe they went to the FWK, too.'

'Maybe,' Tayte said, wondering now why his mother and Karl had given Kaufmann the address of the British Consul-General, and how his mother wound up in Mexico the following year, perhaps on the run from Strobel because she and Karl had come too close to finding him. And where was Tayte's father when his mother gave him away? The sister at the mission had told him his mother had been alone.

'How did my mother and Karl know this man, Johnston?' Tayte asked, thinking aloud.

'He could have been a friend, or family perhaps?'

The idea that Geoffrey Johnston might have been family excited Tayte. If he was, then being British Tayte thought it more likely that the connection would be on his mother's side, and he knew that with some digging he should be able to find that connection somewhere in the UK birth, marriage, and death indexes. But it was just one of many possibilities that for now Tayte put to the back of his mind for investigation at a later date. Right now he wanted to stay on track. He wanted to know why his mother had abandoned him, and more and more he was beginning to feel that the answer was inextricably linked to Volker Strobel.

He was about to ask Jean if she wanted another coffee to go with their next line of research, but when he looked up from his laptop screen, he saw that Jean looked terrified. She was staring past him, out of the window, her lips slightly parted, her eyes wide open. Tayte craned his neck around, following her gaze, and for the first time he saw the man they had come to know of as Max Fleischer. The Death's Head Unit tattoos on his neck were unmistakable. Fleischer was standing just outside the window, no more than three feet away, with only the glass between them. He wore a plain white T-shirt, and now that he had Tayte's and Jean's attention, he lifted it up to reveal a handgun tucked into the top of his black jeans. He began to shake his head slowly from side to side, no expression on his face. He didn't need one to convey the message he was sending them. The gun said it all.

Tayte jumped to his feet and Jean shot a hand out to stop him. 'No, JT! He'll kill you.'

'If these people wanted us dead already, I'm sure they'd have found an opportunity by now.' Tayte continued to rise. 'And I'm sure he's not dumb enough to shoot us in a busy coffee shop.'

He made for the door, thinking about what this man had done to Jean the day before and how he'd threatened to rape her. It gave him both the strength and the courage to confront him, but when he got outside, Fleischer was gone.

Tayte was shaking as he returned to the table and sat down. 'How do you suppose he found us again? Surely he's not been following us since we left the hotel this morning.'

Jean scoffed. 'He might well have been, or maybe he was watching the gallery and knows we went to see Rudi Langner. He obviously knows we're still asking questions, which isn't good.'

'It's not good at all,' Tayte said, wondering whether any of Fleischer's associates had followed them into the coffee shop, and had perhaps sent a text message to him. He looked around. A few people were already staring back at him, no doubt wondering what all the fuss was about, but the place was mostly filled with couples enjoying their coffee. Just the same, Tayte didn't want to stick around.

He closed his laptop. 'Come on,' he said, collecting his briefcase from the floor as he rose.

Jean got up with him. 'We should report this to the police.'

'Yes, and we will, but I don't fancy spending the evening at the police station, and I still can't see how there's anything they can do beyond telling us to go home. I know it's not going to be easy, but let's try to forget about it for now and go find somewhere to eat. We'll drop by and report it in the morning.'

Chapter Nineteen

They dined at the *Spatenhaus an der Oper* on Residenzstrasse. Having been denied taking lunch there by Max Fleischer the day before, Tayte had wanted to go there all the more to spite the man. He'd be damned if he was going to let Fleischer's appearance outside the coffee shop deny them the pleasure of sampling the restaurant's traditional Bavarian cuisine for a second time. Jean had wanted to forget about the research while they were there and just enjoy the meal—to pretend, for a few hours at least, that they were like any other sightseeing couple on a city break. Although Tayte managed to avoid talking about it, his mind was often elsewhere, going over everything they had heard that day.

He wondered again whether Karl was his father, and why he and his mother had gone to see Elijah Kaufmann about Volker Strobel in connection with finding Karl's own father. Had a child come from Strobel's marriage to Trudi Scheffler? And what about Johann Langner's marriage to Ava Bauer? Another possibility for a child existed there. By the time Tayte and Jean arrived back in their hotel room, having had a quick nightcap in the hotel bar, Tayte was all the more eager to get his laptop out and continue digging into these lives that he felt more and more were connected to his own. It was just after eight in the evening, the orange glow at the window fading rapidly now as the sun began to set on Munich's busy city streets.

'That was a very pleasant evening,' Jean said, kicking off her shoes. 'Thank you.'

'I'm sorry if I seemed a little distracted,' Tayte said as he hung up his jacket.

Jean put her arms around him and gave him a squeeze. 'I think you did very well.'

'I just feel there's so much at stake here. I want to stay focused in case I miss something.'

'I know.'

Jean unzipped her dress as she continued into the room. She let it fall to her feet and slowly stepped out of it, catching Tayte's eye as she stooped to pick it up.

'That's not helping.'

Jean laughed. 'Don't get your hopes up, big fella. We've got research to do, remember?'

'Touché,' Tayte said with a grin.

Jean swapped her contact lenses for glasses, and got herself cosy for the evening in her pyjamas and dressing gown while Tayte set up his laptop at the desk. He thought he'd look into Johann and Ava first, while the conversation with Rudi Langner was still fresh.

'I don't expect we'll find much,' he said as Jean sat beside him. He turned to her, drawing in her scent. 'You smell great. Have I said that already?'

'You don't know?'

'I remember thinking it. I don't think I actually said it, did I?'

Jean shook her head.

'Well you do,' Tayte said. 'You smell amazing.'

Jean gave him a wry smile and tapped his laptop. 'Focus. Remember?'

'Of course,' Tayte said, turning back to the screen. 'As I said, I don't suppose we'll find much without access to the records. I hope the Kaufmanns come good on that soon. We can run some general searches, but that's about it. We know plenty about Johann Langner, but until this afternoon, we didn't know that he married Ava Bauer during the war. Let's see if we can find anything out about her.'

Tayte entered her name into the search field on his Internet browser. There were several hundred results, many of which were links to social media websites.

'Do you want to check through those on your tablet?' Tayte said. 'I'll see if any of the other references lead anywhere.'

Jean stood up with a yawn.

'Sounds like someone's ready for bed.'

'It's probably just the wine,' Jean said as she sat up on the bed and woke up her tablet.

Tayte turned his attention back to the search results in front of him. He scrolled through the list, and a few pages on he followed an entry that matched Ava Bauer's name to the Billion Graves website, which had proved useful to him many times in the past as it often listed other family members who were buried together in the same plot. It made sense to Tayte that he might find reference to a child born to Johann Langner and Ava Bauer on such a website, but the date of birth shown against this particular Ava Bauer meant that she would have been too young for marriage during the Second World War.

He followed the further results at the bottom of the entry, clicking on a link to the Genealogy Bank, but that only led him to a newspaper archive containing a birth announcement in 1987, which was too late. There was another link to a service called People Finders. It was a US based service, but as Tayte couldn't rule out that Ava Bauer hadn't wound up living in America after the war, he thought it worth a look. There were a few listings, although the current ages of the women he was looking at were all too young, mostly in their sixties. If Ava Bauer was still alive, Tayte knew she would be a little older than Johann Langner.

Thirty minutes passed while Tayte followed links to one dead end after another, and Jean's silence told him she was having about as much luck as he was. He stood up, collected his laptop, and sat up on the bed beside her.

'No luck?' he asked her.

Jean shook her head. 'Nothing. If Ava Bauer lived long enough to meet the social media revolution, I expect she'd have been too old by then to care about it.'

If she lived long enough . . . Tayte thought, his mind wandering back to the art gallery and the conversation with Rudi Langner. Clearly something had prevented Johann and Ava from being together after the war, something Johann didn't like to talk about. Tayte wished he knew what it was, but as he didn't, he decided to keep an open mind for now. All he did know was that Johann and Ava seemed to have fallen very much in love.

Chapter Twenty

Munich. August 1942.

Having arrived home for a short period of leave the previous evening, and having spent almost every waking hour since in the close company of Ava's parents, with whom Johann was staying, he and Ava were alone together at last. They were balancing awkwardly on Ava's bicycle, running an errand for her father, Gerhard, who had been forced to sell his motorcar in order to provide for the family's essential needs. His Beckstein grand piano, the one thing that Gerhard obstinately refused to part with because he believed it would help get the family back on its feet again after the war, had a broken hammer shank that could not satisfactorily be repaired. He had managed to locate a spare that belonged to the family of a former pupil who lived on the other side of Munich, and Johann, tired as he was from battle and an inherent lack of sleep, had readily agreed to go and fetch it, glad of any excuse to be alone with Ava.

It was late in the hot afternoon and Ava was giggling in his ear. 'Slow down!'

Johann was freewheeling the bicycle down a hill, Ava on the seat behind him as he stood on the pedals. He didn't want to slow down. The faster he went, the tighter Ava held him, and he wanted that feeling to last. They were on the outskirts of Munich, travelling along a lane that ran parallel to a farmer's field, which was tellingly devoid of the wheat Johann imagined would ordinarily be coming into harvest. They reached the bottom of the hill with the summer wind rushing at their smiling faces, and that simple pleasure made Johann so happy that he wished the war was over so he and Ava could stay like this forever.

'Hold on!' Johann called, squeezing the brake levers as he turned off the lane, still carrying enough speed to solicit an excited squeal from Ava.

There was an opening into the field and Johann took it, sure that they had plenty of time to spare before Ava's parents would begin to worry about them. A sunlit patch of bleached grass to the side of the field drew Johann towards it and the bicycle bounced over the rough, baked earth, which was so hard he could feel Ava bouncing in the saddle. Just before they reached the grass the wheels caught in a rut and Johann lost control of the steering. They were carrying little speed by now, which was just as well as they were thrown off onto the grass. They were both laughing as they rolled together, Ava landing on top of Johann who had momentarily had the wind knocked out of him. The bicycle clattered to the ground a few feet away.

Johann sat up with Ava still in his arms. 'I thought we could stop here and rest a while,' he said with a grin, as though tumbling off the bicycle was all part of the plan.

Ava laughed at him as she straightened her hair. 'If I'd known we were coming out for a picnic, I'd have brought some *Schnaps*.'

'I didn't think you had any *Schnaps*.'

'Papa has a bottle. Volker gave it to him the last time he called.'

'Volker's a good friend. He's been looking after you, hasn't he?'

'Yes. He brings Mama food every now and then, and Papa says he gave him a very fair price for his motorcar. I think they've both grown rather fond of him.'

'He can be very charming.'

'Yes, he can.'

'Is that so,' Johann said, fancying that he saw a glint in Ava's eye as she spoke. He smiled playfully and reached an arm around her. 'I hope he hasn't been too charming with you,' he added as he pulled her to the ground and began to tickle her.

'Stop it!' Ava started screaming with laughter. 'Of course he's not been charming with me.' She screamed again. 'Stop! You know I can't take it!'

Johann let her go. He rolled back onto the grass and Ava lay beside him with her head on his shoulder, each gazing up at the drifting clouds, which Johann thought were one of the few constants that remained unchanged by and oblivious to the war raging beneath them.

'I don't suppose you've given much thought to where you'd like to live when the war is over,' Ava said. 'I'm sure my parents wouldn't mind, but we can't live with them forever.'

Johann didn't care to think that far ahead. 'With you,' he said. 'That's about as far as I got. As long as it's with you, I really don't mind.'

'I've often thought how nice it would be to live in the mountains. I know the winters would be cold but we'd keep each other warm.'

'How would I make a living?'

Ava shrugged. 'I don't know. I hadn't thought very far ahead, either. How do you want to make a living?'

The question stumped Johann. In many ways he felt as if he'd been a soldier since the day he could walk. His father and the Hitler Youth had seen to that. Soldiering was all he knew.

When he didn't answer, Ava rolled on top of him and said, 'Would you like children?' With Johann having been away so much since their wedding the year before, she hadn't raised the question before. 'Please say you would.'

'Yes, of course,' Johann said, smiling. 'And you can teach them all to play the piano.'

'And a dog?'

'I doubt you could teach a dog to play the piano, but you can try.'

Ava slapped him and he laughed. 'Yes,' he said, 'and a dog if you like.'

Lowering her head onto Johann's chest, Ava asked, 'Do you ever think that if you imagine yourself in the future then that future will come true?'

'What an odd question. How do you mean?'

'Well, I've been picturing us living in the mountains after the war, with three children and a dog. I think if I keep imagining you there then you'll come home to me when all this is over and we'll be happy.'

'I thought we were happy.'

'How can I be truly happy when I worry about you so much? After our wedding, when you went back to your soldiering, I cried myself to sleep for weeks. I still do.'

'I'm sorry, Ava,' Johann said. 'I wish it could be different. I wish this war had never begun, but then of course, we might never have met.' He wrapped his arms around her and held her close as his lips found hers. And in that moment the war became so distant to him that he lost all concept of the fact that he had to return to his unit in just two days. When at last their kiss ended and reality caught up with him again, he added, 'I'm going to survive this, Ava. I'll survive it for you, you'll see.'

'I believe you will, Johann.'

He felt Ava's warm breath on his neck as she spoke, and he just held her in his arms. She seemed so fragile to him—so vulnerable. His gaze returned to the clouds, and he wished with all his heart that he could be with her always, to love and protect her, and while he didn't think it would do much good to imagine any kind of future against such cruel uncertainty, as he closed his eyes he pictured that house in the mountains Ava had spoken of, and the many children he hoped they would have once the war was over.

Chapter Twenty-One

Present day.

Sitting up on the bed in his hotel room next to Jean, having exhausted the limited research he felt they were able to conduct into Ava Bauer, Tayte put his thoughts about her aside for now, in favour of more certain odds of finding some new information useful to his search.

'Let's move on to Volker Strobel's marriage to Trudi Scheffler,' he said. 'Without access to Ava Bauer's vital records, we could be chasing our tails all night looking for the right person. At least Strobel's and Scheffler's marriage was notable enough to get a mention online. Supposing for now that Karl had come to believe Strobel was his father, for that to be true Strobel had to have fathered a child. Given that he'd married Scheffler during the war, there's a good chance she'd be the child's mother.'

Jean brought up one of the web pages she'd saved from previous searches. 'There's a bit about Strobel's marriage to Scheffler on this website about the world's most-wanted war criminals,' she said as she scrolled down to the pertinent information.

Tayte edged closer to get a better look. He scoffed as he began to read. 'That's quite an infamous guest list,' he said, noting the names of some of the more prominent Nazi Party members to have been invited to the Strobel family *Schloss* for the wedding.

'I read somewhere that Heinrich Himmler was a friend of Volker Strobel's father,' Jean said. 'There can't have been many German families as well-connected as the Strobels during the war.'

'What's that further down?' Tayte said, pointing to a section about Volker Strobel's parents. 'Suicide,' he added.

Jean scrolled down so they could better see the details.

'Suicide pills taken as Berlin falls,' Tayte read aloud. 'So, given that Volker Strobel vanished after the war, did Trudi Scheffler inherit the Strobel fortunes?'

A moment later, Jean said, 'No. It says here that the entire estate was seized by the authorities. Trudi Scheffler was left with next to nothing.'

'Wasn't Scheffler's family also well-connected? Surely the marriage of the only Strobel son and heir would have been matched in terms of status and wealth.'

'Look here,' Jean said, pointing to a section that wrapped up the information about Volker Strobel's marriage.

'Her family cut her off,' Tayte said.

'She became an embarrassment to them,' Jean read. 'She refused to denounce her love for Volker Strobel, and because she kept his name after the war her family wanted nothing more to do with her.'

Tayte and Jean slowly turned to face each other, and Tayte knew they were both thinking the same thing: that a love so obviously blind back then could be just as strong today. It made Tayte think that there was every chance Trudi Strobel née Scheffler knew where her husband was, and that she had perhaps been instrumental in keeping him hidden all these years. Trudi was high on Tayte's list of people to see, but he and Jean had already tried several times to get an interview before coming to Munich, and every time she had refused to talk to them. He began to think about how they might be able to change her mind when his phone beeped and vibrated in his trouser pocket. He took it out and checked the display.

'What is it?' Jean asked.

Tayte read the message. It was short, but it set his pulse racing. 'There's an address in an area of Munich called Laim. The message says to be there at nine thirty tonight if I want answers.'

'It's late for a meeting. Who's it from? The Kaufmanns?'

'I guess so. Or maybe it's from the insider they told us about at *The Friends of the Waffen-SS War Veterans*. Maybe he's got some information for us.'

'Is there a caller ID?'

'No, but perhaps that's understandable if it's from Kaufmann's insider.'

'I saw Laim on the map,' Jean said. 'It's on the other side of Munich. I can't say I like it, but we'd better hurry if we're going. We don't have long to get there.'

Tayte checked his watch. 'Not long at all,' he said. 'And there you are all ready for bed. If Laim's on the other side of Munich, maybe I should go by myself while you keep digging into Scheffler. We can share information when I get back—if you're still up.'

'Oh, I'll be up,' Jean said. 'I'll be too worried about you to sleep. You will be careful, won't you?'

'Of course,' Tayte said. He scribbled the address he'd been sent onto the hotel-room notepad and tore off the sheet. 'Here's where I'm going,' he added, handing it to her.

Just in case I don't make it back.

He knew Jean was right to be wary. He was putting a brave face on things so as not to add to her concerns, but the real reason he wanted to go alone was that he didn't know what he was heading into and he didn't want to put Jean at risk, too. A big part of him wanted to stay right there with her and continue the research, but he'd be the first to admit that he was too inquisitive for his own good at times. He knew he had to go along with this, if only to find out who had sent him the message and why.

'You'll have to get a taxi,' Jean said as Tayte swung his legs off the bed. 'That nightcap in the bar will have put you over the driving limit.'

'I feel fine,' Tayte said, 'but sure, I'll phone down to reception and have them call one for me while I get my things together.'

With that, Tayte made the call, hoping that his text message really was from the Kaufmanns or their insider at the FWK. He recalled pushing his business card through the letterbox when he and Jean had visited the FWK the day before, so they also had his number. The last person he wanted to see when he arrived in Laim was Max Fleischer.

Chapter Twenty-Two

The taxi that had picked Tayte up from the Hilton Munich City hotel twenty-five minutes earlier came to a sudden halt. Looking out of his window Tayte couldn't see how the driver had brought him to the address he'd given him. There were no buildings to be seen. Just trees and bushes, and a few street lamps lighting a railed walkway that disappeared into the distance over the bridge they had stopped before. Ten feet or so below the road ahead, he could see railway tracks, shining icy blue in the moonlight.

'Why have we stopped?' Tayte asked.

The driver, Tayte had quickly learned, didn't speak much English. Although Tayte had to concede that it was far better than his German.

'*Die Strasse ist gesperrt,*' the driver said.

Tayte didn't know what that meant. He thought it was something about the road. A second later the driver confirmed it.

'Road closed,' the driver said, slowly, as he pointed ahead through the windscreen.

In the low light Tayte couldn't fully make out what the driver wanted him to see. He opened his door, leaned out and saw the bridge that arched over the railway tracks more fully. There was a barrier with a temporary road sign in front of it. It appeared that the bridge had been closed for repairs. Tayte checked his watch. He had less than ten minutes to reach the address he'd been given and he hoped whoever had sent him the text message asking to meet him was prepared to wait. He took out his phone and brought up the 'maps' app. He punched in the address and the GPS soon found him. It showed that he wasn't far away. He saw the bridge and the road layout, which turned to the left after the bridge, running alongside the railway tracks for a short distance. The address he'd been sent was no more than a few hundred metres away.

Tayte got back into the taxi. 'Can you wait here for me?' he said, pointing his finger at the ground.

The confused look on the taxi driver's face was far from promising.

'You,' Tayte said, now pointing at the driver as he tried to think how to say 'wait' in German. 'Stay,' he added when nothing came to him.

All he got back from the driver were several German words that this time he did recognise. The driver wanted his fare. Tayte sighed and shook his head as he handed the money over, thinking that he could call another cab to come and get him when the time came to go back. He grabbed his briefcase and got out of the car. Then he made for the walkway that led over the bridge, which was thankfully still open to pedestrians.

For a moment he thought the driver must have understood him after all because the taxi was still there as Tayte began to cross the bridge. But then he heard the car's engine rev up and he turned back to see the taxi speed away to collect his next fare, leaving Tayte alone on the bridge, wondering what the hell he was doing there.

'Why couldn't they have picked a busier place, or waited until morning?' he said to himself, knowing that if he wasn't so desperate for answers he wouldn't have come out at such a late hour, especially if he'd known how isolated the area was.

He took a deep breath and continued over the bridge until he reached the last of the street lamps. There were no other lights in the area as far as he could see. As he followed the road around to his left—as the map on his phone dictated—it became so dark that he had to use his phone as a torch to light his way between the trees, which now seemed to have thickened around him. He kept going and it grew so quiet that, being the great lover of Broadway shows that he was, he felt the urge to whistle a show tune to keep himself company. But he thought better of it. If he had been lured there for some nefarious reason, he didn't want to draw attention to himself until he had to.

When at last the trees cleared, Tayte walked beside the rail tracks for a short while, and he enjoyed the openness, thinking that he'd at least be able to see anyone or anything that came at him out of the darkness. Nothing did, and after a while he began to relax. There were buildings ahead. A few had lights at their windows and that calmed him further. He checked the map again and turned to his right at a small junction in the road he'd been following. The area appeared to be some kind of industrial estate, which accounted for how quiet it was, given the hour. He saw a number on one of the buildings, which was essentially a long brick wall with an aluminium door and a few small windows higher up. At the end of the brick wall he came to a wire fence with a few spotlights at intervals along it, shining into a yard where large wooden cable drums sat here and there like rolls of hay in a farmer's field. There was an office-like building partway along the fence and when Tayte reached it, he saw that it was the address he was looking for.

'Why here?' he said under his breath, supposing that the place might hold no significance beyond the fact that it was in a quiet location, where conversations wouldn't be overheard.

He imagined that if he had been called there by Kaufmann's undercover insider at the FWK, then this was just the type of place he'd pick to meet someone he didn't know. What did this man have to tell him? Something about Strobel coming to Munich? Tayte didn't know, but he figured he was about to find out. The office was in darkness, which did nothing to settle his nerves. He tried to peer in through the windows, but he couldn't see anything through the shutters, which were only half open. He stepped up to the door, thinking that the sender of his text message couldn't have arrived yet—and there he was, just a few minutes after the allotted time and nothing bad had happened. It made him feel easier again, but then he saw something that changed all that in a heartbeat. The door to the building was ajar.

Tayte's heart rate instantly picked up a few beats. He took a deep breath and looked back along the street and out across the road to the other buildings. Apart from the security lighting here and there, they were also in darkness. He stepped closer to the door and gave it a gentle poke with the tip of his finger. It opened further and he stepped back.

Why is the damn door open?

Given that the place was so dark and that there didn't appear to be anyone else around, Tayte could think of no good reason. He could feel his heart kicking in his chest now and all his instincts told him to get out of there—to run back across that bridge and call another taxi once he felt safe again. He turned to go, but as he did so a telephone began to ring inside the office and every nerve in his body seemed to ring with it. He turned back to the sound, which seemed so loud in the otherwise still night. His first thought was that the caller could be the same person who had sent him the text message, perhaps to let him know why he was late, or maybe they had further instructions for him.

So why not call my cell phone or send me another text message?

Tayte quickly checked. There were no calls and no messages.

And who in their right mind would leave the door open just so I can go in and answer the phone?

Inside the office, the phone kept ringing and Tayte gravitated towards it.

What am I doing?

He stepped up to the door. Having come this far, he had to find out what was going on.

'Hello?' he called through the gap.

He nudged the door further open and peered in, but with just the moonlight and the light from the yard coming in through the shutters at the windows he could see very little.

'Is anybody there?' Tayte said as he stepped inside.

He couldn't see how anyone could be or they would have answered that phone by now. He supposed it was loud like that so it could be heard from across the yard when the office was empty. Whatever the reason, Tayte had had enough of the sound. He just wanted to make it stop. He turned to the desk beside him, and he could just make out the shape of the phone on it. He stepped closer, leaving the door wide open behind him for comfort. Tentatively, he picked up the handset and put it to his ear, saying nothing at first, waiting for the caller to speak. No one did. He began to say hello, but as he did so he heard a click and knew the caller had hung up.

Tayte realised something was wrong as soon as he went to put the handset down again. It felt slippery in his hand. Then he was distracted by headlights at the window, which lit up the room, and in that moment he saw blood on the handset and a body lying on the floor at the end of the desk.

There was a screeching of tyres outside and car doors slammed. Tayte was frozen to the spot in disbelief, looking down at the dark silhouette of a man on the floor as someone burst into the room, pointing a handgun at him. The man was shouting in German and Tayte didn't understand most of it, but he did know what *'Polizei!'* meant, and he recognised the police uniforms on the officers who rushed in after the first man and forced him over the desk before they cuffed his hands behind his back.

Chapter Twenty-Three

'I was set up,' Tayte said.

Two plain-clothes detectives were standing on the other side of the table he was handcuffed to. One of them was a tall, lean man in white shirtsleeves, rolled up to his elbows. The other was an equally tall, slim woman with what appeared to be a fresh cut across her forehead that had been patched up with butterfly stitches. She kept her suit jacket on.

The room Tayte had been brought to was all but empty—just the table with a few chairs around it and a water cooler by the door. Three of the walls were painted white. On the wall with the door, Tayte could see a reflection of the room in what was obviously a two-way mirror, from where his interrogation was being monitored. The woman sat down opposite Tayte and stared at him for a few uncomfortable seconds. Then she made the introductions.

'I'm detective Brandt. This is Detective Eckstein.'

Thankfully both detectives spoke excellent English. After Tayte's arrest, he'd imagined the difficulty he was going to have trying to explain himself to someone who didn't understand him.

'Who was the man lying on the floor in that office?' Tayte asked. 'Is he dead?'

'Yes,' Eckstein said, still standing. 'He's very dead, and you've been arrested on suspicion of his murder. As for who he was, perhaps you can tell us. We found no ID on him.'

Tayte shook his head. 'I have no idea who he was. As I've already said, I just went to the address to meet someone. I don't know who, and I didn't get a chance to look at him before your officers wrestled me out of there.'

Brandt slid a photograph across the table. 'You can look at him now.'

Tayte studied the image. It had clearly been taken at the scene of the crime after his arrest. It showed the man he'd briefly seen lying on the floor. The back of his head appeared to have been struck with something, Tayte thought, because that's where the blood on the floor was most concentrated. He realised then that the fatal wound had most likely been inflicted by the telephone handset he'd still been holding when the police came in and handcuffed him—the handset that no doubt had the victim's blood all over it.

'I've never seen this man before,' Tayte said, supposing he might well have been the Kaufmanns' insider. He wondered whether the FWK had found out who he was, or perhaps they had known for some time and had now used this opportunity to get rid of him, and at the same time frame Tayte for his murder. He thought that perhaps this man had been lured there, too, but to his death. 'Look, I already told you,' Tayte added. 'I've been set up for this.' He heaved a frustrated sigh. 'Check my cell phone. You can see the text message that was sent to me. It proves I'm not making this up.'

Brandt leaned closer. 'We have checked, Mr Tayte. I'm afraid all it proves is that someone gave you an address to go to. Perhaps they sent you there to get these answers the text promised you, and maybe you didn't care too much about the methods you used to get them.'

'That's crazy,' Tayte said. He sat back, shaking his head. Then something occurred to him. 'How did you know to turn up at that address? And right at that moment?'

The two detectives exchanged glances.

'We received a telephone call,' Brandt said. 'The caller told us he thought he saw someone breaking into the property.'

'I'll bet that call was anonymous, wasn't it?'

'People don't always want to get involved,' Eckstein said.

'And was the door broken in?'

'No.'

'No, of course it wasn't. Because there was no break-in.'

Brandt slapped her hand down onto the table, regaining command of the conversation. The sound jarred Tayte's already fragile nerves. 'So the victim opened the door for you. Whoever made the call was wrong about the door being forced. It's academic.'

Tayte didn't like where this conversation was going. 'I took a taxi there, for Christ's sake! You can verify that with the Hilton Munich City hotel. I mean, who does that if they're heading out to murder someone?'

'Perhaps you didn't know you were going to murder the man you were going to meet,' Eckstein said. 'Not all murders are premeditated.'

'Is that what happened?' Brandt said. 'You went there to meet this man and things got out of hand? You grabbed the nearest thing you could lay your hands on and beat him to death with it?'

'No!' Tayte said. He was so frustrated now that he was almost shouting. 'I didn't kill him!' he reiterated. 'Look, are you going to charge me? If you're not, can I go?'

'You're not being charged at this time,' Brandt said.

'But the night is young,' Eckstein said with a thin smile.

'You're keeping me in overnight?'

Brandt drew a deep breath and sat back. 'Mr Tayte. A man was murdered tonight and you were found standing over his body with what appears to have been the murder weapon in your hands. Of course we're keeping you in.'

Tayte had to admit that despite everything he'd told them, he appeared to have been caught literally red-handed. 'Well, can I make a phone call? I'm entitled to do that, right?'

'In good time, Mr Tayte,' Brandt said. 'Can you tell us exactly why you're in Munich? You're a long way from home.'

'I'm here looking for answers,' Tayte said. 'I'm trying to find out who my biological parents are.'

'And you think they're German?'

'I think my father is. And I think sooner or later I'll be able to prove it if I just keep digging. That's why I went to that address tonight. I was hoping for information in connection with a wanted war criminal called Volker Strobel. I'm convinced there's a connection either to him or to a friend he had during the war called Johann Langner. I just need more time to make sense of it all.'

'Sounds complicated,' Eckstein said.

'Fortunately, we have plenty of time,' Brandt added. 'Why don't you explain it to us. There's no rush. Start from the beginning and bring us up to date. I'd like to know everywhere you've been and I'd like the names of everyone you've spoken to.'

Tayte drew a deep breath and tried to rub the tiredness from his eyes. Then he told Brandt and Eckstein everything that had happened since he and Jean stepped off the plane the day before. It took close to an hour to go over everything in detail, and to answer the questions the detectives kept firing at him as Brandt wrote everything down. By the time Tayte had finished he felt exhausted.

'The contents of my briefcase will confirm everything I just told you,' he said. 'And you can check your own records to confirm that

I didn't just make up everything about this man who threatened Jean yesterday. I believe he's called Max Fleischer, and I believe he's working with the FWK—*The Friends of the Waffen-SS War Veterans.* He threatened us again earlier today. He flashed a handgun at us.'

'Did you report that, too?' Brandt asked.

Tayte wished now that he and Jean had gone straight to the police to report it. 'No,' he said. 'I didn't want it to spoil our evening any more than it already had. We were going to report it first thing in the morning.'

'I see,' Brandt said.

She stood up and Tayte gave a sigh of relief to think that for now at least the interrogation appeared to be over.

'So what happens next?' Tayte asked as Brandt and Eckstein made for the door.

Brandt turned back. 'You'll be taken to a holding room. Then you'll be allowed your phone call.'

Tayte was beginning to think that detective Brandt had been teasing him about getting his phone call. For close to forty minutes he'd been sitting in another sparsely furnished room at Munich's police headquarters with only a sour faced, uncommunicative uniformed officer standing by the door for company. It felt as though hours had passed by the time the door finally opened again and Detective Eckstein walked in. To Tayte's almost overwhelming joy after everything he'd been through since he'd last spoken to Jean, he was carrying a telephone.

'Five minutes,' Eckstein said, handing the phone to Tayte.

Tayte was smiling as he took it. Not at Eckstein, but at the telephone because he was looking forward to hearing Jean's voice again. As he entered the direct number for their hotel room, he hoped she was still awake. The clock high up on the wall told him it was now just after one o'clock in the morning. The phone only rang twice before it was answered, and it was Jean who spoke first. She sounded overwrought.

'JT!'

'Jean! It's okay. I'm all right.'

'Thank goodness. I've been worried sick.'

'I'm sure you have, and I'm sorry. That text message. It was a setup. I've been arrested.'

'I know.'

'You do?'

'Yes, the police called about twenty minutes ago. They wanted me to confirm what you'd told them. They wouldn't give me any details. Is this serious?'

'It's about as serious as it gets,' Tayte said. 'A man was killed— probably the man I was supposed to meet tonight. I've been arrested for his murder.'

'Christ,' Jean said. 'Do you want me to find you a solicitor—a lawyer? Maybe I should go to the American Consulate.'

'I sincerely hope it doesn't come to that. I've not been charged yet, but as I was told earlier, the night is young. I don't know what the local rule is around how long I can be detained without charges being brought, but they're keeping me in for now. You should try to get some sleep.'

'Will you be able to call me tomorrow? Can I come and see you?'

'I don't know,' Tayte said. 'I guess I'll find out more in the morning.' He paused, and then in a lower voice he said, 'I've got to go. The detective is tapping his watch at me.'

'Wait,' Jean said. 'I found something after you left—something about Trudi Scheffler. I think it's important.'

'I'd love to hear it,' Tayte said, but he knew he didn't have time. Eckstein was now holding his hand out for Tayte to pass him the phone. 'Hopefully you'll be able to tell me all about it tomorrow,' he added. 'I've really gotta go.'

'Okay. So, I'll wait to hear from you?'

At that moment, Eckstein reached out and grabbed the phone. 'Time's up.'

Tayte didn't want the time to be up. He held on to the phone between his cuffed hands just long enough to say, 'Goodbye, Jean. I miss you.'

Then the call was over.

Chapter Twenty-Four

Disturbed by unfamiliar sounds and a deep concern for his future, Jefferson Tayte was woken from a troubled night's sleep in his holding cell at Munich's police headquarters by a key rattling in the lock to his cell door. Having eventually fallen into a deep slumber through sheer exhaustion, he had trouble peeling his eyes open again. When he did he watched the door to his cell open and a uniformed officer he hadn't seen before called in, 'Get dressed. Ten minutes.' As Tayte stirred further from sleep and the reality of his situation caught up with him, he had the feeling that today was going to be a bad day.

Exactly ten minutes later, Tayte was escorted from the holding cell to a room that had an altogether more pleasant feel to it than any he had so far been in since he'd been arrested the night before. He thought it must be a witness statement room. It was bright from the light at the window, the furnishings were soft, not hard, and he saw posters and pamphlets here and there, none of which he could read, but it was clear from the images on them that they were about crime prevention. Detective Eckstein was already in the room as Tayte was brought in. On the table Eckstein was standing beside, Tayte saw his personal effects: his briefcase, wallet, phone, and watch. The sight of these items confused him for a minute.

'You're being released,' Eckstein said, clarifying the situation.

And just like that, Tayte felt the weight of his predicament lift from his shoulders. He drew a deep breath as he took in what Eckstein had just said. Then he smiled at the man, and he almost laughed to himself as he tried to contain his delight. He collected his things from the desk.

'Thank you,' he said, feeling a strong urge to get as far away from the police station as he could before someone changed their mind, although he was curious to know why he was being released. 'Did you find out who killed that man? Do you know who he was?'

'We're hoping that Tobias Kaufmann—the man you told us about last night—will soon be able to help us identify the body. We're no closer to finding out who killed him, but we've learned enough to know it wasn't you. Everything you told us checked out. The taxi driver confirmed what time he dropped you off, and we've confirmed that someone called the telephone you were found holding when our officers turned up and arrested you. More importantly, the telephone handset wasn't the murder weapon.'

'It wasn't?'

'No, the wounds on the victim were caused by something with a sharper edge—a brick or a rock perhaps. And the telephone handset was too light and flimsy to have caused such damage. It would have broken long before the man's skull. Then there's the time of death. Rigor mortis had already begun, which tells us straight away that the victim had been dead for at least two hours. Your friend, Ms Summer, was able to verify that you were with her earlier in the evening. Whoever set you up, Mr Tayte, either knew very little about the changes the human body goes through after death, or they were just sending you a message—another threat perhaps. Maybe you should take this one more seriously. I don't want to have to investigate your murder, too.'

It was a sobering thought, and one Tayte planned to give some very serious consideration. 'The name I gave you last night,' he said. 'Max Fleischer.'

'Yes, we know who Max Fleischer is,' Eckstein said. 'He'll be brought in for questioning as soon as we can locate him. Do you plan on staying in Munich long? We may have further questions for you.'

Tayte had no idea how long he was going to stay in Munich in light of what had happened. 'I don't know,' he said. 'Do I have to stay?'

'No, and in all honesty I'd advise you to go home on the next available flight. Your investigation is obviously upsetting the kind of people you don't want to upset. You should leave that to us. Whatever you decide to do, I have your contact details.'

'Well, just let me know if there's anything you need from me.'

'Thank you. I will.'

'So that's it?' Tayte said. 'I can go now?'

'More or less. I just need you to sign some release papers and you can be on your way.'

That sounded good to Tayte. He couldn't wait to see Jean again, to tell her he was a free man, and to learn what she'd discovered about Trudi Scheffler that she thought was important. As Tayte picked up his briefcase and followed Eckstein out of the room, he began to wonder what that something was, and how it might influence the decision he had to make about whether or not to remain in Munich.

Outside Munich's police headquarters, Tayte ended his call to Jean with a wide smile on his face. He'd said he was going to get a taxi back to the hotel, but Jean had insisted on picking him up, so he didn't argue. He checked his watch. It was just after nine in the morning, and although the hotel they were staying at wasn't far away, he figured it would take her at least twenty minutes to reach him, probably longer if the traffic was bad. He sucked in the cool morning air and gazed up into another clear blue sky, thinking he would call the Kaufmanns as soon as he'd seen Jean. He wanted to confirm whether the man who had been murdered the night before was their insider at the FWK as he'd supposed, and he wanted to know whether they had managed to get him access to the records he wanted to see.

He took a stroll along the pavement outside the building he'd just been released from on Ettstrasse, and he began to wonder again what Jean had discovered about Trudi Strobel née Scheffler, and how it might help to find the answers they were looking for. That's if they were going to carry on at all. He'd never been one to walk away before, but then he'd never felt he had anything much to lose before. Now he did, and the only way he could see Jean backing down was if he backed down first.

He reached the end of the street and began to amble back again, not wanting to wander too far from where Jean was going to pick him up. Ten minutes passed slowly by, and then another ten. He cursed the traffic for keeping Jean from him and decided he'd better stay put now in case he missed her. He leaned back against the wall in the shade of the building and considered whether he really could just pack his bags and go home. He felt closer now to the answers he was looking for than he'd ever felt before, and if Volker Strobel and Johann Langner held those answers somewhere between them, then given their ages he knew he might never have a chance like this again. He drew a deep, contemplative breath, and by the time he let it go again he had the answer. He would do it for Jean, without question. He was going to take Detective Eckstein's advice and book the next available flight back to London.

Tayte closed his eyes and began to drift with his thoughts, still feeling tired after what had amounted to little more than a few hours of quality sleep. When he opened his eyes again, he checked his watch and saw that forty-five minutes had passed since he'd spoken to Jean. She'd said she was ready to come and get him, and that she was leaving straight away, so he thought there had to be a problem with the traffic. But after another fifteen minutes passed, he began to worry. He called her number again. After ringing several times the call went to voice mail. He tried the hotel room, just in case there had been a hold-up, although he thought she would have called him by now if there was. There was no reply.

She must be stuck in traffic, he told himself. *That's gotta be it.*

He figured that was why she hadn't picked up his call—she was driving and needed to concentrate, especially as she was driving on the opposite side of the road to the side she was used to. But as the time continued to tick slowly by with no sign of her and no phone call, he instinctively knew something was wrong. He called her again and this time he left a message.

'Hi, Jean. It's JT. I was getting worried about you, so I'm taking a cab back to the hotel. I'm sorry if you're just stuck in traffic somewhere, but I didn't know what else to do.'

He ended the message and immediately went looking for a taxi, which he found just around the corner on Maxburgstrasse.

'Hilton Munich City hotel,' he said to the driver, and on the way there, knowing the route was likely to be similar to the one Jean had taken, he kept looking out for their hire car and signs of heavier than usual traffic. He saw neither, and he began to feel very concerned as the taxi pulled up outside the hotel, little more than fifteen minutes after it had set out.

Tayte handed the driver a large currency note, and didn't wait for the change. He sprinted into the hotel lobby where he took the stairs and ran up to the first-floor room he and Jean were sharing. 'Jean!' he called as he opened the door.

She wasn't there. He hadn't really expected her to be, but he had to be sure. He saw that her jacket was gone, the car keys, too, so he left his briefcase by the bed and ran down to the lobby again. He was panting as he asked the concierge whether there were any messages for him, but there were none.

Where is she?

He could feel the anxiety of not knowing—of believing without a doubt that something must have happened to her—begin to knot in his stomach. He ran out into the car park and looked for their hire car. The space where he'd parked it the day before was tellingly empty, which told him that Jean had left to pick him up as planned. But then what? Tayte sank his head into his hands, wishing now that he'd made the decision to fly home after Max Fleischer had flashed his gun at them outside the coffee shop. The familiar ringtone of his phone startled him then, and he almost dropped it in his haste to answer the call.

'Jean!'

'Is that JT?'

It wasn't Jean. Tayte didn't recognise the caller's voice, but it belonged to a man with a German accent, and it immediately put his hackles up.

'Who is this?'

'I'm calling from the general hospital in Schwabing,' the man said. 'I saw that you'd left a message for Jean Summer earlier this morning and I didn't know who else to call. Are you a family member, or a friend perhaps? Are you in Munich?'

Tayte felt the blood drain from his cheeks. 'I'm her partner,' he said. 'We're staying in Munich together. What's happened? Is she okay?'

'Jean Summer has been involved in a car accident. She was admitted to the hospital a short while ago.'

Chapter Twenty-Five

Tayte wasted no time getting a taxi to the accident and emergency unit at Munich's general hospital in Schwabing, which was a short drive north of the city centre via one of the city's major multi-lane parkways. The hospital staff member who had called Tayte from Jean's phone hadn't been able to give him any information about Jean's condition, which made him all the more anxious as he sat in the back of the taxi, imagining the worse. He cursed himself several times over for not making his own way back to the hotel after he'd been released from police custody, telling himself that if he had then none of this would have happened and Jean would be okay. If only she hadn't been so insistent. If only he hadn't got himself arrested in the first place. If only this and if only that, but how could he have known? If Jean had been there, he knew she would have been the first to tell him it wasn't his fault, but that gave him little consolation.

He was running again as soon as he got out of the taxi, only slowing to a fast walk as he entered the hospital and approached the information desk.

'My friend, Jean Summer, was in a car accident earlier this morning,' he said to the young woman behind the desk. 'I just received a call to say she'd been admitted here. Can you please tell me how she is? Can I see her?'

A few minutes later, Tayte was led into a ward on the accident and emergency wing. Maybe it was the shock of seeing Jean lying in a hospital bed with a bandaged head and a brace around her neck, or perhaps it was just the relief of knowing she wasn't dead or in intensive care, but when he saw her he wanted to cry.

'Jean, I'm so sorry.' He held her hand and squeezed it.

'It wasn't your fault.'

'I knew you'd say that.'

Jean tried to shake her head, but her neck brace restricted her. 'No, it really wasn't. I was turning off the main road towards the city centre. At the last minute another car cut inside me and I had nowhere to go. What's going to happen with the hire company? The car must be a write-off.'

'Don't worry about any of that. I'll deal with it. Just tell me what happened.'

'Well, this other car forced me into the barrier and before I knew what was happening I'd hit it and the car flipped over. I was so scared. Thank God no one else was hurt.'

'So someone did this to you on purpose? Did you get a look at the driver?'

'No, it all happened so fast. I've already told the police what I could, which wasn't much. I didn't even see what type of car it was, let alone get the registration.'

Tayte's blood was boiling. Within a period of twelve hours he'd been set up for murder and someone had potentially tried to kill Jean.

'You're hurting my hand,' Jean said, and Tayte let go.

'Sorry, it just makes me so mad. These people are clearly prepared to do whatever it takes to stop us looking into Strobel.'

'They must think we're a very real threat then,' Jean said. 'Strobel has successfully managed to evade the authorities for decades, so why does he think we have any chance of finding him?'

'It must have something to do with our research—the connection to my parents perhaps. Supposing for now that Karl is my father—'

'Which he probably is,' Jean cut in.

'Yes, which he probably is. Well, I've been thinking that my parents might also have become a threat to Strobel, maybe as a result of looking for Karl's father, my grandfather, who we're now looking for. If that does turn out to be Volker Strobel, then I can see why they're prepared to go to any length to stop us.' Tayte paused, thinking about the decision he'd made to give it all up and go home. He looked into Jean's eyes, which were bloodshot from the head injury she'd received and the concussion he'd been told had followed as a result. 'I shouldn't have let you get involved in this, Jean. I knew it could be dangerous.'

Jean smiled at him, although Tayte could see that it hurt her to do so. 'What, and miss the opportunity of spending a romantic week in Munich with you?'

Tayte laughed. 'Did they say how long you have to stay in here? I've decided we should quit this, while we still can. I was going to suggest we catch the next available flight back to London, but I guess that can't happen just yet.'

Jean frowned. 'You mean we're running off home with our tails between our legs?'

'Yeah, something like that.'

'Do I get a say in the matter?'

Tayte ran his eyes over the hospital bed and back to the bandaging wrapped around Jean's head, considering that her 'accident' could have been a whole lot worse. He shook his head. 'No, I think this has to be my call, and I've already made it.'

'Well, we can't go today,' Jean said. 'The doctor told me he wanted to keep me in overnight because of the concussion. I'm a little bruised, but nothing's broken.' She flicked at her neck brace.

'This thing's just a whiplash precaution. I'm sure it can come off soon. The car's airbags really saved me from anything worse.'

'So we'll leave as soon as you're able to travel.'

'What will you do in the meantime? You can't sit here and hold my hand all day.'

'Are you sure? Is there a rule against it? Because right now I don't want to leave your side.'

'That's very touching, JT, but I'm sure I'll be fine in here. It's you I'm worried about. Knowing I'm safely tucked up in bed, I know you're going to keep digging all the while you're in Munich. Where are you going next?'

Tayte thought Jean clearly knew that part of him all too well. 'That depends.'

'On what?'

'On what you found out about Trudi Strobel née Scheffler last night.'

'You see, you really can't help yourself. Now I'm not sure I should tell you.'

'I'll be super careful,' Tayte said. 'And it's not like we can send a message to whoever's out to get us that we give up. All the while we're in Munich they're going to assume we're still digging—or at least that I am. And you're right, what else am I going to do?'

'I expect they'll know you're still digging for sure if you follow up on what I found last night.'

Tayte grinned. 'Stop teasing. Now I really want to know.'

'Okay then,' Jean said. 'After you left last night, I kept looking for information on Strobel and Scheffler. I knew I had a few hours to kill and I'd already planned on staying up until you returned. Well, we'd pretty much exhausted everything we could hope to find online about Volker Strobel, so I focused on Trudi. I found a reference to another marriage, but this time Trudi Strobel was only a guest. It was a high-society affair in 1993, well documented online, having made several newspaper social columns and medical journals.'

'Medical journals?' Tayte said, furrowing his brow.

'Yes, the groom was a prominent cardiologist.'

Tayte looked even more confused. 'I can't imagine where this is going.'

'Well, be quiet and I'll tell you. It was the bride I was interested in, and my jaw literally dropped when I saw who it was.' She paused. 'Could you pass me that glass of water,' she added, pointing to a tray that was just out of reach beside her bed.

Knowing full well that she was teasing him again, Tayte handed her the glass of water with a sigh. He took it back from her once she'd finished with it and impatiently asked, 'Who? Who was the bride?'

'The bride's name was Ingrid. In the absence of her father, her mother, Trudi Strobel, gave her away. The groom's name was Dr Keller.'

'Ingrid Keller?' Tayte said.

Jean nodded, smiling.

'Johann Langner's nurse, Ingrid Keller?'

'The very same.'

'Wow,' Tayte said, already considering the implications. 'So, Johann Langner's personal nurse is his former best friend's wife's daughter.'

'It can't be by chance, can it?'

'No, it can't,' Tayte agreed. 'So there was no father-of-the-bride present at the wedding?'

'No. And I thought at first that made sense. If her father was Volker Strobel, he'd obviously want to keep his name off Ingrid's birth certificate. Then again, if Strobel was her father, given that Langner's and Strobel's friendship ended badly during the war, why would Langner want to have anything to do with Ingrid, let alone employ her as his personal nurse? On top of that, Langner did seem very fond of her when we went to see him, didn't he?'

'Yes, he did,' Tayte said. 'So you think the old man could be Ingrid's father? That Langner had an affair with Trudi?'

'It's a possibility. It would explain this otherwise highly unlikely arrangement between nurse and patient.'

'And having a leading cardiologist in the family could certainly have its benefits for someone in Johann Langner's condition, too.'

They fell quiet for a while as Tayte thought it through. It was a great find, but what to make of it? By itself he couldn't see how it brought him any closer to finding the answers he was ultimately looking for, but it occurred to him that it might open a door that had previously been closed to him.

'I'm going to try to see Trudi Strobel again,' he said. 'I think when she hears this, she'll agree to talk. She clearly doesn't want this connection to be made public knowledge. I'll tell her I know that Johann Langner is Ingrid Keller's father.'

'But we don't know that for sure.'

'I know, but Trudi Strobel doesn't know that. I'll tell her I'll keep a lid on it if she'll agree to an interview. If there's any truth to it, I can't see how she can refuse. If she does refuse, then at least we'll know we're probably barking up the wrong tree.'

Chapter Twenty-Six

Tayte stayed with Jean at the hospital for as long as he was able to. When she was taken to radiology for a CAT scan he kissed her goodbye, called the car hire company to explain everything, and then took a taxi to the city centre. Along the way he called Tobias Kaufmann.

'Mr Kaufmann, it's Jefferson Tayte,' he said as soon as Kaufmann answered. 'I'm coming to see you. I have a few things to do first, but I shouldn't be long.'

'Have you found something?' Kaufmann asked, a note of excitement in his voice.

'Possibly. I have some information about Trudi Strobel I'm sure you'll be interested in.'

'Trudi Strobel? I can't wait to hear it. And I have some news for you, too. I'll tell you when you get here.'

'Great. I'll see you soon.'

When Tayte ended the call, he sat forward in his seat, and to the taxi driver he said, 'Can you take me to a florist?'

To anyone following him, Tayte figured it would appear as though he were simply buying flowers for Jean. He was, but he had another motive. The taxi dropped him close to Marienplatz and once inside the florist he purposefully took his time over the bouquet selection, watching the street through the window for signs of anyone lingering outside, waiting for him to leave again. He wasn't taking any chances now. He had little doubt that someone had to be following him. He thought the FWK would want to make sure he'd got the message at last and was going home, and he wanted to give them every indication that he had. Once he felt he'd done enough to convince them, he needed to disappear before going to see Tobias Kaufmann, which he didn't think would be a problem amidst Munich's busy city streets.

It was late morning by the time Tayte left the florists, his flowers in one hand and his briefcase in the other. He headed across Marienplatz towards the highly ornate Old Town Hall—a fourteenth-century neo-Gothic hall and clock tower, where on 9 November 1938 Joseph Goebbels had delivered his speech as a prelude to *Kristallnacht*. Tayte paused in the middle of the plaza, in plain view of anyone following him, and took out his phone. Now that he had his flowers for Jean, he was calling the airport to see if he could get a flight home. At least, that's how he hoped it would appear to anyone nearby.

Instead, he pulled up the number for the German Heart Centre. He wanted to see how Johann Langner was, and to ask if he could see him again to continue his wartime story. Before he pressed the call button, he put on a loud, touristy voice, and said, 'Yes, hello. Munich Airport reservations?' A moment later he pretended the connection was bad, facilitating the need for him to shout his next line. 'Could you please check availability on flights to London, England.'

Tayte pressed the call button then and continued walking again. When his call was answered he lowered his voice and said, 'Hi, I'd like to enquire about a patient called Johann Langner. I wonder if you can tell me how he is. Or better still, is it possible to speak to him?'

'Your name, please.'

'Jefferson Tayte.'

'One moment, please.'

Tayte waited, walking slowly, his eyes scanning the plaza to see if anyone was looking at him. He saw that several people were, which he supposed was because of the shouting. They probably thought he was a madman.

The receptionist came back on the line. 'I can put you through to Herr Langner's personal nurse,' she said. 'Please hold.'

The call only took a few seconds to transfer. When it did, Tayte heard the almost offensively direct and harsh tones of Ingrid Keller, whom he now saw in a somewhat different light following Jean's discovery. There was no introduction.

'Herr Langner is very ill, Mr Tayte. You must leave him to rest.'

'I just wanted to ask whether he was feeling any better.'

'So you can come back and make him worse again?'

Tayte didn't quite know what to say to that. Keller made him feel instantly uncomfortable. 'I just wanted to . . .'

Tayte trailed off, aware that the volume of his voice had risen again, and that he wasn't going to get anywhere talking to Ingrid Keller. He could see why Langner's son, Rudi, let her get on with things, and why they communicated with one another about the state of his father's health via text messages.

'I'm sorry to have troubled you,' he added, and then he ended the call thinking that if Johann Langner was Keller's father, then her protectiveness, not only as his nurse, but also as his daughter, was perhaps understandable. Although he didn't see why she had to be so rude about it.

He put his phone away and picked up his step as he went back to his subterfuge. Now he was looking for a gift shop or a travel accessory shop, further adding to the idea that he would soon be leaving Munich and perhaps wanted to buy a few souvenirs to take home, or maybe an inflatable neck cushion for the flight. He found a gift shop partway towards the Old Town Hall and he paused outside to peruse the postcards before going in, making sure that whoever was following him saw that he was simply killing time while he waited for Jean to get the all clear from the hospital. It was a small shop, like a pop-up shop that had been filled with low-quality touristy items. Once inside, he continued to browse the bags and T-shirts, the pens, key-rings, and confectionary, much of which bore the words 'I love *München.*'

As before, Tayte kept an eye on the door and the street outside, looking for anyone who seemed familiar to him, or who appeared to be paying him too much attention. He recognised no one and no one seemed to be watching him. *These people are good, though,* he reminded himself, knowing that he and Jean had been followed since leaving the offices of the FWK earlier that week. Tayte supposed he wouldn't know that these people were there unless they wanted him to, so after a few minutes he left the gift shop, heading back across the plaza for what appeared to be a market of some kind. It was busier there, which suited his purpose. When he reached the first stall he saw that it was a daily food market called the *Viktualienmarkt,* which occupied a large square in the centre of the city.

Tayte quickened his pace as he ventured further between the stalls, often having to slow down again as the shoppers and browsers thickened around him. He took his jacket off to change his appearance, in case his followers had become accustomed to looking out for his bright tan suit jacket. A white shirt was no less conspicuous perhaps, but it was a different look and he thought it might help. He turned around one stall and another, not stopping until he felt lost himself. Then he walked out of the market with his knees bent and his shoulders stooped to keep his head down, taking the nearest side-street he came to. When he felt sure he was in the clear, he began to run, fuelled by a sudden rush of adrenaline as a cat-and-mouse sense of danger kicked in.

Tayte found a taxi soon after leaving the pedestrianised Marienplatz area. He checked the street map on his phone and asked the taxi driver to drop him off a few blocks from his intended destination, just in case he'd underestimated his opponents' resourcefulness. If the address of *Kaufmann und Kaufmann* was known to the FWK, which Tayte fully imagined it was, then Tobias Kaufmann's door was the last door he wanted them to see him knocking on.

He thought Tobias looked tired and more than a little distressed as he greeted him. His eyes were red and his beard was knotted, as though he'd been pulling at it all night and half the morning. If Tayte was right about who the man that had just been murdered was, Tobias Kaufmann had every reason to be distressed.

'Come in, quickly!' Kaufmann said. He was looking past Tayte and his bunch of flowers as he spoke, looking out into the street, which had been quiet when Tayte arrived. 'I hope you weren't followed.'

'I don't believe so,' Tayte said.

'Good, good. Well come on up.'

Tayte followed Kaufmann up to his offices and through to the same back-office area he and Jean had visited before—to the Strobel room, as Kaufmann had called it. There was no sign of Herr Kaufmann senior on this occasion.

'The police contacted me this morning,' Kaufmann said as they sat down.

'I know,' Tayte said. Then he told him about the text message he'd received the night before and how it had been the catalyst to a series of events that saw him being arrested for murder. 'It was a setup, of course,' he added. 'I believed the message I received must have been either from you or your insider at the FWK, which was clearly what I was supposed to believe. When I saw the dead body lying at my feet, I realised what was going on. I told the police I thought you might know something about who their murder victim was.'

Kaufmann drew a sharp breath. 'He was our insider, yes. He was also the son of a good friend of mine.'

'I'm very sorry to hear that. I had no idea.'

'No, of course you didn't. I suspect now that this whole story about Strobel coming to Munich was just a ruse to draw him out. I fear that his is yet another life to chalk up to the Strobel death toll. I sincerely hope it will be the last, but of course we're no closer to finding him.'

'My partner, Jean Summer, found an interesting piece of information last night,' Tayte said. 'Right now I don't know if it means anything, but—'

'I'd be glad to hear it,' Kaufmann cut in, clearly eager to listen to any new leads.

'Well, I can't prove anything just yet,' Tayte said, 'but I believe that Trudi Strobel's daughter is Johann Langner's personal nurse, Ingrid Keller.'

'I see,' Kaufmann said, raising his eyebrows. 'We know a little about Trudi Strobel, of course. Although she's never given any statements about her husband. She consistently refuses to talk to anyone about him. One thing that's always struck me as odd is where her apparent wealth comes from. She's set up very nicely, and yet she was left close to penniless after the war.'

'Yes, I read about that,' Tayte said. 'The Strobel fortunes were seized and her family disowned her, cutting her off from any inheritance. Although there's been plenty of time to make a little money between then and now.'

'Well, that's just the thing. Trudi never remarried, and we know from various records that she's neither worked nor owned a business. There's a lot of speculation suggesting she gets her money from Volker Strobel, for her silence perhaps, but nothing has ever been proven.'

Another possibility occurred to Tayte. 'Or the money could be coming from Johann Langner,' he said. 'We know Langner is a very wealthy man, and I believe there's a strong possibility that Langner is Ingrid Keller's father. What if he's been paying her child maintenance, off the record?'

'Hmm . . .' Kaufmann mused. 'An affair between Trudi Strobel and her husband's former best friend?'

'It fits well enough,' Tayte said, 'and I can't see how else Keller came to be Langner's personal nurse. I'd put Ingrid Keller in her mid-fifties, so she was born around 1960. Langner served ten years in prison for war crimes from 1945 to 1955, so maybe he went to see Trudi soon after he was released. Whether it's true or not, I aim to bluff it and tell Trudi Strobel I know Langner's the father. I'm hoping neither she nor Langner will want that made public, at least enough for Trudi to agree to see me.'

'I'd love the opportunity to talk to Trudi Strobel,' Kaufmann said, 'and I wish you luck, but as I've said, she's never given any interviews about Volker Strobel before.'

'I figure it's got to be worth a shot,' Tayte said. 'And I'll be coming at it from a new angle—Johann Langner.'

'Anything's worth trying at this stage,' Kaufmann agreed. He began to pull thoughtfully at his beard. 'If this discovery does get you an interview, be sure to come back and tell me all about it, won't you?'

'Yes, of course,' Tayte said. 'That's if I can get in touch with her before I head back to London with Jean.'

'You're going home? When?'

'As soon as Jean can leave the hospital and it's safe for her to fly. She was in a car accident this morning. She says it was deliberate.'

'Is she okay?'

Tayte nodded. 'She seems to be, but it's made me think again about whether we should stick around any longer than we need to. Munich's becoming too dangerous a place for us.'

Tobias Kaufmann shook his head with an air of despair. 'I've been attacked myself. We even had a fire here about fifteen years ago. I'm sure that was deliberate, too. Thankfully, it was put out before too much damage was done. I think by now the people protecting Strobel know us Kaufmanns won't be scared off, so they leave us alone. Either that or after all these years of trying they know we'll never find him. These people will scare anyone off the Strobel scent if they believe them to be a threat. Which is what excited me about you when you first came to see us.'

Tayte thought Kaufmann had made a good point, as Jean had earlier. He and Jean had to be a threat to Strobel, or why go to such lengths to scare them off? Tayte didn't like to think of anyone scaring him off an assignment, especially his own assignment, but he knew it was selfish just to consider himself in this. Jean had been right, though. All the while he had to remain in Munich, he was determined to dig as deeply as he could for the answers he hoped to find, and if that meant bringing Volker Strobel to justice, whether the man was his grandfather or not, then that was fine by him.

'When I called to say I was coming to see you,' Tayte said, 'you told me you had some good news for me?'

'Ah, yes. Possibly some very good news. We've had clearance for you to go and see a woman called Jan Statham at the *Standesamt München*—the civil registration office where the births, marriages, and deaths for Munich are recorded. She's been briefed to let you have access to the records you need to see, although you're not permitted to remove or photocopy anything.'

'Can I take notes?'

'Yes, of course. I'm told Jan Statham is British, so you won't have any language issues, and she'll be able to help you with document translations. She's lived and worked in Germany for a good many years.'

'That's great,' Tayte said, smiling broadly. 'When can she see me?'

'Whenever you're ready. She has your name. I'll give you her telephone number at the *Standesamt* so you can call ahead.'

———

The Munich *Standesamt* was on Ruppertstrasse in the Ludwigsvorstadt-Isarvorstadt district, a short distance southwest of Munich's city centre. It was just after midday and Tayte was in a taxi on his way there, having called the number Tobias Kaufmann had given him for Jan Statham, who had been able to see him right away. Before Tayte left the offices of *Kaufmann und Kaufmann,* Tobias had also given him the contact details he had for Trudi Strobel. Tayte already knew where she lived, having written to her twice before leaving England. He'd planned to go and knock on Trudi's door that very afternoon while he waited for Jean to get the all clear from the hospital, but as Tobias had been able to furnish him with a telephone number, he now punched it into his phone.

Tayte's palms began to feel clammy as he waited for his call to be answered. From what Tobias had told him about Trudi's financial situation, he didn't expect her to answer the phone herself, and he wasn't wrong. The voice that greeted him belonged to a female, but she sounded far too young to be Trudi. He thought she must be a housekeeper or perhaps a carer of some kind.

'*Familie Strobel, Guten Tag.*'

'*Sprechen Sie Englisch?*' Tayte said, hopefully.

'A little. Who is this, please?'

'My name is Jefferson Tayte. I'd like to speak to Trudi Strobel.'

'*Frau Strobel nimmt keine Anrufe entgegen.*'

'Excuse me?'

'No calls.'

Tayte wasn't going to be put off this time. 'Please tell her I know about Ingrid Keller. Do you understand?'

'Yes. Wait please.'

Tayte waited, absently watching the city streets pass by outside the taxi window. He didn't have to wait long.

'This is Trudi Strobel. What do you want?'

Tayte wasn't sure why he felt so nervous, but he did. 'My name's Jefferson Tayte,' he said, thankful that Trudi appeared to speak very good English. 'I wrote to you about—'

'Yes, I know who you are,' Trudi cut in. 'I told you I didn't want to speak to you.'

But you are speaking to me, Tayte thought, considering it a good sign. He thought she could just as well have told her young helper to hang up the phone, but she hadn't. 'I know about Ingrid Keller,' Tayte repeated. 'I know she's your daughter.'

'Yes, and what of it?'

It was time to deliver the bluff. 'Well, I also know that her father is Johann Langner, who used to be your husband's best friend, and I have the feeling you'd rather I kept that to myself.'

'Are you threatening me, Mr Tayte?'

Tayte didn't like to think of it that way; he knew it was an idle threat he wouldn't follow through with, but his time in Munich was fast running out and he really wanted this interview. 'Look, as

I said in my letters, I'm just trying to trace my family, and I believe you might be able to help. I'd like to come over and talk to you, that's all.'

The call went silent for so long that Tayte thought he'd lost the connection. 'Hello?'

'Yes, I'm still here,' Trudi said. 'Very well. You can call at five this afternoon.'

Tayte was only partway through thanking her when the call ended. He put his phone away, considering that his hunch seemed to have been right. Trudi had certainly not denied that Johann Langner was Ingrid Keller's father, but he wondered again whether it meant anything in the context of his investigation. If it did, then right now Tayte couldn't see what. The discovery had given him an interview with Trudi Strobel, though, whom thus far he couldn't rule out as being his paternal grandmother.

As the taxi turned into Ruppertstrasse and pulled up outside the offices of the Munich *Standesamt*, Tayte thought ahead to the records Jan Statham was about to show him, hoping they might shed some light on the matter. Perhaps they would give him some insight into what had happened between the two friends and the girl during the Second World War. He felt sure that Johann's and Ava's relationship had not continued beyond it. Langner's son, Rudi, knew very little about Ava, and he had certainly never met her, or heard his father mention her outside of that brief period during the war when they were married.

So what had become of Ava Bauer?

Chapter Twenty-Seven

France. The Western Front. 5 August 1944.

Neither the onset of evening, nor the warm breeze at the window offered Johann any perceptible respite from what had been yet another hot and sticky day in Normandy. He drew contemplatively on his cigarette as he sat in his room and blew the smoke along with the breeze where it began to spiral into the room. He had been billeted in a house with three other officers of similar rank near Flers while the *Leibstandarte*, now a full Panzer Division, assembled prior to their next action, which Johann knew would be soon. The familiar pre-battle nerves he always felt as he awaited orders, which had been stretched to breaking point several times over since the war began, were suppressed for now because of an alarming message he had recently received from Volker. He took the slip of paper from his pocket again, still ruminating on its contents, when a tap-tap at the door denied him the chance to read it again.

'*Monsieur?*'

Johann turned to the door as it opened, and he saw Marie's delicate young face appear through the gap.

'Supper is ready, *Monsieur*.'

Johann put his slip of paper away again as he stood up. 'Thank you, Marie. Did your mother manage to make good use of the provisions we brought you?'

'She has made a cassoulet, *Monsieur*.'

'Ah, very good.' Johann extinguished his cigarette with his fingers, pinched off the tip and put the remainder back into its packet for later. 'At least when I go back into battle, I shall do so with a full stomach.'

He reached the door and opened it further, smiling at Marie, whom he thought could not have been more than twelve years old. He followed her along the passageway outside his room, which was lit only by the moon at the bare windows.

'Have you and your mother eaten?' Johann asked as they began to descend the stairs. They creaked at his every step.

'*Oui, Monsieur*. A little.'

'Good. You must keep up your strength.'

They arrived at the door to the dining room and Johann could hear the voices of his *Kameraden* beyond.

'The table is already set, *Monsieur*,' Marie said as she opened the door for him.

'*Merci*, Marie. Please thank your mother for me.'

Johann entered to the faint but stirring music of Wagner, which was coming from a small Bakelite radio set at the far end of the room, where the shutters were closed against the night. The room was dimly lit by several candles set at intervals along the table, which cast wavering shadows against the walls.

'Ah, here he is,' someone said. It was Horst, an *Obersturmführer*, like Johann, whose voice sounded strained and coarse following his recovery from a Soviet bayonet wound to his throat. 'Here, have some wine, Johann. It's very good.'

Johann sat down and took the proffered glass of wine. 'The cassoulet smells good, too,' he said, helping himself to a hunk of bread from the board.

'A good German sausage has to be among the world's most versatile foods,' the man sitting opposite Johann said. His name was Friedrich, and as *Hauptsturmführer* he was the senior ranking officer at the table.

'That's very true,' Johann said, reaching across the table to fill his plate with a ladle of sausage and bean stew from the pot.

'We were just telling Karl here about the *Ostfront*,' Friedrich said.

Karl was the most junior officer. He was a young *Untersturmführer* who reminded Johann of himself as he had been when the war began—only Karl had left the training school at Bad Tölz at an even younger age. Johann had seen many young faces on the battlefield in recent months, and he had fought alongside many *Kameraden* who were inexperienced, such as those among the ranks of the 1st SS Panzer Division *Hitlerjugend*, a *Waffen-SS* armoured division drawn from the Hitler Youth, which had only been combat ready since March that year. Johann took it as a sign that Germany's losses were far greater than could be sustained if they did not win the war soon.

'Were you there when Kharkov was recaptured?' Karl asked Johann, his eyes suddenly bright in the candlelight. His tone was full of the eagerness Johann found often accompanied a young *Leibstandarte* soldier's unfamiliarity with the harsh realities of war.

Horst answered for him. 'Johann has been just about everywhere the *Leibstandarte* have been. He's one of the oldest hares around. Isn't that right, Johann?'

'I could say the same about you, Horst,' Johann said with a smile. 'And yes, I'm beginning to feel very old.'

They laughed. 'Nonsense,' Horst said. 'There's plenty of fight left in both of us.'

The *Hauptsturmführer* interjected. 'With Operation *Lüttich* imminent, we shall find out soon enough,' he said, and everyone around the table, except young Karl, gave a sombre nod in agreement.

A moment later, as if wishing to turn the subject away from the war, the *Hauptsturmführer* asked, 'Have you heard from your wife yet, Johann?'

Johann had made no secret of the fact that the last letter he had received from Ava was dated close to three months ago, soon after his last brief period of home leave that May, when the *Leibstandarte* had been withdrawn for a period of rest and refit. He might have thought little of it, given the intense fighting in Normandy since early June, but Ava had been in the habit of writing to him regularly and he knew other soldiers of the *Leibstandarte* who had received letters from home as recently as two weeks ago.

He sat back from his food, thinking about Ava again, recalling the music she had played for him on his last visit and how it had mesmerised him as he watched her slender fingers drift over the piano keys, caressing them as he longed to be caressed. How impatient he had been for night to fall so they could be alone together.

He reached into his pocket and withdrew the message he had received from Volker, whom he had contacted recently to ask if he would call on Ava. Not knowing she was safe and well kept Johann awake at night more than usual, and he envied Volker that much. Having married Trudi Scheffler in the spring of 1942, his friend's position afforded him a closeness to his wife that Johann could only dream of. Having seen so little of Ava during the two and a half years since they were married, coupled with the almost daily uncertainty of whether or not he would live to see her again, was difficult enough. To worry for her as he did, and to be so helpless to do anything about it, was almost too much to bear.

He unfolded the slip of paper and offered it up for all to see. 'I received this message from a friend in Munich just yesterday,' he said. 'He informs me that my wife's family home has been boarded up.'

'Munich?' Friedrich said.

Johann nodded. 'That's right.'

'Well then, as long as the house is still standing, you've nothing to worry about. Didn't you hear? Munich was bombed during several raids a few weeks ago.'

'Does your wife have any family outside the city?' Horst asked. 'Perhaps she and her parents went to stay with them.'

'Yes,' Johann said, thinking back to his wedding day, when he had been introduced to Ava's uncle, a man called Heinz Schröder. 'She has an uncle living in the countryside on the outskirts of Gilching. It's about fifteen miles west of the city.'

'Well, there you go,' Friedrich said. 'I'm sure that's all it is. Your wife and her parents have simply been upset by the bombings and the displacement from their home.'

'But Ava could have written to me just as easily from Gilching.'

'I think you're worrying too much,' Horst said. He topped Johann's wine up. 'Here, have another glass and try to relax. With all that's going on, I'm sure there must be a hundred good reasons why your wife hasn't written to you.'

The young *Untersturmführer* spoke then. 'Why don't you send a message back to your friend and ask him to call at her uncle's house? Perhaps he could see if she's there for you.'

Short of deserting his post to go and look for Ava himself, Johann knew it was all he could do.

Chapter Twenty-Eight

Present day.

Tayte was waiting in a small reception area when Jan Statham came in to meet him. She wore navy blue trousers and a cream blouse with a gold and blue scarf at the neck. He put her somewhere in her forties. She pushed her shoulder-length auburn hair back off her face with her glasses as she approached, greeting Tayte with a warm smile as he rose to meet her.

'Those are lovely flowers,' she said once she'd introduced herself, shaking Tayte's hand with enthusiasm. 'This is all a bit exciting, I must say.'

'It sure is,' Tayte said, reminding himself that it was proving to be more than a little dangerous, too. 'I'm very pleased to meet you.'

'Likewise. It's not every day I get to help track down a war criminal.'

'No,' Tayte agreed.

He knew that was how Jan must have been briefed. He also knew that it was exactly what the Kaufmanns hoped his research might lead to, but while he would have loved to help bring the Demon of Dachau to justice, he remained focused on trying to find out why his mother and Karl had gone to see the Kaufmanns in connection with Karl's family—his family. He didn't say anything to Jan about that, having decided it was best not to get into his own issues, which he thought would only complicate matters.

'What's that accent I'm picking up?' he asked. 'It's subtle, but it's familiar. Whereabouts in the UK are you from?'

'I grew up in Wales,' Jan said. 'Although I was born in Cheshire.'

They left the reception area, taking a flight of stairs.

'I expect you're keen to get stuck in,' Jan said. 'I was given the names of some of the people you're interested in, so I've jumped the gun a bit and started without you. I hope you don't mind.'

'Not at all,' Tayte said. 'Anything that saves time is a bonus in my book.'

'Super,' Jan said, still smiling. 'I've managed to pull a few records together for you. Are you familiar with German family history?'

'A little,' Tayte said. 'But it's not exactly my specialty.'

'I'm sure you'll be just fine. The records aren't so different, apart from the language, of course. Do you speak German?'

'No, I don't,' Tayte said. 'I'm afraid my German is appalling. I'm glad to have someone like yourself to translate things for me.'

They left the stairwell and went through into one of the office areas.

'The main thing to keep in mind,' Jan said, 'is that there's no central repository in Germany for civil records. Most of the information useful to genealogists here is stored at local level. That can make things a little tricky as you need to know in which town, city or municipality the event you're looking for took place, but there are ways to help identify where German ancestors lived. Church records and gazetteers can be very useful there.'

Tayte already knew some of the things Jan was telling him as they made their way through the office area, but there was plenty he didn't know and he was keen to learn as much as he could. He noticed that many of the desks were vacant, which he supposed was because it was lunchtime.

'It becomes more difficult if you need to go back prior to Germany's unification in 1871,' Jan continued, 'when the country was made up of several independent kingdoms, each with their own way of doing things. I think you're only interested in the last century, though. Is that right?'

'Yes, I think so,' Tayte said. 'For now at least,' he added, considering that if Karl was his father, then in time he would be very interested in going back as far as he could. But not today.

'Mind you,' Jan said. 'It can get a little tricky again from 1945, when the country was split into East and West Germany. And because of the war parts of what was once Germany now belong to other countries altogether, so records for German ancestors may no longer be in Germany as we know it today at all.'

Jan showed Tayte into a room that could ordinarily have been a meeting room, but which for today's purposes appeared more like a personal reading room. There was a single large table in the centre with several chairs arranged around it. There was a keyboard and screen, a couple of notepads and pencils, and what appeared to be a folder of documents.

'Do make yourself comfortable. Would you like some tea or coffee before we get cracking? I don't drink coffee myself, but I'm sure I can find you some.'

'Coffee would be great,' Tayte said, thinking that a sandwich would go well with it. With all that had happened that day, he'd had no time or inclination for breakfast and his stomach was beginning to protest.

Jan paused at the door and turned back to him. 'Have you eaten? If not, I can ask someone to bring something back from the deli. Someone's always popping out at this time of day.'

Tayte smiled. He liked Jan already. He thought back to something Johann Langner had said at the hospital, when describing Ingrid Keller as his lifesaver. '*Meine Lebensretterin*,' he said with his hand on his stomach and a cheesy smile on his face.

Jan laughed at him. 'What would you like?'

'Anything's fine. You can surprise me.'

When Jan returned with their drinks a few minutes later, Tayte had already opened the file she'd prepared for him. He'd tried to wait, but he had no willpower when it came to seeing records, especially when they were right under his nose, even if he did feel like a child getting caught under the Christmas tree when Jan came back into the room. Not that any of the records meant much to him, other than a few names and places.

'I couldn't resist taking a look,' he said as Jan sat beside him.

'That's quite all right. I'll take you through what I found and we can go from there. Now, you're interested in two people, the notorious war criminal Volker Strobel, and someone called Johann Langner, who I'm told was Strobel's friend during the Second World War.'

Tayte sipped his coffee and nodded. 'I'd like to identify any other family members from either of these men. In particular, any children they might have had.' He was still firmly of the opinion that one of them might have fathered Karl and could therefore be his paternal grandfather. 'Let's start with Strobel.'

Jan flicked through the copies of the records she'd prepared, and she set a few out. 'These are all I could find for Volker Strobel,' she said, sliding one in front of Tayte. It bore the title *Geburtsurkunde*. 'I found this in the *Geburtsregister*—the birth registry. It's a copy of Volker Strobel's birth certificate. He was born here in Munich so it was easy enough to locate.' She pointed at the other names on the certificate. 'This is his father, Joseph Strobel, and his mother, Mathilde Strobel née Wolf.'

She slid another record under Tayte's nose as he began writing the names down on one of the larger notepads Jan had provided. 'This is from the *Heiratsregister*—the marriage registry,' she said. 'It shows Volker's marriage to Trudi Scheffler. The only thing that's a little unusual about it is that it's more common for marriages in Germany to take place in the bride's home town, but on this occasion the marriage was registered in Munich.'

'I read about it online,' Tayte said. 'They held a formal ceremony at Volker Strobel's family home. I guess you could say it was somewhat self-centred of him to deny the bride marriage in her own parish, but he appears to have been the type.'

Jan agreed. 'I don't know if any of the other names mentioned are of any interest to you. Trudi's parents are there, and the witnesses of course.'

Tayte was interested. He added Trudi's parents to his list: Claus and Kamilla Scheffler, glad to see that both names were present, which wasn't typical for marriage certificates in every country or time period, where often only the father's name was recorded. He also added the witnesses to the marriage, Friedrich Berger and Konstanze Schmidt.

'I'd be interested to know about any siblings,' Tayte said, figuring that if Volker or Trudi had any brothers or sisters, then their birth records should be easy enough to locate via their parents' details. 'I'd also like to know whether Volker and Trudi had any children together. There's plenty of information online about Volker Strobel, but I couldn't find any mention of a child.'

'No, I couldn't either,' Jan said. 'I think if there had been a child, it would be public knowledge by now, what with all the attention Volker Strobel has had over the years.'

'Have you looked for siblings?'

'No, I didn't get that far. Let's have a look now, shall we?'

'Sure,' Tayte said, 'but before we do that, are you able to pull up a birth certificate for Ingrid Strobel? She's Trudi Strobel's daughter.' Tayte didn't expect Ingrid's father's details to be there, but he wanted to be sure. 'I believe she was born in Munich somewhere between 1955 and 1960.'

'That shouldn't be difficult,' Jan said as she began tapping details into the computer.

The door opened then and lunch arrived.

'I'll leave you to eat your sandwich while I go and fetch this birth certificate from the archive,' she said. 'I shouldn't be long.'

'Thanks,' Tayte said to both Jan and the young man who brought his sandwich in. He didn't know how much it cost, so he gave him a ten Euro note and told him to keep the change, which he thought should amply cover the tip.

Tayte was just finishing his sandwich when Jan returned with the record he'd asked to see. She placed it in front of him as he swallowed his last mouthful and hurriedly wiped his fingers on the hem of his jacket. He could see it was only a copy of the original record, but all the same, he didn't want to risk getting mayonnaise on it. He didn't need Jan's help this time to find what he was looking for. The father's details were tellingly blank, which confirmed why Trudi Strobel had agreed to see him. To Tayte's mind, she clearly didn't want anyone to know that Johann Langner was Ingrid's father, or most likely it was Langner who didn't want anyone to know.

'That's exactly what I was expecting to see,' he said. 'Thank you.'

'No problem at all. That's what I'm here for. On to the siblings then?'

They started with Volker Strobel as Strobel's family were local to this particular civil registration office. Trudi Scheffler's information, on the other hand, proved to be rather more time consuming as Jan had to call a contact at the *Standesamt* in Stuttgart, where Trudi's family were from. Because of this it took a while to reach the conclusion between them that Volker Strobel had been an only child, and so had Trudi Scheffler.

Tayte had thought it worth looking to see if Volker Strobel in particular had any siblings. He thought that if Volker had fathered a child out of wedlock, there was a chance the child might have been brought up by someone else in the family, although he knew it was more likely that the child's mother or someone in her family would have taken care of the baby. He'd come across such things before, and he knew from experience that children displaced in such a manner were never easy to find.

He began to think about that. It *was* usually the mother's family who wound up caring for such children, perhaps to hide an indiscretion, or in this case for any number of reasons. It made him think about Ava Bauer—the girl caught in the middle of the friends' affections. He knew Ava had married Johann Langner, but even if she'd had a child, that didn't mean it had to be Langner's.

'Let's move on,' he said to Jan. 'These other records are presumably about Johann Langner?'

'Yes, they show he was born in Dresden and that he was married to Ava Bauer here in Munich, also during the Second World War, as with Volker Strobel and Trudi Scheffler.'

She slid the records she'd found on Langner across to Tayte, and looking at their record of marriage his eyes fell on Ava Bauer's name. He tapped it. 'I'd like to see what else we can find on Ava Bauer,' he said, writing down her parents' names, Gerhard Bauer and Adelina Bauer. He also noted down the witnesses as he had before: Heinz Schröder and Lorenz Richter.

'Do you want to look for siblings again? Aunts and uncles?'

'Let's look at everything. I'd particularly like to know whether she had any children, and whether there's any further record of marriage for her.' He paused as he wondered again whether she'd survived the war, and what had become of her if she had, reminding himself that she was no longer with Johann Langner.

'And do you think that's going to help you find this war criminal, is that it?' Jan said. 'If Ava knew him, she might have had a child with him no one knows about. And if you can find the child, you think that might lead you to Volker Strobel?'

'Maybe,' Tayte said, thinking that if Volker Strobel was his paternal grandfather then his research might well lead to him.

Jan pulled her glasses down over her eyes and started working the computer again, checking the indexes, Tayte supposed. He understood so little of what was appearing on the screen and he'd never felt so out of place in a record office before. He would have loved Jan to explain everything to him, but he thought it would take too long and he knew the best time for explanations was when he had the records he hoped she was locating in front of him. He was idly perusing the records Jan had already prepared for him when his phone rang, playing the overture to *Dirty Rotten Scoundrels*, which Jean had taken him to see in London's West End recently. Her name flashed up on the screen.

'Excuse me,' he said to Jan as he stood up to take the call. He went to the corner of the room and pressed his phone to his ear. 'Hi, how're you feeling?' he asked Jean, speaking softly. 'I hope the tests went okay.'

'I'm fine,' Jean said. 'I've been given the all clear so I don't have to stay here overnight after all, but I do need to pop back in the morning for another check over before we fly home. Actually, I'm a bit bored.' Tayte heard her laugh. 'Can you come and get me out of here?'

'Sure,' Tayte said, thinking about the research and knowing it would have to wait. 'I'll get a cab right over. Maybe we can go and get a bite to eat and I'll tell you all about my day.'

'Perfect. I'll see you soon.'

As the call ended, Tayte checked his watch, remembering that he had an appointment with Trudi Scheffler in what was now less than two hours. He hoped Jean wasn't going to mind it being a quick something to eat because he didn't want to jeopardise his interview with Trudi now that he had one. He went back to Jan.

'I'm really sorry about this,' he said. 'Something's come up and I have to go. Can I leave this with you and come back in the morning? It could be too late to carry on today, unless you can keep the offices open and don't mind working late.'

'Ordinarily I wouldn't mind working late at all, but I've got band practice after work today. I play bassoon in a wind band, you see. I'll keep at it for as long as I can, though.'

Tayte smiled. 'Tomorrow morning then,' he said, collecting his briefcase, his flowers, and the notes he'd made. He shook Jan's hand. 'Thanks for all your help today. I'll try to be here first thing.'

Tayte left the offices of the Munich *Standesamt* hoping that Jean would understand that he had to come back to the record office and finish what he'd started. Although she'd already told him she needed to pay another visit to the hospital in the morning, so he figured he'd have some time on his hands again. As he arrived back in the reception area, heading for the desk to ask if someone could call him a taxi, he began to wonder what information on Ava Bauer Jan might find, and whether or not it would prove useful to his search.

Since learning that Ava Bauer and Johann Langner had married, it had puzzled Tayte that Langner had never mentioned it while he and Jean were talking with him at the hospital. Or perhaps he would have got around to it if they had been with him long enough to hear the full story he had begun to tell them. He wondered how Langner's story would have played out, and whether he would have talked about Ava and what became of her. Tayte could only guess for now. Whatever the answer, he thought the last years of the war must have been very difficult for Johann, both on and off the battlefield.

Chapter Twenty-Nine

Near Vienna, Austria. 17 April 1945.

As night fell, exhausted and in need of sleep, elements of the fragmented *Leibstandarte* set up defensive positions along the Vienna-Linz road. Johann Langner knew none of the soldiers he now found himself keeping company with, all acquaintances formed through war having also been destroyed by it. As the senior ranking officer amidst the small unit he now found himself a part of, he was in command of a handful of machine-gun squads and twenty or so riflemen, in part made up of boys whose uniforms barely fitted them, and whose heads had not yet grown sufficiently to fit the helmets they wore. How these young and inexperienced soldiers had made it out of Vienna at all, Johann could not imagine.

The advance of Germany's Seventh Army in Normandy during Operation *Lüttich* the previous year had quickly been brought to a juddering halt. Bombed into retreat by superior Allied air power, Johann and what was left of the *Leibstandarte* soon found themselves outflanked and encircled near Falaise, but managed to break through in a hard-fought retreat that forced them to leave their armament and artillery pieces behind. With the loss of around 5000 men of the elite *Leibstandarte*, Johann knew he was lucky to have made it out of France alive.

By the end of 1944, in what the Allies would call 'The Battle of the Bulge', the *Leibstandarte* were back on the Western Front in the forested Ardennes mountains, spearheading Operation *Wacht am Rhein* under the command of Wilhelm Mohnke. But, low on fuel and with their ranks bolstered by many inexperienced replacements, by the end of January 1945 the *Leibstandarte* was once again forced into retreat, and Johann soon found himself in Hungary, returned to the Eastern Front as part of Operation Spring Awakening—*Frühlingserwachen*.

Germany saw early gains as they tried to secure some of the last oil reserves still open to them, but the offensive proved too ambitious, and so the *Leibstandarte*, with the 6th SS Panzer Army under Josef 'Sepp' Dietrich, withdrew to Vienna to hold defensive positions against the fast approaching Soviet Army. By the beginning of April the Soviets had arrived. After a week of intense street fighting they had breached the city centre, and Johann and his *Kameraden* had fought to hold Vienna against overwhelming odds. The city he had once visited as a wounded soldier, and the Prater parkland area through which he had walked with Ava, had become a battleground. Even the Ferris wheel beneath which he had proposed to her was now, like much of this once beautiful city, all but destroyed.

By the middle of the month Vienna had fallen and the battle-weary remnants of the *Leibstandarte* were in retreat again, hotly pursued by the Soviet 46th Army, stopping now and then in an attempt to slow the inevitable red tide that threatened to wash over them if they remained in one place too long.

Having been spared further Soviet attacks for some hours, once Johann had established his unit's defensive positions, he began his inspection.

'*Obersturmführer?*' one of the young *Schütze* said.

Johann didn't know the boy's name, but he thought him no more than fifteen years old. 'Yes, what is it?'

'We don't have much ammunition, *Obersturmführer.*'

'Then use what you have sparingly. If 'Ivan' comes for us, make every bullet count.'

'*Jawohl, Obersturmführer.*'

Those who could sleep would do so in shifts among the cover of the shrubs and trees by the roadside, while the rest of the troop kept watch. As an extra precaution, Johann had sent a small three-man reconnaissance squad half a mile back towards Vienna as an early warning measure. He would send three others to replace them at midnight. Johann shared the command watch with a *Rottenführer* called Protz. The squad leader had clearly seen little combat, but he had been all Johann could muster for his small troop in the chaos of their bloody retreat. The man instilled so little confidence in Johann that he sat awake through the first two hours of Protz's watch, lying on a bank beside the shrubbery, listening to every sound the night had to offer while he counted the stars in the night sky to ward off his fatigue.

With an hour of Protz's watch remaining, Johann finally began to drift, and thoughts of Ava came to him, as they often did. He had still received no word from her—no clue as to her whereabouts, or even whether she was alive or dead. He had sent a letter to Volker the previous year, as the young *Untersturmführer* he had briefly shared a billet with in Normandy had suggested. Volker had later replied to say that he had visited Ava's uncle in Gilching, but that her uncle had seen nothing of the Bauer family in recent months. Ava and her parents had not then gone to stay with her uncle to escape the Munich bombings.

So where was she?

Volker had said he would look into Ava's whereabouts further, but that was now months ago, and Johann had received no further news. As his eyelids became too heavy to keep open, his thoughts drifted to his parents and the news that his home city of Dresden had been all but flattened by ceaseless bombing raids that February. He had been denied leave to return home, and he had later heard that the area where his parents lived had been among the worst hit. Soon after that he received news that their bodies had been recovered from the debris. Johann shed no tears for his father, but for his mother, whom he had seen so little of in recent years, and who had endured more hardship than any wife deserved from her husband, he wept in phases for several days.

Thinking about the bombing of Dresden again made Johann wonder where Ava had been when the bombs fell on Munich the previous year, and whether she and her parents had been buried somewhere beneath the rubble and the devastation that typically followed such random destruction. His last waking thought was that Munich was only two hundred miles west of his current position. And how he wished he was there, where he knew the answers to these questions that tormented him must lie.

'*Nachthexen!*'

Johann had no idea how long he'd been asleep, but it felt as if only a matter of seconds had passed before his eyes shot open again. At hearing the cry, his first instinct was to roll closer to the bush beside him. His Luger was drawn in seconds. Then he heard the familiar sound of the wind whistling through the bracing-wires of one or more Soviet Polikarpov U-2 biplanes and he holstered his sidearm again, knowing it would prove useless against the attack.

The biplanes had been nicknamed *Nähmaschinen*—sewing machines—because of the rattling sound their engines made. But their engines were now switched off to facilitate a stealthy approach to their target. Flown by the all-women pilots of the Soviet 588th Night-Bomber Regiment, who were referred to as *Nachthexen* or night witches, their chief objective was to disrupt and to deny the enemy sleep.

The first fragmentation bombs took out one of the machine-gun placements, and Johann could only hope that the men operating it had managed to leap clear in time. The hitherto still night air suddenly erupted with the sound of the explosions and the quick return of machine-gun fire, and cries went out in all directions as members of the *Leibstandarte* ran for cover.

The Polikarpovs glided in low to deliver their payloads, some skimming the treetops, over which they began to drop phosphorous pellets, which ignited everything they touched. The trees and shrubbery were soon ablaze, and Johann knew that those soldiers unlucky enough to receive phosphorous burns would die a slow and painful death.

'Take cover!' Johann called to his remaining machine-gun units. Experience told him that his men were unlikely to bring one of these *Nachthexen* down. The biplanes, which were essentially modified crop dusters, were strongly built, and his men, gathered in clusters around their gun emplacements, were easy targets. Their best defence was to scatter and wait out the attack.

The snick-snick of the biplanes' engines started up again as soon as they passed by, and Johann peered up from his cover to watch their shadows pass overhead in the darkness like the winged, fire-breathing beasts they were. It seemed the enemy would not allow them a moment's rest in their retreat from Vienna. The *Nachthexen* had done their job well, but their raid on Johann's position was only the beginning. Within half an hour the shelling began, and now that their position was lit up by the burning trees and foliage, Johann and his unit were easy targets.

The first barrage landed short and Johann gave the order to push on along the road towards Linz. The only vehicles he and his makeshift unit had managed to pull out of Vienna with were an

open top VW *Kübelwagen* and two *Zündapp* sidecar motorcycles—
one of which had run out of fuel several miles back. Thankfully they
had not yet been hit, but even so, while the vehicles had proven
useful for carrying supplies and a few wounded *Kameraden,* the unit
as a whole could only move as fast as those who were on foot.

Johann made for the *Kübelwagen,* which was parked a hundred
yards or so along the road, beneath a canopy of branches at the
roadside. Further in, the burning trees continued to crackle and
flame, illuminating the way. He called over to one of his men.

'Bring the wounded. *Schnell!*'

As Johann turned back to the car, he saw someone jump in. It
was *Rottenführer* Protz. The car's engine started and the vehicle
pulled away, wheels slipping in the loose dirt beside the road.

'Protz!' Johann yelled.

He pulled out his Luger and took aim, knowing that this man's
cowardly attempt to save his own life would mean the wounded
would have to be left behind. He fired a shot and saw the bullet clip
the car with a spark, but Protz did not stop. Johann took aim again,
but this time as he pulled the trigger he did not hear the gun's report
over the shells that suddenly burst around him. The ground shook
at his feet, unsteadying him. He saw the car take a hit and flip into
the air. Then he heard screaming behind him and he turned around
to see a man staggering towards him, flames consuming him as
others ran into the trees in wild panic.

Johann was reminded of the woods near Romanovka, where
he had earlier received his wounds, and he wanted to warn his men
to stay out of the trees, but at that very moment he felt a searing
pain at the back of his head as another hail of Soviet shells erupted.
Something struck him out of nowhere, and for the briefest moment
he was aware that he was falling.

Then darkness fell with him.

Chapter Thirty

Present day.

It was apparent to Tayte as soon as the taxi pulled up at the gates to Trudi Strobel's significant home that Tobias Kaufmann had not understated her wealth. She had clearly done very well for herself since the war, despite having been left with next to nothing because of her association with her war-criminal husband. Given that Tobias had said she had never remarried, worked, or owned a business herself, the main question turning through Tayte's mind as he approached the intercom and pressed the call button was where her wealth had come from. He had a few ideas, which he expected Trudi would soon confirm, and he hoped he could also persuade her to talk about Volker Strobel.

Jean was beside him. By the time Tayte had collected her from the hospital with his wilting bunch of flowers and had taken her back to the hotel, there had been little time left before his appointment with Trudi—just long enough to book them both onto a return flight to London the following evening while Jean fetched her jacket and changed into her jeans and a pale yellow, V-neck sweater.

Having brought Jean up to date with everything that had happened since he'd left her that morning, and despite Tayte's suggestion that she might like to rest at the hotel, she had insisted on seeing Trudi with him and he could do little to dissuade her. Her neck brace was off. Her hospital test results were good. Apart from a few bumps and bruises here and there she was her usual self again. Only now she seemed to have a renewed sense of determination to make the most of their now limited time in Munich. As the main gates powered open and Tayte and Jean walked the drive towards the house, they had time to take the estate in.

'It must be worth millions,' Tayte said.

'Not when Trudi bought it,' Jean countered.

'No, but it would still have cost a fortune, relatively speaking, and the upkeep must be a huge drain. There's a few acres of land to tend and—' He paused and whistled. 'Well just look at the place. How many bedrooms do you think there are?'

'At least a dozen.'

'At least,' Tayte agreed.

The house, arranged on three floors, was painted white, which made it stand out all the more amidst the lush greenery of the landscaped gardens it was set in. A balcony ran around half of the top floor, where Tayte imagined the master bedroom was. He couldn't think why someone Trudi's age would choose to run such a sizeable estate all by herself. By all accounts she had no other family to share it with than Ingrid Keller, but he imagined she lived with her husband when she wasn't caring for Johann Langner. It was another indicator to Tayte that Trudi didn't need the money. She could have made a fortune from the sale, but clearly she didn't need to sell.

They were greeted at the front door by a smart young woman in a black dress, whom Tayte supposed was the person he'd spoken to when he called the house earlier. When the young woman greeted them, the familiarity in her voice, and her awkwardness with the English language, confirmed it. She led them through a marble-pillared hallway to a bright sitting room at the back of the house, which looked down over a wooded area and what appeared to be a recreational parkland. In the distance, Tayte could see Munich's Olympic park with its various domes sprawled over the landscape like vast Bedouin tents.

'Very nice indeed,' Tayte said as they sat down and waited for their host to join them.

Trudi Strobel didn't keep them waiting long. She came into the room alone, dressed in a light-green gown and cardigan, aided by the fanciest looking walking stick Tayte had ever seen. It had a gold filigree handle over polished ebony, the gold tracery weaving between colourful enamelwork that extended partway down the cane. Tayte knew from seeing Trudi's vital records that she was ninety-two years old. She was tall and slim, but without appearing frail. Her grey-white hair was impeccably styled and set, and her skin, though lined with the inevitability of old age, had a quality to it that belied her years. Tayte and Jean stood up as she approached them, and Tayte thought she appeared as elegant in her demeanour now as he supposed she had been in her youth.

'Mr Tayte,' she said, coldly and without the slightest hint of a smile. She made no suggestion that she wanted to shake Tayte's hand. 'I can't say it's a pleasure.'

If Trudi had been born with a silver spoon in her mouth then it showed in the plummy way she spoke. There was a haughtiness to her tone and very little trace of the German nuances evident in the accents of most of the people Tayte had spoken to since arriving in Munich. He imagined she'd received the finest education money could buy.

Trudi turned to Jean. She tilted her head back and raised her glasses slightly to peer beneath them, giving the impression that she was looking down her nose at her. Then as if Jean wasn't worthy of being addressed herself, she turned back to Tayte and said, 'And who is this?'

'This is my partner, Professor Jean Summer,' Tayte said. He could see from the glance Jean gave him that she was glad he'd got the 'professor' part in.

'A professor?' Trudi said, studying Jean more closely, as though she couldn't quite believe it.

'Royal history,' Jean said. 'Particularly the constitutional history of England, specialising in the Plantagenet dynasty.'

Trudi didn't continue the conversation. She made a slight but disdainful sound in her throat as she turned away and sat in a chair that looked uncomfortably upright. 'Well, sit down,' she said. 'Let's get this over with.'

No refreshments were offered, so Tayte got straight to the point. 'Firstly, I'd like to apologise to you for the manner in which this interview has come about.'

'You mean how you threatened me?'

'Yes,' Tayte conceded. 'And I'm sorry it had to come to that. It's not my usual style at all.'

Trudi made a point of eyeing Tayte up and down, from his perennially ruffled black hair to the comfortable, if bordering on worn out, beige loafers on his feet, as if to suggest that style of any kind wasn't really something Tayte gave much thought to. She made him feel so uncomfortable that he found himself trying to press the creases out of his jacket with the palms of his hands.

'I won't ask how you made your discovery about Johann Langner,' Trudi said. 'It doesn't matter. Only the consequences are important. You said you knew that Johann was Ingrid's father. Yes, he is. Now if I have to talk to you about other matters to ensure your discretion, I will. No one wants to be associated with the Strobel name, least of all a highly successful businessman such as Johann Langner.'

'Look,' Tayte said, offering Trudi a smile. 'I'm sensing we've got off to a bad start here, and—'

'A bad start?' Trudi cut in. 'Believe me, Mr Tayte, it won't get any better until you leave. Now what is it you want to talk to me about?'

Tayte drew a deep breath, wondering how anyone could be so rude, yet at the same time he thought he deserved it for the way he'd forced Trudi's hand. He thought about showing her the photograph he had of his mother, but he didn't suppose he'd gain anything from it, and he didn't feel that Trudi Strobel was someone he wanted to share such a personal image with.

'I'm just trying to find my family,' Tayte said. 'That's all. I believe Volker Strobel could be my grandfather.'

That seemed to amuse Trudi. She gave a small chirp of a laugh, but there was no warmth to it. 'Poor you,' she said. 'It wouldn't surprise me, although I'm certainly not your grandmother, if that's what you think. Ingrid is my only child.'

'Why wouldn't it surprise you?' Jean asked.

Trudi turned sharply to Jean, as though she'd forgotten Jean was there. She sighed. 'I suppose we have to talk about this, don't we? Volker wasn't exactly what you would call a faithful husband. He had a penchant for a particular kind of intercourse. His love-making, if you could call it that, was often violent, and I endured it, both before and after we were married. I suppose the novelty with me wore off, thank goodness, because after a while Volker took to seeing prostitutes—women he could pay to smile through their sufferings as if they were enjoying it.'

Trudi paused, closing her eyes for a few seconds. When she opened them again, she said, 'I remember the first time. We had been to a restaurant here in Munich called the Osteria Bavaria— Volker and I, Johann and an older girl called Ava Bauer, whom I quickly came to despise, though more out of my own jealousy than any fault of hers. You see Volker was besotted with Ava. I think he'd hoped to win her hand that night, but when it became clear that it was Johann she wanted, Volker became very moody. Late that night, he came to me at the apartment my aunt had rented for us while we were staying in Munich. I couldn't really say he raped me because I wanted him, but I'll never forget how violent he was, and how uncaring he seemed towards me afterwards. I've realised since then that it was because he couldn't have Ava, so he took it out on me—and all those prostitutes, perhaps trying to find someone who was more like her, but of course he never could.'

'Why did you marry him?' Tayte asked.

'My family had always wanted the marriage, and I suppose at the time I was as besotted with Volker, for all his faults, as he was with Ava. There were always three people in our relationship, and I knew I was the consolation prize he didn't really want. Whenever Volker was with me, I knew he was thinking about her.'

'But you kept his name after the war,' Jean said, shaking her head, clearly at a loss to understand why.

'I kept the name I had taken when I married Volker Strobel because I believe in the sanctity of marriage. I had taken my marriage vows unto death. Is that so hard to accept?'

'No, I suppose not,' Tayte said, thinking that her decision to do so, however righteous, had cost her a great deal: her family and her fortune, not that she hadn't turned that around remarkably well. He began to feel a little sorry for Trudi as he considered that the family who had pushed her into her marriage with Volker Strobel had then turned their backs on her when the man they had wanted her to marry became an anathema to them.

'Johann Langner was very different,' Trudi said. 'Quite the antithesis of the man I married. He came to me when he was released from prison, and at first, although it sounds peculiar to say it now, I saw it as a way to strike back at Volker. That was in 1955. Johann's family had been killed during the Dresden bombings, so I suppose at the time he had nowhere else to go.'

'What about his wife?' Tayte asked, still wondering why Johann hadn't gone to Ava when he was released from prison. 'Do you know what became of Ava Bauer?'

'No,' Trudi said. 'We lost touch somewhere amidst the chaos of war. I never saw Ava again after she and Johann were married. When Johann came to me he never spoke of her, for which I was glad. I had already shared one relationship with Ava Bauer and I did not wish to do so again. My affair with Johann lasted a few years, but as Johann found his feet and started to become successful, he wanted less and less to do with me. He left me for the last time just after Ingrid was born. He paid for this house and gave me a handsome sum of money in advance for our daughter's upkeep, and my discretion.'

'And I suppose when Ingrid found out who her father was,' Tayte said, 'she later took the job as his private nurse to be closer to him without anyone suspecting he was her father?'

'Exactly that, yes.'

Tayte sat back, wondering where to take the conversation next. Trudi seemed to have volunteered plenty of information, perhaps just to get this over with as she had earlier said, but he couldn't see how it helped him with the bigger questions he still hoped to find the answers to before he and Jean had to leave Munich—apart from the knowledge that Volker Strobel had potentially sown more seeds for his family tree than Tayte cared to think about. After a few seconds of uncomfortable silence he glanced at Jean, who gave a slight shake of her head as if to say she didn't know what to ask next either. So Tayte asked the obvious question in the hope that something might come of it.

'Can you tell us anything else about Volker Strobel?'

'So you can find him and ask him whether he's your grandfather?'

'Something like that, I guess.'

Trudi shook her head. 'I can't help you, Mr Tayte. I've had no communication with Volker since before the war ended, which of course is now more than seventy years ago.' She looked suddenly upset. 'Why is it that people wish to make me relive these things that happened so long ago when I would sooner forget? This is why I refuse to give interviews about my husband. It's painful to me. Do you understand? By coming here as you have, you're hurting me.'

Tayte couldn't have felt any more uncomfortable than he did right then. He could see that Trudi's eyes had glazed over and he knew it was time to go. If Trudi did know anything about Volker Strobel that might prove useful in locating him then it was clear she wasn't going to tell him and Jean about it.

'I'm really sorry to have upset you, Mrs Strobel,' he said. He got up to leave and Jean stood with him. 'We'll leave you in peace.'

'And you'll keep what you know to yourselves?'

'A deal's a deal,' Tayte said. 'You have our word that we won't tell another soul.'

'Another soul?'

'We mentioned it to someone when we found out, but I'll make sure he keeps it to himself.'

'And how will you do that?'

Beyond asking Tobias Kaufmann not to tell anyone, Tayte didn't know. He supposed Tobias had already shared the information with his father.

'I'm sorry,' Tayte said again, making for the door.

⌣

As Tayte and Jean walked back along the drive towards the main gate, Tayte checked his watch and noted that it was almost six o'clock, their visit with Trudi Strobel having lasted less than an hour. He took out his phone and called the taxi firm he'd been using, thinking that he'd take Jean into the city centre to find somewhere nice for their last evening meal in Munich.

'That was awkward,' Tayte said to Jean once he'd booked the taxi.

'I don't think she liked me at all,' Jean said.

'Maybe she's got a problem with other women in general.'

'You mean she's psychologically scarred after having shared her husband with Ava Bauer, whom she could never live up to, and a host of prostitutes?'

Tayte snorted a laugh. 'Yeah, something like that.'

They reached the gates and Tayte watched them close slowly behind them. 'She really opened up to us back there, didn't she? About her personal life, I mean.'

'Yes, I didn't expect that,' Jean said.

'Me neither. It makes me think that if she did have anything to say about Volker Strobel, she probably would have said it. She can't have much affection left for the man.'

'I'm surprised she had any at all after the way he treated her. If she knew where he was, I'm sure she'd have given him up long ago.'

'Maybe,' Tayte said, but with a degree of doubt.

'You don't think so?'

'I don't know. Something just doesn't seem quite right to me. I mean why tell us all that intimate stuff about her husband at all? It's like she wanted us to think she hated him. She practically spelled out the reasons. I could be entirely wrong here, but it strikes me as a good way to put us off the idea that she might still care for Volker. Then there's the maintenance money. It all seems to wrap up very nicely. She had a child with Langner, as we suspected, and he paid her off for the child and for her discretion, which explains her wealth.'

'Put like that, it does seem as if she's left us with nowhere to go—no story to pursue.'

'Precisely,' Tayte said. 'But does it explain her wealth?'

'How do you mean?'

'Well, we know that Ingrid was born a few years after Langner left prison. And Trudi told us that Langner left her for the last time just after Ingrid was born. It didn't click at the time, but do you recall the conversation at the hospital where the chauffeur, Christoph, told us Langner started out with nothing, and that it took several years for him to even make a proper living from his business?'

'Yes, of course,' Jean said. 'So Langner wasn't a wealthy man when Ingrid was born.'

'Far from it,' Tayte said. 'Seems he wasn't anywhere near wealthy enough to have bought her that house, even back then.'

'She also said that Langner had paid her a tidy sum of money as well.'

Tayte nodded. 'She was clearly lying. And even if Langner had somehow paid Trudi off, barring her having made some very lucky investments over the years, it was a long time ago. Where's she getting the money to maintain all this from?'

'Where else could the money have come from?' Jean asked, and they both stared at one another, clearly thinking the same thing.

'Volker Strobel,' they said together, although Tayte had to remind himself that Tobias Kaufmann already suspected as much and had been unable to prove it.

The taxi arrived and Tayte gave the driver the name of the restaurant Trudi had mentioned, thinking it would be good to go somewhere that the subjects of his self-assignment had once been.

The driver, an older man in his sixties with grey stubble on his face and a leather flat-cap on his head, turned back with a blank expression.

'It's a restaurant in the city,' Tayte added, speaking slowly in case the driver was having trouble understanding him, but it seemed he understood well enough.

'You mean the Osteria Italiana on Schellingstrasse. It hasn't been called the Osteria Bavaria since the war ended. They say it's the oldest restaurant in Munich.'

'I guess that's the place then,' Tayte said. He turned to Jean. 'You like Italian, don't you?'

Jean smiled and nodded and the taxi took off, heading for the city centre. Settling back for the ride, Tayte put his hand on the back of Jean's and said, 'I'm glad you're okay. You had me so worried this morning.'

Jean leaned in and kissed him. 'And I'm glad you're not going to jail,' she said with a smirk.

'Yeah, me too. Let's try to stay out of trouble for the next twenty-four hours, shall we? Nice meal . . . Early night . . .'

Jean laughed at him. 'Did you just wink at me?'

'I think I had something in my eye,' Tayte said, and Jean slapped his arm.

At that moment, their frivolity was interrupted by Tayte's phone buzzing in his pocket. He took it out and checked the display. There was a number, but he didn't recognise it.

'Hello,' he said. 'Jefferson Tayte.'

'Mr Tayte, it's Tobias Kaufmann. Is it all right to talk?'

'Sure,' Tayte said. 'It's good timing, actually. We've just left Trudi Strobel. I was going to call you later to let you know how it went, although we didn't really learn anything new that's likely to help with your hunt for Volker Strobel.'

'That's a pity.'

'Yes, it is. Look, I told her we wouldn't say anything about Langner being Ingrid Keller's father. I know I've already told you, but I don't see how we have anything to gain from telling anyone else.'

'You might not feel the same way once you've heard what I have to tell you,' Kaufmann said. 'Since our last conversation about Trudi's wealth, I've been following the money, so to speak. At least, some associates of mine have. We'll talk more when I see you. Is now a good time?'

'What, right now?' Tayte said, thinking about a bowl of pasta or a pizza, or maybe both.

Jean had been listening in. She gave Tayte a nod, and Tayte couldn't help but feel a little disappointed with the timing.

'Okay,' he said. 'We'll be right over.'

'I'm not at the office at the moment. One of the staff, Amir, is working late. He'll let you in if you arrive before me. I shouldn't be long.'

'Great,' Tayte said. 'We'll see you soon.'

Chapter Thirty-One

Because of the hour, the tree-lined avenue that was home to the offices of *Kaufmann und Kaufmann* was markedly changed from Tayte's previous visits. The various offices were mostly now closed, the people who staffed them having gone home for the day, and the car-parking spaces that had made the road appear all the more narrow during office hours were now largely vacant. The taxi pulled up in front of a line of motorcycles and Tayte paid the driver as he and Jean got out.

'I can't wait to hear what Tobias has found,' Tayte said as they approached the entrance, but in his next breath he realised he might have to. A familiar feeling of unease churned through him as he looked at the door. It was ajar, just like the door to the premises he'd visited the night he was framed for murder, only this time the doorframe was splintered. It looked as if it had been kicked in. He put his arm out to hold Jean back. 'I think our "friends" have been here.'

'Maybe they're still here,' Jean said, drawing Tayte's attention to the motorcycles. She was holding out her phone.

'What are you doing?'

'I'm taking a photo of the number plates.' She took the photograph and put her phone away again. 'We should go.'

'What about Tobias? He's on his way here. We can't just let him walk in on whatever this is. He also said someone called Amir might be working late. What if Amir's in trouble?'

'So let's call the police and go and wait further down the street. We can warn Tobias when he gets here.'

'What if Tobias is already here?'

It troubled Tayte to think that Kaufmann or his employee, Amir, might already be in trouble. What if one or both of them was in mortal danger? By the time the police arrived, he thought it could be too late. He pushed the door open and peered inside.

'You call the police,' he whispered, stepping over the threshold. 'I'm just going to take a look.'

Tayte set his briefcase down inside the door and watched Jean take her phone out again. He made for the stairs, but as he started to ascend them he heard a clatter from the offices above and he froze. Fear and self-preservation rooted him to the spot for a few seconds, but he found the courage to continue. He took two more steps and then he heard voices, agitated voices speaking in German. There was another clatter and this time the din continued, as if the people he'd heard were destroying the place.

He turned back to Jean and instantly caught his breath. She was staring right back at him, a knife pressed to her throat. Behind her with his arm around her chest was a taller man in blue jeans and a white T-shirt. He wore a black full-face crash helmet. The visor was up but all Tayte could see of his face was his eyes, which looked determined.

'Move!' the man demanded, shuffling Jean towards the stairs. 'Go up!'

Tayte's heart began to pound. What to do? He realised this man must have been posted on the street, out of sight, to watch for trouble after the rest of the gang broke into the building. Tayte's hesitation caused the man to reaffirm the pressure on the knife at Jean's throat, and Tayte knew he had little choice but to do as he was told. He continued up the stairs, taking his time. He reached the small landing area that led to the offices of *Kaufmann und Kaufmann,* and there he stopped. A few seconds later the knifeman arrived with Jean. Tayte thought she looked surprisingly calm given their predicament—at least, she appeared considerably calmer than he felt.

'Inside!' the man ordered, his tone full of aggression.

The sounds of breaking office equipment and splintering desks gave Tayte little desire to obey, but he could think of no alternative that wouldn't endanger Jean's life. He wanted to charge the man down, but that knife was already pressing into Jean's skin. He couldn't risk it.

'Go!' the man insisted again, and this time Tayte pushed the door open.

The room was a mess. Most of the desks had been tipped over and papers had been ripped and scattered. There was an assortment of office hardware from plastic paper trays to big old-fashioned computer screens, most of which had been thrown across the room and smashed. On the walls someone had spray-painted black Nazi swastikas. The clatter stopped as soon as Tayte entered. A gun was drawn and the muzzle was suddenly aiming directly at Tayte's face. Instinctively, he thrust his hands high into the air as the knifeman followed into the room after him with Jean. He kicked the door shut behind him.

Now that there was a handgun trained on Tayte, the knifeman shoved Jean away and Tayte caught her as she stumbled into him. Tayte counted three men in crash helmets: the knifeman, the gunman and a heavily muscled man further into the room. All wore jeans and white T-shirts, although the man with the gun was the only one wearing black jeans, just as Max Fleischer had been when he'd appeared outside that coffee shop window.

'Well, well,' the gunman said. 'Look who it is.'

The chin guard of his helmet rocked back as he spoke, and Tayte glimpsed the skull tattoo of the Nazi Death's Head Unit insignia on his neck, confirming his suspicions that the gunman was Max Fleischer. Fleischer came closer. He went up to Jean, grabbed her arm and pulled her away from Tayte. Then his helmet began to roll from side to side as if he were studying her.

'I told you what would happen to you if you didn't go home,' Fleischer said, and Tayte could imagine the sickly grin on his face.

'*Wir haben keine Zeit,*' the muscular man towards the back of the room said.

Tayte turned towards him as he spoke, and then he saw another man, bound and gagged and lying on the floor at the back of the office towards the Strobel room. He figured it had to be Amir. At least he was still alive.

Fleischer leaned closer to Jean, 'Oh, we'll make time,' he said in reply to the other's words. Suddenly he turned on Tayte and levelled the gun at his head again. 'But first I'm going to take care of you.'

Tayte had been shot at and threatened at gunpoint before, although it wasn't an experience he felt he'd learned anything from; he was just as scared now as he had been then. His senses were particularly heightened. He could feel the adrenaline begin to boil in his veins, preparing him for fight or flight. He knew if he didn't do something, he and Jean were likely going to die, and the thought of what Fleischer and his gang might do to Jean before they killed her only served to fuel his determination to fight. He was thinking fast, looking for a way out. His eyes flitted around the room and settled on the muscular man again, and while Tayte had plenty of natural strength on account of his size, this man looked unstoppable. He knew he needed the gun—the gun Fleischer was pointing at him. He thought that if any of the other men had guns they would have drawn them by now. Whoever had the gun had control of the room.

'You can't shoot me,' Tayte said. 'I'm Volker Strobel's grandson.'

He didn't yet know if that was true, or whether Strobel would care, come to that. But right now he was happy to say anything he thought might buy him some time.

Fleischer laughed at him. 'Is that so?'

'You know otherwise?'

Fleischer shook his head, and Tayte thought he must have planted an element of doubt in the man's mind. He could see it in Fleischer's eyes—a questioning look that asked, 'What if it were true?' Tayte helped Fleischer's thoughts along in that direction.

'What if I'm right?' he said. 'What if I'm right and you shoot me? How's that going to reflect on you when Strobel finds out?'

'*Wir sollten sie mitnehmen*,' the knifeman said.

'What was that?' Tayte asked. 'What did he say?'

'He says we should take you to see him.'

'Well, maybe you should. Maybe this isn't your call to make.'

Tayte thought that if he and Jean were taken to see Strobel, it would at least postpone the sentences hanging over them. But while he had plenty of questions he wanted to ask Strobel, he preferred to do so on his own terms. These thugs had already said too much. They had admitted to knowing Strobel, and more importantly they had made it clear that they knew where he was. Tayte knew there would be no way back once they had seen him, if indeed there was any way back now. Getting that gun still seemed to offer the best chance of getting out of there. But how?

'Bring them,' Fleischer said, and the knifeman grabbed Jean as the muscleman came for Tayte.

Fleischer relaxed the gun a little then, and Tayte's eyes fixed on the broken display monitor on the desk beside him. He didn't think he'd be able to turn and pick it up in time to hurl it at Fleischer before he managed to squeeze a shot off, but he was all set to give it a go when an alarm bell started ringing, and suddenly the room was being showered with water from the sprinkler system. The building's fire alarm had been triggered and Tayte could only think that Tobias Kaufmann had arrived and realised that Tayte and Jean, and his member of staff, were in trouble.

Tayte didn't waste a second. As the alarm bells began to ring and the water came down, Fleischer momentarily turned away. At that moment, still high on adrenaline, Tayte grabbed the monitor and launched it at Fleischer, sending him crashing into one of the upturned desks. The gun went off, sending a bullet into the ceiling, and Tayte leapt on top of Fleischer as he tried to get up again. He could see the muscleman still coming for him, but faster now. He had to get the gun, but where was it? Fleischer had dropped it in the fall.

A split second later, Tayte saw it resting among the strewn papers to his left. He leapt at it, aware that Fleischer had grabbed his legs in an attempt to stop him. But Tayte was tall and he had a long reach. He managed to curl a finger around the trigger-guard just before the muscleman arrived beside him. Then as Fleischer climbed on top of Tayte, he twisted around, and with both hands gripping the gun he shoved the muzzle into Fleischer's chest.

'Stop!' he yelled, his eyes wide with fear, his heart now thumping at an alarmingly fast rate. He could see his hands shaking as he clenched them tighter around the gun.

The muscleman stopped in his tracks as Fleischer's hands went up. There was no move either man dared make to disarm Tayte. With the gun pressing into Fleischer's T-shirt, he would have known Tayte could pull that trigger and put a bullet in him as soon as he so much as twitched. Tayte didn't know whether he could actually pull the trigger, but Fleischer seemed in no hurry to find out.

'I didn't have you down as the hero type,' Fleischer said.

'It's called self-preservation. Now don't try anything or I *will* shoot you.'

'Calm down, cowboy,' Fleischer said. 'It doesn't have to end this way.'

Someone else spoke then. 'Drop the gun,' the knifeman said.

Tayte's eyes were locked on Fleischer's, reading the situation between them. In his peripheral vision he saw that the man with the knife had Jean again.

Jean called out. 'Don't you dare!' she said, and Tayte knew she was right. If he dropped the gun now, they were both as good as dead.

'Tell your friend to drop his knife,' Tayte told Fleischer, his tone firm.

Fleischer scoffed. 'He never listens to me.'

Tayte shoved the muzzle of the gun harder into Fleischer's chest. 'So we'll wait here like this until the police arrive. Who do you think set the fire alarm off? There isn't a fire, and it didn't go off by accident.'

Fleischer's expression soured, and Tayte saw in his eyes that he had him beat. A second later Fleischer raised his hands higher.

'*Lass die Frau gehen*,' Fleischer said, and the knifeman let Jean go. She took his knife from him and tossed it across the room, where it became lost in the debris that was now Tobias Kaufmann's main office.

'Now tell the big guy to back off,' Tayte demanded, and once he had, Tayte snarled at Fleischer and added, 'Now get off me!'

He kept the gun trained on Fleischer the whole time, and slowly, carefully, they disentangled themselves from one another until they were standing several feet apart, the gun locked in Tayte's grasp between them.

'Now I want you to empty your pockets,' Tayte said. 'All of you!' He didn't want any surprises. 'Throw everything down onto the floor where you're standing and walk slowly to the back of the room.'

To Tayte's surprise there were no complaints. Fleischer and his men did exactly as they were told. Jean came and stood beside him.

'I feel sick,' Tayte said, quietly out of the corner of his mouth.

'Hang in there. You're doing great.'

Together they watched Fleischer and his gang unload their pockets: more knives, a set of brass knuckles from the muscleman, some coins and the keys to their motorcycles. Jean picked up one of the knives and went over to the man who was lying bound and gagged on the floor. She cut him loose and without saying a word he ran from the room as though it really was on fire.

'Now move,' Tayte said to Fleischer and his men, flicking the gun towards the back of the room. Since he did now have the gun, he didn't plan to run or let anyone go. He hoped it was Tobias who had set off the fire alarm, and he hoped he really had called the police. In which case, all Tayte figured he had to do was to keep everyone there until help arrived. He followed the gang slowly towards the back of the room until they reached the door to the Strobel room. It was already open and Tayte could see from the mess beyond that they had already been to work in there.

'Inside!' Tayte said, and as Fleischer backed into the room after his men, his eyes locked on Tayte with a hateful stare.

'I'm going to find you,' Fleischer said. 'And when I do, I'm—'

'Yeah, yeah. Whatever,' Tayte said, cutting him short. He stepped closer to reassert his command of the situation, forcing Fleischer back into the room until Tayte was standing in the doorway, ready to close it on them. 'Just get in there. I'm tired of your threats.'

Tayte was about to shut the door when he heard the main office door open.

'The police are on their way,' Tobias called in, and the distraction, which had served Tayte so well before, now served Fleischer.

Tayte lost his concentration for just a second, but it was long enough for Fleischer to turn the situation to his advantage. As Tayte's eyes fixed on him again, he saw Fleischer dodge to his left in a blur so as to avoid any bullet Tayte might have had time to fire. But Tayte did not have time because Fleischer's next move sent Tayte's gun hand smashing into the edge of the aluminium door frame. It sent such a shock of pain through him that he was forced to let go of the gun. It clattered to the floor somewhere inside the Strobel room and Tayte knew he wouldn't be able to get to it first this time. As Fleischer turned to retrieve it, Tayte slammed the door shut.

'Go!' he called to Jean and Tobias, and in his next breath he pulled a filing cabinet over so that it was partially blocking the door. He turned to see Jean fumbling among the clutter, wondering what on earth she was looking for. Then as he ran to her he saw that she'd picked up a set of motorcycle keys. A shot was fired, and behind them now as they went, Tayte could hear the metallic thump of the door to the Strobel room being kicked against the filing cabinet. He knew it would only hold the gang back for a few seconds.

They caught up with a confused Tobias Kaufmann in the stairwell. Tayte grabbed his arm. 'We've got to get out of here!' he said. 'Where's Amir?'

'He took off,' Tobias said. 'That's why I came up. The police are—'

'They won't get here in time,' Tayte interrupted. 'We have to go.'

They reached the street and Jean went straight to the parked motorcycles. Tayte gave Tobias a gentle push in the opposite direction.

'Run!' he said. 'Just like Amir. Keep going and don't stop until you're safely away from here.'

Tayte heard a door slam in the offices above and knew Fleischer and his men were at the top of the stairwell. There wasn't much time. As Tobias set off, Tayte ran to Jean, who was trying the key she'd picked up in one of the motorcycles. She shook her head and moved on to the next one.

'They're coming!' Tayte said. 'We need to go now!'

'I'm going as fast as I can,' Jean said. She'd moved on to the third bike. She turned the key and the motor fired into life. 'It's always the last bloody one, isn't it? Get on!'

It was a BMW motorcycle, the same make as the one Jean had back in London, only this was much smaller. Hers was a tall, enduro machine, which was more suited to Tayte's size, whereas this was more like a sports bike, but without the fairing. Jean kicked up the stand and revved the motor, and Tayte honestly didn't think there was room for him on the postage stamp of a seat behind her, but a shout from behind him quickly forced him to try. He barely had to swing his leg up to mount it. The suspension sank as he lowered himself and locked his arms around Jean's waist, and then the front wheel suddenly lifted off the ground momentarily as Jean opened the throttle.

Above the sound of the engine Tayte thought he heard sirens wailing in the near distance. As they sped off, he glanced back and saw Fleischer. He was aiming the gun at them, but he must have thought better of pulling the trigger. Contrary to how Tayte felt about riding pillion again after what had happened the last time, he was never more glad to be on the back of a motorcycle again.

Chapter Thirty-Two

Conscious of Max Fleischer's threat to find him again, and not wishing to discover what the man was going to do to him if he did, Tayte had suggested to Jean that they relocate to a different hotel for their last night in Munich. Following another restless sleep, he was now back at the hospital with Jean, sitting in the waiting area with several walk-in patients.

After their ordeal at the offices of *Kaufmann und Kaufmann* the evening before, Jean had ridden the motorcycle hard until Tayte felt the need to tell her they were safe and that she could stop. If he hadn't, he thought her adrenaline would have kept her going until the bike ran out of fuel. They had abandoned it somewhere close to the city centre, and from there they took a taxi to the police station to report what had happened. Tayte let the police know where the motorcycle was, and Jean forwarded a copy of the licence plate photograph she'd taken in the hope that it might help to identify the members of Fleischer's gang, although Tayte figured the bikes had probably been stolen or had false plates.

On the way to the hospital that morning Tayte had asked the taxi to stop off at Tobias Kaufmann's office to check that he was okay. He also wanted to collect his briefcase. Since leaving it behind he'd felt as if a part of him was missing and he was keen to get it back, but he'd found that the entrance to the premises had been secured with a heavy chain and padlock, and he couldn't raise an answer from within. He'd tried Tobias's mobile phone a few times that morning, but every call had gone straight to voicemail. Tayte had learned from the police that Tobias was okay; he'd been picked up at the end of the street as the police arrived. Tayte hadn't been surprised to hear that Max Fleischer and his two sidekicks had fled the scene just moments before the authorities arrived.

'Jean Summer!'

Tayte's ears pricked up at hearing Jean's name.

She stood up. 'Shouldn't take long,' she said, and then she went over to the nurse who had called for her.

Tayte watched them talk for a moment. Then Jean came back.

'That was quick.'

'I wish,' Jean said, frowning. 'Some of yesterday's test results were inconclusive and they want to run them again. It could take a while.'

'Inconclusive? What does that mean? You're okay, aren't you?'

'It doesn't mean anything yet. Just that they don't know. They said they would hurry things through so we don't miss our flight.'

Tayte checked his watch, aware that he'd told Jan Statham he'd be with her at the Munich *Standesamt* first thing.

'Look,' Jean said. 'I know you told me you weren't letting me out of your sight until we're back in London, but we don't have a lot of time left. Why don't you go to the record office while I do what I have to do here? We can meet up afterwards.'

Tayte shook his head. 'I don't want to leave you. After what happened last night these people know we're still digging.'

'Good,' Jean said, a little indignantly. 'Personally, I'm tired of these people trying to scare us off. Remember they're only doing it because we're on to something. We must be.'

Tayte liked her spirit, and he couldn't argue with her logic. 'I suspect Tobias Kaufmann must be on to something, too,' he said. 'Why else turn his place over like that?' Tayte had been wondering about the motive and the timing of the attack on the Kaufmanns' offices all night. He figured the reason had to be connected with whatever Tobias had found from 'following the money' as he'd put it.

Jean agreed. 'And he's going to be excited when we tell him we know Strobel is still very much alive.'

'He sure is,' Tayte said. 'And if Fleischer was going to take us to him, he can't be too far away. He must have come to Munich after all, as Kaufmann's insider said he would.'

'So keep digging,' Jean said. 'I was fine here all by myself yesterday, and I'll be fine again today. Besides, Jan Statham might be too busy to see you later. What if she's found something?'

The thought put a smile on Tayte's face. 'She was looking into Ava Bauer for me.'

'Yes, you told me.'

'I think Ava could be pivotal in this.'

Jean laughed. 'You don't have to convince me. Go and find out while there's still time. You know you'll only regret it when we get back to London if you don't.'

Tayte knew Jean was right. 'You'll wait here until I come back for you?'

'Right here,' Jean said. 'This area of the hospital's always busy. Fleischer would have to be crazy to try anything.'

'That's exactly what I'm worried about.'

'You know what I mean,' Jean said. She gave Tayte a playful smile. 'Besides, it's you he's after now, remember?'

'Only too well,' Tayte said. He leaned in and gave Jean a kiss. 'You'd better go. The nurse is waiting. Call me as soon as you're ready to leave.'

'I will. And I know I keep saying it, JT, but be careful.'

Tayte gave her a cheesy smile as he made for the exit. 'Careful is my new middle name,' he said. 'Don't you worry about me. I'll be back before you know it.'

—⌣—

As Tayte sat in the back of the taxi on his way to Munich's civil registration office, his thoughts were preoccupied with Ava Bauer and the idea that she was the most likely candidate for his paternal grandmother. As for his paternal grandfather, all Tayte knew was that his mother and her husband, Karl, had gone to see the Kaufmanns in connection with tracing Karl's father, which suggested to Tayte that Karl had at least considered the possibility that Volker Strobel was his father. Yet, if Ava was indeed Karl's mother, then given that she was married to Johann Langner during the Second World War, there was every possibility that Langner was Karl's father. Tayte closed his eyes and shook his head as he wondered how on earth he was going to prove any of this. He had to remind himself that he was still working on little more than a hunch. He thought it was a pretty big hunch, given his findings, but in his line of work he knew that it was the facts that really mattered. He just had to find them.

'Find the child,' he told himself, 'and you'll find your family.'

Tayte had become so lost to his thoughts that the journey seemed to take no time at all. He only snapped out of them fully when the taxi pulled up outside the Munich *Standesamt* and the driver asked for his fare. Tayte checked his watch. It was just before ten—a little later than he'd hoped. He took his phone out as he walked towards the entrance and tried Tobias Kaufmann again, but as before, his call went straight to voicemail. He supposed Tobias must be busy sorting out the mess Fleischer and his gang had made.

'Mr Tayte!'

Tayte spun around to see Jan Statham pacing towards him with a spring in her step as she tried to catch up. She was wearing a light green trouser suit today. He stopped and met her smile, noticing that she had a paper tray of hot drinks in her hand.

'Good morning,' he said. 'I'm sorry I'm a little later than I said.'

'That's quite all right,' Jan said. 'It's not like we're running to any kind of schedule, is it? I thought you wouldn't be much longer so I popped out and got you a fresh coffee.'

She handed one of the paper cups to Tayte. 'Jan, you really are a lifesaver,' he said. 'And please call me JT.'

They went inside, taking the stairs up to the same office area as before.

'Did you manage to find anything?' Tayte asked.

Jan's reply didn't sound too promising. 'Not as much as I'd hoped to,' she said. 'I've found some basic records for Ava Bauer, but . . .' She trailed off as she opened the door to the small meeting room, which was just as it had been when Tayte left it the day before. 'Well, here we are,' Jan added. 'You'll soon see.'

They sat down with their drinks and Jan slid a folder between them. 'I found three records for the Ava Bauer we're interested in,' she said, opening the folder. She laid out the records. 'You've already seen her marriage certificate, and I couldn't find anything else to suggest she ever remarried. This is a copy of her birth certificate. It tells us she was born here in Munich in 1917, to Adelina and Gerhard Bauer.'

Tayte recalled Ava's parents' names from the marriage certificate he'd seen the day before. From his jacket pocket he took out the piece of paper he'd written their details on, glad that he hadn't put it in his briefcase. '*Musiklehrer?*' he said, picking up on one of the many German words written on the certificate. 'Did her father teach music?'

'Very good,' Jan said. 'See, you're picking up the lingo already.'

Tayte saw a name he recognised then. 'Schröder,' he said, more to himself than to Jan.

'That was Adelina Bauer's maiden name,' Jan said, highlighting the entry for Ava's mother with her finger.

Tayte unfolded his piece of paper, knowing that Schröder was one of the names he'd written down the day before. 'Heinz Schröder was one of the witnesses on Ava's and Johann's marriage certificate,' he said, knowing now that Heinz was another family member on Ava's mother's side.

Jan brought the copy of Ava's and Johann's marriage certificate into view. 'Yes, here he is,' she said. 'You're quite right.'

Tayte drew a line under his name. So far he'd seen Ava's birth and marriage certificates, but there was one other record Jan had found for him. 'Is that Ava's death certificate?' he asked, supposing that if it was, it would soon enlighten him as to why Johann Langner's son, Rudi, had never known the woman his adoptive father had married during the war. Jan's answer was unexpected.

'No, I couldn't find a record of death for Ava,' she said. 'I did manage to obtain a copy of her christening record, though.' She slid it towards Tayte. 'Apart from telling us the religion of her parents, the only other information it gives us that we don't already have is the names of her godparents, who I've already confirmed are her maternal grandparents.'

Tayte added their names to his list: Gottfried and Krista Schröder. 'So there's no record of death for Ava?' Tayte asked, seeking clarification.

Jan shook her head. 'It doesn't mean there isn't one, of course. Just that her death wasn't recorded here in Munich. I even contacted a few colleagues in neighbouring offices to see if they could find anything.' She shook her head again. 'We'd need to know where she died, really. Assuming she has died, of course.'

Tayte thought Ava might even have emigrated after the war. Many people did. In the absence of being able to locate a death certificate for her, he decided he would have to keep an open mind for now about whether Ava was still alive or not. It was a possibility, although she would be almost a hundred years old. If she was alive, he thought it all the more curious that she and Johann had not remained together after the war. From everything Langner had told him, Tayte was of the impression that he'd been besotted with Ava, and yet his son, Rudi, had never so much as met her.

Tayte thought back to his first day in Munich, when he and Jean had gone to see Johann Langner at the hospital. He thought about Langner's parting words again, and now more than ever he considered that the answer to these questions could very well be related to the 'terrible thing' Langner had told them Volker Strobel had done. But while Tayte knew he could begin a long quest to find out precisely where and when Ava died, and whether she was still alive, that wasn't why he was there. He had to stay focused. He was looking for a child—his father.

'Did you look for any dependants?' he asked. 'I'm particularly keen to find out whether Ava had any children.'

Jan nodded. 'Yes, I did.' Her nod turned into a shake of her head. 'I couldn't find any.'

'That's okay. I didn't expect this to be easy.'

Tayte turned to the names on his list and began to go over his earlier thinking about the possibility of a child having been brought up by another member of the family. Ava's parents were good candidates, but apart from them only one other name really stood out for Tayte. It was the name he'd previously underlined: Heinz Schröder. Tayte figured he was most likely Adelina Schröder's brother—Ava's uncle. Ava's christening record told him that her maternal grandfather was called Gottfried, so Heinz couldn't have been Ava's grandfather, which Tayte thought might have made him too old to be a potential candidate. The fact that Heinz had been a witness at Ava's and Johann's wedding also told Tayte that they had been close at the time, which to Tayte's mind made Heinz Schröder, along with Ava's parents, the obvious choices. He didn't know who the other witness, Lorenz Richter, was—perhaps a friend or neighbour, or even someone provided by the registration office on the day of the wedding. He couldn't rule anyone out, but it made sense to start with the strongest candidates.

'I'd like to see everything you can find for Ava's parents, Gerhard and Adelina Bauer, née Schröder,' Tayte said. 'And for Heinz Schröder here,' he added, tapping the witness section on Ava's and Johann's marriage certificate.

Jan looked at it again. 'I see he lived in Gilching at the time of the marriage,' she said. 'I'll have to call the Starnberg *Standesamt*. It's not far from Munich. Gilching is a municipality of Starnberg, you see.'

'Great, and as there's a family connection to the area, perhaps you could ask them to dig out whatever they can find on Ava's parents, too. Do you know how long it's likely to take?'

'Hard to say. I'll tell them it's urgent and have them send the results over electronically. While they're working on all that, I'll see what I can find here.'

'Thank you, Jan,' Tayte said with a smile. 'I'll sit on your shoulder, if you don't mind—see if I can learn something.'

Jan laughed. 'I shouldn't do that,' she said. 'Big fella like you. You'll squash me flat!'

Tayte was smiling at Jan's joke as they stood up. He followed her out into the large office area to make her call to the civil registration office in Starnberg, and as she dialled, he began to feel optimistic about the results he hoped would come back. Family history was all about making connections, and as Jan began to give her counterpart in Starnberg the information they had on Heinz Schröder from Ava's marriage certificate, the back of Tayte's neck began to tingle at the thought of what new connections he might soon discover. More importantly, he wondered where they would lead him next.

Chapter Thirty-Three

Gilching. 22 April 1945.

'There's no one home. Hasn't been for months.'

Johann turned away from the house he'd been directed to on his arrival in Gilching and saw an elderly woman standing by the gate in boots and a long overcoat. The wide-brimmed hat she wore was still dripping rain from the downpour Johann had just been caught in. She was a short, stocky woman. She had a sour expression on her face and a quizzical squint in her eyes.

'What's your business here?' she added.

Johann approached her with caution, unsure from her brusque tone whether her interest in him was well meant. 'I was told that my wife's uncle lives here. Herr Schröder?'

'This is Heinz Schröder's house,' the woman said. 'He's not here.'

'Do you know where I can find him?'

'Your guess is as good as mine. His last letter was from Holland, but that was several weeks ago.'

'Holland?'

'That's what I said. Has the war made you deaf? Both his boys were in the *Wehrmacht*. They died on the Russian Front. At hearing the news, Herr Schröder took off.'

'And what of his wife?'

'*Frau* Schröder died more than ten years ago.'

'I see,' Johann said, already contemplating what to do next. It occurred to him then that Volker could not have called on Herr Schröder to enquire into Ava's whereabouts, as he had said in his last letter. How could he have if Herr Schröder was not there? Johann wondered why Volker would lie to him, or whether there had been some mistake. Clearly, his next move was to contact his friend to find out.

'You're SS?' the woman said, eyeing Johann's apparel.

The *Sieg* runes on his tunic were barely visible beneath his greatcoat, but her keen eyes seemingly missed nothing. Johann nodded.

'Why aren't you fighting?'

Johann was about to explain how he came to be there when it began to rain again.

'Never mind,' the woman continued. 'You can tell me later. You look as though you need something to eat more than you need to stand around in the rain explaining yourself to an old busybody like me.' She took Johann's arm and led him out into the lane, which was no more than a muddy track between hedgerows. 'Look at you,' she added. 'You need dry clothes, too. You're shivering.'

'I must go back to Munich,' Johann protested. 'There are things I have to do.'

'*Ja, ja.* All in good time. If you don't take better care of yourself, pretty soon you won't be able to do anything.'

Johann found that he didn't have the strength to resist the woman, and how his stomach groaned. He'd lost track of how long it had been since he'd last eaten. They came to another gate and turned onto an even muddier track that ran to a single-storey dwelling with a smoking chimney. Johann couldn't deny that it looked inviting after all he'd been through since fleeing Vienna five days ago. The woman took him inside and led him to a bedroom where she began to undress him. It was only then that she could see how dishevelled he really was. His wet clothes were close to threadbare in places and torn in others.

She tutted. 'If you're all that stands between me and the Russians, heaven help us!' she said. She soon had Johann stripped to his underwear. 'I'll leave you to deal with the rest. You'll find blankets in the closet.'

'Thank you,' Johann said, and the woman left the room with his clothes over her arm.

Johann could have collapsed onto the bed beside him and not cared if he ever woke up again were it not for his need to find Ava. For now he found the blankets and began to wrap them around him, catching his pallid, malnourished body in the dressing table mirror as he did so. He wondered how it was possible for one man to collect so many cuts and bruises and yet still be able to stand long enough to look upon himself as he did.

Drawn by the heat from the fireplace, he found the old woman in the sitting room. She was putting more logs onto the glowing embers as he entered.

'Sit down,' she said, indicating the chair closest to the fire.

As the logs began to flame, instantly brightening the otherwise grey afternoon, the woman left Johann to gaze into them with his thoughts. A short while later she returned with a steaming mug in one hand and a hunk of bread in the other.

'It's soup,' she said. 'It's all I can offer you for now.'

Johann took it and immediately began to devour the meal. The soup was almost too hot to drink, but he didn't care. He gorged himself for a full minute until it was all gone. 'Thank you. I'm Johann. What's your name?'

'I'm Frau Olberg,' she said. Her tone softened. 'You can call me Martha.' She sat down opposite him. 'Now what are you doing in Gilching? Are you a deserter?'

Johann didn't like to think of himself as such, but he was unable to deny it. His reasons seemed justifiable to him under the circumstances, and they were certainly not borne out of fear or cowardice. But as he had made no attempt to rejoin what remained of his regiment, he doubted a court martial would see it that way.

'I plan to find my unit again as soon as I've finished my business in Munich,' he said. 'I've come from Vienna. The Russians overran the city and we retreated.' He went on to tell Martha about the air attack and the shelling. 'Something struck my head,' he continued. 'When I regained consciousness I found myself alone with nothing but the bodies of my *Kameraden* around me. If anyone survived the attack, they must have fled for their lives, but it seems the shelling was only a farewell as no Russians came for me. They must have had another objective in mind. Berlin, I suppose.'

'You were lucky. I've heard what the Russians do to their prisoners.'

'Yes, I was lucky,' Johann said. 'But then only the lucky survive such things.'

'That's likely true enough. How's your head? Let me see it.'

Martha stood up and began to inspect Johann's head. It took no time to find the wound. 'The blood has dried in your hair. I'll have to clean it. Does it hurt?'

'Not any more.'

'Good.' Martha sat down again. 'So why are you here?'

Johann briefly explained the situation with his wife and her parents, and how he had decided he must return to Munich to find out what had happened to them.

'I had a motorcycle,' he continued. 'It had taken a little damage, but it still ran, so having no idea where else to go, I rode through Linz and then to Salzburg. The fuel ran out soon after I crossed the border into Germany. After that I was forced to make the rest of the journey by bicycle and on foot.'

'You have a bicycle?"

'No. I picked it up near Rosenheim, but I was forced to take a less direct route, off the main road, across the countryside. Both tyres punctured and I had to abandon it. I had to be careful to avoid the Gestapo and the SD, who I'm sure would have taken me in for questioning had they spotted me. My reconnaissance skills came in handy, I can tell you.'

Johann paused. The effort to talk had begun to make him feel dizzy, and he could still feel himself shivering, despite the dry blankets and the heat from the fireplace.

'You're sweating,' Martha said. 'I felt your head just now. You have a fever. You should lie down and rest.'

'No,' Johann said, thinking of Ava. 'I'll be okay in a moment.' He closed his eyes and took a few slow breaths before he continued. 'When I reached Munich I went straight to my wife's parents' house. It was boarded up as I expected it to be, but I had to see it for myself. Then I came here, hoping Ava's uncle could help.'

'And what will you do now? How will you find her?'

'I must return to Munich. Perhaps a neighbour knows something, and there's a friend I need to speak to.' Johann started to get up. 'Do you have a bicycle I could borrow?'

'Yes, but your clothes . . . They will take hours to dry and you need to rest.'

'No, I can't,' Johann insisted. He stood up and immediately began to sway. He put a hand on the back of the chair to steady himself. 'Thank you, but I must—' He paused. The room was suddenly spinning. He took a step towards the door, and then another. And then he collapsed.

Chapter Thirty-Four

Present day.

Tayte had been at the civil registration office in Munich close to two hours, and it was approaching midday by the time Jan Statham had exhausted her search for records on Ava's parents. They were still waiting on the records concerning Ava's uncle, Heinz Schröder, from the Starnberg office, which Tayte hoped wouldn't be too much longer. He was conscious of the time, thinking that Jean could call him away at any minute.

As they went back into the small meeting room and sat down, Jan set the documents out between them, and having paid close attention to everything she had done, Tayte found that he had now picked up many of the basic words and phrases that were relevant to genealogical research in Germany, giving him a better understanding of what he was looking at. Jan had also run a search for records relating to Heinz Schröder, but she had found nothing more than an entry in the *Geburtsregister*, recording his birth in Munich in 1887. All other events had clearly been registered elsewhere, such as at the Starnberg office, under whose jurisdiction Heinz was living at the time of Ava's and Johann's wedding.

Tayte picked up the copy of Adelina Bauer's birth certificate. 'There are fewer records here than I'd hoped for,' he said. There was another birth certificate, this one for Ava's father, Gerhard Bauer.

Tayte held the two records side by side. 'Between these two birth certificates we have the names of both sets of Ava's grandparents, and the names of both her maternal and paternal great-grandmothers. It would all be highly useful information if I was trying to build Ava's family tree, but that's not why I'm here.'

'No,' Jan agreed. 'I'm sorry we couldn't find any record of death for either of Ava's parents. I'd have thought perhaps their deaths might have been registered in Munich as they were born here and lived here. Still, you can't say we didn't try. People are prone to moving about, aren't they?'

Searching for Ava's parents' death certificates had taken up most of the time, not least because finding them would have given Tayte hope of locating a last will and testament, and because of that he hadn't wanted to stop searching until every avenue had been exhausted. He figured that if Ava had had a child that had been brought up by Ava's parents then there was a good chance of finding mention of that child in their will. But they had found nothing, suggesting that Adelina and Gerhard Bauer had died outside the areas covered by the Munich *Standesamt*, necessitating a wider search, which, unless those records were covered by the Starnberg office, would take time—perhaps more time than Tayte had.

The only other record they had found for Ava's parents was from the *Heiratsregister*—Adelina's and Gerhard's marriage certificate. Tayte picked it up as he set the birth certificates down.

'This at least gives us another name to look into,' he said, looking at the witness section. 'I'd imagine Kurt Bauer here is Gerhard's brother. Maybe he was his best man at the wedding.'

'That seems likely,' Jan said. 'He's not mentioned on any of the other certificates. He's not his father or grandfather.'

Tayte highlighted Kurt Bauer's place of residence. 'I don't suppose this address falls under the Munich *Standesamt*, does it?'

Jan adjusted her glasses and took a closer look. 'No, Ingolstadt is to the north of Munich. I can call them.'

Tayte checked his watch again. He had no idea how much longer Jean would be at the hospital, but he supposed she must be waiting on her results by now. As for his research, he wanted to follow every lead open to him while he was there.

'Would you mind?' he said, starting to feel a little awkward because of all the running around Jan was doing on his behalf.

Jan didn't seem to mind in the least. She sprang to her feet. 'Wait there and I'll see if I can rustle up another cup of coffee for you while I'm at it.'

Tayte didn't know what he'd done to deserve such kindness and enthusiasm, but he was grateful. 'Thank you,' he said with a wide smile on his face. 'I really do appreciate it.'

As Jan left the room and Tayte sat back with his thoughts, he took out his phone and pulled up Jean's number. He thought he'd try to see how she was doing, to gauge how much time he had, but his call went to voicemail. He figured she was somewhere inside the hospital complex, where phones had to be switched off. As he cleared the call down, he saw Tobias Kaufmann's number on his recent calls list and tried him again. This time Tobias picked up.

'Tobias, it's JT. I've tried you a few times already. I figured you must be—'

'What a morning!' Tobias said, cutting Tayte short. 'The police have been back. I've had the fire service in, and the security people. It's a disaster!'

'I'm sure you must be very busy, so I won't keep you,' Tayte said. 'I was just wondering what you were going to say last night. You told me you'd been following the money.'

'Yes, I was going to show you something, but now I can't find it. I have some interesting financial records for you to see, but the place is in such a state, I'm afraid they could be anywhere. That's if they're still readable. Everything's wet from the sprinklers!'

'I see. Well, perhaps I could drop by with Jean this afternoon. If you've not found them by then we could lend a hand.'

'I could certainly use a few helping hands around here, that's for sure,' Tobias said. 'Amir refuses to come in. Mind you, who can blame him after what happened? By the way, I have your briefcase.'

'Great. I meant to ask you about that. Is it okay?'

'It's about the only thing in this place that is.'

In the background, Tayte could hear Tobias moving things around, presumably while holding his phone to his ear. There was a grating sound, followed by a thud and a curse. Tayte thought he'd better leave him to it.

'We'll come over just as soon as we can,' he said, feeling more than a little sorry for the man.

'Okay, I'll see you.'

There was another clatter in Tayte's ear, and he thought Tobias must have dropped the phone because a second later the call ended. He heaved a sigh as he turned back to the desk and the records in front of him. His thoughts turned to Ava again. He hoped he was right about her having had a child. He began to doubt himself, wondering whether his need to find his family hadn't driven him to make rash decisions, led by nothing more than wishful thinking.

'There has to be a child,' he told himself, considering that he had biological parents and grandparents, just like everyone else. He had to come from somewhere—from someone. 'And why not Ava Bauer?'

Keep digging, Jefferson . . .

Those familiar words echoed through Tayte's mind, but they were not his words. They belonged to his old friend, Marcus Brown. Tayte could see his face now, uttering words of encouragement as he had always done in the past. 'Keep digging. Never stop until you find what you're looking for.' It was something of a genealogist's mantra between them, and Tayte planned to adhere to it.

'There has to be a child,' he told himself again.

Chapter Thirty-Five

Munich. 26 April 1945.

Johann Langner spent four days in Gilching. Having collapsed by the fireside in the company of his host, she had put him to bed where he drifted in and out of consciousness in a state of constant delirium. In his wakeful moments he was aware of Frau Olberg watching over him, soothing his brow with cold towels, until gradually the savage images of war that would make him cry out in his sleep succumbed to peace. On the morning of the third day, his fever broke, and by the afternoon he felt well enough to get out of bed, his determination to recover having been fuelled by his need to find Ava.

Johann's legs still felt weak as he pedalled through the outskirts of Munich on Martha's rattling old bicycle. Whatever its state, Johann was grateful for it. He had set out from Gilching early, beneath an overcast sky, and he had taken frequent breaks out of necessity along the way, avoiding the busiest places as best he could. Johann was also grateful for the civilian clothes he now wore, which belonged to Ava's uncle, Heinz Schröder. He had chosen the dullest clothing he could find in Herr Schröder's wardrobe so as not to stand out, and he wore a cap pulled down over his brow. Martha had warned him that many of the people had turned against the military, the SS in particular, because the people blamed them for the lack of food, and the destruction and poverty the war had brought about. She feared that if he wasn't picked up by the Gestapo and shot for desertion, then the people of Munich would almost certainly try to lynch him from the nearest tree if they knew he was a member of the once elite *Leibstandarte*.

It was late morning by the time Johann turned the bicycle onto Landsberger Strasse, which followed the main railway tracks to the station terminal. Here, evidence of the bombings was soon everywhere he looked—the railway having been a key target for the Allied air strikes. He was looking for a public telephone booth. He was desperate to speak to Volker and he knew he couldn't just cycle up to the gates of the concentration camp at Dachau and ask to see him as he had before. Things were very different now that he had no papers allowing him to be there.

As the bomb damage only seemed to increase the closer he came to the main railway terminal, Johann decided that any telephone booths still standing in the area were unlikely to work. So he made a turn and headed towards the centre of the city, which he had hoped to avoid. As the streets became busier he found himself looking away from everyone he passed, and from every vehicle that passed him. Then somewhere along Sonnenstrasse he saw the word *Fernsprecher*—long distance. The red telephone booth had a small queue standing outside it, which was a good sign. Clearly it was in working order.

Johann cycled past it and turned into a narrow alley. He propped the bicycle against the wall and pretended to adjust the chain so as not to arouse suspicion as he watched the booth. He had a frustrating wait as it seemed that every time someone left the queue, another person joined it. This pattern continued for thirty minutes. Then when the last person entered the booth, he pulled his cap further down over his eyes and left the alley to wait outside it, hands thrust deep into his pockets, nervously flicking at the coins

Martha had given him. His shoulders were scrunched and his head was bowed low. When the occupant came out, he turned away and coughed into his hand. Then he slipped inside.

Volker had previously given Johann a telephone number for the administration building at Dachau concentration camp, and Johann had written it in his *Soldbuch*—the personal identification and pay book given to him as a new recruit when he joined the *Leibstandarte*, which he had since been obliged to carry everywhere with him. He lifted the handset from its hook on the side of the receiver box, inserted his coins, and dialled the number. A few seconds later the call was answered.

'Hello?' Johann said. The line was poor. 'Could I please speak to *Lagerführer* Strobel?'

'Please state your business.'

'It's a personal matter. I need to speak to him urgently.'

'Are you family?'

'No, I'm a friend.'

'Well, I'm sure you can understand that *Lagerführer* Strobel is a very busy man. I cannot interrupt his duties without first verifying the urgency of your call.'

'I told you, my reasons for calling are personal. If you can just let him know I'm on the line, I'm sure he'll want to speak to me.'

Johann was squeezing the handset tightly in frustration. He wanted to slam it against one of the telephone booth windows, but he constrained himself. Outside he could see that there were already two people waiting.

After a considerable pause, the man at the other end of the line sighed and said, 'What is your name, please?'

'Does it matter?'

In a more aggressive tone, he asked again, 'Your name, please.'

'It's Langner. He'll know who I am.'

'One moment. I'll see if *Lagerführer* Strobel is available.'

Johann inserted the last of his coins as he waited, listening to the static clicks on the line for what felt like an eternity. Outside, he saw that the queue had built further, and he could see that those who had been waiting longest were growing impatient. Someone tapped on the window and he turned his back to them.

'Hello? Herr Langner?'

'Yes, hello,' Johann said with urgency.

'I'm afraid *Lagerführer* Strobel is not available. I'm sorry.'

It was not what Johann wanted to hear. 'Did he give you any message for me?'

'No, there was no message.'

Johann couldn't believe it. He began to doubt then whether this man had found Volker at all. Surely his friend would have something to say to him.

'Did you speak to him yourself?'

The man's tone became impatient. 'As I said, *Lagerführer* Strobel is a very busy man. Goodbye.'

The call ended and Johann just stared into space for several seconds as he tried to understand the situation. Volker, it seemed, did not wish to talk to him. Another tap-tap at the window snapped him out of his thoughts and he quickly hung up the handset. There was a sarcastic cheer from someone in the queue as he opened the door and left at a pace with his head bowed low, knowing that if anyone so much as saw the youthfulness in his eyes, they might stop him to question why he was not fighting for the *Reich* in what now seemed to Johann to be its dying days.

Johann continued south along Sonnenstrasse, pedalling as fast as his limited strength would allow before dizziness threatened to overcome him. He slowed down, and he was panting hard as he turned off onto Lindwurmstrasse in the Ludwigsvorstadt district, heading for the borough of Sendling, southwest of the city, where Ava and her parents lived. He had hinged so much hope on the belief that his friend would have at least some answers for him, but now that hope had been dashed. He tried to tell himself that Volker was simply too busy to speak to him—as the person he had spoken to on the telephone had suggested. With the Allied forces pressing in from the west and the Soviet army coming ever closer from the east, he supposed that Volker had far more important matters to attend to. He suspected there was more to it, however, and that troubled him.

Johann's only idea now was to return to Ava's home. He thought perhaps a neighbour might have seen or heard something that could prove useful to him in his search. He knew he would be running a great risk as he would have to knock and ask questions at every door without first knowing who would answer, but it was a risk he had to take. The road he was on ran into Sendling, which was essentially a residential quarter. When he reached the end of Lindwurmstrasse, he turned left, heading towards the spire of St Margaret's church at Margaretenplatz. The area seemed eerily quiet, as though the soul had been stripped from the place in the time since he last saw Ava there.

He passed the church and turned into the road where Ava lived, wondering whose door to knock on first. He could see Ava's home further down on the right. He rode up to it, thinking to start with the immediate neighbours, but when he pulled up at the kerbside and dismounted the bicycle, he glanced at the house again and noticed that some of the boards were missing. He was sure of it. A week or so ago, when he had called at the house before going to Gilching, the doorway had been fully boarded. Now there were at least four planks missing from the lower section. His hopes lifted when he thought that perhaps Ava and her parents had returned home, but he was equally conscious of the fact that the boards could have been removed by looters.

Johann approached the house with caution and saw the missing boards in a loose pile to the side of the porch. The door was set back and just visible through the gap, enough to see that it was ajar. He ducked his head and passed through, teasing the door further open. Once inside, he was greeted by a stale and musty odour. The air was cold and it was too dark to see much at first, but his eyes quickly adjusted and he knew the place well enough. Ahead of him, a narrow staircase ran up from the entrance hall to the first floor. The family room was on his left and the kitchen and dining areas were straight ahead. He stepped further in and suddenly froze as he heard a rattling sound coming from the family room. The door was open and Johann stepped carefully towards it, until he was standing in the frame.

The sound came again and Johann's eyes were drawn towards it. This room was partially lit by the gaps in the boards at the window, and in the half-light he saw the silhouette of a man in an overcoat, bent over a cabinet, rummaging for something—valuables, Johann supposed. He despised looters, who preyed on the misfortune of others. He leapt at the man, grabbed him by the shoulders and spun him round, pinning him back against the cabinet.

'Get out of here!'

Johann drew his fist back ready to hit the man, whom he could now see more clearly. He was an older man, perhaps in his fifties. He looked terrified.

'Candles!' the man said. 'I was looking for candles.'

'Johann?'

Johann's muscles went limp at hearing his name, but it was not the man before him who had spoken. It was a woman's voice. She sounded weak and frail, and so very old. He let go of the man and turned around. And there, sitting in an armchair with blankets piled around her, he saw a woman he barely recognised. The grey daylight from the gaps in the window boards revealed a gaunt and pallid face. Her head was shaved, and her hollow eyes seemed to stare back at him. Johann was immediately reminded of those unfortunate souls he'd seen at Dachau when he went there to see Volker. It was Ava's mother, Adelina, and in her lap . . .

No, it can't be.

Johann had to step closer, convinced that his eyes were playing tricks on him in the half-light. But it was true. She was holding a baby.

Chapter Thirty-Six

Present day.

Following Jan Statham's phone call to the civil registration office in Ingolstadt, having asked them to retrieve the vital records they held for Ava's paternal uncle, Kurt Bauer, Jan came back into the meeting room where she had left Tayte, and he thought she had even more of a spring in her step than when she'd left. Her face was full of smiles. She had several printouts in her hand, and Tayte imagined they were the reason she was so excited.

'Wow, I've heard about German efficiency,' he said with a grin. 'Don't tell me they've sent the records for Kurt Bauer over already.' He was grinning because he knew full well that such a feat was impossible in such a short time frame.

'No, silly. They're from Starnberg,' Jan said as she sat down.

She placed the printouts onto the desk in a pile in front of Tayte, and he immediately began to share her excitement. On top of the pile was a printout from the *Sterberegister*. It was for Adelina Bauer.

'Ava's mother,' Tayte said as he recognised her name.

'Month of death, May,' Jan said, showing Tayte the corresponding column on the record. 'Year of death, 1945.'

'So Ava's mother died just as the war was ending.'

Jan nodded. 'The cause of death says *Lungenentzündung*. That's pneumonia.'

Tayte took a deep breath as he wondered whether the record offered any significance to his search. Adelina Bauer had died prematurely, but he imagined many people did for one reason or another during those dark years. He turned to the next record. It was from the *Heiratsregister* showing Heinz Schröder's marriage in 1910 to Frieda Schäfer. Jan had already found Heinz's birth certificate, which Tayte slid across to keep Heinz's vital records together. The following printout showed another entry from the *Sterberegister* and Tayte sighed to himself at seeing it.

'Heinz's wife also died prematurely,' he said, noting that the death certificate, or *Sterbeurkunde*, for Frieda Schröder had been issued in 1933, twenty-three years after their marriage. 'She was only forty-two years old.'

'Some of the records I see are enough to make anyone weep,' Jan said. 'It took me a while to get used to seeing people's lives laid out like this—sometimes a birth certificate one year, and then a death certificate for the same child a few years later. You deal with it, don't you, but I don't think it's something you ever really get comfortable with, or want to for that matter.'

'I know exactly what you mean,' Tayte said. 'I find it can help to look for the positives. In this case I'd like to think that, although Frieda's life was cut short, she spent twenty-three happily married years with Heinz before she died.' Tayte turned to the next record. It was a birth certificate. 'And look, they had a son, Franz Schröder, born in 1913, just before the Great War.'

'That must have been a hard time for Mrs Schröder.'

'I'm sure it was,' Tayte said, turning to the next record and reading the word *Sterbeurkunde* again.

'Oh dear,' Jan said when she saw it. 'That's her boy's death certificate. 1942.'

Tayte nodded. 'What does this mean?' he asked, pointing to the section where the reason for death appeared. '*Gefallen.*'

'It simply means fallen,' Jan said. 'Heinz Schröder's son was killed in action during the war. Look here, it shows the place of death as Russia.'

Tayte shook his head. Whatever side a person was on during a war, he imagined that every parent shared a common grief at such a loss of their child. He turned to the next record. It was another birth certificate—a *Geburtsurkunde*—for a second son, Werner, born little more than a year after his brother Franz. Tayte hung his head over the next record when he saw that it was almost identical to the previous death certificate.

'Two sons killed on the Russian Front in the same year.'

'Perhaps it's a mercy their mother had already passed away by then,' Jan said. She shook her head. 'Terrible times. I don't know how any mother could cope with such news.'

'Or father, come to that,' Tayte added. 'By the end of 1942, poor old Heinz Schröder seems to have lost all his immediate family.'

'There's a couple more records to go,' Jan said, prompting Tayte to look at the next one.

'This is another marriage certificate,' he said, scanning the details. 'In July 1945 Heinz Schröder married Helene Schmidt.'

'It's nice to know he remarried.'

Tayte smiled. 'See, that's a positive, right there.'

There was nothing particularly noteworthy about the marriage. The bride's address told Tayte she was a local woman, perhaps someone Heinz had known for some time, given that his first wife had died more than ten years earlier. The witnesses were a neighbour called Martha Olberg and another member of the Schmidt family. Tayte turned to the last record, and as soon as he saw it a shiver ran through him. His breath caught in his chest as he scanned the details.

'Karl Schröder?' he said, unable to believe his eyes.

'Does that name mean something to you?'

Tayte nodded. 'It's what I'm looking for. At least, I think it is.' His eyes were all over the document, taking everything in, and at the same time trying to understand what this discovery meant. He was looking at a copy of Karl Schröder's birth certificate. The father was listed as Heinz Schröder, the mother as Helene Schröder née Schmidt. The place of birth was shown as Gilching. 'This was issued in September, 1945,' he added.

'So it gets even more positive for Heinz,' Jan said. 'He had another son. This time with his new wife, Helene.'

Tayte scrunched his brow. 'I don't think so. See here. The date of birth is shown as February, 1945, yet this certificate wasn't issued until September that year, seven months later. The date of birth is also five months before Heinz and Helene were married.'

Jan looked more closely. 'That's curious then, isn't it?' She pointed to something written on the record. 'And this field asks whether the child was born legitimate or illegitimate, and it says "*legitim*", which is something of a contradiction, too.'

'I think that what we're looking at here is an amended birth certificate. I don't believe Heinz and Helene are Karl's biological parents at all.'

'You think he was adopted?'

Tayte reminded himself that if this was the Karl he was looking for, the same Karl who had later married his mother, then he had gone to see Tobias Kaufmann's father, Elijah, back in the 1970s with a view to tracing his parentage. If Karl had believed that Heinz Schröder was his biological father, Tayte could see no reason why Karl would have done that. There would have been no need to look any further.

'I'm sure you're aware that it's common practice to change the facts on amended birth certificates so it appears as if the adoptive parents are the child's biological parents. The place of birth can be changed to suit the adoptive parents' address, even the date of birth can be altered. I think on this occasion the date of birth must be correct, or it would likely have been amended to something closer to the date when the child was named.'

'That makes sense,' Jan said. 'They don't call them "amended" certificates without good reason, do they?'

'No, they don't,' Tayte said, thinking that his own birth certificate showed he was born in Washington, DC, where his adoptive parents brought him up, but he had later come to see that for the falsification it was.

'So, do you think Karl is Ava's child?'

'I think there's a very strong possibility,' Tayte said. 'We don't know what became of Ava yet, but it's fairly certain she was no longer with Johann after the war. I don't know why just now,' he added, thinking again about the terrible thing Langner had said Strobel had done. 'If Ava had a child, though, it's possible that by the end of the war, she might not have been able to look after it. And here we have a child adopted by Ava's maternal uncle. The timing of the adoption certainly fits, and Heinz's birth record tells us he was born in 1887, so he would have been fifty-eight years old in 1945, when he and Helene adopted Karl. That could be considered a little old to want another child, don't you think?'

'Yes, I suppose so,' Jan said. 'Although I imagine there were plenty of displaced children in Germany around that time, because of the war. I shouldn't think his age was so much of a barrier to adoption as it might be today.'

'No, and especially if the child was from your own family and there was no one else around who could look after it. We already know Ava's mother, Adelina, died in May the year Karl was adopted.'

'The original birth certificate should be able to confirm it,' Jan said. 'Although it might not be so simple to find it, let alone obtain permission to see it.'

'I'm sure it would take too long,' Tayte said, knowing that such sealed original birth certificates could be very difficult to get at, even if you were the person named on the certificate. He turned to the last record. 'Here's Heinz Schröder's death certificate. He died in 1959, age seventy-two.'

Tayte did a quick calculation, noting that Karl would have been fourteen at the time of Heinz's death. He thought Karl couldn't have known he was adopted until sometime afterwards. Perhaps his adoptive mother had told him. He suspected Heinz must have taken the story of how Karl came to be adopted to his grave, or Karl wouldn't have had such a hard time trying to find his family after Heinz died.

Jan began to tidy the papers on the desk. 'Looks like we've run out of records. Any idea where you want to go with your research next?'

Tayte nodded. 'Yes, I do,' he said, considering that Johann Langner must know the truth.

He also considered the now strong possibility that Johann Langner was his paternal grandfather. Langner was married to Ava. That fact made him the obvious candidate for Karl's father, and yet there was that terrible thing Volker Strobel had done. Given all that Tayte had heard since arriving in Munich, he still couldn't rule out the possibility that Strobel was his grandfather.

Tayte sat back in his chair, his thoughts spinning wildly through his mind. He had plenty of information gathered in the records before him. They painted a picture of several interwoven lives, telling a story that in many ways backed up his hunch that Karl, who was in all probability his father, had been born to the Bauer family. But who was Karl's father? Tayte had to find out. He had to find a way to see the ailing Johann Langner again, to confront him about the matter while there was still time.

Chapter Thirty-Seven

Heading for the street outside the Civil Registration Office, Tayte took out his phone and called the German Heart Centre again, preparing himself for another clash with Ingrid Keller. Only this time he wasn't going to back down. If it turned out that Langner and Ava were Karl's parents, then he figured Keller had to soften a little when he told her they could be related.

'Hello,' he said as his call was answered. 'I need to speak with a patient in your care—Johann Langner. It's urgent.'

'One moment, please.'

Tayte kept walking as he waited for Keller's harsh tones to come on the line. He reached the street and started to look for a taxi to take him to the hospital, whether Keller refused him or not.

'Mr Tayte?'

'Yes, hello,' Tayte said. It wasn't Keller. The voice belonged to a man.

'I understand you wish to speak with Johann Langner. I've been in charge of his care while he's been with us.'

'Can I speak to him?'

'I'm afraid Herr Langner is no longer with us, Mr Tayte.'

Tayte stopped walking. 'He died?'

There was a hint of laughter in the man's tone as he spoke again. 'No, no, Mr Tayte. To the contrary. He was discharged this morning. Is there anything I can help you with?'

Tayte sighed with relief. He smiled. 'No, that's okay,' he said. 'Thank you.' He was about to hang up when he thought to ask, 'Do you know where he went?'

'Home, I should imagine.'

'Home,' Tayte repeated. 'Yes, of course. Well, thanks for your time.'

Tayte ended the call and stuck out his hand as a vacant taxi approached. As he climbed in the back he looked up the contact information he had on Langner from his earlier research. He had an address, but no phone number.

'Grünwald,' he said to the driver.

Then Tayte sat back for the ride and tried Jean's number again. As before it went straight to voicemail, telling him he still had some time left to follow his instincts before returning to the hospital. When the beep sounded in his ear, he left another message.

'Hi Jean, it's JT. I tried to speak to you earlier. I hope everything's okay. Anyway, I'll try again later. Call me as soon as you can. I think I've made a breakthrough. I'm pretty sure I've found Karl—in the records at least.'

Tayte ended the call thinking about Jean waiting around at the hospital for more results, and he imagined she must be bored senseless by now. As he put his phone away, he reminded himself that he'd promised to take her back to the Munich Residence before leaving the city, and he would do everything he could to keep to that promise, despite the decision to fly home earlier than planned. He thought that was sure to cheer her up.

Within the hour, Tayte was standing outside a pair of high wrought-iron gates in Munich's well-to-do residential suburb of Grünwald, which was to the south of the city centre. It was a green, parkland area on the right bank of the river Isar, which the taxi driver had informed him was the most expensive municipality in Germany. It was populated with lavish mansion houses and was home to the rich and the prominent, which Tayte thought suited Johann Langner's obvious success very well.

The early afternoon sun felt hot on Tayte's back as he strode up to the gates and gazed along the driveway, to the house he could only just glimpse through the low branches of the trees that partially obscured his view. He stepped up to the intercom, reached out his index finger to press the button, and then he hesitated, considering that he could be on the brink of discovering a truth he had spent the last twenty-five years of his life looking for.

'Are you ready for this, JT?' he asked himself.

He thought back to his visit with Langner at the hospital again, and he was reminded of something else Langner had said. 'Are you completely sure you want to find out?' he'd asked Tayte. 'Wherever it may lead? Whatever the repercussions?'

Tayte took a deep breath and straightened his back. 'Hell, yes,' he said under his breath. Then he extended his arm to the intercom and pressed the call button. 'Hello, it's Jefferson Tayte,' he said, leaning closer. 'I don't have an appointment, but I really need to speak to Johann Langner.' After a brief pause, and with a note of desperation, he added, 'Please.'

Tayte withdrew from the intercom and waited. When nothing happened he stepped closer again, pressed the button and said, 'I believe Johann Langner is my paternal grandfather. I just want to talk—to confirm things.'

There was still no response, and Tayte began to wonder whether there was anyone home. As his desperation deepened, he pressed the button a third time and said, 'I know Ingrid Keller is your daughter, Mr Langner. Mrs Keller, that means we could be family.'

Tayte doubted whether Keller had a soft side, but he figured if she did, and if she was listening, that ought to do it. After another thirty seconds passed in silence it was clear to him that he was either wrong, or no one was listening. He stepped away from the gates, turning his back on the house, and gave a frustrated sigh. He thought over all the research, all the discoveries he and Jean had made, and he felt sure he had to be right about Ava Bauer and the child. He turned back to the gates, and this time he almost sprinted up to the intercom.

'I know about Karl Schröder,' he said, his voice rising. 'He's my father.' He let go of the call button and in a softer voice, just for himself, he added, 'I know he is.'

When nothing happened, Tayte stepped away again. He began to walk back to the road, thinking to sit there and wait for someone to either go in or come out, but as he did so he heard a click and a whir, and he wheeled around to see the gates begin to open. There was no sound from the intercom, but he took it as a clear sign that his last words had reached someone inside. Now he was being invited in.

⁓

Not having his briefcase with him felt odd to Tayte. He missed it, although, as he hadn't been allowed to copy any of the records he'd seen at the Munich *Standesamt*, it didn't really matter that he didn't have it with him now. Just the same, he still didn't feel himself without it. The hand he usually carried it in felt awkward and somehow surplus to requirements, so he thrust it into his pocket and tried to forget about it. He hoped Johann Langner didn't have cause to ask him to prove any of what he'd just spoken into the intercom, because all he had was the list of names he'd scribbled down, and he didn't imagine that would carry much weight if it came to it.

But being right would, Tayte thought, and he supposed he was only being invited into Langner's home now because he was.

Partway along the drive, Tayte saw a man he recognised from his first day in Munich. It was Christoph, wearing the same grey suit he'd been wearing when he'd collected Tayte and Jean from the airport. He conveyed little warmth as they met, the limited familiarity between them seeming to curry no favour. Christoph's only words were, 'Please follow me,' which Tayte duly did, thinking the man polite and efficient, if rather more conservative with his words than Tayte would have liked under the circumstances.

He was led through the mansion's grand, marbled hallway, past a wide sweeping staircase and into a sunlit drawing room that looked out over what appeared to be a bowling green. Johann Langner was sitting in a wheelchair by one of the many windows, covered almost from head to foot in a barber's gown. Behind him, Ingrid Keller was trimming his hair. She didn't once look up from what she was doing, even to acknowledge Tayte's presence.

'Mr Tayte is here to see you, Herr Langner,' Christoph said, and with a sharp bow of his head, he left the room.

'Ah, Mr Tayte,' Langner said. 'Well, come and sit down. You must be weary. I know you've made a very long journey to get here, haven't you?'

'Yes, I suppose I have,' Tayte said, thinking that Langner was referring to the journey Tayte had set out on to find his family all those years ago. 'Thank you for seeing me again,' he added as he sat down on the sofa, facing Langner. 'How are you?'

'Good of you to ask, Mr Tayte. I'm pleased to say that I'm much improved.' He raised a hand towards the window, pointing. 'Do you play lawn bowls?'

Tayte looked out at the green, and then back to Langner. 'No, I can't say I've ever tried it.'

'I find it very therapeutic, and I'm sure the activity has helped to keep me going longer than I perhaps should have. Unfortunately, it's not very popular in Germany. I saw the game being played in England some years ago and I took quite a liking to it.' He laughed. 'Ingrid here has been my fiercest opponent,' he added, and Tayte didn't doubt him.

Langner's dry laughter trailed off. 'So, your research here in Munich has led you to believe that I'm your paternal grandfather, and that I have a son called Karl, who you believe is your father?'

'Yes,' Tayte said, knowing he still couldn't rule Volker Strobel out, and at the same time hoping that perhaps Langner could. He was more keen than ever now to hear about the terrible thing Langner had said his wartime friend had done. 'At least, I believe Ava Bauer is my paternal grandmother,' Tayte added. 'I know my mother married someone called Karl, and I found a Karl in the records, adopted by Ava Bauer's uncle—your wife's uncle—Heinz Schröder. I've come here in the hope that I can clarify that, and to confirm whether you're Karl Schröder's biological father.' Tayte paused and chewed his lip. 'Or whether perhaps you know of someone else who is.'

'Ah, you're referring to Volker Strobel, of course?'

Tayte nodded. 'You said previously that Strobel had done something terrible. Did it concern Ava? Why weren't you with Ava after the war? And how come your own adopted son, Rudi, knows so little about her?'

'So many questions,' Langner said, dry laughter in his voice again.

Tayte thought it sounded forced, perhaps to make light of a darker memory that had stirred within him. A moment later, Langner coughed and fell silent, as if composing himself. Then he swallowed hard, and Tayte thought a lump must have risen in his throat.

'I'm sorry to be so direct,' Tayte said to break the silence.

'That's quite all right. There's little point now in beating about the bush, as the saying goes. Rudi knows so little about Ava because until now I've chosen not to talk about her. As for the rest . . .'

Langner trailed off, and Tayte watched him lift his eyeglasses and wipe a tear from the corner of his one good eye. He reminded himself then to tread carefully. He didn't want to upset Langner to the point where Keller would once again feel obliged to ask him to leave.

Langner sniffed back his emotions, straightening his posture as best he could. Around him, fine wisps of white hair continued to fall to the snip, snip of Keller's scissors. 'I think perhaps it would be best if I concluded the story I began to tell you and your friend when you first came to see me. Then I think you might have the answers you're hoping to find.'

'That would be great,' Tayte said, beaming with enthusiasm.

Langner gave a slow nod. 'Very well then,' he began. He cleared his throat. 'Towards the end of the war I lost contact with Ava, so when the opportunity presented itself I came back to Munich to look for her. Vienna had fallen. Germany's once mighty military machine was beating a fast and final retreat to Berlin. The country was in chaos, but somehow through the smoke and the debris, I found my answers.'

Tayte saw Langner clench his fists then, as though angry at the memories that were fighting to free themselves from his obviously troubled mind.

'You want to know what terrible thing Volker Strobel did?' Langner continued. 'I'll tell you what that man did. Heaven knows I must tell someone, while I still can.'

Chapter Thirty-Eight

Munich. 26 April 1945.

At the boarded-up house of Ava's parents in the borough of Sendling, Johann Langner continued to stare at the baby cradled among the blankets in Ava's mother's arms with disbelief. At last he fell to his knees, his face lined with anguish, his mind full of questions to which he sensed the answers would reveal a terrible truth.

'Adelina! What happened? Where's Ava?'

A tear fell onto Adelina's cheek. She sat forward and held out the baby. 'She is here, Johann.' Her voice sounded laboured.

Johann shook his head. 'Where is she, Adelina? You must tell me.'

Adelina looked down at the baby and then back to Johann. 'Can't you see her?' She held the baby out again, this time into the light that shone in through the gaps in the boards at the windows. 'Look. He has his mother's eyes. Can you see her, Johann?'

Johann looked, and as his eyes met the child's he was taken back to the very first time he saw Ava Bauer. His own eyes began to well with tears. 'What are you telling me, Adelina?' His voice wavered as he spoke. He already knew the answer. 'Please, I need to hear you say it.'

Adelina turned away then, and Johann heard her sob.

'Say it, Adelina!' Johann's tone was firm now. 'I can't believe it otherwise.'

Adelina turned back to him and he knelt closer. 'Ava is dead, Johann. My daughter is dead.'

Johann held Adelina then as they both began to cry unreservedly. He could feel her frail body beneath the blankets she was wrapped in—feel her fragile bones shaking in his arms, the baby between them, silent and peacefully oblivious to the horrors of the world into which he had been born. When he felt he had no more tears left to cry, Johann withdrew, but he remained on his knees beside the armchair. He knew that if he tried to stand up at that moment he would only fall down again.

'And your husband? Is Gerhard also—'

Johann didn't need to finish his sentence. Adelina began to nod her head almost as soon as he began to ask. He let out a long sigh and wiped the tears from his cheeks.

'Tell me what happened, Adelina.'

'Don't you want to meet your son first?' Adelina said. She turned the baby to face Johann, and the baby's tiny hands began to grab at the air between them.

'My son?'

'Of course.'

All these months and Johann had no idea. He thought back to the last time he had seen Ava. It was in May the previous year, when he had been granted home leave. He had received only one letter from her since then, which was soon after his return to the Front. He realised that whatever had happened to the Bauer family must have happened soon after the child's conception, which by his calculations had to have been eleven months ago.

'Hello,' Johann said to the baby. He placed his hand over the baby's chest and felt his heartbeat. It was strong. He held the baby's hand, and those tiny fingers curled around his. 'I'm Johann. I'm your father.' The baby was smiling, but Johann could not. 'He's very quiet,' he said to Adelina.

'He's had to be,' she said. 'He would not have survived otherwise.'

Johann looked at Adelina again and thought how gravely ill she appeared. Only now did he think to ask, 'Have you eaten?'

The man Johann had confronted when he first came into the room was still standing by the cabinet he had been rummaging through, looking for candles. He answered for her. 'She's had soup. It's all she could manage.'

'And the baby?'

'Yes, my wife saw to it.'

Johann nodded. Turning back to Adelina, he asked, 'So where have you been? Dachau?' It was clear from her appearance that she had been held in a concentration camp. 'Is Volker Strobel responsible for this?' Johann didn't want to believe it, but why else had his friend lied to him about having visited Ava's uncle in Gilching, and why had Volker seemingly ignored him when he telephoned the camp earlier that day?

'The Gestapo came for us early one morning,' Adelina said. 'They took us to a cell and refused to answer any of our questions. We had no idea why we'd been taken. The following day we were told it was because we had been harbouring a Jew.'

'A lie?'

Adelina nodded. 'They brought a girl in and she pointed at us and told them we'd hidden her and fed her for several weeks. She was able to tell them things that could only have been known by someone who had been inside this house and knew it well. It was all the Gestapo needed to prove the allegation.'

'Volker?'

Adelina nodded. 'Although we didn't know it at the time.'

Johann felt his strength return to him in a heartbeat. It coursed through his veins as a rage unlike any he had felt before, even in battle, raced through him. The man he had called his friend had not only betrayed him, but the family that had welcomed him in with open arms.

'A short while later,' Adelina continued, 'we were sent north to the concentration camp at Flossenbürg, where we were allocated to sub-camps. I never saw Gerhard again after that. I heard that he'd been shot for protesting his innocence, and I almost lost the will to live, but Ava kept me going. She was already pregnant, of course, and when the guards found out they made her sign a form to say that the baby would be taken away from her as soon as it was born. She didn't want to sign it, but the guards were very persuasive. It was a euthanasia consent form.' Adelina paused and smiled at the child. 'As you can see, Johann, your son was not taken away. Ava died during the birth. She was so weak and malnourished, as every-one at the camp was. So it fell to me to look after her baby—my grandson.'

Adelina reached out a frail hand and began to stroke the baby's forehead. 'Several women in my hut helped to look after him, and if he had been any trouble, I'm sure he would have been taken away. I don't think anyone expected him to live long under such condi-tions, but he's strong, Johann. He's a survivor, like his father.'

Johann couldn't help but blame himself for Ava's death. Had she not been pregnant, she would likely have survived the ordeal along with her mother. But how could he have known? He looked at the child, and he certainly could not blame him. He reminded himself then that Ava's death was no fault of anyone's but the man he had once called his friend.

'Do you know why Volker had you arrested—why he set you all up with this story about harbouring the Jewish girl?'

Adelina nodded. 'He came to the camp twice. The first time was just a few weeks after we arrived. He spoke in private to Ava and Ava passed on what he said to me. He told her he loved her, and that he wanted her for himself. He told her she was to leave you, and that while it pained him to punish her as he was, he thought she needed to see just how much power he commanded. He told her he would keep us all at the camp until she changed her mind.'

Johann began to grind his teeth. Now he saw through Volker's visits to the Bauer house, bearing provisions to help ease the family through the hardships of war. It was all for himself, working his way into their trust, their friendship, with no other goal in mind than to have Ava for himself. 'And the second time?'

'On Volker's second visit he begged Ava to agree to his terms, saying that it tortured him to know she was suffering. But Ava resisted him, even then. She loved you so much, Johann.'

The thought of something so pure between them having been so cruelly destroyed, and by his best friend of all people, forced Johann to bite his lip to hold back his tears.

'A few months passed,' Adelina continued. 'I think Volker must have heard about Ava's death, and I think perhaps he was responsible for letting me look after her baby. I know he signed my release order. That was just a week ago. The Americans were close to Flossenbürg and we were being prepared to march out of the camp, but they let me go—just like that—with a simple piece of paper.'

Adelina reached a bony hand beneath her blankets, which seemed to take a great effort. Several seconds later, she showed Johann the slip of paper. 'These are my release papers, in case anyone stopped me.' She unfolded the document very slowly, as though every movement required all her strength and concentration. And there on the form Johann recognised Volker's signature.

'So his guilty conscience finally got the better of him,' he said. 'But it won't save him.'

'What will you do?'

'I'll take care of you and my son, and then we'll see.'

Johann turned to the man he had confronted when he first came into the room. 'Who are you?' he asked. His tone was short.

'I—I live across the street.'

'They can't stay here. It's cold and they need help. Will you care for them until I return?'

The man shook his head. 'My wife won't—' He paused. 'Look, we don't want any trouble.'

Johann sighed. 'Well, do you have a motorcar?'

'No, I—.'

'Can you borrow one?'

'Yes, but—'

'I need you to take us to Gilching. Will you do that much?'

The man seemed to think about it. Then he nodded. 'Yes, all right.'

'Good. We must go at once.'

Chapter Thirty-Nine

Present day.

At Johann Langner's home in Grünwald, Jefferson Tayte had been listening to the continuation of his host's wartime story with great interest. During the course of Langner's monologue, Tayte had also become knotted with anger over what had happened to Ava and her parents. Volker Strobel had done a terrible thing indeed, and while Tayte would have felt anger at hearing such a story about anyone's family, more and more he was coming to regard the Bauers as his own family, especially as he'd just heard that Johann Langner and Ava Bauer did indeed have a child together.

Ingrid Keller had finished cutting Langner's hair, and Tayte and Langner were now alone in the sunlit drawing room. Tayte appreciated his time together with the man he was now coming to think of as his grandfather, although he supposed Keller wouldn't be gone long. He sat back on the sofa he'd been perched on since his arrival at Langner's home and took a deep breath to calm himself.

'Thank you, Mr Langner,' he said. 'You don't know what it means to me to hear that you and Ava had a child. And you've cleared a few more things up, too,' he added, thinking about the Bauer family and the records he'd previously seen, and those he had not been able to see.

'How do you mean?' Langner asked.

'Well, there were no death records for Ava or her father on file at the Munich record office. They could have been recorded elsewhere, but I now know that's not the case. If they died at Flossenbürg concentration camp, maybe their deaths weren't recorded at all.'

'I see,' Langner said. He nodded. 'Yes, I'd say it was highly unlikely, particularly as they died close to the end of the war.'

Tayte thought about Ava's mother then and he recalled that she'd died in 1945. Now Tayte understood why. 'I saw a copy of Adelina Bauer's death certificate,' he said. 'I don't know if you're aware, but it appears that Flossenbürg killed her, too. She died soon after she was released, and it seems likely to me now that her death was as a result of her ordeal at the camp.'

'I didn't know that,' Langner said. 'I'm sorry to hear it.'

It was a sorry affair altogether as far as Tayte was concerned. No, not altogether. Something good had come out of it—the child. It seemed likely to Tayte now that he had become Karl Schröder, and if Karl really was Tayte's father then he had been born in a concentration camp at Flossenbürg, not in Gilching as was recorded on Karl's birth certificate, supporting Tayte's belief that he'd been looking at Karl's amended record, and that Karl had indeed been adopted. Tayte knew such seemingly miraculous births existed, although they were few. He'd read about them in newspapers and online, and with great fascination over how such fragile life can emerge and survive under such atrocious conditions. Yet here was another example of life finding a way.

Tayte was distracted from his thoughts when the door to the drawing room opened behind him and Ingrid Keller returned. She still hadn't spoken a word since Tayte arrived. He didn't know what he'd done to upset her, but it was clear that she'd taken a dislike to him. He thought perhaps she just had a sour disposition, and that she was the same with everyone. Rudi Langner had certainly backed up that notion, but Tayte couldn't see what he could do to win her over, so he dismissed it. He turned back to Langner to see Keller produce a nail file with which she began to manicure his fingernails.

'Someone's being pampered,' Tayte said in an attempt to lighten the atmosphere he felt Keller's presence imbued. 'Are you just glad to be out of hospital, or do you have a party to go to?'

Langner looked up from his hands, showing a hint of a smile. 'I'm being fussed over because I have an anniversary party to attend this evening.'

'For the gallery?' Tayte said, knowing it couldn't be a wedding anniversary. 'That's great. I'll bet you're thrilled to have made it out of that hospital in time.'

Langner chuckled to himself. 'I'm thrilled to have made it out of there at all,' he said. 'Now shall I continue my story before I forget where I was?'

'Absolutely,' Tayte said. He wanted to hear what became of the child, sure now that he'd been adopted by Ava's uncle, Heinz Schröder. He figured there had to be a story to explain how and why that came about, too, but for now he couldn't get past Langner's account of the terrible thing Volker Strobel had done. 'So what did you do about Strobel?' he asked, supposing that a fighting man in the ranks of Germany's elite *Leibstandarte* could not have let such a thing go without retribution.

Tayte knew at once that his question had stirred further dark memories within Langner. His fleshy cheeks sagged as he began to shake his head. A moment later he sighed heavily and said, 'I was so full of hatred. And one terrible deed can so easily lead to another, can't it?' He nodded slowly to himself, as though answering his own question. 'What did I do?' he repeated. 'I'm afraid an equally terrible repercussion followed Ava's death.'

Chapter Forty

Dachau. 26 April 1945.

It was late in the grey afternoon as Johann Langner continued to watch the main gatehouse at Dachau concentration camp from the cover of a ditch a hundred or so yards back. He was observing the vehicles coming and going, and he had noted that far more attention was being paid to those vehicles leaving the complex than to those entering, which was as he had expected. Vehicles leaving were searched so thoroughly he doubted anyone trying to escape could avoid detection. Vehicles entering, however, were given no more than cursory glances by the guards. After all, who in their right mind would choose to break into a concentration camp?

Johann was not in his right mind.

Upon his return to Martha's house in Gilching, the kindly woman had taken Adelina and his son in without question, and Johann knew she would care for them as best she could until his return. Just the same, he feared for Adelina. He had noted her decline even on the short drive out of the city. It was as if she were at last giving up her will to live now that she knew her charge, Johann's son, was delivered to him and was in safe hands. It made Johann all the more resolved to do what he knew he must now do.

As soon as Adelina and his son were made comfortable, Johann had changed back into his uniform, thinking that in the fading light of the afternoon, should he be seen at the concentration camp, he would blend in better than if he were wearing civilian clothing. Closer inspection of his now clean but battle-weary uniform, however, would single him out as a member of the *Leibstandarte* in an instant, potentially raising questions he knew he could not satisfactorily answer. He would have to be careful.

A supply truck approached the camp and Johann ducked back into the ditch so as not to be caught in its headlights. He listened, and when the truck drew level he climbed out from the ditch and ran along behind it, using it as a screen. The truck was ten feet high and covered with a tarpaulin that was lashed with ropes, which Johann thought he could use. As the vehicle approached the gate, it slowed. He had to act fast. As soon as the truck stopped, he grabbed the ropes and pulled himself up onto the roof, where he lay still and silent, listening to the words being exchanged between the guards and the driver as the driver was ordered to show his papers.

A moment later the truck's engine started up again and the gates were opened. Then the truck passed through, beneath the ever watchful gaze of the giant black eagle Johann had seen on his previous visit. He remained low as the truck moved through the outer layer of the complex, keeping still so as not to draw attention to himself should anyone glimpse the truck from above. But it was almost dark now, and he imagined the guards' eyes would naturally be focused towards the concentration camp. At least, Johann hoped they were.

A few minutes passed, and with every second Johann felt his pulse quicken. The supply truck turned one corner and another, and he tried to glimpse where it was taking him, but although he had been to the camp before, he was not well acquainted with its layout, especially in the fading light. When at last the truck came to a stop, he waited, breathing slowly to calm himself. He was outside an open-fronted, single-storey building, and seeing an assortment of military vehicles parked inside, he realised the truck had pulled up outside a garage block. He kept his head down as he heard the truck's doors open. Then the loading ramp at the back was dropped with a slam that jarred his nerves.

He heard talking, and within a minute the footfalls of several men could be heard as they began to unload the vehicle. Johann realised then that he had to climb down before they finished or he would find himself heading out of the camp again, and if that happened, there was no doubt in his mind that he would be caught. He crawled closer to the front of the truck's roof, away from the activity, and peered out over the bonnet, wondering where to head for once he'd climbed down. He thought his best cover was among the parked vehicles inside the garage block, but then he heard a clanking sound ahead and to his left—metal tinkling on concrete, as if someone had just dropped a wrench. He thought a mechanic must be working on one of the vehicles further along, and he reminded himself to be cautious.

A moment later, the conversation at the back of the truck became suddenly lively, and it seemed to Johann that someone was telling a joke because the men were soon laughing riotously. Johann used the din to mask any sound he made as he swung his legs out over the edge of the roof and lowered himself onto the bonnet. He looked around to make sure the way was still clear, and then he walked ahead at a regular pace, using the truck for cover as he had before, staying in the blind spot of the men unloading it. When he had taken ten paces unchallenged, he ducked into the garages, dropped to the floor and rolled beneath the nearest vehicle, where he planned to wait until the supply truck had gone and the fading sky had turned to black.

Close to an hour passed before Johann ventured out from the vehicle he was hiding beneath. With no moon or stars visible in the overcast sky, only the dim camp lights lit his way as he headed back out from the garage block in the direction the supply truck had brought him in. He kept to the shadows as best he could, which were thankfully plentiful. The complex was busier than he had hoped it would be, but everyone he saw or heard seemed so heavily wrapped up in their duties that he managed to make good progress. He sensed the heightened activity was in no small part related to the news that must surely have reached the camp commandant that the Allies were at Munich's doorstep.

The darkness that now helped to conceal Johann, however, also hindered his ability to recognise the buildings he had seen on his last visit. Because of this it took him a while to get his bearings. Having left the garage block, which was a small complex of buildings in itself, he crossed the road he had come in by to the trees opposite. Looking back he could see the buildings at the end of the SS troop barracks Volker had previously shown him. Volker's accommodation then was back towards the administration buildings, across the courtyard by the main gate and past the bakery. The thought of crossing such an open space, which was well lit, did not encourage Johann, but there were few options left open to him.

He kept to the shadows for as long as he could, and when he came to the courtyard, he watched and waited for what he considered to be his best opportunity. Guards came and went, as did several vehicles and SS officers, and seeing those officers come and go with such ease made Johann think he would have to appear as one of them. After all, he was an SS officer himself, and he was in uniform. He just had to hope no one came close enough to see its condition, or to notice the regiment he served with. When the way was clear, he stuck his shoulders back and set out, telling himself to act as if he was supposed to be there. He reached halfway without challenge, but his resolve began to crumble when two guards turned the corner beside the bakery. They were heading straight for him.

Johann wanted to look away and change direction so as to avoid them, but he knew that to do so would only arouse their suspicion, so he kept going, and the guards drew closer. They seemed to straighten their postures as Johann approached. Would they notice the state of his uniform or that he was a member of the *Leibstandarte*? Would it matter to them if they did? Johann's heart began to thump as he asked himself these questions, and then they were upon him, no more than a few feet away. Both men saluted.

'*Guten Abend, Obersturmführer*,' one of the guards said, leaving Johann in no doubt that they had at least noticed his rank insignia.

'*Abend*,' Johann replied, his eyes fixed on the other side of the courtyard as they passed one another.

Johann kept going, but he was soon forced to stop.

'*Obersturmführer?*'

He turned back. The guard who had wished him a good evening approached.

'Please excuse my impertinence, *Obersturmführer*, but you have come from the Eastern Front?'

Johann nodded. Clearly the guard had indeed noticed the state of his uniform as well as his rank, but there was something about the guard's tone that put Johann at ease.

'I have a young brother,' the guard continued. 'He served alongside the *Leibstandarte* in the 12th SS Panzer Division *Hitlerjugend*. I've not heard from him in six months and was wondering whether you have any news from the Front? We receive so little information.'

Johann thought the guard sounded desperate to hear whether there was even the slightest chance that his brother might still be alive. He wished he could give the man hope, but how could he know? He shook his head. 'I'm sorry. I've come from Vienna. If your brother was there, you should pray for him.'

'*Jawohl, Obersturmführer.* I do, every day.'

With that the guard clicked his heels and saluted again, and both men continued on their patrol, leaving Johann to finish crossing the courtyard, now with a degree of reassurance that his presence at the camp had not so far raised suspicion. All the same, as he neared the first of the SS residential houses he was heading for, he thought he'd better not take any chances, so when he was sure no one could see him, he slipped back into the shadows of the trees that he'd noticed some of the houses backed on to. He recalled that on his previous visit, Volker had taken him through a gate to show him the SS officer housing. There had been guards at the gate then, and Johann supposed there would be now. He also thought they would be far more inquisitive than the two guards he had just met if he attempted to walk nonchalantly past them.

Johann soon came to a brick wall that was about eight feet high, which he imagined ran along the line of houses he was trying to reach. Assessing the situation, he saw that there was no barbed wire running along the wall, and he thought it would be easy enough to climb. He wondered then whether this wall was regularly patrolled by the guards. He suspected it was to some degree, but high security had clearly not been deemed necessary here, because again, he doubted those in charge of camp security expected anyone would wish to break in to the residential area beyond.

Johann looked along the wall and listened for signs of activity. He found none. The further along he went, the more dense the trees became until it was difficult to see anything at all in the darkness. He knew that Volker's residence was at the end of the line of houses he was moving perpendicular to, and as he followed the wall, using his fingertips to guide him, it occurred to him that the higher up the chain of command you were the further you lived from the sounds and smells of the concentration camp.

When the wall turned to his left, he thought he must have gone far enough, so he stopped and listened for activity again. Once he was sure there was no one around, he leapt at the wall and pulled himself up. He didn't dare linger for a moment. He swung his legs over and dropped to the other side where he landed with a thump. A quick appraisal of his surroundings told him he was in a well-tended garden, partially screened from the house by several shrubs of one kind or another.

Johann remained still for several seconds in case anyone had heard him enter the garden and was drawn to the sound. Then he looked out from the shrubs and saw that he had hit his mark. To his left he saw the row of houses, some with lights at their windows, others in darkness. They were a mixture of what appeared to be semi-detached family homes between small terraces that accommodated perhaps five or six SS officers each. He could see no more houses to his right, telling him that this was the last house on the appropriately named *Strasse der SS*, which fronted the buildings. The house before him, a small detached building no more than twenty yards away, was Volker's accommodation.

Johann thought there were sure to be guards in the street beyond, and perhaps even at the residence itself. He imagined that Volker, as the main camp's *Lagerführer,* might even have a small staff. There was a dim light at one of the windows on the ground floor. He couldn't know who was there for sure, but the light told him the house was not empty. Taking no chances he crawled through the garden on his belly, as if he were back at the *Ostfront,* until he reached the house, wondering now how he was going to get inside undetected.

He stood up with his back pressed against the wall. He was no expert at housebreaking, but he had to find a way to get inside now he was there. He stepped away and checked the windows. All appeared to be closed on both levels. There was a drainpipe that ran close to one of the upper windows, and it crossed his mind to try to climb it and break the window to gain entry, but he quickly decided that even if he made it to the window without falling, the sound of the breaking glass was sure to draw attention. This was a particularly quiet area. There was no sound here to mask his activity.

A path ran alongside the house. It was poorly lit by a pale and distant street lamp on the other side of *Strasse der SS*. Keeping low, Johann went around to the front of the house, his eyes peeled for the slightest sign of activity. There were lawns at the front of the houses and a few more shrubs here and there, which Johann used for cover as he left the pathway. From there he had a good view of the street. He peered along it and quickly ducked back again as he saw the flare of a cigarette lighter not thirty yards away. It illuminated the faces of two guards as they leaned in and lit their cigarettes. They were on the same side of the street as Johann, heading towards him, and at seeing them Johann was glad he hadn't tried to break into Volker's accommodation by smashing a window. If he had then the guards would have been on him in an instant.

He sank into the shrubbery as low as he could, and he kept still as they approached. Out of the corner of his eye he watched them amble past, and his eyes continued to follow them until they were lost to distance and darkness. They would return again, that much was certain, and Johann had no idea how long he had before they did. Wasting no time, he crawled out from his cover just enough to see the house more fully, hoping to find an open window, but there were none. The house appeared to be locked up tight. The light inside the house drew his attention and he crept up to the illuminated window, thinking to peer inside, but as he did so, the light went out.

Johann hurried back to the side of the house, and a moment later he heard the front door open and close again. Someone was leaving. He wondered whether it was Volker, but he soon saw that it was not. It was a woman, and at first Johann thought it must be Trudi Scheffler, to whom Volker had been married now for the past three years. But unless Trudi had put on considerable weight in that time, it was not her. He watched the woman button her coat as she set off at a stomping march down the street, and he supposed she must be a housekeeper or a cook. Perhaps she had prepared Volker's evening meal for when he returned. Johann couldn't know and it didn't matter. What did matter was that the house now appeared to be empty.

Voices from the direction the two guards had set off in suddenly drew Johann's attention. The guards were already returning on their patrol. Johann moved further back into the deeper shadows along the pathway at the side of the house until they passed, wondering again how he was going to get inside. He could see no quiet way to do it. Then it occurred to him that he would have to wait in the shrubbery for Volker to return.

Johann watched the guards come and go so many times that he soon learned their timing: three minutes beyond the house and back, twelve minutes in the direction the woman had gone. He had soon lost count of how many times they passed him and it was now quite late. He checked his watch. It was almost midnight. Then a short while later he heard a sound that was different from those he had grown accustomed to as he lay in wait for Volker to show. Someone else was approaching. His or her footsteps sounded markedly different from the guards' plodding footfalls. These steps had urgency—authority.

Johann felt his whole body tighten. Then he saw him and his heart began to pound in his chest as the rage he had felt earlier that day, at hearing what this man had done, burned once more inside him. There at last was Volker Strobel. Johann watched him stride up to the house in his immaculate uniform. He reached to unlock the door and by then Johann was already on his feet. As the door opened, he drew his Luger from its holster, and as Volker entered the house and switched on the hall light, Johann burst in after him, knocking him to the floor at the foot of the staircase. He kicked the door shut behind him.

'What did you do?' he seethed.

His head was shaking with rage and disbelief, even now, at the idea that anyone could imprison someone in a concentration camp simply because they had chosen to love someone else. He aimed his pistol at Volker's head and stepped closer. He had always had a steady aim, but now his whole arm seemed to shake as he extended it.

'Johann,' Volker began, but Johann silenced him.

'Get up!'

Volker got to his feet.

'In there,' Johann ordered, flicking his pistol towards the door on his left.

'You know if you shoot me the guards will come?' Volker said.

'Do you think I care? My parents are dead, and now, because of you, I have no one to live for.'

'What about your son?'

Johann didn't answer. He grabbed Volker by the collar and spun him around. He took Volker's pistol and slipped it into his pocket. Then he shoved him towards the door.

'Get in there!' he said again.

Chapter Forty-One

Present day.

Another interruption at the drawing room door caused Johann Langner to pause his wartime account of how he had dealt with Volker Strobel for the terrible things he had done to Ava Bauer and her parents. Tayte followed Langner's gaze as the old man was snatched back from his memories, to see Christoph enter the room.

'Excuse me, Herr Langner, but your car is almost ready. We should leave soon.'

The announcement, although it had not fazed the seemingly imperturbable Ingrid Keller, who had now moved on to shining Langner's shoes, seemed to surprise Johann Langner.

'Thank you, Christoph,' he said. To Tayte he added, 'The time goes by so quickly, don't you think? Even at my age, the long life I've led now seems little more than a blur to me. I'm afraid we don't have very long to finish my story.'

'Is there long enough?' Tayte asked, hope evident in his tone. He really did not want Langner to leave his account there. It wasn't a story Tayte felt could keep for another day, especially as he and Jean were booked on a flight back to London that evening.

'Oh, I think we might have just enough time,' Langner said. 'Now where were we?'

Tayte sat forward. 'You'd gone into the concentration camp at Dachau, looking for Strobel,' he said. 'You found him and forced him into his own accommodation at gunpoint. I'm keen to know what happened next.'

'Ah, yes,' Langner said. He nodded to himself, as though recalling the details that followed.

Tayte thought he was about to continue, but instead, he paused and fixed his eye on him.

'Are you absolutely sure you want to know what happened next?'

Tayte scrunched his brow. 'Yes, of course. Why wouldn't I be?'

'Perhaps because this is a past you might not wish to be connected with. Wouldn't you rather walk out of here now, go on with your life and forget about it?'

Tayte had come too far to throw in the towel now. He was in all the way.

'There's still time,' Langner continued. 'But if I go on, I'm afraid it will be too late for you to reject who you are.'

'I want to know who I am,' Tayte said, determined. 'It's all I've ever wanted to know. Please, go on.'

'Very well, but don't say I didn't warn you.'

Chapter Forty-Two

Dachau. 26 April 1945.

The light from the street lamp across the road outside Volker Strobel's accommodation at Dachau concentration camp shone a pale glow into the room, casting long shadows over the few items of furniture that occupied it.

'Draw the curtains,' Johann ordered.

By his estimation the guards would be passing the house again soon and he couldn't risk being seen, especially now that he'd made it this far. As Volker went to the window, Johann went to the table lamp he'd seen on entering the room. When Volker drew the curtains, Johann switched the lamp on.

'Now sit down.'

Johann flicked his Luger at one of the armchairs by the fireplace. It had been lit, in all likelihood by the woman he had seen leaving the house earlier, but at this late hour it was now reduced to glowing embers.

'Are we alone?' Johann asked. 'Where's Trudi?'

'We are perfectly alone, Johann,' Volker said, lowering himself into the armchair. 'Such beauty as Trudi possesses cannot exist in a place like this. Besides, Trudi would not live here any more than I would allow her to, but she visits often enough.'

Johann remained standing. 'You don't deserve her, or any woman for that matter.'

'Ah, so we come down to it. I cannot say I haven't been expecting you. I knew you must have discovered what had happened with the Bauer family when you called the camp this morning. You've done well to get this far.'

'It was easy,' Johann said. 'Although I had expected you here sooner. I've been waiting a long time for you to return.'

Volker scoffed. 'Haven't you heard? The enemy is at our door. There is much work to be done at Dachau.'

'Yes, the Devil's work,' Johann said, imagining the kind of work Volker was referring to. Ava's mother had told him that the camp at Flossenbürg was to be evacuated the day after her release. The *SS-Totenkopfverbände*—the Death's Head Units—were trying to cover up the atrocious things they had done in their concentration camps—things that people such as Volker Strobel would surely be made accountable for. 'You must be more than a little concerned about what will happen to you when the enemy arrives,' Johann added.

Volker laughed to himself, and although it was with a degree of sardonicism, it sickened Johann to think that the man before him could draw even the slightest amusement from any of this.

'Look at us, Johann,' Volker said. 'What happened to you and me, eh?'

'Do not compare us, Volker. I still know myself, but you! You've become a monster. A demon!'

'Then shoot me,' Volker said, his fingers digging into the arms of his chair. 'Shoot me and send me back to hell, where I belong.'

Johann raised his pistol. All he had to do was pull the trigger. It was that simple. He would pull the trigger and take another man's life, as he had done many times on the battlefield—only this man sitting before him was far more deserving of death than any of those soldiers who were only doing their duty, as he had been doing his. So why wasn't it that simple?

Friendship. Johann knew it came down to that. And for all the terrible things Volker had done, even now he wished his childhood friend, with whom he had spent so many happy years before the war, would say something to redeem himself. He had been the brother Johann had never known—the brother he had yearned for since learning that his flesh-and-blood brother had died as an infant. Johann stared into Volker's eyes, but he saw no trace of remorse. Even if there had been, even if Volker were kneeling on the floor in penitence, begging for forgiveness, Johann knew there could be no stay of execution for this man who was ultimately responsible for the death of his wife.

'Well, *Blödmann!*' Strobel said. 'What are you waiting for?'

Johann's arm began to shake again. He willed himself to pull the trigger and be done with it, but something, or someone, now prevented him. It was his son. Volker was right. If Johann fired a single shot, the guards patrolling the street outside would be at the door in seconds. It had been easy enough to get into Dachau, but he imagined it would be much harder to escape, especially with the camp on full alert after discovering the body of their *Lagerführer*.

'You can't do it, can you, soldier boy?' Volker continued, as if he were deliberately taunting Johann in an attempt to make him pull the trigger.

But Johann did not fire. As much as he wanted Volker to pay for all he had done, he could not deliberately leave his child fatherless as well as motherless. He was suddenly resolved to do all he could to return to Gilching. He had not yet held his son as a father should—as he doubted his own father ever had. Johann lowered his pistol and Volker sat up with a look of bewilderment on his face.

'You really can't do it, can you?' Volker said, his shoulders slumping as he spoke.

'You sound disappointed.'

Volker drew a long and thoughtful breath. 'Yes, perhaps I am. Perhaps in moments of weakness I'm shocked myself at the things I've done. And if you can't stop me then who will?'

'You can stop yourself.'

Volker laughed. 'You don't really know me at all, do you, Johann? You always look for the good in people, and I've always loved you for that, but there is no goodness in my heart. I used to look for it, questioning why I do the things I do, when I know I've caused pain and suffering. I've long since stopped looking. There is nothing there to find.' He relaxed back into his chair and pressed his fingers together in front of him, as if in contemplation. 'Let me make this easier for you, Johann. I'm going to tell you a story, and then you're going to shoot me. I promise you will.'

Johann frowned, wondering how Volker could be so sure.

'There was an adjutant here at Dachau before the war called Max Koegel,' Volker began. 'He became a good friend of my father's, and in turn of mine. When the war began, he was commandant of the concentration camp at Lichtenburg, and then at Ravensbrück. Currently, he's the commandant of Flossenbürg.' Volker paused and smiled at Johann. 'Now you begin to see where my story is going, eh?'

Johann felt his muscles tighten again. He already knew what Volker had arranged for the Bauer family, but he sensed he was about to learn something that Ava's mother had not told him.

'I'm telling you this,' Volker continued, 'because it's important for you to understand just how easy it was for me to incarcerate the Bauer family at Flossenbürg. And how easy it was for me to arrange special treatment for them if I so chose.'

'What kind of special treatment?'

Volker looked very pleased with himself now. 'Well, since you ask, let me tell you. The first time Ava refused me, I had her father shot.'

Johann's breath began to quicken. His hand tightened around the grip of his pistol, but he kept it at his side.

'The second time Ava refused me,' Volker said. 'The very last time she turned me away . . .' He paused, as though teasing Johann. He gave a sigh. 'I told you there was no good in me, Johann.'

'What did you do?' Johann asked through gritted teeth. A part of him did not want to hear the answer, yet he was compelled to know. 'Tell me!'

Volker sat forward again. 'The main camp at Flossenbürg is split into male and female sections,' he said. 'Perhaps you already knew that. Well, as a special treat for those prisoners who performed certain camp duties, a selection of the prettier looking women were sent into the male camp to satisfy their sexual needs.'

'Stop!'

'No, Johann. You have to stop me, remember?'

Johann put his hands to his temples and tried to knock the images Volker had put there from his head.

'The second time Ava refused me,' Volker repeated, louder now, 'I had her placed into this ring of whores, to be abused by so many filthy, sexually deprived men, over and over again until their animal desires were satisfied.'

'She was pregnant!' Johann seethed. He had tears in his eyes, and his muscles were bound so tightly now that his whole body began to shake. He aimed his pistol again.

'Yes, even while she was pregnant with your son,' Volker said. 'But then I'm sure that only added to the entertainment. Still, at least I got my ring back. It wasn't really my grandmother's, you know. I took it from an old Jewish woman who had no further need of it.'

When Volker punctuated his words with a satisfied grin, Johann could take no more. But instead of pulling the trigger, he hurled the gun at Volker.

'Shooting you would be too easy!' he said, and before the gun had clattered to the floor, he hit Volker hard in the face. He heard bone crack and he hit him again. He pulled Volker from the chair and threw him to the floor where he pinned him down with his knees and rained blow after blow down onto him until his face was a blood-red mask. Images flashed through Johann's mind of the first time he had met Volker. He was back in that corridor at the Hitler Youth training academy. Back then it had been the bully, Günther, who had rained punches down on Volker's face. Now it was Johann. Volker wanted Johann to kill him, and now Johann would do so gladly.

Volker offered no fight. Just as Günther had beaten him that day in the Hitler Youth, Johann now continued to beat him. He beat him until his arms felt too heavy to continue, and when at last he could not find the strength to throw another punch, he stopped. He looked down at the lifeless body beneath him, to the man he had just killed, and he could now barely recognise him as the friend he used to know. He rolled off Volker's body, his hands dripping with blood, and he lay silent and still for several minutes, until gradually his rage subsided and his strength returned.

At length Johann got to his feet, weary and exhausted. His only thought was that he had to leave Dachau and return to his son, but as he reached the door he heard a cough behind him and he stopped. He wondered how Volker could still be alive, yet he knew as he turned to face him that he was. In his hand, Volker was holding Johann's Luger.

'I lied to you, Johann,' Volker said, garbling his words as he wiped his own sticky blood from his jaw. 'I would not have allowed Ava to be violated. I worshipped her, don't you understand?

I wanted you to shoot me for what I did to her, but you let me down, my friend.'

With that, Volker aimed the pistol at Johann's head, pulled the trigger twice, and watched him slump to the floor.

Chapter Forty-Three

Present day.

At hearing what the old man in the wheelchair opposite him had just said, Jefferson Tayte felt the colour drain from his cheeks. He felt suddenly light-headed and nauseated, not least because he knew his life was in danger. He wanted to run for the door, but confusion and a degree of curiosity rooted him to the spot.

He swallowed hard and said, 'You're Volker Strobel?'

The old man nodded gravely. 'Yes, I'm Strobel. I'm *Der Dämon von Dachau*. And so you see, the second terrible thing I had to do, as a result of being responsible for the death of Ava Bauer and her family, was to kill my best friend. Now, as I warned you, I'm afraid it's too late for you to reject who you are.'

'I'm Johann's grandson,' Tayte said, almost to himself, still shell-shocked by the revelation that this man sitting before him had killed the real Johann Langner and hidden behind his name all these years. It pained Tayte to think that his grandfather had as good as survived the war, only to be killed by his best friend.

'So it would appear,' Strobel said. 'I know Johann's son, Karl, also had a child. From what you've told me I imagine that was you. But now we come to the consequences of who you are.'

With that, Ingrid Keller, who had been standing behind Strobel's wheelchair as he finished telling Tayte his story, produced a handgun and pointed it at Tayte. A moment later the door to the drawing room opened again and Max Fleischer entered, grinning from ear to ear. His gun was already drawn and now it, too, was trained on Tayte.

At seeing Fleischer, Tayte said to Strobel, 'So *The Friends of the Waffen-SS War Veterans* have been protecting you?'

Strobel laughed. 'The FWK don't know who I am. Max here has dealings with them, but he works for me. I knew his grandfather during the war.'

'Then the FWK had nothing to do with this?'

Strobel shook his head. 'I sent Max after you and your friend as soon as you left the hospital when you first came to see me. I arranged your friend's car accident, and prior to that I set you up for murder. We knew who the Kaufmann's insider was. By having Max kill him we were doing the FWK a favour, not that we could ever tell anyone. But you just wouldn't give up.'

'I see,' Tayte said.

'Do you? Do you really see?'

Volker Strobel removed his barber's gown in a flourish. Beneath it was not a smart business suit as Tayte had expected the old man would be wearing for his anniversary, but the uniform of a Nazi officer of the *SS-Totenkopfverbände*, replete with its Death's Head Unit skull insignia on the right collar tab.

It was suddenly clear to Tayte what kind of anniversary Strobel was being prepared for. An overwhelming flood of questions raced through his mind as he wondered how Strobel had managed to pull this change of identity off. Right now, though, he had other things to worry about. He had unwittingly walked straight into the lion's den with little to no hope, it seemed, of getting out alive. He thought about Jean, and he realised she would have no idea where he was. He hadn't even told Jan Statham at the record office where he was going. He'd been so caught up in the chase that he hadn't given it a thought, or felt the need to. As far as he knew he was visiting with Johann Langner, whom he had rightly believed was his grandfather.

Keller put her gun away and wheeled Strobel closer. She left the two of them facing one another and was replaced by Christoph, whom Tayte had not seen enter. He was still aware of Fleischer to the side of him, though—still aware that the man had his gun pointed at him. For now at least Tayte understood that he was at Strobel's whim.

Strobel sighed so heavily that Tayte could smell his decaying breath. 'I had long since thought this business was over,' Strobel said. 'But here you are. When you came to my gates and said you knew about Karl Schröder, I had to find out what you knew, and I quickly realised you knew very little. You should have taken the opportunity to walk away when it was offered to you, but you're so persistent, aren't you, Mr Tayte? Now I expect you'd like some answers for all the trouble you've gone to?'

'What does it matter if you're going to kill me?'

Strobel raised his eyebrows, as if shocked by the idea. 'Who said I was going to kill you, Mr Tayte? On the contrary, I'd like you to do something for me, in return for which I'll give you all the answers you could wish for, and your freedom.'

'And what if I won't do what you ask?'

That seemed to amuse Strobel. 'Oh, I'm sure you will, but if you truly can't then of course I'll have to kill you. The choice will be yours to make.'

Tayte was understandably sceptical. 'My choice? Really? So what is it you want me to do?'

'That's the spirit,' Strobel said. 'But first I'm going to finish my story. Don't you want to know what happened after I killed your grandfather?'

Tayte just gritted his teeth, supposing it didn't matter whether he wanted to know or not. He was going to hear the rest of the story anyway.

'Afterwards,' Strobel continued, 'I'm going to tell you about the time a young couple came to see me, much as you and your lady friend came to see me a few days ago. Their names were Karl and . . .' He trailed off. 'Now what was his wife called?'

Tayte wasn't about to remind Strobel of his mother's name, but it didn't take long for the old man to recall it.

'Sarah!' he said as the name came to him. 'That was it—Karl and Sarah. It was in 1963, when I opened my education centre. You remember, don't you? I'm sure you want to hear more about that.'

Tayte felt suddenly claustrophobic, as if the walls and ceiling were closing in around him. Knowing that his parents had unwittingly had anything to do with Volker Strobel made him fear what the old man was going to tell him.

'But, all in good time,' Strobel said. 'I'm running late.'

Tayte's stare was fixed on Strobel. Right there and then he wanted to reach out and wring the rest of the story from his scrawny old neck, but even if he could have been so brave, or foolish under the circumstances, the opportunity was quickly denied him. He saw Strobel nod his head briefly, not at Tayte, but past him. Then Tayte felt Ingrid Keller's cool hand press down on one side of his neck as a needle was thrust deep into his skin on the other. He winced, then his head rolled back and he saw Keller grinning down at him, right before he blacked out.

Chapter Forty-Four

Tayte had no idea how long he'd been unconscious. When he awoke he initially thought he was going to be sick, which he put down to whatever drug had been pumped into him. As the feeling passed and he opened his eyes, he found he still couldn't see anything. Wherever he was, he was in total darkness, although he quickly realised he was no longer in Volker Strobel's drawing room. The air was much cooler here and there was a dampness to it he could smell, as though he were in a basement somewhere. He was still seated, but when he tried to stand up he found himself unable to. He had been bound to something that rattled when he rocked back and forth in an attempt to free himself, although he was surprised to find that there was no gag at his mouth. He was about to shout for help when he heard a familiar tune. It was the show tune he'd set up as a ringtone on his phone. He snapped his head towards the sound and saw his phone glowing in the darkness as the call came in.

Jean . . .

Tayte struggled with his bonds again, but it served no purpose. He couldn't break free. A moment later he heard another sound and he froze. There were footsteps in the distance, growing louder. A few seconds later the room was flooded with light to such an extent that Tayte had to shut his eyes again and turn away from the door that had just opened in front of him.

'So, you're awake. It's about time, sleepyhead.'

It was Max Fleischer. Tayte was getting tired of hearing his accented English tones. Fleischer was also now dressed as a member of the *SS-Totenkopfverbände*, and Tayte supposed he must have walked in on Strobel's preparations for a neo-Nazi gathering of some kind.

Fleischer strode over to Tayte's phone and picked it up. He looked to see who was calling. 'It's your lady friend,' he said. He laughed. 'Don't worry. If you don't make it through this, I promise I'll take care of her for you.' With that, Fleischer opened the back of the phone and popped the battery out. 'We can't be too careful, can we?'

Make it through this? Tayte thought. *Through what?*

As Tayte's eyes adjusted to the light, he saw that he was strapped to an old wheelchair. He was in a small stone room that had been stripped of everything it had once contained, apart from the bright strip light above him and a crate of some kind, upon which his few personal effects had been set out. He heard more footsteps then and his attention was drawn back to the door as another wheelchair was pushed into the room. It was being guided by the taciturn Ingrid Keller, who Tayte now knew was not Johann Langner's daughter, but Volker Strobel's. Trudi Strobel's story about Johann coming to her after he was released from prison was a blatant lie. It had been Volker Strobel, returning to his wife, whom Tayte now imagined he had been seeing in secret all these years.

'Ah, Mr Tayte,' Strobel said. 'I'm afraid you missed my cere-mony. I was being honoured for my former services to the *Führer* and the Fatherland, and for the past fifty years to the Fourth Reich.'

'What time is it?' Tayte asked, sounding a little groggy from the drugs. He was no longer wearing his watch, which he supposed was on the crate with the rest of his things.

'It doesn't matter what time it is,' Strobel said. 'The only thing that matters now is whether or not you want to get out of here. Do you want to get out of here, Mr Tayte? Go back to your sweetheart and fly home, eh?'

That sounded good to Tayte, but after all he'd seen and heard, whatever Strobel promised him, he knew it wasn't going to happen. Even so, he had little choice but to play along for now. 'Yes, I'd like that very much.'

'Good! That's a very good start indeed. Now, you remember I said I wanted you to help me?'

Tayte nodded.

'Well, as I said, do this one thing for me and then you can go. But I don't want to do it in here.'

Strobel nodded to Fleischer. 'Bring him, Max.'

With that, Fleischer took hold of the wheelchair Tayte was strapped to and they followed Strobel and Keller out of the room. They were soon in a corridor that led along a stone-walled passage where Tayte saw exposed pipework, confirming his belief that he was in a basement somewhere. At the end of the corridor a procession of Nazi flags adorned the walls, lit by more of that overly bright and harsh strip lighting. They came to a door on which was hung a framed photograph of Volker Strobel as a young SS officer, shaking hands with a man Tayte recognised as Heinrich Himmler. Strobel must have noticed Tayte staring at the photograph as they waited for Keller to unlock the door.

'It was taken on one of Himmler's visits to the camp at Dachau,' Strobel said. 'I remember that his daughter, Gudrun, was with him.'

'Really?' Tayte said, sounding uninterested.

'Oh, come now, Mr Tayte. Your grandfather was a Nazi. It's in your blood, too.'

Tayte had feared as much since he'd first heard that his parents had gone to see the Kaufmanns in connection with Volker Strobel, looking for connections to Karl's father.

You can't choose your ancestors, JT, he reminded himself, although he imagined there had been all kinds of Nazis and he was sure they were not all like Volker Strobel. From what he'd heard about Johann Langner, Tayte liked to think he was perhaps a good man at heart, and under different circumstances who knows how his life would have turned out. But these were feelings Tayte would come to terms with in his own time, if he had any time left.

The door was wedged open and one after the other, Strobel and then Tayte were wheeled through into another room. Tayte was no longer surprised by what he saw. He was in a shrine of sorts, that much was apparent as soon as his eyes fell on the larger than life portrait of Adolf Hitler, which was lit up on the far wall. A single candle glowed before it as a remembrance offering. Tayte noticed then that there were portraits of other key Nazi Party officials lit up all around the room, which were interspersed with fine art paintings and golden symbols of the Third Reich. The ceiling was adorned with a large Nazi banner, the central swastika hanging directly over a polished brass swastika set into the stone floor beneath it.

'These are the paintings I'm forced to keep in my private collection,' Strobel said, waving a hand around the room. 'Of course, I used some of them to help get my business started, and as an act of goodwill I repatriated a few with the families of their former owners. It put me in good stead with the community as my business grew.'

'Stolen war treasures?' Tayte said with disdain.

He got no answer. None was needed. The two wheelchairs were pushed further into the room, and when they came to a stop Tayte found himself directly beneath the portrait of Adolf Hitler. The wheelchairs were then turned in so that Tayte and Strobel were facing one another. They were so close that their knees were almost touching, and Tayte couldn't imagine what the old man wanted him to do.

'Now to the business at hand,' Strobel said, his tone deathly serious. 'Instead of me killing you, I want you to kill me.'

'What?' Tayte's face was suddenly creased with disbelief.

'You've caught me at a good time, Mr Tayte. I'm making you part of my exit plan. My life for yours. That's the deal.'

Tayte shook his head, unable to comprehend what he was hearing. He stared at Strobel, wide eyed. 'You're crazy!'

'Yes,' Strobel said, almost laughing. 'I'm sure I am. But I'm also very tired. I'm in constant pain, and I'm told by my doctors that it will only get worse before the end. In short, I've had enough.'

'Well, can't you kill yourself?' Tayte said. 'Or get your daughter to do it with one of her needles? Why me?'

'A father cannot expect his own daughter to kill him, Mr Tayte, and Max here is like a son to me. I can't ask him to do it. I've thought about suicide—a cyanide capsule and a bullet to my brain in the manner of my *Führer*—but I can't do it, either. For now at least, my beautiful Aryan son, Rudi, knows nothing of who I really am, so I can't ask him. Besides, the more I've thought about it, the more appropriate I believe it would be for Johann's grandson to do it. I've never got over killing my friend. Of all the things I've done, his is the only face that continues to haunt me. It will be a kind of justice for him if you can do this one thing he could not.'

Strobel gave a nod, and this time Fleischer stepped beside Tayte and cut his right arm free. Then he tossed a pistol into his lap.

'It's the Luger that belonged to your grandfather.'

Tayte just stared at it, thinking he must still be unconscious, caught in a bizarre nightmare from which he couldn't wake up.

'Leave us now,' Strobel said. To Fleischer, he added, 'You know what to do, Max.'

Fleischer nodded and strode off towards the door.

'You, too, Ingrid,' Strobel said. 'I don't want any harm to come to you should Mr Tayte get any wild ideas of his own. Stay outside the door until you hear the shot.' To Tayte, he added, 'There is only one bullet in the chamber. Use it wisely.'

Tayte was surprised to see that Ingrid Keller had tears in her eyes as she leaned in and kissed her father goodbye. He imagined she believed it was for the last time. A moment later she followed Fleischer out of the room.

'You're not kidding, are you?' Tayte said as soon as he and Strobel were alone. 'How can you be so sure I'll do it? I don't think for a minute that Fleischer or your daughter are going to let me walk out of here afterwards.'

Strobel sighed. 'When you leave, Max and Ingrid will both receive a tidy sum of money. Max will disappear, and Ingrid and her husband will retire early to whichever tropical paradise they choose. Tonight this building will be burned to the ground. The authorities will find my bones and blame the anti-Nazi groups that have so long campaigned to shut this place down. You will be a free man again, and as long as you keep your silence about what happens here, you will not be implicated. But try to leave this room without killing me first and it will be you who dies. That I promise you.'

'We're in the basement of your museum, aren't we?' Tayte said. 'Your education centre?'

Strobel nodded. 'It has been little more than a cover for my operations with the Fourth Reich. I think it fitting that my body should be cremated here beneath the image of my *Führer*.'

'You really are crazy,' Tayte said, still unconvinced that he would be allowed to walk away from this. Strobel surely understood that he would go straight to the authorities and tell them everything, regardless of the consequences he might have to face as a result. No, Tayte wasn't buying any of it. He knew he was a dead man whether he ended Strobel's life or not.

He gave a firm shake of his head. 'I won't do it.'

'Yes, you will, Mr Tayte. My story, remember. I haven't finished it yet. Now, where was I? Ah, yes. It was the 26th of April, 1945, and I had just killed your grandfather.'

Tayte had heard enough of Strobel's story. All he wanted to do was to get out of there, find Jean, and board the plane back to London. But how was he going to do that? He had a gun in his lap with a single bullet in the chamber, no knife with which to free himself from the wheelchair he was bound to, and even if he could reach the door, Keller and Fleischer were beyond it, armed and most certainly dangerous. One bullet would not be enough. On top of that, no one had any idea where he was. He realised then that he had no way of knowing how long he'd been unconscious, either. He had no idea whether it was day or night, or even if it was the same day. The flight back to London might already have left for all he knew. He concluded that for now, as before, he had no choice but to play along with Strobel's bizarre game and listen as the old man continued his story.

'Within seconds of shooting Johann,' Strobel said, 'the guards patrolling the street were at my door, and naturally, after hearing the shots, they were full of concern for me. I dismissed them easily enough. I was, after all, their *Lagerführer*.'

'They didn't question the state of your face?'

'They never saw my face. It was dark and I barely opened the door. They were soon gone and I was glad to be alone again. I had to think, and think I did. By morning I had it all worked out, but I had to make sure Johann's body was never found.'

'Don't tell me,' Tayte said. 'You buried him in one of your lime pits.'

Strobel gave Tayte a sharp smile. 'You're on the right track, but I had to be very sure. So while it was still dark, I went out and removed the striped uniform from a dead Jew. I put it on Johann, and in the morning I had his body collected and taken to the incinerators. No one cared who he was, and I was accustomed to my orders being obeyed without question. Johann appeared as just one more Jew for the pile.'

'You're despicable.'

'Yes,' Strobel said, eyeing the gun. 'Perhaps I'm the kind of man you'd like to rid the world of, eh?'

Tayte didn't answer. He closed his eyes instead, unable to look at Strobel a moment longer.

'With Johann gone and the Allies close to Dachau,' Strobel continued, 'all that remained for me to do was to dress myself in my friend's uniform and take off with his papers. Johann was very strong, and he beat me so hard. I should have gone to a hospital to have my jaw and my eye treated, and my eye might have been saved if I had, but that would have been too risky. Instead, I bandaged myself up as a wounded soldier and I endured the pain as I went into hiding. My wounds left me disfigured, as you see, but that, too, served its purpose. By the time I was picked up, some months later, I looked enough like Johann and was virtually unrecognisable as the man I truly was. Not that anyone came forward to verify that I was Johann. Most, if not all, of Johann's close companions in the *Leibstandarte* had been killed at one time or another, particularly during their retreat from Falaise on the Western Front, and later, when Vienna fell to the Soviets.'

Strobel paused and Tayte opened his eyes again to see the old man smiling to himself, as though gratified at how well everything had worked out for him.

'You know the really clever thing about it?' Strobel added.

'No, do tell,' Tayte said with more than a hint of sarcasm, knowing that Strobel was about to tell him anyway.

'The clever thing was that I didn't try to hide behind the papers of a simple soldier from the *Wehrmacht,* as many other SS officers did, or as a former concentration camp prisoner, as I later came to learn that Max Koegel did when the camp at Flossenbürg was taken. No, I hid behind the papers of another SS officer. Who in their right mind would have done that?'

'Yeah,' Tayte scoffed. 'You'd have to be mad, right?'

'Yes, it was madness, and it was a gamble, but it saved my life. As you know, I faced trial for Johann's alleged war crimes. I knew there was a chance I might still have been executed, but as Volker Strobel the death sentence was guaranteed. As it was, I served my time and later recovered the treasures I had stored for my future. I've avoided detection all these years because of one simple rule, Mr Tayte—eliminate all threats.'

Tayte was getting tired of this. 'Look, Strobel. Talk all you want. I'm still not going to shoot you.'

Amusement danced across Strobel's lips. 'I would have been disappointed if you had pulled the trigger so soon,' he said. 'I have so much more to tell you, such as the time I hunted your father across the Karwendel Mountains.'

Chapter Forty-Five

'You'd like me to tell you about your father, wouldn't you?' Strobel said.

The sense of amusement continued to hang on his face as he waited for Tayte to answer, but Tayte wasn't so sure he wanted to hear what was coming next. He gave no reply. Instead, he knotted his hands together and clenched them tight to keep him from picking up the gun in his lap. He just stared at Strobel, noting the obvious satisfaction the man felt at seeing him fight his growing desire to end this. A moment later Strobel continued, as Tayte knew he would.

'Like you, your father was equally determined to find out who he was,' Strobel said, 'and that, as you know, led him and your mother to me. They posed little threat at first. When they came to ask whether I was Karl's biological father, I simply turned them away, saying I had no children, but it seems that turning Karl away only made him more determined to prove it. He kept digging, and people digging into my background worry me, Mr Tayte. Especially people related to Johann Langner. I knew it would only be a matter of time before he found something.'

Strobel gave a long sigh. 'Thankfully, Johann's parents were already dead, and I knew of no other friends or family who had survived the war, or who were close enough to take any interest in Johann afterwards. I did, however, become quite paranoid about

Ava Bauer's uncle, Heinz Schröder, for a time. He knew Johann. What if he came forward to denounce me? As it turned out, I suspect that if he even knew of my trial then he chose to distance himself from it, and from Johann. I had thought myself in the clear, and I was, until your father learned that he'd been adopted, and of course in doing so he became a threat.'

'So you eliminated him,' Tayte said. 'You eliminated the threat. I think I've already worked that part out.'

'Doesn't it matter to you that Karl was your father?'

It did matter, but Tayte wasn't about to break down in front of this man if he could help it. He knew it was just what Strobel wanted, and all the while Tayte had the strength to keep his emotions in check, he would do so to spite him.

'I had been keeping a close eye on your father since the first time he visited me,' Strobel continued. 'Much as I've been keeping an eye on you since your arrival in Munich. Some years later it became clear to me that Karl was close to discovering the very thing that could expose me.'

Strobel raised his left arm and tapped the area close to his armpit. 'Blood type,' he said. 'It has been my greatest concern. For quick identification the majority of SS personnel had our blood type tattooed in black ink beneath our left armpits in case we fell in battle. I've long since had my tattoo removed, but of course our blood type was also recorded in our military records, which is where I imagine Karl made his first discovery. It was when I learned that he'd taken an interest in my blood type that I knew I had to act, but I couldn't very well do so as the reputable Johann Langner. No, I had to call on Volker Strobel for that. I lured your father to a meeting place with the promise of some useful information.'

'That sounds familiar,' Tayte said, recalling how he had been lured in much the same manner when he was set up for murder.

Strobel laughed to himself. 'Yes, and like you, your father came so willingly. But I'm afraid he came to his own slaughter.'

'You said you hunted him.'

'In a manner of speaking, yes, and he gave good sport. I mentioned the Karwendel Mountains earlier—they're not far from Munich to the south. It was there that I made my first home when I was released from prison. You see, I feared discovery for many years, so I initially sought solitude in the mountains. It was there that I took your father, but while I was deciding what to do with him, he escaped, high into the mountains. I sent men after him with dogs, and for a time he led them a merry dance. But I knew the area well. Given the direction in which your father had fled, I knew where he would go. There was a mountain hut, easy to see by anyone traversing the higher passes. So, I drove to it via a mountain track and waited for him, having lit a fire to keep out the cold, and to help draw him in. I waited with my shotgun in my lap, and inevitably your father walked in.'

'And you shot him,' Tayte said, finishing the story, or so he thought.

Strobel laughed again. 'No, I didn't shoot him. I didn't want to have to deal with his body afterwards. As with Johann, I thought it best that no body should be found—at least not that could be easily identified.'

Tayte felt his jaw begin to tighten. 'What did you do?'

'I bound your father to a chair,' Strobel said, speaking slowly now as he gazed at the gun in Tayte's lap. 'Then I left the hut and secured the door. I had already nailed the windows shut. There was no way for your father to escape this time.' He paused. 'I wonder if you can guess what happened next?'

Tayte was fast losing his battle to control the anger rising inside him. He had a good idea what happened next, but he didn't answer.

Instead, he continued to grind his teeth, knowing he was about to find out.

'I took a jerry-can from the back of my vehicle and I doused the hut with fuel,' Strobel said. He leaned forward, grinning at Tayte now as though excited by the images replaying through his mind. 'Pick up the gun, Mr Tayte. If my story is proving too painful, you can end it right now.'

A part of Tayte wanted to, but he didn't. Then he wished he had.

'I cremated your father while he was still alive!'

At hearing those words Tayte's free hand began to drift towards the gun.

'That's it! Just do it!' Strobel said. 'Don't think about it.' He grinned again, and as if to give Tayte further encouragement, he added, 'You know, I can still hear your father's screams as he burned. I found it intoxicating!'

Tayte's hand found the gun, cold metal against his hot and clammy skin. 'You evil bastard. You really are a demon!'

'Then shoot me! Put an end to my life, or must I tell you about your mother, too?'

Tayte's breath caught in his chest. He shook his head. 'Don't you say a word about my mother.'

'I'm afraid I must, if you'll let me. You see, your mother was a loose end, and I couldn't have that. She was pregnant when I sent my associates to kill her.'

Tayte lifted the gun and Strobel's one good eye widened with anticipation.

'I had no idea what your mother knew,' he continued, 'but I had to assume she knew as much as your father. Karl was missing by now, and although I'd made sure his disappearance couldn't be tied to me, she had become a threat nonetheless. I already knew she was staying with her brother in a rented apartment here in Munich.'

'Her brother?' Tayte cut in, recalling his and Jean's earlier visit to the apartment where his parents had been staying with British diplomat Geoffrey Johnston. Now he knew the motive for Johnston's murder. He had simply been in the way and was drowned in the Eisbach to make his death seem accidental.

'Yes, her brother,' Strobel said. 'Which of course means he was your uncle. But apart from having to deal with him, there were other complications.'

'I'm glad to hear it,' Tayte said, scowling at the idea that Strobel was responsible for the murder of yet another member of his family.

'Don't get your hopes up, Mr Tayte,' Strobel said. 'Your mother got away from me that time, but I made sure she knew it was Volker Strobel, the Demon of Dachau, who had killed her husband and was now after her. It served to remove suspicion from the respectable Johann Langner, and of course, your mother already knew that Karl had been interested in Strobel. She must have wondered what he'd found, but what could she do? Indeed, what could the authorities have done when she went to them with her story? Volker Strobel was a ghost. So your mother fled the country in fear of her life, and the lives of her as then unborn children.'

'Children?' Tayte felt an icy chill run through him.

Strobel gave Tayte a wry smile. 'You didn't know, did you? But how could you?' The revelation seemed to amuse him. 'You were not your mother's only child.'

'I have a twin?' Tayte said. It was a possibility he'd never considered before.

'Yes, and your mother was right to fear for your lives as well as her own. I'd learned my lesson with your father, you see. I let Johann's child live and that mistake came back to haunt me. I wasn't about to make the same mistake twice.'

The gun began to shake in Tayte's hand.

'It took several months to find your mother again,' Strobel said. 'She was first traced to England, and then to Atlanta, Georgia. She was doing so well, but how could I let her go? What if she did know something? What if she returned to Germany someday, drawn by vengeance and the need to understand what had happened to her husband? No, I had to eliminate all threats. So when your mother was found again I took care of the matter personally, and let me tell you, it gave me great pleasure.'

Tayte's grip on the gun tightened. Then as if he had no control over his forefinger, it slowly found the trigger.

'She was no longer pregnant when I finally caught up with her,' Strobel continued. 'You and your sibling had emerged into the world, and it was my aim to kill all three of you—to remove the threat once and for all—but your mother had sense enough to separate you.' Strobel paused then and smiled at Tayte before adding, 'You were already out of my reach, but your brother, as I discovered, was still with her.'

My brother, Tayte thought as he subconsciously reasserted his grip on the gun. But as much as he wanted to end this story, he was compelled to know what happened, or spend the rest of his life wondering, not that he felt he had a very long life ahead of him at this juncture.

'What did you do?' he said through his teeth.

'I found your brother in an open basket in the passenger foot-well of the jeep your mother was driving. He was wrapped so snugly in so many blankets, I almost missed him. But then he began to cry. If my curiosity to look at Johann's grandson hadn't got the better of me, I'm sure I could have driven my knife into that bundle without giving it a second thought, but look I did, and then I knew I couldn't kill him. Unlike you, he had Johann's blue eyes, you see. He was a beautiful Aryan boy—my beautiful Aryan boy.'

A sudden onset of dizziness almost overcame Tayte as he realised who Strobel was referring to. The gun suddenly felt so heavy, but he held it up. 'Rudi?' he said, his brow set in a deep furrow. He could scarcely believe it, yet if it were true it meant that his brother was still alive, and living right there in Munich. His fraternal twin.

Strobel nodded. 'I saw that baby boy as my opportunity to repent for what I had done to Johann. I would raise his flesh and blood as though it were my own. I would give his child everything, and in so doing I would sleep all the better for having made amends. And for a time, I did, but it didn't last.'

'That's the most twisted thing I've ever heard,' Tayte said.

'Would you rather I'd killed him? Believe me, Mr Tayte, if it had been you wrapped in that bundle—if your mother had hidden your brother away first instead of you—I would not have hesitated.'

Tayte fell silent, considering how his life had hung in the balance according to which of her children his mother chose to protect first. He thought back to his visit to the Catholic mission in San Rafael, Sinaloa where she had left him, and he heard Sister Manriquez's words again as she told him what his mother had said as she handed him over. *For the child's own protection* . . . Tayte knew now how true those words had been.

'How can I believe you'll let me go, when you know I'll tell Rudi everything?' Tayte said. 'He'll know who you really are, and what you did. He'll hate you for it.'

'But don't you see? I want Rudi to know.'

'Why, so you can mess with his head, too? You want that to be your parting gift to him after you're dead?'

'After I'm dead, he's going to find out sooner or later. I've provided well for those who know who I really am, but after I'm gone they will have no one to fear. Eventually someone will talk. I don't want Rudi to read about it in the newspapers, and who better to tell him than his own brother? It's because of my love for

Rudi that I want you to live, Mr Tayte, so you can be there for him when the time comes. But you must pull that trigger.'

'So you won't be around to face the music? You're a coward!'

'Yes, perhaps,' Strobel said. 'It doesn't change anything.' With that, he lifted his hands to the gun and held the muzzle between his open palms, steadying Tayte's aim.

'I can't do it,' Tayte said.

'Yes you can. You just need a little more encouragement. I'm going to finish telling you about your mother, and then you're going to pull the trigger and this will all be over.'

Tayte shook his head. He didn't want to hear about his mother. He could feel his checkbones throbbing painfully as he fought to hold back the tears welling inside him.

'Now as I was saying, when I finally caught up with your mother she was in Mexico. I'd followed her along a dusty track in the middle of nowhere and I ran her jeep off the road. Then I walked calmly up to her as she lay tangled in the wreckage, and I slit her throat.'

A sigh trembled from Tayte's lips, as if the life had just drained from his own body. He pictured the photograph he had of his mother and the first tear broke and fell onto his cheek. He could hold them back no longer. His lips were still trembling as he extended the gun closer to Strobel, and with the muzzle now no more than two inches from Strobel's face, Tayte watched the old man bow his head towards it, as though he knew he had done enough to make Tayte pull the trigger.

Chapter Forty-Six

Tayte had suddenly lost all concept of where he was and why he was there. Through a thick veil of hatred and tears, all he could see was the gun shaking in his hand and the man who had destroyed generations of his family: his parents, Sarah and Karl, his paternal grandparents, Johann and Ava, and his great-grandparents, Adelina and Gerhard Bauer. And he was responsible for the murder of his uncle, Geoffrey Johnston. Tayte had never felt so much loathing towards anyone in his life, and he'd encountered a few candidates in his time. All of them combined didn't come close to how he felt about Volker Strobel.

Tayte tried to tell himself that Strobel deserved to die, and that he would be doing the world a favour, but he reminded himself then that his family were not Strobel's only victims—far from it. The Demon of Dachau had been responsible for the murders of thousands upon thousands of people. He thought about Elijah and Tobias Kaufmann, and their life-long quest to bring Strobel to justice, to face trial for his crimes against humanity, and it was then that the idea of pulling that trigger seemed entirely selfish to Tayte. He withdrew the gun, and a moment later he tossed it away, removing any last temptation he might have had to pull the trigger.

At hearing it clatter to the floor, Strobel looked up again, disappointment written all over his face. 'So you can't do it, either,' he said. 'Just as your grandfather couldn't do it when he came after me that night at Dachau.' Strobel sighed. 'But I must thank you for the thrill you've given me. I haven't felt that much exhilaration in a long time.' His expression became suddenly quizzical. 'But what is it that makes us so different?' he asked. 'I would have shot you to save my own life, and without a moment's hesitation or remorse. But you . . . Why should you place such value in the life of someone you have every reason to hate? I really can't understand it.'

'I think you just answered your own question,' Tayte said, choking back his emotions. 'If you understood, you wouldn't have done the terrible things you've done.'

'Perhaps I would have been more like Johann, eh? You know, you shouldn't think ill of your grandfather because of who he was or what he represented. I knew him. He was a kind and considerate man. If you had been a young boy growing up in Germany in Johann's place, don't think for a moment that you wouldn't also have been a member of the Hitler Youth. You, too, would have been so proud of your country, and by the time your education and training was complete, you would have gladly fought alongside your *Kameraden* for the things you had come to believe in.' Strobel paused and smiled to himself. 'I, on the other hand, am quite Johann's opposite. But they say opposites attract, don't they?'

Tayte wiped his eyes. He really didn't want to get into a conversation about Strobel's psyche and the things that made him tick. 'So what happens now? I suppose you get to shoot me instead, right?'

'My education centre must still burn tonight,' Strobel said. 'By now Max will have seen to it that the place goes up in flames at the slightest spark.' The prospect seemed to excite Strobel. 'Perhaps I'll give the order and we'll both sit here like this, beneath the image of my beloved *Führer*, until the flames come for us.' He laughed. 'Then we will both be fighting over that bullet, won't we?'

Tayte was about to answer, but just as he went to speak, his attention was drawn to the door. He heard a thud, followed by a gunshot that reverberated around the corridor outside the room. When the door opened a few seconds later, he expected to see Keller or Fleischer walk in, one perhaps having betrayed the other for reasons he could not yet fathom, but instead it was Rudi Langner who entered, and Tayte now saw him as though for the first time. There stood his own flesh and blood.

'*Ist das wahr?*' he called. *Is it true?*

'*Mein Sohn,*' Strobel said under his breath.

Tayte thought Strobel's expression looked as confused as his own. 'He's not your son.' He watched the old man cower from Rudi as he strode towards them, his enraged face red and glistening with tears. For the first time Tayte thought Strobel looked terrified. Tayte noticed then that Rudi had a gun in his hand. He thought it was Ingrid Keller's gun. He was just thinking that his day couldn't get any more complicated when he saw someone he'd thought he would never see again.

'Jean!'

She followed into the room soon after Rudi, shaking her right hand, as though she had just hit it on something, or someone. Beyond the door, Tayte could see Keller lying on the floor. Jean ran to Tayte as soon as she saw him, and by now Rudi had already arrived at Strobel's side. Words were exchanged in German, which Tayte couldn't understand, but he gathered from Rudi's tone and body language that he was both angry and distraught. A moment later Tayte flinched as Rudi slapped his father across the face. Suddenly Jean was beside him.

'What's going on?' he asked her. 'How did you find me?'

Jean leaned in and kissed Tayte hard on the lips, as if she, too, thought she might never see him again. 'I'll explain later,' she said. 'We have to get you out of here.'

She removed a shoe and smashed the heel into the portrait of Adolf Hitler. The glass shattered and she began to cut Tayte free with one of the pieces. In the background, the conversation between Rudi and Strobel was growing more and more aggravated, the gun in Rudi's hand waving with abandon.

'Rudi knows who his adoptive father is,' Jean said. 'He's inconsolable.'

'I'll bet he is,' Tayte said, thinking that was only the half of it. 'He's my brother. Rudi's my fraternal twin.'

Jean stopped cutting away at the tape for a moment and just stared at him, motionless and clearly dumbfounded. Then she continued working the piece of glass. 'Well you'd better hold off telling him for now,' she said. 'He's too wound up. I don't think he can take any more surprises today.'

As soon as Tayte's arms and chest were free, Jean went to work on the tape around his legs. 'I could smell some kind of fuel when we came in,' she said. 'It's what led us down here.'

'Strobel plans to turn the place into his own cremation oven.'

Their attention was drawn to Rudi then as he aimed the gun at Strobel.

Strobel's hand shot out in front of him. *'Mein Sohn, bitte!'*

'Sie sind nicht mein Vater! Ich kenne Sie nicht!' Rudi replied, and Tayte could see in his eyes that he was going to pull the trigger. He saw that Strobel knew it, too.

'Don't do it, Rudi!' Tayte called, but his words didn't seem to reach him.

All Tayte could think at that moment was that Strobel had to face his accusers—justice had to be served. And for Rudi's sake, Tayte couldn't sit there and witness another innocent life, his brother's life, being destroyed because of Strobel. As Rudi stepped closer, his gun arm stiffened with determination, and before Tayte's bonds were fully cut, he leapt out of his seat, taking the wheelchair with him. There was a clatter and the gun went off as both men fell to the floor, and it was then Tayte knew he'd been shot.

The pain in Tayte's side from the bullet that had just hit him was surprisingly mild at first, but it soon intensified. He thought perhaps he was merely having a psychosomatic reaction to the stress he'd been under since going to see the man whom he'd thought was his grandfather, Johann Langner, but the sight of his own blood seeping through his shirt as Jean knelt beside him and lifted his suit jacket away told him the trauma was very real.

Jean grabbed his hand and placed it over the wound. 'Keep it there,' she said. 'I'm sure it hurts, but you need to put pressure on it to slow the bleeding.' She shook her head at him. 'What were you thinking? You could have been killed.'

'Sorry,' Tayte offered. He winced. 'I'll think twice before I do it again, believe me.' He lay still as Jean cut the rest of him free from the wheelchair. As he looked up, he saw Rudi, who was already on his feet.

'It's me who's sorry,' Rudi said. 'I don't know what came over me. I didn't mean to—'

'It's okay,' Tayte cut in, smiling, despite the circumstances, at the man he now saw as his brother. 'I'm sure I'll be fine.'

Tayte hoped he was right. He saw Volker Strobel again then, now ashen faced as he peered down from his wheelchair. Tayte thought it ironic that he'd just taken a bullet for this man, not that he expected any gratitude for it. From the look on Strobel's face, Tayte thought his actions, and the fact that he'd just saved the old man's life, had only served to annoy him, which was fine with Tayte.

He extended his free hand to Rudi. 'Here, help me up, will you?'

Tayte wanted to tell Rudi he believed he was his brother right there and then. He wanted to tell him so much, but now was not the time. He gripped Rudi's hand as he reached out to him, and despite the pain he was in, Tayte was still smiling at Rudi as he was helped to his feet, his hand still pressed firmly to his wound. Tayte wanted to give Rudi a hug, but he was barely standing when the whole room seemed to shudder and everyone's attention was drawn to the door, which had just been slammed shut.

'Keller!' Tayte said.

Jean sprinted to the door and tried to open it. 'It's locked. I can smell smoke!' She began to thump the door.

Strobel was smiling again now. 'That's my girl,' he said. To Rudi, he added, 'She must have thought you'd shot me, or perhaps this is her way of fulfilling my wish to die.'

He began to laugh at the situation, but Rudi soon silenced him. He stepped up to the old man's wheelchair and pulled him out and up over his shoulder in a fireman's lift. Then he carried him to the door. When he reached it he began to kick it, but the door was solid.

'The gun,' Tayte said to Jean, pointing at the wall beneath one of the paintings, to the gun Rudi had been holding. 'Maybe you can shoot the lock through. Be careful, the safety's off.'

Jean retrieved the gun and helped Tayte to the door, where Rudi was still trying with all his strength to break it down.

'Stand back,' Tayte said. He could smell the smoke fumes now, too. He only hoped the fire hadn't yet taken hold of the building. Even if it hadn't he knew they didn't have long.

'I've never fired a gun before,' Jean said.

'It's easy. My adoptive father took me to a shooting range a few times when I was a boy. Just aim for the lock at an angle in case the bullet ricochets and squeeze the trigger.'

Jean held the pistol with both hands to steady her aim. A second later she fired, and she jumped at the sound it made, which was deafening in such a closed space.

Rudi approached the door again and gave it another kick. There was a cracking sound this time as the splintered wood began to give. 'Again!' he said, stepping back.

Jean fired at the lock again, and the next time Rudi kicked the door, it swung wide open. Smoke billowed into the room, followed by a wave of heat that told Tayte the flames were already out of control.

'Quickly!' Rudi said as he carried Strobel out. 'Stay low. Cover your mouth.'

They were all coughing by the time they reached the end of the corridor, where the Nazi flags that lined the walls were all either burning or had already burnt out, presumably having been set alight by Keller as she left. Tayte was grateful they were in the basement where the foundation walls were made of stone, but that soon changed. Some of the walls further on were clad with wood and the staircase out of the basement was also wooden. Everything that could burn had begun to, including a small section of the stairs, which they had to pass through quickly so as not to set their clothes alight.

When they emerged onto the ground floor, heading for the main entrance hall where Tayte and Jean had previously bought their admission tickets, it was clear to see that Max Fleischer had been busy with his preparations for the inferno that was now well under way. The first floor had already collapsed in places and the heat was suddenly suffocating. They ran on as hot ash and burning debris began to fall around them. As they reached the main entrance hall, Tayte saw a familiar face. It was Tobias Kaufmann, standing just outside the entrance. He was with several officers of the Munich police, with Detectives Brandt and Eckstein among them.

'Thank God you're okay,' Kaufmann said to Tayte as soon as he stepped outside. To Jean he added, 'I came as soon as you called.'

It was almost dark out, the immediate area made brighter by the flames that were now raging through the building. As everyone moved away, coughing and spluttering as they made for the safety of the open car park, Tayte thought to check his watch, forgetting for a moment that he no longer had it. It was just an old digital watch, but it had been a gift from his adoptive parents that he'd had so long it pained him to think he would never see it again. He supposed by now that it was burning inside the building along with the rest of his things: his phone and his wallet. And while he was glad he hadn't had his briefcase with him, he knew none of these things compared to the loss of all those fine paintings.

A siren began to wail in the distance, drawing closer.

'That should be the ambulance,' Kaufmann said, eyeing Tayte's wound. 'And by the look of you, not a moment too soon.'

Tayte still had his hand pressed over the area that was bleeding. 'It hurts like hell, but I don't think it's too serious,' he said. 'I don't imagine I'd be standing here if it was.'

He saw Ingrid Keller again then. She was in handcuffs, as dour faced as ever as she was helped into the back of a police car. *And good riddance*, Tayte thought.

'How's that hand?' he asked Jean with a smirk.

'I think it's a little bruised, but it was worth it.'

'I'll bet. You're pretty tough for your size, aren't you?'

'You did call me a tough biker chick once, remember?' Jean jabbed her fist at the air and Tayte laughed until his wound forced him to stop.

He turned back to Tobias and pointed over to Rudi, who was surrounded by police officers as he lowered Volker Strobel into their custody.

'Tobias, do me a favour, will you? Don't let that old man out of your sight.'

Kaufmann scoffed. 'You have my word on that, Mr Tayte. I'll see he gets to trial. I don't care how old he is. The Demon of Dachau will face the families of his victims and justice will be done at last.'

Two ambulances arrived and Jean helped Tayte towards them.

'I also found out about my parents tonight,' Tayte said, finding it hard to think about anything else.

'What did you find?'

'Strobel told me he killed them.'

Jean's shoulders slumped. She squeezed his hand, her eyes doleful and sympathetic. 'I'm so sorry.'

'Yeah.'

Tayte was still somewhat shell-shocked by what he'd heard in that basement room, and yet he had to remind himself that he'd seen no hard proof to back up anything Strobel had said. Maybe Tayte was in denial about it, but for now he figured all he had was Strobel's account of events, and he supposed Strobel would have told him just about anything to make him pull that trigger. He liked to think that Strobel had invented at least a part of his story, but he knew that a simple DNA sibling test could prove whether he and Rudi were from the same mother and father, and that would back up Strobel's story of how he came to adopt him. And there was the niggling question that had always haunted Tayte.

If my mother was alive, why didn't she come back for me?

As Tayte and Jean were met by two of the ambulance crew, wheeling a stretcher towards them, Tayte drew a deep breath and moved the conversation on. He didn't feel up to talking about it just now. Instead, he turned his thoughts to Rudi. He would give him a few days to get used to the revelation that his adoptive father was really Volker Strobel, but he was anxious to see him again. If Rudi would agree to take the DNA test and it proved positive, he figured they had a lot of catching up to do. And he wanted to tell him that, contrary to what he believed, his mother did want him. He thought about getting home, too, so he could start digging around in the archives again, knowing he now had everything he needed to start building his own family tree, and to proving, or disproving, the things Strobel had told him about his parents.

But all that would have to wait.

'I guess we missed our flight,' he said as he sat on the stretcher.

'I guess we did,' Jean replied. 'Not that you're in any fit state to go anywhere other than to the hospital.'

'And I guess you've had a pretty busy afternoon,' Tayte added, wincing as he was helped into a lying position by the medics. 'Right now might not be the best time for explanations, though.'

'No, perhaps not,' Jean agreed. 'Let's talk about it in the morning. I'll come to the hospital with you.' She paused, smiling. 'Someone's got to make sure you don't get into any more trouble.'

Tayte smiled back, but his smile quickly faded when he heard a chilling scream. He looked back at the burning building. There was a figure at one of the upper windows. It was difficult to make out who it was because of the bright flames that engulfed him, but Tayte knew it had to be Max Fleischer.

Having thought her father dead, in her haste to cremate him and kill everyone else in the room, Ingrid Keller had clearly not given a thought to Fleischer, who had still been in the building. Tayte watched him climb out of the window onto the ledge, and then, screaming, he jumped to his death.

Chapter Forty-Seven

It was just after ten the following morning, and having spent the night at the hospital, Jefferson Tayte was with Jean, strolling along the Renaissance Antiquarium at the Munich Residence. It was a lavish sixteenth-century hall of some sixty-six metres in length, with painted walls and ceilings, housing Duke Albrecht V's collection of antique sculptures, from which the room took its name.

'A promise is a promise,' Tayte had told Jean as soon as they sat back in the taxi on their way there.

Tayte had also wanted to get away from the hospital as soon as he could, and Jean was in complete agreement that they had spent far too many hours there between them already that week. Tayte's side was still understandably sore from his ordeal the day before, but the bullet Rudi had meant for Strobel had passed cleanly through him, an inch or so below his ribcage, thankfully missing his stomach. He had a few stitches to scratch at, and he would no doubt have the scars to look back on once everything had healed, but it was nothing more than a flesh wound.

'And you're sure my briefcase is okay?' Tayte asked as they walked, sounding more concerned for his old friend than he had been for himself.

'It's absolutely fine,' Jean said. 'I told you, you can have it back when we leave for the airport. I want you all to myself until then.'

'Okay, I'm all yours,' Tayte said with a grin. 'You know, I must thank *Mr Goodbar* next time I see him,' he added, his grin widening. 'I know I'm trying to cut down, but apart from that bar you bought for me on our first day in Munich, I've missed him this trip.'

'Thank him for what?'

Tayte patted his stomach. 'Well, if I didn't literally have a soft spot for Hershey's, particularly *Mr Goodbar*, I wouldn't have built up this protective cushion around me. He might just have saved my life.'

Jean shook her head, laughing. 'If you didn't have your "protective cushion" in the first place, that bullet would have missed you altogether. Have you thought about that? And I suppose I didn't have anything to do with it?'

Tayte paused while he pretended to think about it. 'Well, maybe just a little,' he said, teasing.

Jean gave him a playful slap. Then she put her arm around his waist and hugged him closer. 'Well, I rather like you as you are, so I'll say it for you. Thank you, *Mr Goodbar!*'

They both started laughing then, until they realised they were the only people making any sound in the otherwise reverently quiet hall.

'So,' Tayte said. 'Now we're away from that hospital for what I hope will be the last time, I think you have some explaining to do. How did you find me? I've been trying to work it out all night.'

'The money,' Jean said. 'When I finally cleared the hospital, I picked up your message. I knew you'd left the record office and I tried to call you, but after several attempts I started to worry.'

'How are you? I'm sorry, I should have asked sooner.'

'I'm fine. There was some internal swelling, but it's okay. They wanted to run another scan to be sure. Anyway, when I couldn't reach you I went to see Tobias. It was mid-afternoon by then and he said he'd been expecting us.'

'I called him earlier in the day. I said we'd drop by and lend a hand with the tidying up. He was trying to find a report he wanted to show us.'

'Well, he'd already found it by the time I got there. After we told him Langner had had a child with Trudi Strobel, and that he'd paid her off for the child, he'd had his government contacts look into Langner's business accounts.'

'Tobias said he was keen to follow just about any new lead that came along.'

Jean nodded. 'And it proved worthwhile. They found that Langner was still making payments to Trudi and her daughter. He'd set up an account in the name of a bogus art restoration company, so that without further examination it wouldn't be obvious who was getting the money. There were several business accounts, but this one stood out because the sums of money being paid into it seemed disproportionately high for the services being paid for.'

'And on closer inspection,' Tayte offered, 'they found the company registered to Trudi Strobel and Ingrid Keller?'

'I don't think it was quite as straightforward as that, but that's the crux of it, yes. They found that the money was ultimately being drawn by Trudi and Ingrid. It wasn't a bad setup either. I doubt it was even illegal. It went unnoticed for so long because, until we connected Langner to Trudi Strobel through her daughter, Ingrid, no one had cause to investigate the reputable art dealer Volker Strobel was posing as.'

They were halfway along the expansive hall when Tayte paused beside a piece of illuminated statuary and gazed up at the colourful frescos on the ceiling, glad to see that not everything so beautiful had been destroyed by the war.

'So, what did you do with this information?' he asked.

'I went back to see Trudi Strobel.'

'You did? How did that go?'

'It was quite confrontational to begin with.'

'I'll bet,' Tayte said, recalling how cold Trudi had been towards both of them when they visited her together.

'I stood my ground, though,' Jean added. 'A couple of hours had passed by now and I was worried sick about you. When I went to Trudi's house and mentioned the bogus company she'd been drawing from the gates couldn't have opened faster. I told her what I knew and I showed her the proof. Tobias had made a copy for me, the poor man. His own copier was broken, along with just about everything else in his office. He had to go to another business on a different floor to borrow theirs.'

'He's a good man,' Tayte said. 'I hope he and his father will find some peace now that Strobel's in custody.'

Jean nodded and continued her explanation. 'I came right out with it and asked Trudi why she'd lied to us about the money— why she'd told us Langner paid her off for the child all those years ago, when in truth he didn't have that kind of money back then. She became very uncomfortable, but I wouldn't be put off. For all I knew, your life was in danger.'

'It was.'

'Exactly, so I told her everything that had happened to us since we arrived in Munich, and that I was deeply concerned about you because you weren't answering your phone. Then I came back to the large sums of money she was still receiving from Langner and I asked her why. Well, she seemed to break down in front of me. She became angry at first, but I kept asking her why Langner was still supporting her, and whether the payments were really just to keep her quiet about his daughter, Ingrid. It was then that she began to break down and she told me Langner wasn't Ingrid's father. She just came out with it. I still don't know whether she meant to say it or not, but that was the moment the penny dropped. Trudi went very quiet after that, but she'd already said enough and I think she knew it. I realised that if Langner wasn't Ingrid's father, the money had to be coming from someone else—someone posing as Johann Langner.'

'And who else could that be other than Trudi's husband-in-hiding, Volker Strobel,' Tayte said, smiling at Jean and wondering what he'd done to deserve her.

'I went back to Rudi Langner after that,' Jean continued. 'When I told him what I knew about his father and his nurse, it must have come as such a shock. He was so upset. It was clear to see how much he looked up to his father. Imagine finding out that he was really the Demon of Dachau and that he'd been lied to all his life.'

'I can see why he was so mad at Strobel when you both found me,' Tayte said. 'How did you know I was there? Rudi can't have known what really went on at that place.'

'We tried the house first,' Jean said. 'Langner wasn't there, and neither was Keller, so we called the German Heart Centre to see if he'd been readmitted. They hadn't seen him. Langner's former Hitler Youth building was the only other place we could think to check, and we knew something was wrong as soon as we arrived. As I said when we found you, there was a strong smell of fuel in the air and we followed our noses to the basement. I almost bumped into Ingrid Keller.'

Tayte grinned. 'And then she bumped into your fist.'

'You're not going to let that go, are you?'

'Sure I will—eventually. Just remind me not to get on the wrong side of you.'

As they came to the end of the hall, Tayte held Jean close to him and gazed into her eyes. 'I really thought I was going to die last night. I haven't said it yet, but thank you, Jean. You saved my life. How can I ever repay you?'

'Oh, I'm sure I can think of something,' Jean said. A moment later she stood on her toes and kissed him, and her whole face lit up as she said, 'Marry me?'

Acknowledgements

My thanks to Katie Green for helping to shape and structure this story, to Catja Pafort for copyediting the book and helping with my German, to Emilie Marneur and the team at Amazon Publishing for all the many things that go on behind the scenes, and my continued thanks to my wife, Karen, for her support and the invaluable input that goes into every Jefferson Tayte story. I would also very much like to thank you, the reader, for reading or listening to this book. I hope you enjoyed it.

About the Author

Credit: Karen Robinson

Steve Robinson drew upon his own family history for inspiration when he imagined the life and quest of his genealogist hero Jefferson Tayte. The talented London-based crime writer, who was first published at age sixteen, always wondered about his own maternal grandfather—'He was an American GI billeted in England during the Second World War,' Robinson says. 'A few years after the war ended he went back to America, leaving a young family behind and, to my knowledge, no further contact was made. I traced him to Los Angeles through his 1943 enlistment record and discovered that he was born in Arkansas . . .'

Robinson cites crime writing and genealogy as ardent hobbies—a passion that is readily apparent in his work. He can be contacted via his website, www.steve-robinson.me, his blog at www.ancestryauthor.blogspot.com, and on Facebook at www.facebook.com/SteveRobinsonAuthor.